Lilith

As well as being a very successful writer, MARGARET LEWERTH has had great professional experience as a director in radio and television. She has a well-established reputation in this field and has worked with such stars of television and theatre as Ethel Barrymore, Talullah Bankhead and Victor Borge.

Lilith is the fourth novel in a four-book saga, *The Roundtree Women*.

MARGARET LEWERTH

Lilith

The Roundtree Women
Book IV

This edition published 1994 by
Diamond Books
77–85 Fulham Palace Road
Hammersmith, London W6 8JB

First published in America in 1981 by
Dell Publishing Co. Inc.
First published in the UK by Fontana Books 1981

She's beautiful and therefore to be woo'd;
She is a woman, therefore to be won.
WILLIAM SHAKESPEARE, *1, Henry VI*

PART ONE

NEW ORLEANS 1900

CHAPTER ONE

She pressed the doorbell again, listened through the thickness of the oak door, and heard nothing. The silence lay like dust in the narrow, sunlit street. The house, eyes closed, had withdrawn behind louvred blinds. The hour was unlucky. New Orleans gentility was taking its rest.

Not that she had a choice. Impulsive in all things, Henrietta Roundtree had waited too long to make this journey. Even at this moment the events of the past month could chill her with a horror that made her instinctively reach for the hand of the small boy beside her. Unlike her own, his fingers curled within hers, warm and confident.

'I guess nobody's home.' He was a boy of wide blue eyes and long silences, slight for his eleven years and small-boned like herself.

'Of course there's someone home, Amos. I wrote Tante Charl – Aunt Charlotte,' she said, correcting herself. How easily the old French usage came, despite the years. But the boy must be made to understand. 'I wrote Aunt Charlotte several weeks ago that we would arrive. But this is an old house. The walls are thick. And everybody takes a rest in the afternoon. Especially during Carnival.'

'What is Carnival?'

'Oh, Amos, it's a wonderful time. Parties and balls and the streets filled with people, laughing and dancing.'

'Why?'

'Because everybody is happy at Carnival. And at the end of it you'll see the most marvellous parades. With a king wearing a crown – '

'A real king?'

How much to tell him of reality? How much ever to tell him? The question had twisted deep within her ever since the snow-laced morning two days ago when she had stood in the draughty hall of the white clapboard house in Thatcher, Connecticut, and drawn muffler and mittens close on her youngest surviving child for the last time. When it was time to go, Isaac emerged from his study. He bowed stiffly to her. He did not look at the boy.

'He is your son, Isaac.'

Amos held out his hand. Isaac touched it. His small trunk was hoisted into the carriage. Only once did Amos break the silence.

'When will I come home?'

She hesitated, then answered gaily. 'Maybe you won't want to!'

He turned his face from her. In the next days he had watched in silence from the train window as snow melted into bare earth, bareness into spring, and then, with an abruptness that dazzled him, into a burst of sunlight and colour such as he had never seen. Purple, green, and gold ruffling in flags fluttering in streamers from lamp-posts and railings.

Henrietta shut her eyes against a surge of longing. She had forgotten. It was Mardi Gras time. Forgotten the quickening anticipation, the heart-stopping excitement, the total abandonment to joy. She had forgotten youth. She held Amos to her in an intensity of emotion. And gratitude. It would help Amos through his first loneliness. Tante Charl would never miss Mardi Gras. She would take Amos in her carriage. She would watch with him from the wrought-iron balcony.

Henrietta bought a rosette with ribbons in the same brilliance of purple, green, and gold and pinned it to his jacket. She bought another and laced it through the lock of his small trunk. They would arrive head-high and in splendour, in the colours of Mardi Gras. Purple for justice. Green for faith. Gold for power. She could wish him all three but she did not try to explain. Not yet. It was enough that his face was flushed, his eyes bright. The nightmare was receding.

'Is he a real king?'

'Yes, my darling. A real King of Carnival.'

'On a real throne?'

'On a real throne.'

Small lies. Time enough for him to grow beyond them.

Time enough for her to know the pain of what she was doing.

'Suppose nobody comes to open the door?'

'Then we shall go to a hotel and wait.'

Uncertainty ran through her like a thread of fear. Every hour of this journey had been planned. At precisely four forty-five at the appointed end Isaac would be standing on Thatcher's snow-covered station platform, gaunt, unsmiling, but, as she knew, needing her in the dark hours that came more frequently. Any change in her schedule, any inexplicable delay – Henrietta let a sickening wave of recall pass.

She reached for the massive knocker and hesitated. One did not use a knocker at the doors of quality. If the doorbell went unanswered, one went away until a more appropriate time. Not that the house showed its quality now. The entwining leaf pattern of the overhead railing bore flakes of rust. A few vines trailed through it, disconsolate and dry. The uppermost of the three rounded stone steps gaped in a widening crack.

The massive knocker itself mocked her. An eyeglass mask, neither Comedy nor Tragedy, but inscrutable within an iron crown, was a long-ago whim of her playacting father. Her own childhood years had been measured by her ability to reach up to it. 'The crown is for you,' he had promised, 'if you grow up sweet and good. The mask' – she could still hear the laughter through that spellbinding voice – 'the mask is for you, my little Henrietta, if you don't.'

Thirty years surged and vanished. Sweet and good. She had tried. Until the night docility had vanished and she had flung her fine French name and manners, her young passions, into the arms of a travelling Yankee and gone eagerly, too eagerly, with him to a place she could barely spell. She had made the best of it. She had adjusted to habit and pattern, while Gallic restlessness ran like a small blind mole beneath it. She had paid for that, too, but if she had made a mistake, no man would know it. Nor woman either. Henrietta Roundtree had worn her mask for a long time.

With a quick decisive gesture she gripped the iron crown that formed the knocker. It did not budge. She tugged it,

9

wondering if anyone had ever used it. Slowly, rustily, it lifted. With a sharp clang she sent it pounding against its bronze base.

Motes of dust danced in the sunlight as the old house shook itself from slumber. She leaned close to the door. Surely she heard now the slow, weighted tread of footsteps.

'Someone's coming, Amos!' She could smile now.

Impishly the boy grinned back and stretched his fist to the black knob of the doorbell.

'No, Amos!' It was too late. This time they both heard a distant jangle and a quickening of the heavy steps.

Months later Henrietta would write in her diary that 'it was probably all for the best', but now she could only stand rigid, slight, and erect as a girl, her tight brown silk dress too hot in the sun, her small tilted hat casting a winged shadow against the slowly opening door.

'I heerd you. Who you wantin', boy, shivareein' like that?'

The woman was as broad as she was short. Her skin, the colour of oiled rosewood, was brought to life by the purple and magenta folds of a towering turban. Purple and magenta. Fragments of memory stirred in Henrietta, then slid away. The woman's black, almond-shaped eyes snapped in anger. She had seen only the boy. Amos, in terror, ducked behind his mother.

'I am sorry. My son' – Henrietta stepped through the half-opened door – 'we both thought that perhaps the doorbell . . .' She smiled and her face grew young. 'I am Mrs Roundtree. I wrote two weeks ago . . .' Her voice trailed. The fat little woman's eyes were fastened on her, staring.

'Who you say?'

'Mrs Isaac Roundtree from Connecticut. Miss Martine, my aunt . . .' Explanations were tiring, but the woman's look was unsettling. '. . . this is my son . . .' She did not finish. Two plump hands went to her face. She was swept into an embrace, overwhelming with the nostalgia of starched cotton, geranium water, and kitchen baking.

'Miz Henriette! Miz Henriette! Don't you know me?' The turban shook with embarrassment as the woman stood back. 'I'm Rosalee! Old Jubel's child. Rosalee! You remember, Miz Henriette!'

Henrietta remembered. Rosalee, only a few years older than herself. Skinny once as a firecracker. Rosalee, escaping out of sight of the kitchen on feet of flame. Twirling and lifting her magenta petticoats in the sunlit courtyard outside her father's study while Phillip Martine behind the louvres watched. Often. Henrietta had known about that too.

Rosalee. Time thinned all things. Or, Henrietta hid a quick smile, in Rosalee's case, thickened. She gave the woman another hug. Warmth and comfort. A kindly replacement for the spent fires of youth. For the first time since she had left Thatcher, Henrietta knew the sweetness of relief. She had indeed brought Amos home.

'You're pretty as ever Miz Henriette.'

'Rosalee! I'm past forty!' But the laugh was girlishly pleased. 'And I have seven children. Ten,' she amended, conscious of Amos's solemn eyes. 'God took three of them home.' She added the old unbelieving words as carefully as when her last and youngest, Susannah, lay tiny and worn in white satin and oak. Amos had looked into the stilled, tinted little face and said nothing. As he said nothing now.

Henrietta stifled an impulse to spill the years into Rosalee's ample lap. Instead she flashed Amos a brightening smile and forced gaiety into her voice.

'Amos is our youngest son. He's going to live here with you and Tante Charl. We thought it was better. He – he feels the cold and in this warm climate . . .'

Amos had backed away in the dimmed hall and was clinging to the rosewood pineapple of the newel post. The stairs looked narrower than Henrietta remembered. And darker.

'So if Tante Charl is resting, don't disturb her. Not yet. I want to look around and remember things and show Amos . . .' She rushed on, not willing to release this deep part of herself yet. 'Oh, Rosalee, it's good to be here even for a little while! Nothing has changed! The hall, the settee, the parlour, Papa's den . . .' Impulsively she flung her arm out and pirouetted, supple as a girl, her brown silk dress rustling, her tiny winged hat tilted on the dark, piled hair. 'Home! Tonight I'm going to a ball! The ball of Comus, Rosalee . . . like Maman in white and silver . . .'

'What's Comus?' As he so often did, Amos ended his silence abruptly.

Henrietta spun around and dropped to one knee beside him. 'Oh, my darling, my darling! You have so much to see and to learn. About being happy and laughing. You'll have sunshine and flowers. All the lovely things of life. And Rosalee will make you prawn gumbo and praline pie . . .' She jumped to her feet, the words tumbling from her. 'And, Rosalee, don't you go up to Tante Charl's room. I'll go. I know where she is. Maman's big room on the east corner where the mimosa is. And, oh, Amos's trunk is out beside the front steps. If you could ask someone to fetch it. The carriage driver wanted to carry it in but we were waiting and – Papa used to say never keep a working man waiting, his time is worth more than yours. Come along, Amos, I'm going to show you.'

Rosalee had not moved. The wetness in her eyes now coursed down the folds of her face in two solid tears.

'Rosalee! My dear, dear old friend . . .'

The woman backed away defensively. 'Don't you *know*, Miz Henriette?'

Henrietta had long felt presentiments. She could see a shadow before it fell. She glanced at the rigid little figure at the stairs.

'Amos, go in there – into the parlour. It's cool. You'll find a glass cabinet. Go and tell me what you see in it. Count everything! It's – it's magic.'

The boy went soberly out. He, too, had sensed a shadow.

'Know what, Rosalee? Tell me!'

'Miz Charl's dead.'

'Dead.' She had heard the word too often in her life as a finality. Here it had the toll of a bell. She had never once considered it in her headlong plan. No one had written her. This was her father's house. And hers. Tante Charl was –

'When, Rosalee?'

'Last Mardi Gras. No, two before. I disremember now.' The old woman was shaking. Henrietta's own anguish would have to wait. She put an arm around the woman. 'What happened? Tell me.' It didn't really matter. Tante Charl was gone and now there was nothing. Nothing of the splendour. Only the ash. She must think. She would have to, for Amos. But now –

'. . . sitting right up there on the balcony, waiting for the parade like always. Miz Charl didn't go out any more. Not since – Never further than the balcony. The wind came up. But she wouldn't go inside. I told her. I tried. All she said was, "Rosalee, if all God has left to me is this space, I shall fill it." The wind blew real hard like it was comin' down for her. When the parade gone by, she went in and lay down on her bed. Father Reverre came in the morning. He put the ash on her forehead. And the oil on her lips. She just said *merci* and died.'

'And you've been here alone since?' That might explain the unanswered letter.

'No. I got Pearl, my last child. And her child. An' old George still here. And' – impassivity slid over the heavy features – 'and Madame.'

'Madame? Who?' She saw Rosalee glance at the front door. 'Come in here to Papa's study, Rosalee. You are upset.' A quick look into the parlour told her that Amos had found the glass cabinet. He would be engrossed for some time.

She motioned Rosalee to a chair and sat beside her. 'Tell me everything, Rosalee. If there is someone in this house I should meet, I must know it now. At once.'

'Didn't they write you, Miz Henriette? Or maybe you went so far, nobody . . . knew.' Translated it became clear to Henrietta. The years of treasuring the fragments of her New Orleans childhood had been one-sided. She had married a Yankee. To the proud Creoles he was one with the blue-coated enemy, the hated carpetbaggers, the loathed Anglo-Saxon riffraff who had drifted southward to possess, to destroy, to spit. At barely seventeen Henrietta had become a small and unwitting traitor.

'Who is Madame, Rosalee?'

'She came after your father died. I disremember when. Miz Charl took her into the parlour and closed the door.

When she came out, Miz Charl told us that the – the lady would live in this house and we were to call her Madame Martine.'

So her father, the graceful sorcerer who had spent his years delving into the trunk of his imagination for tinsel and make-believe, had drawn the last card from his sleeve. Had he at the end found consolation for failure?

'And Tante Charl?'

'She went straight upstairs to the small room off the corner of the balcony. And that's where she died.' The mellow voice hardened. 'Madame uses your mother's room.'

Henrietta glanced up, listening to the shadowed silence. Rosalee shook her head.

'She goes out afternoons about three. She comes back most usual after five.'

Henrietta sat rigid, slowly pulling on her half-drawn glove. She needed time.

'What became of my letter, Rosalee?'

The fat little woman did not answer. For a long moment she sat motionless, a polished and inscrutable image. Then she must have come to some inwardly difficult decision, for she rose and in turbaned dignity walked from the room.

She returned carrying a carved mahogany box. With a tiny key drawn from her skirt she opened it. Whatever the box had once held, now only a few shreds of faded green velvet clung to it. Within, Henrietta saw a stack of letters. Uppermost, her own handwriting. *Miss Charlotte Martine.* The letter was still sealed.

'Has no one read it?'

Rosalee's eyes showed a glint of fear. 'Miz Henriette, that letter belong to the dead! I put them all here. Miz Charl would walk this house in torment if anyone touched that letter. She'd come risin' from her grave. I know, Miz Henriette. I *know*. She needs her rest now, poor lady. You understand?'

She understood. A hundred, a thousand years, the immutable timelessness of superstition lay locked in that box. Yet was it so different from the superstition to which she kneeled, bonneted and proper, beside her husband these long years and confessed to uncommitted sins?

She watched the box close. Some day that last forbidden letter of hers . . . but that future was of no concern now. The present had opened at her feet an unguessed hell. Her ears were already tuned to the coming of horses' hooves and carriage wheels.

'Take Amos to the kitchen, will you, Rosalee? I'm sure he could do with a glass of milk.'

'And honey cake, Miz Henriette. You remember Jubel's honey cakes?'

She barely heard. She was seeing Amos again as she had found him that January day on a Thatcher hillside, the icy wind whipping his thin cotton trousers. Shirtless, barefooted, his breath spent, his eyes glazed, globules of sweat standing out on the blue whiteness of his forehead, he was stumbling towards his father as Isaac pocketed his watch. She had screamed and snatched the boy to her.

'Let him be, Henrietta!'

'You're killing him!'

'Last week he could run for only two minutes. Today it is four. He'll be a man yet and a Roundtree. Even if you didn't make him one!'

She let the old taunt pass but before she could slide the shawl from her own shoulders to the boy, she felt her arm twisted to her back. The boy slid limp from her grasp, unconscious to the ground. Her husband's face, close to hers, was stamped with the bitterness of anguish.

Amos recovered. Isaac, as Henrietta knew he would, spent the next nights in remorse and penance on the same hill. On the third morning he lifted his sombre eyes to hers across the breakfast table. She sat small and unsmiling, the white ruffled peignoir tied securely at her throat, her tumble of dark hair swept to the back of her head. Her anger gave a new depth to her beauty.

'I have made a decision, Henrietta.'

She waited, her coldness matching his.

'The boy is not strong enough for this country. He is weak, his health is poor. I have not the time to give to him.

He shall go where life will be . . . more accommodating, shall we say? I have written Havenhall.'

'Isaac, that's an orphanage!'

'It is a charity institution that prepares unfortunate boys to face life. I shall make regular payments to keep him there. The weather is quite mild and – '

'Isaac, in the name of God, he is your son!'

'Like you, my dear, I hold to that position. I have a family to maintain and a responsibility to this town. And Colin Thatcher is no longer here to assert his claim or' – Isaac's thin lips slid back over his teeth – 'take his thrashing. But as you are the boy's mother, you must be considered. If you are set against Havenhall, I will continue the boy's training as you have seen. I am quite willing to support him, and that should satisfy you. I am not willing to have him grow into his father's image, spouting verses, dabbling at pictures, and fouling another man's house!'

Henrietta saw defeat, but fury blinded her.

'Isaac, for ten years I have told you the truth!'

He watched her narrowly, her breasts rising beneath the folds of her gown.

'For ten years you have told me what you thought was good for me. And I am sick to God Himself with it. And with the sight of your bastard!'

'Then I'll take him to New Orleans. Your son, Isaac, but you'll never have to see him again! Tante Charl will take him, my father's sister! She still lives there. In the old house. I'll write her now. This morning. We can leave in a week.' She had managed to steady her voice. 'The sun will be good for him, Isaac. And perhaps some day – '

'There will be no some day.' His eyes, fixed on her, had grown moist and bright. 'But you will not write this morning. If there is to be a bargain, we will talk about it. Tonight.'

He touched his mouth with a napkin and rose. Passing her, he dropped a hand tight on her shoulder, the fingers sliding into the ruffles.

'Tonight.'

Sitting now in the mustiness of her father's den, Henrietta felt her face flush again, while her hands chilled.

16

To stay here with Amos, to sit in the still, sunlit inner courtyard, to walk the beloved streets of Le Vieux Carré with him, watching him grow stronger. She let the dream spin on as if no other children existed, as if in Isaac's deepening shadows . . . who else was there to shelter them, who else to protect the gaunt, sombre man who was her husband from himself? If there was to be a bargain, she had given her word.

Her reverie broke. A clatter of horses' hooves stopped outside the house. She rose. This was no longer her house, but she would meet this woman, whoever she was, on equal terms. Not as a visitor, or a suppliant. Memory played an odd trick. She was a little girl in Communion white, stepping timidly from her father's study . . . into the mystery of incense; the glint of candles; the soprano soaring her mother's faith to the cathedral arches; the thin, cracked chant from the altar: '*Hail Mary, full of grace . . . pray for us sinners, now and at the hour of our death . . .*'

The front door opened. She heard a man's voice, rich and mocking.

'It's Pandora's box of troubles, Fleur, tied up for Mardi Gras. Or maybe your costume for Poseidon's ball!'

'Do you think I'd need a trunk as Venus?'

'It's not very big.'

The woman laughed. It was neither harsh, nor sweet. It was throaty and easy. 'Rosie,' she called. 'Where is she? Roger, my pet, whosesoever joke it is, tell Rosie to have that thing removed from the front step, while I go freshen up.'

There was a silence, a breathless little laugh, a man's endearment, and quick steps.

'Don't keep me waiting or I'll open that trunk. I wager it's your ill-gotten gains of the afternoon. You had the devil's run of luck today, my sweet. They'd need a trunk to send it on.'

The woman seemed at a distance now. Henrietta heard the big laugh again. 'What I win I keep with me, pet. No, don't come up now. We'll have a little champagne downstairs to celebrate our luck and then you must go. Tonight we shall sit in the best seats at the opera.'

Henrietta lifted her head, touched a fleeting hand to her

hair, and slowly walked out into the hall. She saw a sweep of fawn-coloured skirt with jet passementerie on the upper stairs. She saw a tall man, fleshy and solid beneath the careful tailoring of a pearl-grey suit, his hair as black as the disappearing passementerie. At her step he turned abruptly from the mirror.

'Well!' She saw his eyes widen with that quick look of appreciation she had seen in so many men, the instant admiring glance that had stirred the dark jealousies of Isaac and sent her at last to a brief and gentle lover. So long ago. So long ago.

'Madame.' His bow was not without grace, but he kept his eyes on her.

She did not incline her head. 'I have come at an awkward time. I was in the den. I could not help but hear. The trunk is my son's. If it can be left on the step until I can summon a carriage . . .'

She had no plans; the words came heedless but measured. She had no further business in this house. She heard steps. The fawn-coloured skirt was descending the stairs.

'Who are you?' The woman was full-bosomed, tightly corseted. In the dim light beneath the spread of a large black velvet hat, her skin had the smoothness of lard. Ripe, her father would have said. Overripe, thought Henrietta. She caught a cloying scent of perfume and thought of her mother's cool rose water and verbena. The woman had stopped halfway down the stairs.

'Madame Martine?'

'Yes. I am Madame Martine.'

'I am Henrietta Roundtree.' The woman looked blank. 'Henrietta Martine Roundtree.' Then the small devil that could never stay subdued in Henrietta very long took possession of her. 'Henrietta *Beaulaire* Martine.' Creole pride. She had not fallen back on it since the day her mother was buried.

'Henrietta!' Fleur Martine caught up her skirt and came towards her. 'Henrietta! Phillip's daughter! Roger, I told you about Phillip's daughter. From the day I met him he talked about his "little lady". It didn't please me too much,

18

I can say.' She laughed and again it had an honesty that was not unkind. 'The day he married me I made him promise not to say "little lady" again. I know all about quality. It doesn't help you enjoy life. I guess it didn't help you.' She had taken Henrietta momentarily into her orbit before dismissing her. 'But it looks as if you've done pretty well.' She unpinned her hat. 'Roger, Henrietta and I have a few things to talk about, I guess. I don't know why you've come here, but Phillip would expect that much from me. We'll forget our little toast.'

'No, no, please don't, Madame.' Her father's name stuck in Henrietta's throat. 'I did not come here to interfere. My son and I – '

'Your son?'

Roger's laugh interrupted. 'The trunk, Fleur. Pandora's box of troubles. As I told you!' But his eyes were on Henrietta again and Fleur Martine saw it.

'Perhaps you'd better tell me just why you have come, Mrs Roundtree. No, wait, Roger. You might be useful.' Fleur had never managed her life by showing resentment. 'Let's sit down. Rosie can bring coffee if you like.'

Henrietta declined the coffee. In the less dim parlour Madame Martine's face, beneath its careful prettiness, showed lines of fatigue. Her ash-blonde pompadour drained it further of colour. She drew the louvres closer and lit a rose-tinted lamp. She sat easily and gestured Henrietta to a chair, its back to the glass cabinet.

'Your son. You've brought him with you?'

How simple it would be, Henrietta thought, if there were no details, to hurl themselves beneath your feet or into the spokes of your wheels. A forgotten little trunk, foolish with carnival ribbons, and she was reduced in her father's house to suppliant or beggar. Unless she chose to lie.

'I brought him to visit Tante Charl for a few weeks while I – my husband and I – travelled. He is not a strong little boy and . . . my husband and I thought the trip might tire him . . .'

Madame's worldly, tired eyes narrowed.

'You did not know Miss Charlotte was dead?'

'No. I am deeply grieved.'

'Four years ago. You had not heard. Yet you brought your son here with a trunk?' She rose. 'What do you want of me?'

'I want nothing, Madame. I assure you.'

'Quality, Roger. You see. You can do nothing with them. Yet in the end they come to us. Let me tell you something, Henrietta. For that's the way I know of you. Your father married quality. But he came to me for love. In the end, when he was sick and alone, he married me. I never knew when he died. One day I heard. I came to this house with papers and a wedding ring. Quality was sitting right where you are in that chair. But I was here rightfully and I stayed.' Her voice hardened, then suddenly, unexpectedly, she gave a big open laugh. 'So why shouldn't I let quality back? It isn't hard to be gracious when things are all your way. Where is your son? Tell me, are you taking him from home to hurt your husband? Or is he a bastard and your husband doesn't know? It's always a man you must get the better of.'

'Fleur – ' The man's voice held caution.

'Roger, I'm enjoying myself. Time goes round and suddenly you have another chance at the brass ring. I don't think I've introduced you properly but seeing you in the hall I thought . . . Mrs Roundtree, Roger Winters is my friend and adviser. Roger Winters. How's that for a damn-Yankee name? Where's the boy?'

'I'll fetch him myself.' Henrietta moved towards the door. 'And if you, sir, would do me the favour of calling a carriage – '

'Regretfully, Mrs Roundtree – '

'Oh, come, Roger. She's stiff-necked like the rest. I used to call Phillip that. He wasn't quality either though he married it and enough of it rubbed off. But – '

'Madame Martine!' Henrietta spun around. 'I cannot listen to this any longer. It is offensive talk. I have never lived by such ideas. Nor did my father. Whatever you mean by quality, my father, if you knew him as well as you claim, would have told you that quality is behaviour first. And last!'

The words stung, as Henrietta had intended. But she had lost something in the encounter. Temper past, nerves frayed, she had a sense that she had cheapened herself. She wanted to find Amos and escape. Where no longer mattered.

The woman in fawn picked up her flamboyant plumed hat from the divan. She spoke gravely.

'Phillip did tell me that many times. It was what finally gave me the courage to come to this house. We are perhaps more alike than you think. The boy can stay here. My life isn't suited to raising a child. Though if God had sent one . . .' She looked into some secret distance of her own. 'Children sometimes play in the court. He can have the room next to Rosalee's. If that fills your need. It is up to you.'

In the quiet the fawn skirt rustled on the stairs, then stopped. 'By the way, what is the boy's name?'

'Amos,' Henrietta answered in spite of herself.

'Amos. Another damn Yankee!' An open, easy laugh floated down. The rustle of the fawn skirt was lost beneath it.

CHAPTER TWO

Amos thrived.

The courtyard where he played was hot and bright with pink-red flowers, a sweet-smelling tree – lime, he was told – and a second tree where to his amazed eyes real lemons hung. His small dark room, warm with drifting exotic smells from the kitchen, was a cocoon. Here he could nest, alone and untroubled, painting the close walls with new, unspoken images that now began to dance through his mind.

His mother's goodbye had been swift and breath-squeezing. An instant within her arms, a single kiss, and a glimpse of tears he had never before seen in her eyes. They embarrassed him. He stood uncertainly, listening to the quick steps fade and a distant door close. Then he sat down and solemnly finished his honey cake, wondering how long

21

it would be before he could return to the magic of the glass cabinet in the front parlour.

As it turned out, it was quite long. In fact, as the days passed he lost track of the time. He could play in the sunny inner court with Glory, a delicious cream-coloured little girl with tightly pinned black hair, who was too shy of the blond boy to speak until the day the peddler came by with his hand organ and set her dancing. He had tried to follow. Other children gathered, laughing at him. He might have cried. Instead Henrietta's child laughed. As he had never laughed in his father's house. Then, too aware of himself, he had fled to his cocoon.

He was told these were the children he could play with in the courtyard. He could go with turbaned Rosalee to the French Market, to a mind-dazzling array, so far from Mr Bowler's white counters, grey sacks, and brown barrels in Thatcher that Amos felt giddy as he trotted among the stands. Pink- and pearl-tinted fish, ripe oranges vying with tangerines, dark blue and purple fruits he could not name, the alternating greenness of leek and gumbo and lettuce, the yellows or reds of peppers and ripe tomatoes, and the curious striping of something Rosalee called gourds. It was a world of shifting colours to which the warm faces of his playmates belonged. Amos rarely saw a mirror. Once, when he had peeked out of stirring adolescent curiosity into Rosalee's room, he had caught his face in the mirror and hated it. 'I need a shell,' he told the pallid reflection. 'Then I could boil up pink like a shrimp. Or brown like a coffee bean.'

But Amos, too long by himself, had little notion of street playing. Most of all he held to one dream, to return to the glass cabinet. There was magic that could fill his days. From that Rosalee had sternly warned him. 'There's no quality out there in front. You're to stay with me and be what you're supposed to be. Like you belong to this whole house. When your mother comes back . . .'

But Amos knew better than that. He had sensed finality. He would have to figure things out for himself.

So at the hour when the doorbell was not answered and he could hear Rosalee's guttural breathing, heavy in sleep,

Amos crossed the court, went up a flight of steps, pushed open a door, and found himself in a dim upper hall.

Given time, he would have liked to push open each panelled mahogany door in turn. But his goal lay below. He found the banistered staircase. The stairs were polished and bare but they did not squeak. Not like the three top steps home in Thatcher that always gave him away. Here he had only to mind his feet. The silence was so profound that he grew impatient. The parlour door stood half open. He scampered down the four remaining steps, across the hall, and into the room.

One rose-tinted lamp was lit. He saw little else in the dimness of the room except the woman he had met only once and knew as 'Madame'. She lay half reclined against the mustard velvet pillows of the divan. The bodice of her striped dress was open. Amos had never seen such a whiteness and fullness of flesh.

In that first gasping instant he saw neither the napkin-wrapped bottle and two glasses near the elbow nor the buff shadow of a man's coat at the end of the divan. His eyes were transfixed on the white mounds of flesh. He felt a dizziness in his head, a spinning in his stomach, and backed against the half-opened door. It swung closed behind him.

The man rose from a chair opposite the divan. The woman sat up clutching a pale shawl.

'Who is it?' The voice was shrill.

'It's the little bastard.' The man loomed large towards him.

For Amos there was no escape or any sound in his throat with which to answer.

'What are you doing here? Answer me!'

'Let me, Roger!' Madame had by now drawn the striped silk closed and the shawl tightly across it.

'You damned little sneak! I warned you, Fleur.'

'Roger, I said leave this to me!' For a moment, lovers though they might have been, they were enemies too: the older woman and the younger man, eyeing each other across the hidden, hostile realities that lay so near the surface. 'I'll handle this. Please leave us.'

He hesitated, then as usual obeyed, the price of comfort, skilled softness, and the best seats at the opera.

Amos, too terrified to move, felt himself pushed aside and heard the door shut hard behind him.

'Come here.' She had turned off the rose lamp and seated herself in a stiff-backed chair. 'Stand right there in front of me.'

The light was so dim, he could make out little except a towering figure of justice, encased in folds like an ancient Buddha he had once seen in a newspaper, a man infinitely small before him.

'What did you see?'

He swallowed to find his voice and failed.

'I shall tell you. You saw *nothing*.'

He lowered his head.

'Why did you come to this room?' His pale terror must have touched her. Her voice softened. 'You must answer me, Amos. You came against my orders. You know that?'

'Yes.' Speech had returned to him, thin as a reed.

'Why?'

Amos who had learned truth on pain of hellfire, could not lie. But he had also learned that if he told the truth, what lay nearest his heart would be taken from him. Out of his anguish compromise fluttered.

'I came to see what was in the room.'

'What was that?'

He nodded numbly towards the cabinet, glittering like some sunken *Rheingold* in the watery dimness.

'What made you want to see that?' It was as if she were toying with him, playing out the line, then tightening, yielding and drawing, until at last the terrible punishment would be evident.

'I don't know. I couldn't help it.'

The last dregs of truth. Amos was spent. For a long time it seemed she sat looking at him. He had half forgotten the frightening whiteness he had seen from the door. He was aware only that halfway across the room awaited all the magic and mystery his life had ever held and that in another moment it would be shut from him for ever.

At last Madame Martine came to a decision. She rose,

statuesque calm. Hers was a strange beauty that would make his punishment even more terrible.

'Amos, you have done something very wrong. I do not know how to deal with wrong things because I do not always know what made them wrong. Whether you do them or I do them. So I must think. This is what I have decided. Every afternoon, at precisely three-fifteen, you may come to this room and stay for precisely fifteen minutes, no more, no less. Rosalee will bring you. You will not leave the room until she comes for you. Do you understand?'

He did not cry because he was a boy. He stood letting the enormous weight of her words enter him.

She was moving towards the door.

He wanted to thank her, to bow stiffly as he had been taught. Deeper than that, for a powerful instant, he might have flung himself into her arms. But he could never do that. Not now.

She paused. 'Did anyone ever tell you that you looked like someone, Amos?'

'No.'

'It must be the light. Run along.'

He fled through the house. He did not know his first innocence was gone.

In the days that followed, Madame Fleur Martine went through an imperceptible change. Rosalee accepted the violets Roger Winters brought and returned to say that Madame was resting, a slight *mal de tête*. Twice the carriage rolled to the door at three o'clock only to roll away again, empty.

The sultry heat gave way to rain, and the courtyard held three inches of slowly draining water. Amos stayed in his room except for when he went into Rosalee's kitchen to look at the dragging hands of the clock. The servants' talk rose in waves of chatter on one subject: What would the weather be for Mardi Gras? If it rained, would there be parades? Recollections of one year's sudden violent afternoon storm that broke, passed, and left the streets axle deep in mud, miring floats and horses. The voices rose with excitement.

'We'll go up to Storeyville. It won't hurt Amos to see the sights. Those fancy whores will parade no matter what!'

'And the ladies will be out watchin' behind their masks, you bet.' Giggles.

'You got something for Amos to wear, Rosalee?'

'I got Candy's baby rabbit suit.'

'Amos is too old for that!'

'He's little. It'll fit.'

'I want to be a baby doll.'

'You'll do nothing like that. You're staying with me, girl!'

Amos understood none of it. He was sure of one thing: He would not go anywhere as a baby rabbit. But the mounting excitement caught him up like Christmas. Only it was different from Christmas. The store windows were alive with grimacing masks, grinning beneath outrageous, thickened cheeks, enormous mouths. Sometimes, through a window, he glimpsed a mirage of gilt and spangles and feathers. In the narrow streets of the Quarter his pulse suddenly would beat to the savage strangeness of shuttered music, and everywhere purple, green, and gold burst like rainbows beneath uncertain clouds.

But there was nothing he saw or heard, nothing they talked about that could match the magic in the front parlour or lure him from it.

All else was alien. This he had made his. He waited each afternoon, tense lest Rosalee would not look at the clock or would fall asleep or forget. It had not happened. At three-ten she would brush his hair, straighten his shirt, brush the dust off his knees, and lead him wordlessly into the cool, dim front hall. There she would close the parlour doors behind him.

Three days before Mardi Gras, in the thin slanted sunlight that had last broken through, Amos had passed only five of his precious minutes when he heard the door open. Always on knife-edge, he jumped back from the cabinet. A faint scent spun him around.

Madame Martine moved slowly towards him. She wore a

pale white dress, pleated high in front. Her ashen hair, freed from its lacquered pompadour, looked oddly old. She smiled slightly; her teeth, too small for a mouth too wide, revealed her gums. Whatever flair she possessed she seemed determined to hide. Only her large eyes, dark with a meaning he could not read, held him.

'Are you afraid of me, Amos?'

'No.' He remembered Rosalee's admonition. 'No, Madame.'

'Are you satisfied to look into that cabinet through the glass?'

'It's locked.'

'It's been locked a long time.'

He nodded. 'I can see all right.'

'Would you like to know what it is behind that glass?'

He did not, really. It was enough to look at the small figures, three to four inches high, each perfect, each proud, each with a mystery, that both fascinated and awed him. He believed as he stared that they were alive, these knights and dukes, these marvellous, intricate crowns and trains, the ageing king, the young exquisite queen. And the court lady, white as an angel, her arm thrown up as if something had frightened her. In his brief visits he had made up endless stories about rescuing her, about battling the monstrous tiny figures, about . . .

'Come and sit beside me.'

It would mean giving up the last of his precious moments.

'Rosalee is not coming for you today. We have plenty of time. But stay where you are if you like.'

Fleur Martine dropped to a settee beside him. It was not comfortable. For all her vigilance the years were there, the stumbling blocks. It would not be easy to win him. Yet chance had dropped him into her life. In further perversity chance had given him traces of the fine blond face of the man who had at last married her. Respectability had been Phillip Martine's bridal gift and his bequest. Now at long last, filling the hidden emptiness that no man on earth knew, had come this boy. She dared not yet use the word. This . . . son.

27

She sighed. It had begun so badly. What he had seen. What he had guessed. It was useless to pretend he would forget. Children did not forget. She would have to woo him slowly, carefully, filling his mind with so much fantasy of flesh and beauty that her own image would shift and vanish. Some day he would throw his young arms around her neck.

It was the only way Fleur Martine could think, if thinking it was. She would steer Amos for ever from the path of righteousness, as he had been snatched from the coldness of winter.

Madame Martine gestured towards the cabinet.

'Would you like to know what it is?'

Amos hesitated. He was not sure he wanted the fantastic scene behind the glass explained. Not by her. His own dreams had come thickly, glancing off jewelled and ermined figures, like shards of light that became one with this moist, warm, colour-spun new world in which he found himself. They were private dreams, depths he had never guessed lay within himself in the bleakness of his narrow room in Thatcher.

Madame Martine sighed. The boy was indeed difficult.

'I asked you a question.'

Amos nodded without looking at her.

'It is the Court of Comus, the most important ball of Mardi Gras. It is a place to which you will never be invited. Neither will I. Nor was the man who carved and painted those figures.'

'Why?'

For a moment she had his attention.

'Because he did not have the key. You can be rich or poor, young or old, but you must have the key or you will never be allowed in.'

'What key?'

'A name. His wasn't good enough. But he went once anyway. Then he made his own Court of Comus. So when Mardi Gras time came, he could always go to the ball. Watch!'

She leaned forward, pressed a finger against the heart of a magnolia blossom carved into the ornate frame of the cabinet. Inside, the figures began to move. The knights and ladies bowed to each other and began to turn. A jester figure Amos had not seen before jumped up, a tiny jack-in-the-box, before the king's throne. The queen's head turned. The lady's white arms lifted as she turned her back.

Madame pressed the blossom again and the figures began to whirl silently to unheard music.

'If ever I cease to love . . .' Madame Martine sang softly, huskily. 'If ever I cease to love, may the moon be turned into green cheese. If ever I – '

Amos's laugh burst light and unexpected.

'Come.' She took his hands. 'Dance.'

She swung him around once, her cream skirts swirling. But he had never danced. He stumbled awkwardly and broke free, his face red. With a click the pantomime in the cabinet was over.

'Didn't you like it?' she asked.

His eyes were fixed on the cabinet.

'Some day you'll dance to that song, Amos. And love it. It's the song everyone sings at Mardi Gras. I'll teach it to you.' The throaty voice held an intimacy that mocked the words. 'If ever I cease to love, if ever I cease to love, may fish grow legs . . . and cows lay eggs . . .'

It was not what he wanted. He stood stiffly beside the cabinet, searching his mind for the question. She had told him everything but the one thing he could not understand. The one mystery that had brought him back day after day to the cabinet and held him spellbound yet chilled.

'What is it, Amos?'

'They are not people in there,' he blurted. 'They are animals! Look at them! I mean sometimes!'

That was the way Phillip saw them. But the words stuck; the raw truth stayed silent within her. Time had blown that bitterness from the house. The moment for her was now. She wanted to hear him laugh again.

'That depends on which side of the cabinet you look at them from. Come to this side.'

That was the sorcery he had found from the first time he had walked around the cabinet. The gorgeously decked little figures with their human faces that were not human.

The carver's skill had somehow revealed through the humanity the head of hog or ape, wolf or lynx.

'It's a fairy tale, Amos. Some day you can read it for yourself. See. Comus the King, the wizard, holds out a jewelled cup – the Cup of Enchantment. When he gives it to the members of his court, they turn into beasts. But there in the cabinet they are only beginning to change.'

Amos's fingers slid towards the magnolia blossom.

'No. That's enough!' Madame Martine rose. Her emotions had run wide and deep. They were now touching nerves.

She took his hand. It lay lifeless in hers.

'Besides, that's only a toy. A very old toy. I can show you something much more exciting. Would you like to go to a real ball with me, Amos?'

There was no answer to a question he had never before been asked.

'I shall take you to Mardi Gras night. The Ball of Poseidon, the King of the Sea. You will see things there you've never even imagined! Real things!'

She opened the heavy parlour doors and watched him run through the hall, out to the sunlit courtyard, and across it to where the servants lived. She would move him from there. But slowly. One step at a time.

The next day Madame Martine permitted Roger Winters to escort her to the chemin de fer tables. She felt lucky and elated, but her winnings were poor and she came away petulant. Perversely, in the carriage going home, she talked about Amos. When she reached her plan for the ball, he turned on her, his face heavy with anger.

'That you will not do, Fleur!'

'Who is to stop me?'

'Children are not allowed. You know that as well as I do.'

When she smiled, with closed lips, her fading beauty still charmed.

'Amos is not coming as a child. He will be in the living tableau. With me. Cupid, the son of Venus.'

'What are you up to, Fleur?'

'Are you jealous, Roger? Of a boy of twelve?'

He did not speak until they were out of the carriage and at the steps of the house.

'Fleur, listen to me. For your own sake. Don't take the boy to that ball. It is no place for him. It was madness to keep him here. Nothing good can come of dragging him with you. And maybe a great deal of harm.'

'What does that mean?'

'It means I don't want you to do it!'

'Are you so sure of me – and your place here – that you can give me orders?'

For a long moment their eyes held. In that fiery conjunction lay the hostility, the fascination, the sexual duel, that had bound them so long.

His hand slid triumphantly beneath her arm.

'Let me talk to you, Fleur. Now. Let me make you see. The ball is our night . . . ours. You and I . . .' The words, as close and as sure as his touch, were hot with promise. They bore the scent of decay.

She had not expected the decision so soon. Now abruptly the path forked at her feet. Had the boy with his solemn child eyes, his skin like fresh milk, brought her to this? Or had the noon brightness in her unsparing hand mirror?

'Fleur . . .' The man's face flushed; his masculinity pressed against her silks. How often she had yielded, dizzy . . .

She raised her eyes to his.

'I'm really quite fatigued, Roger.'

Without a word he opened the door. She heard it close, the carriage wheels fade.

Silence engulfed her. She recognized it. The silence of the coming years.

'Amos!' she called.

There was no answer. She knew there would be none.

Not yet.

CHAPTER THREE

This day, destined to change for ever young Amos Roundtree's life, was marked, too, on the gilt-edged white calendar on Henrietta Roundtree's writing desk. Marked as invisibly as it was on her own heart.

Outside, the February rain fell cold and relentless, melting Thatcher's snows, blackening the trunks of the maple trees, and baring patches of soaked earth to a false awakening of New England spring.

But Henrietta, this bleak morning, was blind to both rain and presentiment. Nor had she any need to look at the calendar. It was Tuesday in Thatcher. But half a continent away in the sunlit city where she had left Amos, it was Shrove Tuesday. Already men and women were filling the streets, flinging themselves in final abandon to Carnival, before the ashes and penance of Lent. It was Fat Tuesday, Mardi Gras, the riotous farewell to the devil and sin.

She saw herself with Amos, holding his hand, seeing his pale face light up, hearing his rare little laugh at that triumph of buffoonery and beauty, the King of Carnival. *Carne-vale*, the farewell to flesh. Not only to meat eaten, but to the fires of the body's flesh. But she would not explain all that. He was too young.

Too young.

As it had been when she came as a young bride to Thatcher, her Creole blood was still running strong. She had been astonished when, after her first Christmas, Thatcher settled into its long snows, its dark nights.

'But Twelfth Night? Twelfth Night!' she cried out. 'That's when the Wise Men found the child! Why, everybody celebrates! In New Orleans there are as many as five hundred balls from Twelfth Night up to Lent! And the biggest of all is Mardi Gras.' An infectious laugh broke from her. 'If sin is so big in the world, it deserves a big farewell, doesn't it?' The little ripple spread into silence.

She could hear the words 'heathenish' and 'popish', behind her. What was she? French and Spanish? Foreign, Thatcher whispered, and that meant heaven knew what. The very word *Creole* breathed of sorcery and forbidden rites.

That night Isaac read to her from the Bible.

'If thy right hand offend thee . . .'

She was not to talk of such things again. Sins of the flesh were to be left to the pulpit. And pagan ways left to pagans. Then he had closed the Bible, taken off his thick woollen night-robe, and made such loveless love to her that Carnival's own King of Misrule might have brought them to bed.

Henrietta sometimes had wept; sometimes his blunt fears, his lack of joy, wrung her heart. She had wilfully followed this strong man of the soil to what was truly for her the end of the earth. She would keep her bargain. She would not admit her mistake, and she was carrying a child again. But some day she would teach him God's other gift – laughter.

Henrietta shook the memories from her mind and returned to Amos. She would return for him in six months. She could not think of a longer absence. She had told Isaac nothing of the visit, of Tante Charl's death. Nor did he ask. Henrietta saw each day as a coin to be spent as best she could. She had never looked too far into the future. Time would do all things, she believed. Otherwise how could one live at all?

She was not aware until the third knock that someone was at the door.

It was young Bessie Haskell, whose fall from innocence had doomed her from teaching to domestic service.

'Three men downstairs to see Mr Roundtree. They went straight into the parlour, muddy boots and all. They say they're to see Mr Roundtree at nine.'

It was nine-twenty.

'Tell them he's at his office.'

'They say he's not. So they've come here.'

'I'll go down.'

The girl hesitated, burdened with a second thought.

'One of them is my own cousin, Aaron, and I gave him a look that told him what I thought, ma'am. Coming to the front door, mud, rain, and – '

'It's all right, Bessie.'

But it was not. It was a mark of the new times, and the uncomfortable pinnacle on which Isaac Roundtree now stood. Honorary Mayor, chief elder of the church, richest man in Thatcher, his judgement sought before any town decision was made, any official pen set to paper. Thatcher demanded integrity. And the Isaac Roundtree they knew had never compromised himself to politics, to popular applause, or to the gain of money for its own sake. He asked humbly and publicly on his knees for wisdom, or sought God alone up on Preacher Hill behind his farm in the valley, a tall, gaunt figure, as reassuring to the townspeople as the weather vane on the firehouse.

Now a decision had fallen to him that would split the town from the well-to-do in Carriage Lane to the factory workers in Juno's Landing.

But he shared nothing with her. Lately his silences had grown as frequent as his absences at the farm. He had gone last night in the rising wind and rain. She had slept alone and in that grateful circumstance had awakened refreshed and unworried. For all she knew he might still be out on his hill. Yet tardiness to Isaac was like gluttony, the sin of indulgence.

Still there were those three men. She could offer them coffee on this wretched morning. She had a reputation for coffee. Thatcher had never guessed her French trick of adding chicory.

Or she could send them away.

But this was Mardi Gras. Henrietta would never be too old or too settled for that small, single dimple of mischief.

The three men rose.

She recognized two of them at once. Josiah Spooner, third cousin to Isaac and the only living relative he had ever admitted to in Thatcher. She disliked Joe Spooner. He had the crafty look of a man who knew too much and was paid too little for it. Thin and spindle-legged, he was the town mortician and sometimes the sheriff's clerk. He envied his

34

third cousin everything he had, including his fancy wife. Outwardly Joe was as loyal as the sea tide.

Aaron Haskell, big and hearty with sun-seared, veined cheeks and hands like hams. She knew those hands could handle a lettuce seedling or a newly ripened peach with the delicacy of an artist. She was not at all sure of her Royal Doulton coffee cups. Nor did she care. She liked Aaron Haskell. He was rooted to the earth. She had heard things were not going well with him.

The third man was a stranger, and then she guessed. The wiry unruliness of his black hair, the strong gypsy-like face, and the outrageous gold stud he flaunted in one ear. Maxl Krom, the immigrant Hungarian who had somehow made his way from the Boston docks to Thatcher, learned English, found work at the factory at Juno's Landing, and risen to foreman. He was Thatcher's first taste of a labour leader. Rabble-rouser, they called him. But the men followed him like a polestar.

His eyes were bold as they travelled from the grey ruching at her throat to the bottom flounce of her skirt.

'I'm sorry my husband has been delayed. The roads are so muddy.' She smiled. 'Do sit down. I've ordered coffee.' It was a subtle command to the Hungarian. He ignored it.

'It's really a morning that no one should be travelling about in, if they can help it. The rains are early this year.'

'We shouldn't have come here, Mrs Roundtree . . .' Aaron Haskell began. 'But – '

'You're damned right we *should*.' The Hungarian hunched his shoulders. 'And we're staying until we see him. We've heard the Town Council's about decided not to let the new freight-railroad bridge be put through here in Thatcher. If that's so, it'll cross the river fifteen miles below and that means – '

'Max, Mrs Roundtree is not interested – '

'But I am. I know about the bridge, Mr – Mr – '

'Maxl Krom, foreman at the mill and speaking for every man down there who sees his job going if the mill has to pay extra haulage. It'll put the whole factory out of business.'

Bessie entered with a tray of kitchen coffee cups and a

plain coffee-pot, her accusing eyes moving from the men's wet coats to the carpet stains.

'Thank you, Bessie. And some cinnamon cake. The fresh-made.'

Henrietta seated herself on the divan. The day had brightened.

'Mr Krom, I'm very much interested. Like you, I realize that Thatcher must move with the times. Our old railroad bridge of course is not going to be adequate to our future.'

Maxl Krom took the cup from her and sat down beside her.

'You're a smart woman, Mrs Roundtree, as I've heard . . .'

But none of them heard the rest of the sentence. The front door opened. Bessie's murmur reached them.

Isaac Roundtree stood in the entryway. He seemed to fill it, width and height. He looked past his wife.

The men stumbled to their feet.

'Our appointment, gentlemen, was at my office.'

'Isaac, do have some coffee. You must be chilled to the bone driving in.' Henrietta's smile was ravishing. Her small hands moved expertly. Maxl Krom watched her from the corner of his eye.

'So we shall adjourn downtown at once. I regret any inconvenience my tardiness might have caused you but I was delayed by an unavoidable matter of importance at the bank.'

Henrietta sipped her coffee. It was better than revealing surprise. If Isaac had spent the night at the farm, why had he not come home? Why had he gone directly to the bank?

The three men started to talk at once.

'At my office, if you please. That is, if you wish for my time. Otherwise I will bid you good morning.'

'Mr Roundtree, we want your time.' There was an inescapable aura of power and defiance around the Hungarian foreman. 'And we've put in a lot of our own to get it. Mr Spooner here, no hurry about his work. His business can wait all day, unless the weather turns warm.' He grinned and his teeth were white and even. 'Aaron here, those peach trees ain't growing very hard right now. But

I'm on my own time and I'll be docked for every minute I'm out of the plant. It's nine-thirty now and – '

'Isaac, do talk with the men here. It's quite all right and I do think it's fair.'

Isaac Roundtree looked at his wife as if seeing her for the first time. She started to rise.

Whether by accident, courtesy, or something unaccountable, she was aware that Maxl Krom touched her elbow. It was intimate, instantaneous, and gone almost as soon as she was aware of her own awareness.

Isaac smiled his yellowed smile. 'Since my wife's hospitality has put my own business habits to shame, we shall do as she wishes.' He caught sight of Bessie bearing the cinnamon cake. 'But this is not a social hour. So we shall proceed at once. Bessie, take that thing out. Henrietta, my dear, you will excuse us.'

Very deliberately he placed his hand beneath the elbow Maxl Krom had touched and walked her to the hall. As deliberately he turned from her. He neither looked at her nor spoke. But beneath the grey silk she felt a chill, a premonition unlike anything she had known before.

She mounted the stairs to the first murmur of men's voices. It was not long to remain a murmur.

Isaac Roundtree did not sit down. He stood with the muscular confidence of a man who knew the advantage of his height. It obliged his callers to remain on their feet looking up to him as he took their measurement. Josiah Spooner, shrunken with early rickets; bulky Aaron Haskell, stooped with the labour of the soil; and the Hungarian Krom, broad as a wrestler and only half a head taller than Isaac's own wife.

'You asked for my time?'

The men's voices broke out simultaneously.

'One of you must be spokesman.'

Josiah Spooner tacitly asserted his relationship. He was, after all, the only one who could address the honorary mayor by his first name.

'Isaac . . .' he began and caught the unmistakable flash of anger in those brooding eyes. 'Mr . . . Mayor . . . Cousin . . .' He wavered.

37

Maxl Krom stepped forward. The swarthy strength in his face matched Isaac's own.

'Mr Roundtree, I'm not depending on any blood relationship to talk to you. Mr Spooner here came along because he said – '

'Please get to your business. I'm not interested in what Josiah Spooner has ever said.'

That cowed the little cousin and brought a near smile to the Hungarian.

'I got two hundred men behind me at the factory who'd agree with that, Mr Roundtree. They're tired of all the talk that's gone on. They want to know what's going to happen to the factory and to their jobs if the new freight line and the depot goes through downriver at Blaynesville. Instead of here in Thatcher where it ought to. They see the factory being moved – '

'But a man can't move his truck farmin' and fruit orchards . . .' Haskell broke in.

'And they're doing big quarrying up beyond Pinesville, opening up a new dig that'll beat Vermont granite all to hell, if they can move it . . .' chattered Spooner, forgetting his awe. 'Isaac, you're the only man around here who can make Thatcher's stiff-necks give up. They don't want that freight depot because it's where they drive their carriages. And it don't hurt them none if only two trains a day come through Thatcher, one going up, the other going back, four cars for passengers, one for freight. It's about all the old bridge will take anyway. But I tell you, Isaac, unless this valley opens up and Thatcher's high and mighty get off their asses, there'll be grass growing on the one railroad line we got running. People are getting mighty angry watching things getting better for the whole rest of the state, making progress, expanding, while up here in Thatcher they're still worrying if the trains will scare the horses. Hell's fire, Isaac, there ain't going to be no horses pretty soon. Everything's going to move on wheels and gasoline. I'm figuring to get one of them horseless hearses one of these days as soon as I can find someone around here who knows enough to fix it if it breaks down.'

It was the longest speech Josiah Spooner had ever made

to his important cousin. He had the sole satisfaction of seeing Isaac gazing over his head out the window, as if no sound had disturbed the distant contemplation of his private thoughts.

Isaac unclasped his hands behind his black frock coat and bounced his fingertips together, signalling his return.

'Is that all?'

Aaron Haskell cleared his throat. 'Mr Roundtree, you've done a lot for this town. And you've always been good to me and mine. Takin' Bessie in after her trouble. Payin' prompt with no questions. Never returning melons or peaches if they were touched a little. And taking my boy to the hospital when he fell from the rafter at Higgins's barn raising. Mrs Roundtree herself comin' every day with books to see that Neddie did his studying. I remember now what she said with that laugh of hers. "It won't do you any good, Neddie, to get that neck well if you don't have a good head to set on it!"' Aaron let a burly half-chuckle escape. He heard nothing answering him. 'It's this way, Mr Roundtree. I been to all these meetings down at Juno's Landing. I know there's two men on the Town Council solid against any freight line for Thatcher. There's two not sure. And there's you. They're all pretty big men in this town but I know how they listen to you. You could swing 'em any way you want. I got up at the meeting two nights ago and I told 'em it's Mr Roundtree who counts. And he's a good man. He'll do what's right for this town. So that's why we come here today. To ask if you can see it our way because this valley's yours much as it belongs to any of us.'

Aaron took a red handkerchief from his back pocket and wiped his shiny face. Talking was an effort. He preferred the silence of growing things. But he had done his best.

And he knew that Isaac Roundtree had listened, with the attention of a man who shared the silence of the soil.

Isaac's erect stance, like his expression, did not change. 'Has everything been said?'

There was an instant of silence. It might have gone better had not the Hungarian's ancient alienism stirred.

'No, by *Christos*, it hasn't, Mr Roundtree! I didn't come here to beg! I came here to tell you that I and my men want justice. Our fair share. I know your kind. I come from a village like this in Hungary. Only the man who ran things was a count, sitting up in his castle, not doing a thing except playing his music, keeping his women, and counting the money he got off the backs of my people. He never came down from his hill, not even when the wheat crop dried up or the vineyards failed. He didn't have to. He owned that village and everybody in it. Body and soul! He collected first, no matter who starved. That's why I came here. To a country where every man is free and no man can trample on another man's rights. Let them crawl to you, if they like.' He jerked his swarthy head in the direction of the other two, and the gold stud flashed. 'Let them lick your boots, but I tell you that my men want that freight depot here in Thatcher and we'll get it if we have to take the land ourselves. I'm done with oppressors!'

Thatcher had never heard words like it. Nor had the century-and-a-half-old house in which Isaac Roundtree stood with his visitors. The rough voice rasped through the old polished hall, through the pantry doors, as if hurling the violence of a coming century through the settled tranquillity.

Isaac walked to the window and saw that the rain was lessening. Then he turned and faced his angry threatener.

'Who are you?'

Maxl Krom shifted his feet. He had said everything. He was used to ringing cheers. Aaron Haskell and Josiah Spooner stood silent.

'You know who I am,' he said sullenly.

'I know your name. How long have you been in this country?'

'Seven years.'

'Seven years.' Isaac made it seem like a drop of lingering rain, disappearing in the brightening day.

'Well, gentlemen. You've given me what I presume is the best of your thinking. I shall give you the best of mine.'

'When?' demanded Maxl Krom.

'When I am ready. Good day.'

The harsh voice had drawn Henrietta from her room to

the upper hall. She watched them leave, the Hungarian shorter than she had first thought. Isaac stood in the hall, rigid and alone. Then he did an odd thing. He touched the columned wood panelling inside the door, letting his hand remain, as if drawing strength from it. Then he took his overcoat and his tall hat from the antlered rack. He was the last man in Thatcher to surrender to the new derby. He glanced up.

His face bore a sadness she had never seen.

'Isaac, what is it? What happened?'

The sadness vanished.

'Your new friend lacks manners.'

Henrietta watched the door close and wondered if she had ever known the man with whom she had borne ten children.

The short afternoon cleared. Henrietta longed to throw a shawl over her shoulders, put on her heavy-weather shoes, and walk bareheaded through the lifting mists. She had resolutely tried to banish her hour-by-hour fantasies of Amos's little day of magic. They lay in fragments, confetti fallen to the bottom of her mind, beneath a weight she could not define. A premonition that she would not label fear. In Isaac's saddened upward glance she sensed a turning point.

She took embroidery to the back sun-room she had created for herself and sat listening to the dripping melt from the eaves, an occasional clatter of a kitchen pan, and the eventual silence of the dying day. Wheels passed but they did not stop. Twice she pricked her finger. At last she let the frame drop on to her lap and surrendered herself to Thatcher's primal sin of idleness. And to the ghosts that in this greying twilight thronged the house. She left the oil lamp unlit. She chose to let them come.

They were not the ghosts of years past, years present, and years to come in Mr Dickens's comfortable categories. They were faces freed of time. They were her children. Nathaniel Isaac, first-born and heir, with the stain of lust that had swept her into Isaac Roundtree's arms before their wedding day. Dead of God's wrath, Isaac had raged, two

41

days after birth. Divinity unappeased, the next was a girl, solemn eyed and knowing. Isaac had not looked at her for a year. Now nearing thirty, Rachel was drying too soon into schoolroom spinsterhood at the Young Ladies Seminary in Worcester. But Rachel was tight-lipped and loyal. She might outlive them all, lacking the restless fire of Henrietta that sweetened and shortened life.

Then Jonathan, so quickly after Rachel. Henrietta's hand went to her breast with the old pain. Jonathan, his wide, dark eyes full of wonder, trusting the land, the rocks and all animals. Forbidden but flying like the wind on Henrietta's own mare. Until the accident. Isaac had shot the mare and buried his only son, and the brief years of his tenderness iced over.

With that, Divine anger appeared to have abated. Other young faces crowded the old house and Henrietta's thoughts. A son, Josiah, big boned and strong, defying them with logic and surprising them with his love of the sea. Married now into Boston's tight respectability. Another son, Peter Martin, brilliant as a firefly and, like Henrietta's own father, a gambler with life. He would never settle to the law books he found too easy. Henrietta prayed for a steadying woman.

Her face softened. Her daughters. Chastity, air-spun, hair pale as champagne, spirit as buoyant, the goblet of Henrietta's own failed dreams, overflowing to disaster. Chastity – brief radiance . . .

Mary Patience, misnamed, willow-slim in her bridal white, plunging into the blindness of marriage, the rawness of Chicago, and a bed pillowed by a man's whisky breath. She would come with her small son to safety. But Henrietta would not look to the future. She would hold to what she had. Little Amos, a betrayal with his sandy hair and odd ways? He was hers, she told herself defiantly, still within her reach if she chose. As was her last born, Susannah, too fragile for the winds that buffeted this house, this land. Henrietta walked often up the hill to that tiny grave, stooping to feel the earth above it for its warmth.

Her children. Her life's summation. All but one. She shivered and pushed the name away. But he would not be denied. Simon, a harsh, brooding boy, but she had loved him because it was her nature to love. Simon, Isaac's favourite, dark souled as his father. Gone west beneath the shadow of murder. Who knew? *She* had known at last. Not with her mind, but with her being. For an instant the old horror enveloped her. Isaac and Simon, father and son, searching the Ridge for the man they believed to be her lover. Isaac returning to her bed in a silence that bore the finality of a closed door.

Seated in the dusk, she flung out her hands against the memory. They were all her children, all ten. They would live in her as she in them. The tangle of their voices, their laughter, their childish quarrels, their youthful needs cobwebbed the house, like their improbable dreams, their destinies directed by currents they themselves would never understand.

Would she see any of them again? Would this house know them or their children? Haunted by the hour and the uneasiness of her mood, Henrietta saw her own life ending more clearly than she could have ever seen its beginnings. The thought of death mingled with the hard-won wisdom of life. The true pain was not in the agonies of giving birth, small against the triumph. The true pain was in giving life, in opening doors, in time's ultimate victory, to her own defeat. They were gone, her children, sprung from what dark mixing of blood and spirit she could not guess. In the end they would pass her, and she them, as strangers.

'You're sitting in the pitch dark, ma'am!' Bessie's face loomed white in the doorway. 'The master's home and asking for you.'

Henrietta sprang to her feet. 'When . . .' But the question died. The servants had enough to speculate about.

Bessie turned up an oil wick, darted forward, and dropped to her knee.

'You're stitching, ma'am.' She peered closely at Henrietta. 'You've been crying.'

Henrietta touched her own cheek. To her surprise it was wet. She brushed at it hastily, managed a little laugh, and patted Bessie's arm. 'Didn't you know that sometimes tears come just because you love people so much?'

But Bessie was not to be put off. She would walk on hot coals to this fine lady who had given a roof and a floor to her life. They had a special bond.

'Don't you worry, ma'am. The other day Millie was dusting upstairs when the master came up. She saw him stop at the little boy's room and stand looking in. So sadlike that Millie went in afterward and made up the little bed. For luck. In case . . .'

'That was kind of Millie.' Henrietta paused, then added as gently as she could, 'We'll do nothing more like that.'

She went into the bright hall. Isaac's hat and overcoat shadowed the corner. The door to his study was closed. She went upstairs alone, changed quickly. The dark plum silk only heightened her extreme pallor. The day had stifled her.

As she came down the great standing clock in the hall struck six. An odd trick of memory reminded her that after six o'clock on Mardi Gras it was forbidden to wear masks.

Isaac Roundtree stood motionless at the tall parlour window, his back to the room, hands knotted behind him. Henrietta's stylish crimson-and-gold-striped drapes were drawn but not quite closed. The night was a streak of blackness, and the rain had begun again. It was difficult to tell whether Isaac was waiting or listening.

Dinner had been superficially conversational between long silences. The six chairs Isaac insisted be still drawn to the table had been eloquent in their muteness. Henrietta's light step sounded at last. The tall man turned heavily from the window. Faint colour had returned to her face. His wife looked enchanting.

'I had to talk to Millie, Isaac. Would you like coffee?'

'Not now. Please sit down.'

'You look worried.'

'I should look at peace. I've come to a decision.'

The casualness of his tone was in odd contrast to his face. She was aware of a chill passing through her. Once before he had talked so lightly . . .

'. . . I am going to do something I condemn in others and despise in myself. This morning in this living-room I made

44

up my mind to an action I thought honest and right. I have changed my mind.'

She must be patient, Henrietta told herself.

'Well, that's no great thing, Isaac. Everybody does it. Whatever it is, you must have a reason.'

'If you will allow me to continue. Three men sat in this room this morning, at your invitation – '

'Isaac, they were here when I – '

'Tell me which of the servants showed them in here and I'll see that we have better help. Their demands were preposterous. They are men who know nothing of this valley, what it has stood for, what it must remain. They're here for themselves. Cousin Joe, a beggar half of his life. He's got some money in that quarry, but he can't hold it without help. Aaron Haskell – if he'd bother to find out what makes fruit trees grow, he could sell all the crop he could raise, from here to Bollington. As for your new friend . . .'

At last it was out, the two-headed demon of lust and jealousy that Isaac Roundtree had battled all his life. She must be still. She must not answer. Not yet.

' . . . a hunkie millworker who sees his way to power by stirring up honest, hardworking men, killing their pride, filling them with the rot of a thousand years. Turn Thatcher into a freight junction! Let this town and this valley be smoked out, bypassed until there's nothing here but factory squalor, so a foreign devil like Maxl Krom can ride on the shoulders of the workmen as far as he wants to go! I'm a humble man, born of humble people. My father was a miller. His father was a peddler. But old Gideon Roundtree peddled more than pins and pots and women's gew-gaws. He peddled God's Word through this valley until God told him to leave his wagon and take the Book and go up on that hill behind the farmhouse. There he'd be heard. And this town and this valley prospered.'

He had never said so much to her. He was looking back down the years at something he had never shared.

'The decent people who gave it their name knew why. Because my grandfather, Gideon Roundtree, brought God to it. You're a foreigner. You, my own wife. As foreign as that Hungarian your eyes were on. You don't understand any more than he does what happens to a man who gives his strength to a new land and gets his strength from it. But old Nathaniel Thatcher knew. He built this house. And he farmed the valley too. He gave me work when I was a boy. He said even if I was only a miller's son I could amount to anything I wanted to, if I'd stay on the land and work it. One day he called me to this very room and told me he'd give me a bounty if I'd take his son's place in the Union Army. A man could do that in those days.'

The flicker of a young smile robbed his mouth of grimness.

'When I told my father, he would have whipped me but I was too tall. I told him I was going to free the slaves and get three hundred and fifty dollars for doing it. He said nobody could free the slaves but the President of the United States and taking three hundred and fifty dollars to kill somebody and get killed doing it was a sin in God's sight.

'Well, I went and I came back. And Nathaniel Thatcher left me his valley and I swore to keep it. But by that time the Devil had sent me temptation and laid claim to my soul.'

She had heard that before, as she had seen the sweat again appear on his forehead. But in his eyes was heavy-lidded sadness, the sadness she had glimpsed from the upper hall.

'Isaac, it is no sin to love a woman, marry her, and bring her to your house. If I had been another kind of woman – '

'Another kind!' he broke in. 'I've asked God that a thousand times! Why? Why, oh God, wasn't it another woman? A good, plain, kneeling woman who kept her eyes to herself and gave me sound sons. I've grown rich and I thank God for that. But He sent me a woman whose body no man can resist and who has lied to me since the night thirty years ago she lay with me in a field and forced me into the righteousness of marriage!'

Henrietta went quickly and closed the parlour doors.

'I have never lied to you, Isaac.'

'How long have you known Maxl Krom?'

'Isaac.'

'Has he brought you to bed?'

She turned but he barred her way.

'We will have this out now! You begged prettily enough for Krom and his cause this morning. I saw him looking at you, not your face, no, but what he knew better, what he felt he had a right to touch. Your body.'

She stood like stone. He had never struck her, but she knew how the very words he flung at her could excite him more than a whip. Yet this night was different. They were not in the bedroom. The words came oddly, matter-of-factly, with the weight of judgement.

'When I left the house this morning,' he began again, 'I had made my decision. I sent word to the Town Council that under no circumstances would I support the building of a new freight line and depot in Thatcher. Then I walked for a long time. I walked to this house and saw no light. I walked around it and around this town, telling myself that a man's wife should be where he could find her. I tried to guess where you were. Finally I knew what I would do. I was born humble. I was not above humbling myself once more even to the whore I took for a wife.

'So I will bargain with you, madam. I will yield to Maxl Krom's request if it would please you.'

'Please me! What do I know of Maxl Krom and the dirt under his nails? What do I care about a freight line? You can't help accusing me, Isaac. It's your sickness. But I won't let you soil me. And yourself. I came here to love and obey as I vowed. I came here to make you a home and give you children. No man in Thatcher has a finer house. No man in Thatcher speaks or looks better. Little as you've understood, I've done all that. I've endured from you what no woman on earth should endure. But I took you for my husband and prayed to God every night of my life to help me forget the differences between us. You've never forgotten them. You've hated them, and what you hate you blame on God and call sin!' She drew a breath but she could not stop. She would force him to look at what lay between them.

'You've come to hate me, Isaac, because you're ashamed of your own sickness. You tell yourself I've lied when the

47

lies are already waiting in your mind. Look at me, Isaac, and tell me what you see. You don't see a wife. You see some twisted idea of your own madness. I won't bargain with you, Isaac. Nor will I lie. My children have gone. The man I thought I married never existed. What time I have left is my own. God only can help me fill it!'

She turned but he caught her arm.

'You have not lied to me? You have never held anything from me?'

'I said that.'

'Was Colin Thatcher your lover?'

'You know he was. Had he come back for me I would have gone with him.' She said it steadily, without fear, taking some last warmth from that brief summer sweetness.

'Is Amos his son?'

She wavered. A sudden pity almost closed her throat. In the end whatever she said would make little difference. She was as incapable of freeing him as he was of freeing himself.

'Amos is your son. Ours, Isaac.'

She said it with finality.

Now she could walk from this room that had lost any semblance of belonging to her. But he was not finished.

'I was late in meeting the . . . gentlemen . . . here this morning because I went to the bank. Clay Brewster had a message for me. When you took the boy to your aunt in New Orleans, I had an account opened in the Bank of New Orleans with instruction that regular payments be made to Miss Charlotte Martine for the boy's keep. I told you I would hold to my responsibility. This came for me today.'

She saw the trap.

She took the letter wordlessly. She did not have to read it but she had to give a semblance. She followed the words slowly, aware of the ticking of the hall clock.

Dear Sir,

We have been informed that Miss Charlotte Martine died three years ago this February. The Martine House on Dauphine Street is now owned and occupied by a woman who claims to be the second wife of Phillip Martine, deceased. She is one Flora Caylee, part-owner of a gambling establishment on Esplanade Avenue and is connected with several other questionable properties. We therefore return your cheque, assuming you have no further wish to open an account. We remain, sir, your obedient . . .

'Did you know your aunt was dead?'

'I learned it when I got there.'

'Yet you never told me. You were willing to leave the boy who bears my name, if not my blood, with that woman?'

'Would you have let me bring him home?'

The question was futile, any hope of truth between them lay shattered. Only the deepening distrust, only her helplessness to reach this man imprisoned by his need of her and his self-loathing.

He searched her face. For that instant the shadows seemed to lift and she saw the bewilderment of the young soldier she had met so long ago on a dusty road, the raw-muscled, strong man of the earth she could not put from her mind. Had he ever said I love you? She could not remember. But she had known then even in her innocence that she could match him, tame him and that she would go with him to the end of the world.

Then the image was gone. The hard lines returned to his face, the coldness to his eyes. Premonition again touched her. She shivered.

'The boy is there. That is where he shall stay. He will meet his own father some day in hell.' He paused. Then the words broke from him. 'And his mother.'

Henrietta heard the door to his study close. After a while she heard his steps in the hall. The rain began again to lash the windows. She heard him leave the house.

He would not return that night. She saw him in her mind riding the dark, ice-rutted road to the farm, locked in the solitary battle with his inner devils in which neither she nor any other could help him.

She remembered once more the blind young need that had driven her so recklessly to him. She could still have met kindness with kindness but that, too, was doomed by her own confession. It would have been better to have lied

49

about Colin Thatcher. Let Isaac think what he would of that brief summer that made endurable all the winters to come. But her honesty forbade it. Instead she had thrown herself on his mercy and found that his devils denied her even common plea.

In spite of herself the old facts crept from the corners. That winter day so long ago when Colin Thatcher had said goodbye, gone up on the Ridge in the deep snow. Isaac had followed. Colin had never been seen or heard of again. She knew as if it had been thundered into the ice-bound silences between them that Isaac bore the stain of murder. His devils who forbade him love permitted vengeance.

Henrietta drew the long drapes against the storm. She welcomed these long solitudes now. They helped to banish the one emotion that lay deepest of all. She had not until this moment named it. Upstairs, in the ruffled privacy of her own bedroom, she turned to her one last confidante, her locked diary. She had been defeated so often, but here among notes and scribblings, broken thoughts, half poems, lay her defiance, her integrity, the inner self which no man, no god, no devil could violate. She picked up her pen . . .

'Scribbling again, Henrietta?'

The pen dropped from her fingers.

Isaac stood in the doorway, his clothes dripping wet.

She had learned steadiness. 'Isaac, let me get you some dry things!'

'Hear me, will you? I want no more of this town, its committees, its stupidities. Its starings and whisperings at the woman who is my wife. We shall not wait for June to go out to the farm. We shall go in two weeks. And we shall stay. See that the house is closed. Pack what you need. There will be only the two of us.' The dark eyes blazed for an instant at something behind the room.

'God help me, if He will, Henrietta. I must save your immortal soul!'

In the void that held her, she saw for an instant one face, the small boy she loved so intensely, her last and sweetest son.

In that distant, light-filled city women were at their mirrors; gowns of a hundred colours and costs lay splashed across their beds. Rich, poor, social, nameless, the proper and the daring . . . were giving themselves to one last night of revelry.

But Amos would be asleep now, in a little back room, guarded by honest Rosalee. He would be sated, she hoped, on a small cup of pure pleasure.

At her desk, slowly, mechanically, scarcely knowing what she did, Henrietta at last took up her pen.

'. . . fear is a crippler. I shall try to shun it as I always have from my life – my house – and my heart. But I know now that Isaac intends to kill me.'

CHAPTER FOUR

The crowd noise swelled like surf. Madame Martine's carriage slowed and stopped. Faces pressed against the windows, bodies blocked the carriage doors and milled around the horses.

'Keep going, Domic!' called Fleur Martine.

'Too many people, Madame. They're all trying to get into the ball.'

'How far are we from the entrance?'

'A quarter of a block.'

'Keep the horses moving. The crowd will give way!'

She heard shouts, a few curses, but the carriage slowly began to roll.

The boy nodding in the dark corner opened his eyes.

'What is it?'

'It's the ball I promised you, Amos. Wake up!'

'Will I see King Comus?'

She gave a short, hard laugh. 'Not at this ball, you won't. But you'll see a lot of other things. You'll forget all about Comus.'

He knew better. 'What will I see?'

'I told you. You'll see Poseidon. He's the king of the sea and a magician. You'll see mermaids and water-devils – haven't you been listening?' She broke off irritably.

For the second time in the day Fleur told herself she had made a mistake. It was all very well in the loneliness of the house and the unsparing light of day to allow herself the indulgence of long suppressed mother feelings. She supposed every woman had them. But she had chosen a different way. She had always wanted to taste every aspect of life and now the small boy, so suddenly dropped by fate into her life, had touched her. Well and good. To fill a dull afternoon.

But as the twilight lengthened and Pearl had come in to pile her gilded hair high, help her into the ivory satin gown with its emerald velvet trim, the silence jarred. No messenger at the door with flowers, no note of anticipation from Roger. Motherhood, she reflected, did not enrich a woman's life. It impoverished it. And the boy was not even her own.

She had been tempted to leave him at home. But that would have given Roger the satisfaction of victory. She could not hope to hold a man younger than herself by showing defeat. Younger, yes. But tonight, as she finished her dressing and stood before the triple mirror, she told herself no one would know how much. A little, perhaps, but never the truth. And she missed him. His admiring laugh, his slow eyes, his skilled and suggestive touch. A woman like herself without a man at her side? Never again!

She rang for Rosalee.

'Is the boy ready?'

'He is asleep, Madame.'

'Well, wake him up.'

The turbaned woman hesitated. 'He has been on the streets with us all day, Madame. He has seen all the parades. He is very tired.'

'I'm taking him with me, to the Artists' Ball, Rosalee.'

The woman's face remained impassive. 'He's only twelve. He's too young for such things.'

'The French kings were married at twelve.'

Madame Martine, née Flora Caylee, did not hold much with books, but she knew one little authoritative retort could silence this mutely possessive woman.

'If you don't like the way I do things, Rosalee – '

'You just tell me when, Madame . . .'

The arguments never went further. The dark woman and the white woman knew their mutual dependence. The years alone told them.

She had won over Rosalee as she had won over Roger. She had the boy now, half drugged with sleep in the carriage. She had been a fool but she could not afford to think so. It would show in her face. She had only to think what she could do with Amos until the final tableau. He was to be Cupid to her Venus. Was not Cupid the true son of the goddess of love? She had been right at least about that. It would be a sensation. The boy was really quite beautiful.

The carriage stopped.

'Are we here?' He sat up.

'Yes. Amos, you're to do exactly what I tell you tonight. Do you understand?'

'Yes.'

'You will have to wait by yourself for a little while. Then I will come for you.'

'How long?'

'Does it matter? I will come when I am ready.'

The carriage door opened.

Roger Winters extended his hand with a knowing smile. She reached for it. She was young again.

Amos sat on a cot in a brightly lit, closetlike room where he could dimly hear shrill laughter, masculine shouts, and music. It had no beginning and no end but was throbbing inside him like the stifling heat.

He did not want to fall asleep. Even after the hot humiliation of the rabbit suit had worn off, the day had been filled with images that returned to haunt him. He had seen nothing like the tiny figures in the glass cabinet. Instead he had been pressed back and forth by clowns, apes, dominoes, grotesque females with enormous pillowed breasts and male voices, huge grimacing heads on dancing legs, with high voices. He had been separated once from Rosalee by a chain dance of red imps and returned by a carrot head on stilted legs.

53

He had caught glimpses of splendour. A bearded figure in silver and white on a towering throne. A soaring tournament of knights on mock horses. A lofty dance of shepherds and elves, and a real waterfall. All moving, stately as clouds above a sea of heads.

It had been too much. A dizzying surfeit to mind and body that had left him faintly sick. He hoped they would not come for him. Not until they were ready to take him back to the comfort of darkness and the nearness of Rosalee. But his longing stretched further than that. To a cold stark room where he could see his breath over the edge of the quilt. To the familiar rigidity of his days. To the quick smile with which his mother made everything right, until she had last said goodbye. She had not told him she would come back.

The music, louder now, buffeted him. He buried his head in his arms.

In a corridor outside a closed door, Roger Winters lit another cigarette and waited. Madame Martine was changing into her costume for the final living tableau. She would never let him watch her dress. Songs are sweet, she would misquote gaily, but forbidden songs are sweeter. But he really did not care. He understood all her tricks. And it would not last much longer. He had managed the Esplanade place for her much better than she knew.

A girl passed, heavily rouged, wearing a wrapper. One of the nymphs. He winked and tapped her buttocks. She passed him haughtily.

'Roger!' Fleur Martine's voice was light as a bell.

He opened the door without knocking. He had to admit the final effect was superb. She was standing tall and straight. Pale green, diaphanous chiffons wrapped her generous body. Her hair, loose and laced with light-catching brilliance, fell nearly to her waist. She was ageless and she was breathtaking. Phillip Martine knew what he had found so long ago in young Flora Caylee. Yet Roger found himself resenting the man. Had this woman been given any chance in life, she would have outdistanced them all. She would have triumphed on any stage, graced any court. Instead she had set her sights only as far as Martine. She got what she wanted. But life never waited. He himself would make sure he was never trapped as she had been.

'Well, what do you think of me, Roger?'

'You know what I think.' The husky insinuation always warmed her.

'No, don't muss me, my darling. Not yet.' Her body stirred. 'Later.' She let the promise hang. 'Is the boy ready?'

'How would I know?'

'Roger, you said – '

'I said I would help *you*, my sweet. I will have nothing to do with the boy.'

'I told you I'm sending him back.'

'When?'

'Tomorrow if you wish. Or next week. When I've written his mother.'

'Make up your mind. Why you ever let him stay in the first place, I don't know.' He was sulky now and she must reassure him.

'Shall I tell you?'

He shrugged.

'Roger, don't turn away from me. Not now. Not tonight. I need you. I – I took the boy because Henrietta Martine asked me. Imagine! Phillip's daughter asking *me*. She is a Beaulaire. Her mother was a Beaulaire. The boy has Beaulaire blood. My father ran a shrimp boat from the bayou but they had to come to me, Flora Caylee, for a favour. You'd spoil that for me!'

He thought again of the waste. A Bernhardt, a Duse . . . but the world did not wait either. Her intensity returned lines to her face.

A florid man in a velvet tam-o'-shanter, his shirt sticking to his back with sweat, stuck his head in.

'God, you look great, Flora. How do you do it? The boy's sick.'

'Sick? How do you know?'

'Well, he sort of fainted. Polly's been dousing him with cold water.'

'I'll come right away. Get him ready.'

'Forget him, Fleur!' Roger snapped.

If greatness had passed Flora Caylee by, her small dreams would not. She swept out to hold on to them.

The final tableau of the Artists' Ball was a smashing and rowdy success. Flaming torches framed the platform and turned the tableau into an iridescence of watery light. Fleur Martine stood revealed in her near transparent draperies, against a papier-mâché seashell rising pearl-like behind her. Beside her leaned Amos, pale and powdered, a green, gold, and purple sash across his bared body. His limp hand held a gilt bow. His eyes were closed. Around the shell, half-sitting, half-reclining, postured the sea nymphs in skin shades from pale white to the richest coffee and cream, smiling and nude as the day they were born.

A masculine roar went up.

'Annie, my love!'

'Belle, I'd know you anywhere!'

'My sweet little Pansy!'

The band struck up and the crowd began to sing. 'If ever I cease to love . . . if ever I cease to love . . .'

A man holding a bottle of wine stumbled up to the platform. Deliberately he held it above a kneeling nymph and poured the contents over her ripe breasts. She laughed, blew him a kiss, and flung her arms wide to the boy behind her.

'Have your first taste of champagne, boy!'

Amos's eyes flew open. He jumped away. As he did his foot tangled in Fleur's trailing draperies. He stumbled free and fell from the platform, striking the stand that held the blazing torch. It swayed, bent, and toppled into the shell. There was a gasp from the crowd. In another instant the shell burst into flame. From the swirling, fiery, pale green draperies came a scream, hoarse and inhuman in its agony.

The newspaper reported the fire with tart disapproval. Fortunately the building was saved and there were only a few injuries. But, the editorials scolded, the low elements in the city who were using the Mardi Gras as an excuse for orgies must be controlled. The name of Madame Phillip Martine did not appear.

Amos, his hair singed, his back sprained, returned to Rosalee's care.

No questions were asked him, no orders given. The house was silent and he found no one to stop his visits at any time to the glass cabinet. While his body healed, his hands grew active. He began to take sheets of paper and a pencil with him and sketch the figures he saw. Then he began to sketch his own memories of demons and imps and the faces and bodies of women. Time somehow passed and slid into the shadowed corners of the quiet house.

He had quite lost track of the past when one day he looked up to see the front door open and a woman enter. She came at once to the entryway of the parlour because there had been no need these days to draw the double doors.

She walked slowly and stooped; a shapeless cloak wrapped her and beneath a wide-brimmed hat she was heavily veiled. Because of the safety of the world he had made within himself, he was not afraid.

'Do you know me?' Her voice was thin and raspy.

'No.'

'Would you know me if you saw me?'

He hesitated because the question perplexed him. He was looking at her. He did not know her.

Slowly she lifted her veils.

He neither winced nor turned away. His wide blue child's eyes searched her face, steady and interested, looking for signs of recognition in the puckered flesh, the closed nostril, one eyelid drooped and uneven as an old shutter, and the forehead criss-crossed in folded parchment scars. She bore the gaze.

'Yes,' he said finally. 'You are Madame. May I stay here until I finish my drawing?'

She dropped her veils, not to hide her face but her tears. Then deliberately she unpinned the veils, removed her hat and her cloak, and lowered her crippled body into a chair.

'Do you mind if I watch, Amos?'

'No,' he said. His head bent over his pad. 'It's a picture of the jester. But without the animals. I don't think they should be there, do you?'

Rumours spread that Madame Martine had returned, but no one saw her. Sometimes a tradesman caught a glimpse of a veiled and bent woman in grey, walking in the inner courtyard on the arm of a youth.

Before the year was out, Madame received a letter. Haynes and Blodgett, Solicitors, Thatcher, Connecticut. They regretted to inform her that Henrietta Martine Roundtree, mother of the boy Amos, had met with accidental death at the Roundtree farmhouse. The monthly payments made to Madame Martine by Mrs Roundtree would cease. As no provision had been made for the boy, his future must be left to her discretion.

Madame summoned Amos. He now had a larger room above her own on the third floor. From it he could look down into the street, into the new world that was his, yet from which he was already guarded by the pervasive grey-veiled presence below.

Madame told him briefly, quickly, that his mother was dead. Then she drew him to the warmth of her muffled body, grateful that the twisted shell of her face that concealed emotion also concealed her satisfaction.

Amos grieved silently and without witness.

Sometimes he awoke in great lonesomeness and he made sketches of his mother. The flowing silk dress that she had worn at a party so long ago when he watched her through the bars of the upstairs banister, a forbidden child in a forbidden place. Her dark hair was piled high, her face glowing, as she spoke to a tall, sandy-haired man he did not know. Amos would paint her in that ruby-red dress some day, but her hair would fall loose as it did when she would bend over his cot to kiss him good-night. He would paint her smile as she had said her last goodbye to him in this very house. Not quite a smile.

He slept fitfully for a long time. Then slowly he forgot. As he forgot the bruising cold of Thatcher's winter and his father's voice.

*

Madame was patient. Daily she summoned him to walk with her in the courtyard. Daily she joined him in his hour of play with the magic of Comus in the parlour cabinet. Daily she questioned him on what he had seen, what he had found to sketch. Until the dim, shadow-filled rooms no longer seemed unnatural. His young imagination scurried among them, finding its own outlets until nothing seemed strange any longer. If he had any idea that among the backstairs children he was known as '*Le Bâtard*', Madame made no effort to dispel it. Suspicion could only deepen her satisfaction.

For out of the burning had come phoenixlike her own fulfilment. She, Flora Caylee Martine, daughter of a Cajun shrimpman, at last possessed quality. Living, breathing quality that none could take from her, quality that could neither be denied nor claimed.

Within the veils of her self-imprisonment Flora Martine discovered at last the rewards of single purpose.

She would live for ever on its terrible strength.

As the ordered days passed, Madame discovered that this thin, quiet child from the North concealed a tenacity, a hidden pebble within him, to match her own.

He would not relinquish his name.

He was Amos Roundtree and he clung to that as he had once clung to a branch of a three-hundred-and-fifty-year-old oak that stood high on Thatcher Ridge above his father's farm. His father had taken him up the Ridge and swung him up to a branch. Frozen with terror, he had gazed down to the ground, to the Ridge, to the valley far below. But he had held on until his fear had at last dissolved into the oak's own solidity.

Sometimes the ancient tree returned in his dreams. He would wake, clinging fast to all that remained to him. His own name.

Madame yielded. There were more important issues.

The boy must be schooled. Like most transgressors comfortable with their sins, Madame saw the Cross not as a place of agony and contrition but as a sensible solution to problems beyond her. She sent Amos to the Franciscans for catechism, sums, and spelling. The rest she would take care of in her own way.

He soon outgrew Rosalee's chaperonage to taste his first freedoms. He would choose as many different routes home as he could, sliding into the hidden alleys and narrow streets of the old French Quarter, small and curious among the secret dens of indulgence and vice.

His overbright eyes and deeply flushed face did not escape Madame. She was more puzzled when he returned home with nostrils pinched and blue. Those were days of low clouds, gusty rain, when he would race to the levee and let the cold air from a Gulf of Mexico 'norther' stream over him, satisfying something that he could not name, something she feared. She would keep him home until the storm passed.

When he was fifteen, he grew abruptly tall.

A week before his sixteenth birthday he heard the silver bell tinkle from the darkness below. It was after ten, the house was shuttered for the night, the servants closed off in the rear of the court. Disciplined to every whim, Amos made his way from his third-floor room to the door of Madame's bedchamber.

Her hearing had sharpened as her isolation grew. Before he knocked, he heard her call, husky yet oddly mellow.

'Come in, Amos.'

He obeyed.

'Close the door.'

The click of the latch was not as loud as he seemed to hear it.

'What do you see?'

'Nothing.'

The darkness was total. Every thread of light that might have slid into the room from sky or street was curtained off. Yet the air was not stifling. It had the softness, the impenetrability of black velvet against his face, and a giddying, strange sweetness.

'What do you feel, Amos?'

He felt the power of the dark pressing on him. He felt the throbbing echo of his own temples, his racing blood. He felt the weight of an enigma that lay ahead. Yet he could only stand rigid, silent.

'Do you feel nothing?' The whisper was sultry with a music of its own, so low he barely heard it. It was not Madame who lay beneath the silk covers. In the complete darkness, the knowledge and the image vanished for him. The whisper that came was a voice he had never heard, a mysterious beckoning, an invisible thread of enchantment.

'Take off your clothes.'

He breathed a small inaudible sigh.

She must have worn the sheerest of silk on her body, her arms, her throat, her hands. From it an invisible smoothness, subtleties of scent and touch and warmth, flowed over him, draining him of memory and will. At last he was enveloped in an ecstasy that was as complete as it was disembodied.

When her whisper finally came from the depth of the blackness, it was light with youth and mockery.

'Go now.'

On his sixteenth birthday Madame summoned him again. She had let seven days pass before restoring his regimen, seven days while she waited for the forces of guilt and memory and irrepressible triumph to subside. When he entered the room, his slight bow, his direct glance, the new manhood in his face, told her of success. The enigma would remain, with the certainty of her possession. He would not remember, yet he would never forget.

He found her sitting in the parlour, blinds drawn, her grey skirts full around her ankles, her face veiled. A man stood near her. She explained in the grating remnant of voice Amos knew so well that while she was in excellent health and intended to live for a long time, she had rewritten her will. The terms were simple. Amos was to have all she possessed, including the house and its contents. There was one condition. Because she disliked strangers and could not live alone, Amos must promise not to marry until the day after her death.

The man held out a sheet of paper.

Amos read it with self-conscious slowness. Obedience was still strong within him. Even one short week had restored the house to an impersonal normalcy that blanched the witch's night to unreality. He saw the bond implied in the contract. But he saw something more, something that the ageing woman in her veils could not see. The future. He was young. Young people lived. Old people died. Death already seemed layered in Madame's grey veils.

And with that thought young Amos was struck by a compassion that would change for ever the subtle relation of their lives. Madame had suffered. No one but himself knew the racked courage of her days. She endured it to do this for him. If she had snatched one moment of lost youth from him, he had a lifetime of others to give. Emotion washed through him for which he had no words. Its ebbing left him at peace. He would stay with her for whatever time remained to her. It was the least he could do.

He took the pen thrust out to him and signed.

Madame rose. Her step and her bearing seemed more frail as she left the room. The man nodded significantly at Amos. Amos looked past him. He sensed already that the contract was both a bond and a freedom. He had lost his innocence to this house. But he had been set free of – what? Being a Roundtree? Being anything but what he chose?

He had yet to learn that the only predictable pattern of life is its unpredictability.

CHAPTER FIVE

'But it's ridiculous, Amos. What in the world made you sign such a thing?'

'The better part of wisdom. I can't make a living out of painting. Or support you. Besides, she wants it that way.'

He kissed the girl, rolled out of the bed in his studio, and gathered up his clothes.

'But it isn't right, Amos. It's – it's like being kept. To promise not to marry until the day after an old woman is dead!'

He stood looking down at her, his sandy hair rumpled, his blond moustache too thin, his face too pale. His coolness she found disturbing. Only his extraordinary blue eyes seemed alive. And they were distant.

'Your twinge of morality does you credit, Jeanie.'

'Don't you want to marry?' She sat upright. The perfection of her body always pleased him. She was the most popular real-life model in the Quarter and she had brought him to his astonishment not only love but virginity. 'I don't want to wait for ever,' she added petulantly. 'What is she? Eighty? No. Seventy-nine, you told me.'

'Let's not end our times together this way.'

'You don't even want to talk about her.'

'Quite correct.'

'Amos! Amos! What kind of man are you?'

'As you so rightly said – a kept man.'

'I didn't mean it. I know it isn't so. But she acts as if she owns you like a piece of furniture. Oh, it must be hideous! Hideous!'

Her habit of repeating words annoyed him as so many things did these days. He was nearly forty. He was an established artist in this small world now. The freedoms of his life suited him like the warmth of the close, mellow streets. But he was aware of its sluggishness. He was a Roundtree. He bore the name as he bore the memory of that lost icy hillside, the wind that whipped him to his knees, the cold that seared his bared skin with pain. But in the end that memory had instilled in him the triumph of survival.

That is what had gone from his life. The Roundtree need of challenge, of proving himself. It would happen with a child of his own, a son to teach to live as he had not.

'Maybe the next time you come, I won't be here,' the girl said, sulking.

'Someone else will.' He laughed and caught her as she sprang from the bed.

'Doesn't anything touch you, Amos? You – you live in a cocoon. No, let me go! No, I won't come here again!'

On the day after her ninety-third birthday, Madame in her veils, mechanical as an ancient doll, took her last walk on Amos's arm. That evening she summoned him to her bedside. She lay, head bonneted in white ruching, body so shrunken that it made scarcely an outline beneath the white silk cover. But time had dealt kindly with her. The withering had already been done.

She signalled him to lean close.

'Go to the Beaulaires, Amos.' The words faint and dry as her touch. 'The Beaulaires,' she repeated. 'They are Comus.'

She tapped his cheek once and closed her eyes.

Her dust mingled quickly and lightly with the marble dust of the white-templed Martine tomb in St Louis cemetery where he insisted she be buried.

Amos was past fifty years old. The year was 1943.

The following week he quietly married young Lissa, his current model. Seven months later she gave him his only child, a daughter. He named the little girl Elizabeth Beaulaire Roundtree and saw that she was not beautiful. But her eyes were large and blue and as luminous as daybreak. And in her wilfulness and endurance ran the strength of the winter winds.

He called her Lili.

PART TWO

THE LOVERS

CHAPTER SIX

'What are you doing?'

The girl leaning over the balcony was neither pretty nor graceful as convention would have it. She was slight and angular and so were her features. But there was a magnetism in the large blue eyes that snapped and flashed, and in the soft huskiness of her remarkable voice. She was at once as wary and as coaxing as a cat. She was just twenty.

'I asked you a question, Luis.'

The young, well-muscled Hispanic did not look up.

'You know what I'm doing, Miss Elizabeth.'

'I am not Miss Elizabeth, Luis. We've been all through that. Elizabeth was the dreariest saint in the whole catalogue. She was offered a kingdom and chose a convent before she was twenty. If anybody offered me a kingdom . . .' Her laugh was quick. Light and shadows played across her thin face. 'Anyhow, you should call me Lili, and some day if you ever look up from cutting your old bushes, I'll tell you why.'

She laughed again and ran down the outside stairs that led from the gallery to the walled garden below. April heat and rain had combined to touch off a riot of azalea and hibiscus, poppies and roses, bougainvillea and camellias. The earth steamed and the young man had taken off his shirt. His skin shone, oiled and youthful, his face gleaming against the whiteness of his teeth. Whatever Creole still flowed in Lili Roundtree's swift blood recognized the perfection of this specimen.

'I know what you're doing, Luis. You're trying to make your precious moonflowers open before night. They won't, you know.'

He looked at her directly. 'Everything has its own time. I never force anything.'

It was delicious and exciting and it was exactly the kind of titillation Lili enjoyed. It meant nothing. Luis was gardener for the Aunts Beaulaire and the aunts had brought up Lili according to their own notion. Not that they had wanted the responsibility. The bar sinister lay bleak across the child. No matter how famous her father had become among the denizens of art in the French Quarter, the facts remained that Amos Roundtree had led a life of disrepute, taken as a bride a tawdry little model half his age, and he child of the union born questionably soon. Disregarding the name Roundtree, which was only a dismal reminder of their late cousin, Henrietta Beaulaire Martine, and her unfortunate Yankee marriage, the maiden l!dies saw only arrogance in Amos Roundtree's gift to his child of the Beaulaire name.

Little Elizabeth Beaulaire Roundtree might have been passed over and forgotten had not the ladies at their morning café blanc and croissants opened the paper to the headlined crash of Flight 187 out of New Orleans and into a watery grave in the bayous. Mr and Mrs Amos Roundtree were listed among the victims.

It filled the ladies not so much with sorrow as dismay, the pain of recall and outright exasperation. What Amos and his wife were doing on Flight 187 they could not imagine. Why anyone flew the wretched things was beyond them.

But the modern world had hurtled into the circumspect and unchanging ways in the grand house on St Charles Avenue. A Beaulaire was a Beaulaire no matter where found. Abandoning the blood was unthinkable. They drew their skirts close and paid a visit to Dauphine Street. They found a spindly ten-year-old, orphaned, bewildered, and disturbingly secretive. Duty seen was duty done. Little Elizabeth Beaulaire Roundtree was moved to St Charles Avenue. The convent nuns were called upon with firm instructions. And now past twenty, Elizabeth, whom no one called Lili, was as little comprehended by the Beaulaire aunts as she had been at ten. Except that she had been presented and was now safely engaged. The marriage would not be brilliant but it would be suitable.

'Luis!' It was a tone of command. Luis Ortega y Diaz wiped the sweat from his forehead and returned to his bushes. 'Luis, I'm bored. I want to go up to Dauphine Street. Will you come with me?'

'You know I cannot do that.'

'Of course you can. You have a car. You've been working here all day like a stevedore. Besides, I don't like to go into a haunted house alone.'

'It is not haunted, Miss Elizabeth.'

'Oh, but it is. You haven't seen her. The woman with the veils, hiding her scars. She glides through the house, Luis.'

'And if she didn't, you would say she does.'

'Why shouldn't I? It's my father's house. Mine now. I don't want anybody buying it. Please, Luis, it will be lovely and cool inside.'

'No, Miss Elizabeth. The man you are to marry should take you there if you want to go.'

A peal of laughter answered him, bright as a birdcall.

'Dear old Neddie!' She sat herself cross-legged on a stone turtle. Her legs were slender, her skirt short. 'Luis, let me tell you about Neddie. He hates things that are old and musty. He loves figures and shiny bank offices. His father was King of Comus and his father before that and Neddie's older brother will be some day and that leaves Neddie not much. He thinks it's a step downward to marry me, but I'm not sure he could do much better. And the aunts have laid it on pretty thick about the Beaulaires. Anyhow I'm not really going to marry him but I do like staying engaged. If I weren't engaged, I couldn't go up to Dauphine Street with you. But as I am, it's quite respectable. Don't you see? Come on, Luis! Before the whole afternoon goes.'

The young man looked at her legs. They were long and slender and the calves gently rounded to the finest of ankles.

'Miss Elizabeth, I work very hard. Some day I make enough money to go back to Santo Domingo to help my people who are oppressed. Some day I will be a great leader.'

'Would you take me with you? I should adore to be the wife of a great leader!'

'You laugh at me!'

69

'No, Luis, I don't. But don't you like a little fun while you are becoming a great leader? It was always fun at Dauphine Street. I could show you so many things. Luis, if you don't come with me, I shall tell the aunts you brought a girl in here last night.'

'I do not bring a girl here. Ever!'

'But they would believe *me*, wouldn't they?' A quick laugh took the mischief from the words. And because he was young and she showed more of her legs as she jumped up, he laughed with her.

'That's better, Luis! Where's your car?'

'I don't have one.'

'Then we'll take a cab.'

'I cannot afford that.'

'You *are* being exasperating. Then we'll take the trolley and walk.'

The Dauphine Street house had not changed in her eyes. A curio shop flanked one side. A po'-boy eatery with an open counter blossomed aromatically across the way. Other places of small and hopeful business thrust themselves among the old buildings. The street itself no longer slept the afternoon away. It was thronged with shoppers, sightseers, and the new breed of youth, bearded, sandalled, and at stultifying and enormous leisure.

Her father's house had faded into the others. A louvred blind hung paintless and angled. The iron railing on the balcony showed breaks. One front step was missing. An air of mustiness and neglect clung to the whole house like one vast cobweb. But Luis's practical eye caught a new shoring beneath the roofline and a modern drain spout at the corner. Faded, he thought, but firm.

'Remember, it's haunted,' she whispered. 'We'll go in the back way.' She took his hand, which he quickly withdrew, and led him down a narrow alley.

'Don't be afraid.' Her eyes sparkled. Luis had already begun to wish he had not come. Yet his eyes lingered on her legs as she fitted a key to a heavy, paint-shorn wooden door. It creaked satisfactorily.

'This back part was once the slave quarters. Isn't that

dreadful? Then the servants lived here. I'll show you the little room where my father slept.'

They both heard the sound. It was neither a step, nor a creak. It was simply sound, then silence.

'I told you it was haunted.' A shade of lightness faded from her voice. 'Come on, we'll go across the courtyard. It used to be filled with the most beautiful flowers. You'd like that, Luis. My mother loved flowers.'

He followed her. The sound had not been a natural one. He should not leave her here alone. Yet superstition welled deep in Luis. He wished to all the saints he was back trimming his moonflowers, saving his wages to be a leader.

On the far side of the desolate courtyard she pushed open another door. They were in the wide, cool hall, the air musty with dampness.

'Come on into the living-room.' She pulled open the doors. The room was spectral. Pale dust sheets covered every piece of furniture and only the single broken louvre gave a slant of light. She pointed to one swathed object. 'That's the magic cabinet.' The mischief had returned. She stood close to him. 'I'll show it to you, Luis.' Her eyes danced. 'If you'll kiss me.'

He was young and male. In his country women did not invite and tease without knowing what they wanted, what would happen. His senses were stirred, his pulses raced. She was slight, she was tempting. It would be so easy to take her in her arms in her too-brief skirt, her bared legs, push her down on the pale dust sheet that covered the divan . . .

'Are you afraid, Luis?'

She was unaware, he told himself. Could she be so innocent? So unconscious of her own magnetism? How could any man . . .? He clenched his hands and knew the palms were wet. She lifted her teasing face.

'Just one, Luis! To see if you're real.'

He would look back years later to this perilous crossroad and confess to an unseen priest that everything he had thought, happened, that in a blinding instant he had taken this girl, that the image lay for ever, stained, in his mind. For Luis knew nothing about the mirages of Freudian guilt, and even less about skittery female coquettes. He only knew that at this moment his work-hardened muscles ached for her and that he was twice the man of that gringo banker who would get her. And that maybe she had something to learn . . . He swept her roughly to him, bent his head.

Then he heard it. They both heard it. The sound that was now a distinct step in the upper hall. Then another.

Luis Ortega y Diaz fled. Without looking back or even up, he ran across the hall, into the courtyard, and out the rear entrance.

Lili, released from a game that had turned suddenly darkly perilous, stood rigid, her own senses wrenched and displaced, her longing unspent, in a bewildering kaleidoscope of fears. In an instant, in this ghostly dimness, Luis had turned from friendly prey to overpowering conqueror. Is that what happened to a man when you only wanted to share a few high-spirited moments, a release from tedium? She was trembling with emotions she could not define and she was angry with herself.

Worse, there was someone in the house. Over her rapid breathing she heard the footsteps clearly now, slowly, surely, descending the stairs, the stairs she could not see. They were not the steps of a ghostly old lady veiled in grey.

The outrage of ownership added to her turmoil. Whoever the intruder was, tourist, hippie, common thief, murderer – her mind spun on – she would stand her ground. This house was hers. It was the only place in the world where she was sure who she was. Any stranger – She moved to where she could see the bottom of the stairs.

'Well, hello!'

He was above average height, solidly built, a face broad and regular, a thatch of unruly brown hair. He was tieless and carried a jacket, and if he had not been so crumpled, she might have stood staring. As it was, she looked twice, then a third time.

He saw a slim girl with a dead-white face and over-sized eyes that might have been spellbinding if they had not been so definitely hostile. He remembered from somewhere that

72

you approached even small tigers by looking directly at them.

'I hope I didn't frighten you.'

'Not at all. I'm quite used to hearing intruders prowl about my house.'

'You live here?' His dismay was genuine.

'I don't think that has anything to do with it.'

'My apologies. You do own it?'

She could see no reason to answer that. 'How did you get in?'

He grinned, showed a crease line that might once have been a dimple but now gave his face added strength.

'My dear young lady – '

'I am not your dear young lady.'

'You've made that apparent. But when a house is known, or should I say' – the grin returned – 'advertised, so widely as haunted, any ghost-lover worth his salt can get in. I chose that semi-boarded-up window on the alley, which I judge once upon a time looked out on a garden. Once again I apologize. Which I might add I'm not in the habit of doing. Never apologize, never explain, is an old motto of mine. Sometimes it works, sometimes it doesn't.' The grin again. 'But I owe you one this time. I heard two voices so I must have scared somebody.' He looked at her intently.

She felt herself flush.

'You're mistaken. I was here alone. But it's all right. I don't scare easy.'

'I don't think you do. In that case . . .' He slung his jacket over his shoulder. 'Thanks. I'll get along.'

She felt confused and inadequate. It was not at all what she had expected. Nothing that this hot, empty, frustrating afternoon had been. Yet she didn't want him to go. Not yet. She really should put him in his place, take that loftiness down a notch or two, show him that property owners of Le Vieux Carré don't encourage common Yankee sight-seers . . . Instead she giggled.

He released a long breath. 'I thought you never would.'

'What?'

'Laugh.'

'I thought *you* never would.'

73

'What?'

'Stop talking.'

'Bad habit of mine, I admit. All right, now that there's an armistice, may I ask you one question, Miss – uh – Miss – '

'Roundtree.'

'Miss Roundtree . . . there is another name?'

'What's the question?' But her eyes brightened. This kind of banter she enjoyed.

He gave a small grunt. Proceed with caution to Square Two. He took out his wallet and handed her a buff-coloured card.

On it she read in stark block letters, Henley Brocklebank Turner III. National Press Syndicate. He took the card from her, wrote briefly on it, and returned it. The lettering was scratched out. Below he had written Brock Turner. She looked at it blankly.

'Okay? Square Two?'

'What?'

'Never mind. Let's get back to you.'

'I'm Lili Roundtree.'

'Lovely. Short for Lillian?'

'No. Elizabeth. But I prefer Lilith.'

'Lilith? Why?'

'You know Lilith. She was in the garden with Adam before Eve. She was made from the same dust as Adam so it gave her a head start. But I guess Adam couldn't cope with that, so along came silly Eve from his rib.'

'You don't say.' He surveyed her thoughtfully, his face straight.

'Oh, yes. The nuns don't see it that way, of course. They like to say Lilith was all bad. That's why she had to go. But I think she really wanted to. Anyway that's where the Lili comes from.'

He was silent for a moment. The old house was caught in a spell. She was part of it. In another instant it would all vanish like the afternoon. The girl included. For a reason he would look into later he did not want that. Not right away.

'I thought you had a question.'

'All right. Is this house really haunted?'

'Do you want the truth, Mr Turner?'

'It would be refreshing.'

But she missed the point. She was measuring him with her enormous blue eyes. No beauty, no glamour girl, he told himself, and skittish as a colt. Yet he stood there like a gangling schoolboy, hoping very much, very gently.

'It's a long story. Something very sad happened a long time ago. A woman named Fleur Martine . . . Madame . . .'

She was still measuring him. Square Three? He would take a chance.

'What would you think about telling it to me over a drink?' Was that the beginning of a smile? 'Would LaFitte's do, Miss Roundtree?'

CHAPTER SEVEN

The clatter in the newsroom had begun its usual after-five crescendo. WNCS-TV peaked with its six o'clock broadcast.

The news editor sat with a phone crunched into one shoulder while his ball-point doodled on a sheet of script in front of him.

'Yes, sir. Yes, Mr Russell. He ought to be in any minute. I don't know what he's got for a story but they like anything Brock Turner has to say down here. I *know* it's network, sir. I hope it's a big story, too. I'll tell him as soon as he gets in. Like I said, any minute now. *Sir*.'

He dropped the ball-point, snapped his hand in mock salute, and laid the phone gently to rest with two fingers as if it had burned him.

'Where the hell is Turner?'

As he addressed no one in particular, no one answered.

'You can't lose a guy in three hours in this town,' he muttered.

'When he's a guy like Brock Turner, it's easy.' The copygirl laid a yard of Teletype news on his desk and sashayed off. Brock Turner had lightly patted her once and she had sat up half the night narrowing all her skirts.

The news editor sighed. He did not have to ask anyone when Turner walked in. The chemistry would tell him.

'Five forty-four ten, chief. All signals go.' His young subordinate was already aping Brock Turner's rough briskness.

'I can see the clock, son.' Celebrities gave the editor a headache. It was always this way. Wrapped, packaged from New York or Hollywood, encased in enough of the glue of awe and privilege to foul up his schedules for a week. Brock Turner was a good man, a hell of a guy. It was what they did about him that stirred the editor's slow-rising bile.

'Think he'll show, chief?'

'If he doesn't, use the Jefferson Parish flood story.'

'That was the day before yesterday.'

'Sure. And run the fire at Stadley Place – '

'He's here!' yelled somebody.

Steve caught a fleeting glimpse of a large coatless frame dogtrotting down the corridor towards the news studio. It was said that Brock Turner had never missed a newscast in his career. The editor believed that but he also suspected that Turner's wake was strewn with the limp bodies of producers, directors, engineers, and make-up girls who did not believe.

He caught up with Brock outside the studio door.

'You just made it.' It was not bright, but the editor was struggling to keep a low profile on sarcasm.

'What are you talking about, Steve? Six minutes to go. And the Pan-Cake's already on.' He turned a face beiged and flattened of character.

'Your boss called from New York. Again.'

'Thanks.' The answer was sharper than Brock intended. The word *boss* nettled him. Mortimer Russell was network news executive and he liked a show of authority, but both of them understood that Brock Turner was his own man. No one yet had tied him to a long-term contract. They told him he could ask half a million a year for a starter on a ten-year deal. With residuals, raises, and stock options . . . But that was money. What Brock had in his gut was freedom and a

76

long-ago self-promise. No man was going to get inside that.

'He wanted to know if you had a story.'

'Good old Mort. He's given to kidney trouble around air time. And he's got a new dame who likes him to close shop early.' He was climbing into his coat, smoothing his thick, unruly hair. The editor had to admit the guy had style. Macho. No wonder women –

'Don't think I haven't enjoyed your town, Steve. Greatest little big city in the world. As I've just discovered.' He tightened his tie. The effect was better. 'Sure I've got a story.'

He grinned and the news editor could hear another million sets click on.

He would always have a story, Brock told himself, because he knew how to get one and to deliver it with precision, wit, or intensity as the occasion demanded. He had a way of looking at things, a wry detachment that people trusted in this ververbalized era. That was his value in the market place. And that was all. He thought again of Lili and realized she had not been out of his mind since he had first come on her in that boarded-up old house.

He glanced professionally at the second hand sweeping the studio clock.

No sweat. He had a story tonight as he would have another and another, turning them up like minnows until at last, in some corner of the world, he would run down the one story that mattered. The one man. Sunshine, Brock had grimly named him. Brother Sunshine, his obsession. His great white whale. *Call me Ishmael. Call me Turner.* But Br'er Sunshine would never lead him to madness. Only to the most satisfying moment of his life. To the sweet, silent knowledge of revenge. And a promise kept. He wondered where Lili would fit into this chequerboard of his days.

He had never believed in love at first sight. Or in love in any lasting guise. That was a woman's game. He already had the answer to that.

'Sally's got your plane ticket on the nine o'clock.'

He remembered the news editor beside him.

'Thanks. I'll send her a box of candy. I'm not leaving

tonight.' He ignored the look of surprise. 'Ask her to leave it open.'

A red light flashed.

Brock took his seat behind the news desk, wondering if Lili had started dressing for dinner. Whether she would be late.

The engineer, behind his bank of screens in the control, raised his hand.

The announcer arranged his face.

ON THE AIR.

'Good evening, ladies and gentlemen. This is the Six o'clock Worldwide News from Station WNCS-TV. Our special guest tonight is ace reporter and commentator Brock Turner with another of his sensational and newsbreaking – '

'Jesus,' said Brock under his breath. He hunched forward exuding his special brand of authority and intimacy.

'Hi, friends. Brock Turner here from the glamour town of these United States. What I've got to tell you tonight would not strike either of us as sensational, but I promise you it will touch your heart, as it did mine. It's about a woman who chose to live as a ghost . . .' He turned on that getting-to-like-you half-smile known among the staff as the sponsors' delight.

The news editor had a momentary and happy vision of the rating chart and quietly tiptoed out of the studio.

The long April twilight deepened.

In the subdued if faded rosewood elegance of the drawing-room on St Charles Avenue, the Sisters Beaulaire sat dressed and ready with the grace of long-accepted service for the dinner hour. Clementine, tall and spare and at ease with a straight spine, held her embroidery frame at a disciplined angle, her needle leaving a trail of exquisite petit point across it. Clementine did not approve of idleness at any time and now in her sixties her skill had become one of the lost arts of *la vieille société*. Josephine, shorter, given to clear-cheeked plumpness, watched the regular rise and fall of her sister's white sleeve. She saw no reason why hands that had been busy all day should not rest. Besides she hated needlework. And anyway, she had too much on her mind.

She flipped the pages of the historical magazine in her lap, then let it slide to the floor. She glanced at Clem and retrieved it.

In another ten minutes Carrie would come in, light the lamps, and draw the louvres. Promptly at six-thirty she would bring in the silver tray bearing two tiny cut-crystal glasses of the pale Dubonnet the sisters favoured. Promptly at a quarter to seven she would announce dinner. It was already too late, thought Josie. Let the silence deepen with the blue dusk.

She knew they were both aware of the crisis that filled the space between them, uncaged, waiting.

Lili paid off the cab and watched it disappear down the treelined avenue. She was in no hurry. The air was sweet. In the half light the azalea bushes banking the walk glowed with colour. The drawing-room lamps had not yet been lit but through the lime trees she could make out two dim and motionless silhouettes. The aunts were down for dinner.

But it did not matter. None of it. It was a lifetime since she had left the house that afternoon. The childishness of that episode irritated her now. For the brief three-quarters of an hour spent at the little wooden table with a man she had never seen before, sipping a Ramos she hardly wanted, was another lifetime. He had talked about everything, sometimes looking so directly at her that she felt weak, sometimes hardly seeing her. And when he had said dinner at seven-thirty, no answer seemed to be required. She did not remember making one. She would wear her hyacinth silk. He had said something about her eyes. Henley Brocklebank Turner. She had memorized the syllables carefully in the cab home.

As she opened the front door, the lamps went up as if on cue. She heard her Aunt Clem's voice, firm, in the drawing-room.

'Give this to Luis, Carrie. I am disappointed that he left the flagstones untrimmed and neglected to cut back the south portico wisteria but under the circumstances this is for the best.'

Carrie emerged into the hall carrying a pale grey envelope. She hardly glanced at Lili. Lili came back to reality. She had been able to sense disaster since the first weeks when she had come to live in this sepulchre house. When she had broken a Sèvres cup . . . when she had climbed into the attic . . . when . . .

'Lili, my dear, you're home!' Aunt Josie's warm voice was threaded with warning. Lili dutifully kissed the aunts. Clementine said nothing.

'What's happened to Luis? I heard – '

'If you heard, there's no need to ask, Lili. Because I think you know what's happened.' Clementine, having embarked, could not reverse sail. She tucked the needle with deliberation into the canvas and set the embroidery frame aside. 'Luis left his duties at three-thirty this afternoon, did not return until nearly five, and – '

'But he was with me!' It was out before she realized it. Indignation was always to come before judgement with Lili.

'So I understand. Cook saw you.'

'Lili, dear, whatever the reason was . . .' Josie began. Aunt Clem squelched her with a look.

'There could be no possible reason why Elizabeth would leave this house with a young man who was a servant on the premises and not return for nearly two hours.'

'He is not a servant. I mean, even if he is, he knows more about plants and flowers than anybody on St Charles Avenue. You said so yourself, Aunt Clem. Besides, he's not going to be a gardener much longer. He's going to be a leader of his people.'

'A what, dear?' Josie heard clearly but the whole scene needed some braking.

'A leader of his people, who are oppressed.'

It smelled faintly, unpleasantly, to Aunt Clem of something she would rather not name. Pink, she would have said delicately. While it darkened the episode, it had little relevance now. Something bigger was at stake that she must at all costs point out to this baffling, self-willed girl.

'. . . besides,' Lili was rushing on, 'I asked Luis to go to Dauphine Street with me this afternoon because you said I shouldn't go into that empty house alone.'

'We both did, Clem.' Josie liked a winning point.

'I see no reason for Elizabeth to go to Dauphine Street. If she must, I certainly never suggested she take a *man* with her. A strange man. Did anyone see you?'

'There were plenty of people in the street. We went down the alley and in the back way.'

Clementine ejected a breath of dismay. Once she had given up her youthful dreams, she had come to look on her virginity as a holy chalice, proud of its preservation. By now she was even able to pity once-married Josephine for her irreparable loss. But beyond the whiteness of purity a fragment of her mind scurried, forsaken, alone, a blind mole ferreting out unmentionable dark acts, secret lusts and pleasures that could only be enjoyed through condemnation.

'You were in the house alone with him?'

'That's no reason to fire him.'

Clementine saw her triumph. 'Luis was not fired. He gave notice on his return this afternoon.'

Tried and found guilty, Lili told herself. In the end Luis had the last word. It might not have mattered at all to her now, except that it gave her the beginning of a very large idea. As plain now as Aunt Clem's rigidly aristocratic features. Clementine herself provided the clue.

'You will, of course, have to tell this to dear Edward.'

'Tell what, Aunt Clem?'

'Whatever happened in that house this afternoon between you and – and that servant.'

'I don't see why I have to.'

Even Josie looked dismayed. 'Lili, he's your intended husband.'

But Clementine was sharper. She pounced.

'Did anything happen?' She paused. 'Tell me the truth, Elizabeth. I must have the truth. Your Aunt Josephine and I have done everything we could for you. We have taken you into our home, given you background, position – '

'Clemmie . . .' protested Josie.

81

Clementine ignored her. 'You are engaged to a most suitable young man of fine family. His grandfather was King of Comus. A beautiful life is ahead of you. And now this! I must know, Elizabeth – what did that young man do?'

Imagination had made the ephemeral solid. Fancy had become fact. There was nothing she could do that would hurt Luis now. Some day, when he was a leader, he might laugh at it. As for her . . . Lili lowered her eyes, 'I'd rather not say, Aunt Clem.'

Even Josie glanced up in dismay.

'You will tell me, Elizabeth. Or I shall call Father Gregory.'

Lili shrugged. 'All right. If I have to. But it will shock you, Aunt Clem. And you will hate that.'

'I think I know my duty.'

'Yes, Aunt Clem.' Lili hesitated, summoning suitable reluctance. 'We went in the back way as I said. We crossed the court into the hall – '

'I want the whole story, Elizabeth.'

'I'm trying to tell you. I wanted to go into the living-room and see if the cabinet was all right. I – I asked Luis to wait in the courtyard. Instead' – she hesitated and Clementine leaned forward a shade – 'he followed me. It was sort of dim, the dust sheets were all over. He came up behind me . . . we were near the divan . . .' She could almost see Aunt Clem's dry, tight lips moisten.

'Go on, Elizabeth.'

'Must I, Aunt Josie?'

'Really, Clem – '

'*Tais-toi*, Josephine!'

Lili's shoulders sagged. 'Anyhow, he – he tried to kiss me. I . . . wouldn't let him. Then he – he . . . the divan was there . . . don't ask me any more!' She covered her face with her hands.

'No, dear. We understand.' Josie was patting her shoulder. Clementine sank to the back of the chair. Her hands were trembling.

'Can I go now, Aunt Clem?'

82

The gaunt-faced woman nodded. 'Perhaps we'd better talk more, Elizabeth, before you see Edward.'

'No. No. You're right. I see it now. I couldn't marry him letting him think I – I'm something I'm not. It wouldn't be fair to him. Oh, Aunt Clem, I was so . . . foolish.'

Lili turned and ran from the room. They heard her steps, like a running scale up the stairs. In the distance they heard the door close.

Josie broke the silence with a small sigh, its reason known only to herself.

'Times have changed, Clem.'

'Not that much.' Clementine straightened her spine. 'More Roundtree than Beaulaire, as I always suspected.' She folded her hands.

Carrie was entering with the silver tray and the two tiny cut-crystal glasses.

'I believe I shall have to write a letter. I see no other solution. Set it down, Carrie. We're quite ready.'

Lili was late.

Brock met the situation with both regret and relief. Regret that among all her other surprises, she did not surprise him with promptness. Relief that she was not made over eager by the thin veneer of his so-called fame. He gave no thought to what the evening might or might not hold, nor to tomorrow or the day after. He simply very much wanted to see her again, to delight in her rarity, to hear her laugh, and to feel that at thirty-two youth had not entirely slipped his grasp.

Tomorrow would take care of itself.

She came in from the last of the light in something blue, something soft and white over her shoulders, and a blue ribbon holding her hair high on her head. The gravity of her expression made her face oddly younger.

He rose and pulled out a chair.

'Thank you,' she said without smiling. *Never apologize, never explain.* She learned quickly, he told himself. She looked around. 'Where are we?'

'If you read the sign outside, we're at Les Trois Piques. A discovery of mine. Strictly a family place. Run by three generations. And possibly the best red-snapper chowder in this hemisphere.'

The room was long and narrow, the walls bare except for some yellowed posters of the French Opera House, the *Natchez Belle* at an antebellum wharf, and Sarah Bernhardt as Hamlet. The diamond pattern linoleum floor showed both wear and polish. Narrow tables with bentwood chairs hugged the walls. The tables, covered with immaculate coarse white cloths, were occupied by couples engrossed in each other.

No glamour. He was not trying to impress or flatter her. She doubted that Edward T. Lettlier had ever set foot in the place. But Neddie was out of her life now, for all practical purposes. As he had been only a practical purpose in the first place, he was receding rapidly. It was part of the curious new sense of freedom that was leaving her so strangely solemn. Handling freedom, she was discovering, was not as easy as achieving it. The tissue of lies that had given it birth lingered to haunt her. What had life on St Charles Avenue been but lies from the very beginning? Secrets she had slowly pried from the old house, hidden away behind manners and discipline that made a mockery of growing up. But now suddenly, miraculously, everything had changed.

'Why the hair ribbon?'

'What?'

'You look different tonight.'

'I need to.' Her answer was enigmatic, but that was part of her fascination. Iceberg conversation, he called it. Nine-tenths of her beneath the surface. But he was patient. When he had to be.

He gave the order, selected a wine.

'I chose the chowder for you instead of the shrimp. There are no other choices. You eat the family speciality of the evening.'

'Thank you.'

He looked at her sharply, suspecting sarcasm. There was none. Only the seriousness of her face. But at least she was attentive.

'What's wrong with my hair ribbon?'

'Not a thing.'

'But you don't like it?'

'Sure I like it. It's different, that's all.' He grinned. 'I expected the same girl.'

'I'm not the same girl, but we needn't go into that now. I should have said I was sorry to be late.'

'Don't.' He had no idea what she was talking about but he sensed a confession coming, he in the role of fatherly forgiver. The very words could curdle the evening. He would bring a smile if he had to draw faces on the tablecloth. Anything to get back to, if not basics, something nearer the astonishing and tender delight of that brief gin-Ramos half-hour at LaFitte's.

'Never apologize . . . remember?'

'And never explain. I remember. Though it could get a person into a lot of trouble sometimes.'

'Not any worse than trying to fib your way out of a mistake.' He had said something wrong. Her face shadowed.

'I'd rather forget all about it.'

'So would I.' He gave her the most honest smile in his arsenal. 'Look, we spent thirty-seven minutes talking about me this afternoon. Let's talk about you. Incidentally, you should always wear that colour.'

'I know. But I get tired of it. Anyway, we didn't talk about you. We talked about what you thought about New Orleans. And things. I don't know anything about you. Except that you're some kind of reporter, I guess.'

She had a disconcerting way of fixing her large eyes directly on his face. He realized again that she had no idea who Brock Turner was. While the thought nicked his vanity, it gave him an odd sense of being young, with an untried future ahead. A future that would take a different turn from this day forward. He had no idea that his smile had turned suddenly boyishly shy. She returned it. Her hand lay on the table. He touched it. She did not draw away. For an instant the circle of candlelight barricaded the outside world. A heady instant. Then he remembered. He tapped her fingers lightly and left her free.

'So tell me who you are, Lilith Roundtree.'

She laughed. 'It really isn't a very pretty name put together like that, is it? I told you my father, Amos Roundtree, was an artist and my mother was very beautiful. She loved birds. She never caged them. They used to come into the courtyard, even humming-birds. I'd watch her working with her flowers. The birds coming right down beside her. I knew why my father married her. No matter what people said.'

He heard the unsteadiness that she covered instantly with a quick laugh.

'She called me Lilibet, which I thought was silly but she said was elegant because that's what the Queen of England was called when she was little. She wanted me to be elegant even if I wasn't pretty. She said elegance was more important than anything and that anyway I would be beautiful when I was forty. *Forty!* As if it would matter then!'

Was she younger than he thought? He guessed twenty-two or twenty-three. He hoped twenty-five. It would not be easy to know this girl. Brock was not used to complicated women.

The red-snapper chowder arrived. And the wine correctly chilled. He discovered he was healthily hungry. She sipped at a half-empty spoon. She would have to do better than that if – He checked the thought. He was leaving tomorrow. He could stretch it one more day. But should he?

Her eyes were on him, large, lustrous, grave.

'It is good – the chowder.'

'I thought you'd never say so.'

'You don't always have an appetite after a big crisis in your life.' She set down her spoon. He had an uneasy sense of foreboding. 'There's something I think I should tell you, Brock.'

The foreboding deepened. But, dammit, not at this moment of gastronomical pleasure.

'It was why I was late.'

He put down his spoon. 'Dear, dear Lili. Would it interest you to know that I don't give a damn why you were late? You're here. You look wonderful. If you'll just eat

86

your chowder like a good girl, I think I'll fall in love with you.'

He said it lightly, a try-on, and instantly regretted it. Nothing worked the same with this girl. Her eyes grew graver. He lifted the wine bottle.

'Pouilly-Fuissé, good vintage. The cup that cheers – '

'. . . and clears . . . today of past regrets and future fears . . .' she murmured.

'What?'

'Omar. I love poetry. My mother always read it to me. I learned old Omar by heart. I used to read him at night and cry. When the nuns caught me, they'd give me two more Latin declensions. They said poetry was for recreation and anyhow, I should read Longfellow or Elbert Hubbard because they were more Christian.' Light danced for an instant in her eyes. 'I hated studying but I love poetry. Real poetry. Do you?'

'I don't know much about it.'

'I'll teach you! Listen. "There was a door to which I found no key: there was a veil past which I could not see: some little talk awhile of me and thee . . . there seemed – and then . . ."' Astonishingly her eyes glistened.

'Hey, wait a minute.'

'Brock.' She leaned across the table and he caught the scent of something as sweet as it was subtle. 'I have to tell you. I don't want to – to fib my way out of anything. Not with you.' It was as near a declaration as he had ever heard without words. He was for an instant nineteen. Then he was old. Very old.

She reached into her handbag and brought out a small felt sack. From it she took a ring. A dazzler. Two and a half carats, minimum, he guessed. It might as well have been two and a half stones in his gut. 'My engagement ring.'

He took a large swallow of wine. To hell with the sentiment of a toast.

'You've made your point. Let's enjoy dinner.'

'You might hear me out. I was engaged. Until ten minutes to six tonight. I am not now. I wanted you to see this because I want you to know everything about me. Tomorrow I shall return it. That's all. Do you see?'

87

'Who's the guy?'

'Does his name matter?'

'You come on a little sudden, Lili. Why would you dump him like that?'

'I've known him a long time. When he asked me to marry him, I thought it was a good idea. I don't think it is now.' She dropped the ring on the table. It bounced. He covered it with his hand.

'Lili! For Pete's sake – '

'He wouldn't want me now. Anyhow.' She returned the ring to its tiny sack. 'Brock, can't you see? I didn't want to come out to dinner with you tonight . . . *engaged*.'

Like a man looking into an abyss towards which he was irresistibly drawn, he saw.

Lili, her face serene, sipped her wine, her eyes teasingly on him over the rim of the glass. A way no girl should drink with a man she hardly knew. He would tell her that some day too.

He was barely aware of the soul-reaching drama of trout Rochambeau. But she released a sigh of contentment.

'Now I am hungry.'

Out of this new giddiness, Brock told himself, could come only disaster.

It was to come sooner than he expected.

CHAPTER EIGHT

They would each remember that evening as long as they lived.

The dazzle of lights of the young-old city. The April night sky, white with moon-concealing mists. The blackness of the enduring river that spoke to him of home and history. The great hulks of anchored cargo ships, delighting her with the mystery of their distant ports.

But mostly Brock would remember her face, as she first lifted it to his.

And Lili would remember that he never said good-night.

They walked wordlessly from the restaurant called Les Trois Piques. Through the narrow streets of the Quarter, across Jackson Square, as impervious to the throngs of springtime strollers as to the insistent spontaneity of the bearded players of street jazz. They passed the French Market. At the river's edge they found a bench on the deserted esplanade.

They held hands. They talked. They were silent. They talked again. It was enough to let anticipation flower through strangeness to certainty. She was a woman, he discovered, who liked silences. He was a man, she told herself, to whom she could say all that had been stifled in her lonely growing up.

'The house was so big. And so empty. Although it really wasn't. It was filled with furniture and things on tables that mustn't be broken. I did dreadful things.' She giggled. 'Oh, I tried not to break anything. But I looked in every room and every closet. There wasn't much else to do and nobody to stop me. That's when I found Aunt Clem's court dress hanging in back of a third-floor wardrobe. Imagine! Aunt Clem had been a court lady at the ball of Comus a million years ago. After that you're expected to be married within a season or two. Aunt Clem never married, and I guess she never got over the disgrace. It must have been a great tragedy for her. Especially if nobody asked her. I discovered about Aunt Josie too. She was widowed at thirty-two but she had a lover. His letters were tied up –'

'In blue ribbon?' he teased.

'No. Plain string in a shoe box. But he couldn't marry her so he went away.'

He stirred and looked across the river.

'Were you in the Court of Comus?' he asked.

'No. Aunt Clem had it arranged but I refused. I thought all that fuss was silly and I had no intention of just getting married that soon anyhow.'

'Why not?' After the brief fire of candour at the dinner table, all this talk seemed to be putting distance between them. Yet he had to know all he could about her. 'What else would you do?'

'A lot of things. I went to the university for two years.'
She hesitated and her hands twisted. 'I was a misfit, Brock.
I came from the convent and I could do Latin verbs and
French knots and I could set a dinner table for twenty-four
and I knew how to keep linen sheets – '

'And Omar.' He grinned.

'That was part of the trouble. If I hadn't spent my time
reading that poetry . . .' She gave a wry little laugh. 'One
day a beau I had at the university took me downriver on one
of the harbour ferries – Why are you smiling?'

'I haven't heard the word "beau" since my grandmother
in Kansas – '

'Well, that's what we say here and it isn't considered
funny. Anyhow, Chuck showed me some rusty old wharves
further down the river and he told me that was where the
Liberty ships in the war were put together. You remember
the Liberty ships?'

'Instant freighters.'

'But Chuck said they were sent here in pieces and riveted
together. And you know who did it? Women. All women
putting those ships together. He told me women did a lot of
things like that and when was I going to join the twentieth
century? And didn't I ever want to do anything besides be a
girl?'

It seemed in the softness of the night adequate to Brock.
But she was caught up in the intensity of her vision.

'I did want to do a lot of things, Brock. But I didn't know
anything. Really. And there were the aunts. If I had just
gone off . . . but how long do you go on being grateful and
trying not to hurt people?'

'So you got engaged?'

She was silent.

He put his arm around her and drew her to him.

'Do you know what I think, Lili Roundtree?'

'What?' It was a mere breath; her lips were open.

'I think you can do anything in this world you want to.
And I hope you will.'

He kissed her, lightly, more deeply, until her body
surged towards his, and in the melting splendour of the
night the knowledge came and the promise was made.

When he at last released her, she did not move from him. Darkness and certainty wrapped them.

'I have no place to take you, Lili.'

'I know.'

'But we'll plan tomorrow.'

'I'd like that.'

Finally she straightened. He stirred. He did not kiss her again. There was no need. His voice was husky with desire.

'Tomorrow.' He looked out into the night. How long was tomorrow? And after tomorrow? Then he heard somewhere in his mind a silent promise that he had never made before. Or wanted to. He would not lose this girl no matter what the cost.

'You look so solemn, Brock.'

'Thinking. It never came easy.'

'There ought to be a better way.'

Silly half-talk that set them both laughing because they wanted to laugh and to love and to know each other better, already feeling that they had known each other all their lives.

'Okay. I'll let you make the decision. Coffee and doughnuts over at the Market or a jazz spot.'

'Both,' she said promptly. 'Coffee first.'

'Good girl! One vote for the lady who can make up her mind. They'll make you President one of these days.'

He pulled her to her feet and slipped her hand through his arm. 'But not if I can help it.'

His happiness at that moment was so complete that he was afraid to look at it. A night moth, as luminous as the girl on his arm, which daylight, reality, tomorrow, could sweep from him.

The famous French Market Café was almost empty at this off-hour. Three girl tourists near the centre of the room were bored with each other. The fourth, an older woman, was wondering why she had ever agreed to come, except the tour was cheaper if you came in couples. She sat moodily gazing at a half cup of cold café au lait. French coffee indeed. Half chicory, if you asked her and bitter as gall. As for the doughnuts, she would never try to pass these square lumps they called *beignets* for the crullers she used to make for Herb. Herb, gone these two years, and here she was where she never in her right mind wanted to be, a million miles from Des Moines with three silly girls half her age.

The girls were scanning the place. Like that radar thing that followed Sputnik, Herb used to explain to her. It was easy to see what they were after. She'd go back to the hotel room, if she could trust a cab to take her, and let them do as they please. As she opened her purse she heard a squeal.

'Look, it's him!'

'Sure it is. I'd know him anywhere.'

'He's even handsomer off TV!'

'Millie, look! It's Brock Turner!'

Millie shut her purse. Brock Turner. Herb used to turn Brock Turner on every night. 'Too good-looking for his own good, but he makes a lot of sense. He ought to be a comer one of these days.' Now here she was in the same place with Brock Turner. It was like seeing Herb.

'Where?' she asked nervously.

'Over there in the corner. With that girl in blue.'

'She's not much to look at.'

'That wouldn't bother him. He's got one in every town, I'll bet.'

'Well, he could sure put his shoes under my bed any time he wanted.'

'I wonder if she knows he's married.'

'He isn't!'

'Oh, yes, he is. My girl-friend has a cousin in Kansas. She says Brock Turner's got a wife living out there, daughter of a big shot, a judge or something, who won't let Brock get a divorce.'

'That's gossip and I think it's mean,' said the older woman.

'What's with you, Millie? I'll bet you have a crush on him too. Who'll dare me to go over and speak to him?' The thin redhead, nubile in a black sweater, started to rise.

'If you go, I'm going with you, Ginnie.'

'Me too.' The plump blonde, pulling her mini-skirt taut to the seams, giggled. 'I'm going to ask for his autograph. Boy, that girl he's with is a real nothing.'

The redhead hid her mouth with her hand. 'Wanna see me break it up?'

Lili cupped the hot coffee in her hands. Its warmth seeped through her like a second happiness. So much to say, yet so little. So much to know and yet she knew everything she wanted. She smiled dreamily. He caught it.

'Nice.'

'What is?'

'This. You. Being here.'

'Oh . . . Brock . . .' She was giving herself away like a schoolgirl. But she dropped her hand on the table and he reached for it.

'Is it too soon to tell you, Lili – '

'Much. You hardly know me.'

'Would you consider a formal – ' But he did not finish. The table was suddenly overshadowed. Three girls in a mingled scent of perspiration and cheap perfume crowded close.

'You're Brock Turner, aren't you?'

'I'd know you anywhere, Mr Turner.'

The redhead was silent, abashed by the quick release of held hands.

Brock, without looking at Lili, was aware of her startled face. He swore silently, but he knew the business and knew what must be done. He was on his feet, moving as if to shield her.

'What can I do for you young ladies?'

'Could we have your autograph?'

'Easy.' The famous half-grin. He conjured three white cards from his pocket and with a slender gold pen scribbled something on each one.

'Thanks, Mr Turner!'

'Oh, thanks!'

'Could we have one more for Millie?'

'Nothing simpler.' On a fourth card he wrote 'For Millie'.

The girls giggled. The redhead found her voice.

'I heard you tonight, Mr Turner. You were wonderful. I just shivered. That story about the old lady in the grey veils

– the ghost. I'd love to see that house. We're just in New Orleans a few days . . . if you could tell us – '

'I'm afraid not. I never reveal sources. Thank you for stopping by.' The professional, warm dismissal that would not hurt the ratings.

The girls trailed away, awed and envying. Brock sat down. Lili was examining her cup.

'Well, say something, for Pete's sake.' The lights were too glaring. She looked small as a bird.

'I didn't know you were famous.'

'Not very. Would it matter?'

'I thought you were a reporter.'

'I am. A damn good one, too, when they let me.' He would keep this light. Her eyes were unfathomable. 'Do you ever watch television?'

'We have a set. But it's in the back room.'

'I see.'

She seemed to realize that something more was called for.

'Aunt Clem doesn't believe anything she doesn't see in print. Aunt Josie says there's too much talk in this world anyhow.'

'And you . . .'

'I just don't like being told what to do. Eat this, drink that. Too many orders.'

It was as neat a disposal of his chosen career as he had ever heard. He wondered what Mortimer Russell would think. But Mort Russell was a long way off, and Brock had a problem.

'Well, I suppose that's one way to look at it. But it isn't all bad. There was a nice programme the other day on fish life in the upper Amazon.'

She saw the grin but there were things she had to know.

'What time?'

'Seven-thirty Sunday morning.'

They both laughed. But it did not clear the air.

'What do you do on television?'

'Special news spots. Usually at six in the evening.'

'Oh.' The syllable fell into silence.

'Look, it doesn't make all that difference, does it?'

94

'I suppose I should have known. But you didn't say anything.'

'You didn't ask me.' But it was inadequate. There was something bigger here.

She looked around. 'Could we go? I don't like being stared at. I guess everybody knows you.'

'Not quite. Lili, don't be silly about this. It's the way I make my living. I'm a reporter first. But it's what happens when you get your face on that damned screen every day.'

'I understand, Brock. I just never knew anybody famous before. But it makes a difference, doesn't it? Any place we went, anything I might say . . .' She hesitated. 'Well, you're a reporter and I suppose you've got to report. Like the ghost story – the old lady in grey veils.'

So that was it. 'Now wait a minute! That story is known all over the French Quarter.'

'But it was my family . . . my house. Here in New Orleans, nobody likes being in public like that.'

If she were serious, the convent and the aunts were certainly showing. But he sensed again something even deeper.

'Lili, Lili! You're talking like a school kid. Ten minutes ago we were sitting here as deeply in love, if I know what that word means, as any two people ever found themselves. It was magic and it was wonderful. And it was all that mattered to me. I've fallen for you, Lili, in a way I don't understand and have never known. I'm not going to let you spoil it because three silly girls – Or maybe you're jealous,' he added bitingly.

'Jealous! I'm never jealous! We're sitting here all right and I've told you everything I can about me.'

'Have you?' They were quarrelling now. And they had not even made love.

'Yes. But I don't know anything about you. I wouldn't even have known what you did.'

'Then ask, for Christ's sake. But maybe it's like that guy, your "beau" on the ferry said. You'd better join the twentieth century first.' His well-known voice was rising, with his less-known temper. He was angry and he felt helpless. The place was filling up. 'Let's get out of here.'

But now she made no move. Her hands were around the cup again. Her eyes were solemn. She seemed to be engaged in an inner dialogue. Important and alone. When she finally spoke her voice was soft and without expression.

'Brock, is there anything else I should know? I mean, about you. I mean, before tomorrow?'

He saw the delicate flush on her face. Would he ever know her? Light and shadow. Shallows and depths. For an instant he was tempted. It would take only a little lie. They would have tomorrow. That would persuade her.

If not, he told himself, she still had that damned little grey felt sack in her purse. She could marry the guy and live comfortably cocooned the rest of her life, with her linen sheets and her French knots, whatever they were. He, Brock, would have learned a lesson. An old lesson he thought he had mastered until four o'clock this afternoon.

'I guess you'd rather not answer, Brock.'

He unclasped one of her hands from the cup and held it.

'What do you want to know, Lili?'

She hesitated. Her eyes had a melting tenderness, an intensity he would never forget as long as he lived. Happiness was something he had never believed in, a name for someone else's state of being. Yet for the first time in his life he almost saw it, palpable and shimmering between them on the table. When did a man take what he wanted and the devil take the rest?

'Are you married, Brock?'

He returned her look and drew a slow breath. There had never been any real choice of answer. Not to her.

'Yes,' he said simply. The mundane phrases followed. 'I didn't work at it. We've been separated for five years. I can't get a divorce. For a lot of reasons. I don't know how much you want to know.'

'Nothing else really.'

'Where does that leave us, Lili?'

She was too calm, too quiet. The serenity he had seen in her face returned. Yet with a difference. She was light-years from him across the narrow table. He had no way of reaching her.

'I'd like to think about it, Brock.'

'And tomorrow?'

'I'd like to think about that too.'

The lights were still on at the St Charles Avenue house. That meant the aunts were still up. No doubt the talk of her 'ruin' had gone on many hours. If there had been any laughter left in her, it would have bubbled. But that all seemed so long ago, so childish.

'Is that you, Elizabeth?'

Aunt Clem sat alone in the living-room, upright, fully dressed. Aunt Josie was nowhere to be seen. That meant that judgement had been passed, but Aunt Josie did not agree and would not be present at the deliverance. Lili had reached a judgement of her own, so it was just as well to settle things now.

'Come in, Elizabeth.'

Oddly, as she crossed the room, Lili felt a rush of compassion for this gaunt woman so nearly at the end of her life, a life as unbending as her spine, as empty as the sheathed court gown banished to the darkness of the third-floor wardrobe.

Yet truer instinct, a latent wisdom already deep in Lili, warned her that she had no right to pity. Her own life was still untested, her youth suddenly jolted into confusion. But here in the quiet order of this room, this stern, ageing woman sat formidable and enduring. Clementine Beaulaire with her stifled tragedy knew who she was.

'*Know who you are, Lilibet.*' Her father's dim words came back, back from the sunlit courtyard, the cool studio where he painted fretfully and fitfully. '*You are yourself and no one else. No one else can be you. Know that individual grain inside you and keep to it. Then nothing can break you. Hurt you, yes. Even scar. But never defeat or destroy you.*' He had added, as if he had forgotten the listening child, '*I never knew.*'

Nor do I, thought Lili, standing in Clementine's orbit. How to learn? Where to learn?

'Edward was here tonight.'

Lili came back to the troubled present. 'Oh?'

'We thought you had gone out with him.'

'No, Aunt Clem.'

97

'We were rather concerned.'

There was no answer to that.

'Such a fine young man. So well-bred.'

There was no answer to that either.

'It is a pity but we shall say no more about it. I am sure you intend to speak to Edward yourself. Tomorrow, I should advise.'

'Yes. Of course.' It was mechanical. Tomorrow had evaporated. Lili longed for dismissal.

But the old woman did not move. She sat sibyl-like in the ring of lamp-light.

'Your Aunt Josephine and I have come to a decision, Elizabeth. We have done everything we can to give you the proper background, the upbringing, we believe you should have. But of course we must face the fact that there is another – There are other claims on you, other blood in your veins that we, perhaps, are not in a position to understand. I have written a letter – and dear Edward was kind enough to post it for me – to Mr Willard Roundtree in Thatcher, Connecticut. He is a cousin of your father's. He came here at the time of your father's death. He seemed a most reliable man. He said that if at any time you should want to go north . . .'

To Lili's surprise, the rasping voice quivered. She heard a sound. Aunt Josie had entered the room. Her cheeks were lard-like. As if on cue she picked up her habit of alternating Clementine's conversation.

'But of course, there is no hurry, Elizabeth. You can take all the time you wish. Isn't that so, Clem?' The round face was beseeching.

'I think too much time could only be awkward for us all.' Clementine Beaulaire rose with no seeming bend to her spine. 'Good-night, Elizabeth.' She turned off the too revealing lamp-light.

So that was how it was done. In an irresponsible moment of rebellion, Lili had placed herself in a different world, where different rules prevailed. But rules nonetheless. She had fallen from their grace, the pattern was as inevitable as it was final.

She felt the giddiness and saw the quicksands. With a

second vision she caught a glimpse of something deeper, as she glanced from one stern and sorrowing face to the other. How easy it was to be young. How clever to mock, to belittle, to rebel. To have time before her without boundary and without end. And to be so sure that no one ever before had known the ecstasy and the pain of new encounter.

Unaware, she had brought to them the contagion of living. With her it would go. The lamps would be lighted at six, the louvres drawn on the lavender dusk retreat. But the silence would grow until –

She could not live life for them, she thought hotly. She could not even share the enormity of Brock Turner's existence. Or burst out in confusion that it was not hers alone to claim.

'I'm sorry, I truly am, for disappointing you.' She heard her own voice break. 'I do love you both so much!'

She fled and tears dimmed the old and gracious curving staircase. She would not let them come until she reached the darkness of her room. When they came, she was not sure why. For the lives greyed so nearly to their end downstairs? For the waves of emotion sweeping through her, devastating in their rapidity?

A man unknown to her twenty-four hours ago filled her mind and her being. They had parted without a good-night. She longed to say good-morning.

She held the pillow close as if it were his body.

At last, because she was young and untried, she wept without reserve or reason. For the simple inscrutability of life. Its anguish. Its wonder.

The new dawn woke her with its freshness. In the pallor at the window tomorrow already took shape.

Destination unknown.

Lili unknown.

CHAPTER NINE

It was the telephone's fourth ring, but Mortimer Russell did not hear it because he did not want to hear it. He was heavy with satisfied sleep. He rolled back the night table and flung his arm across the girl beside him.

She sat up, pushing back a mop of tangled yellow hair. Her face had the good-natured pout, her body the untroubled sensuality of a Barbie doll. Within it, as Mort knew, lay the shrewdness of a pocket calculator. But her lush insatiability blew old embers to new flames that ringed him like a hopeful Brunhild against the chill of approaching fifty.

Mortimer liked metaphors, particularly those he had to explain to the girl beside him. If culture had not gripped the inner man, it had at least spread adequately thin and wide to befit a network vice-president.

'Mort, answer it. Or he'll keep ringing the rest of the night.'

Mort reached over and pushed down the turn-off button. The ringing stopped. In the darkness he slid a hand across her warm breasts. She moved obligingly, but he let himself return to lassitude. It was enough to know that she was there. Two divorces had taught him that nothing in life was as sweet as a waiting woman. Trishanka Bliss had a talent for waiting.

But not when self-interest was aroused.

She leaned across Mort's thickening rib cage and lifted the switch. The ringing resumed, like an impatient presence.

'You know who it is at this hour. If he's in trouble – '

'What the hell do you care?' But he decided not to ask. She might give him an honest answer. He had caught her more than once, her small tongue between her lips, her eyes glued on the handsome head and the enigmatic smile on the screen. Women and Brock. He'd like just once to see the network's number-one news asset fall on his face. Or his prat.

'Who is it?'

'Good evening, little brother.' The precise, carefully oiled syllables told him all he needed to know.

'Brock! For Christ's sweet sake . . .'

'The top of the evening, or the bottom, to you, friend. I am at Carny's.'

'And drunk.'

'Possibly. But not completely. I would share the malt and a few well-chosen words.'

'If there are any words to choose, I'll choose 'em.' Mort was awake now and perspiring and none of this was good for his blood pressure. 'Why the hell weren't you back last night after the broadcast? And what in the name of holy Monday was all that tripe about little old ladies in grey veils?'

It was wellknown that the network executive never gave away his own secret awe of celebrity.

'I thought you'd never ask, Mort.'

'You promised a big story!'

'I never promise.'

'So you use forty thousand dollars of sponsor money to –'

'I'll come right up and explain.'

'You will not!'

'I'll hold a second table, next to mine.'

Mortimer Russell grunted and slammed down the phone. Three-ten in the morning. The night shot, the mood gone. His head had begun to pound and Trisha was sitting in the middle of the big circular bed, hugging her knees, naked as the moment he had carried her there. She had no sense of the subtlety of clothing. Before or after. If there wasn't a law, she'd walk down the centre of Park Avenue . . .

'Is he bad?'

'I wish to God he was unconscious.'

He went into the onyx and gold bathroom, liberally speckled with the initials M.R. like the dropping of security, popped a tranquillizer into his mouth, and began brushing his teeth. Mortimer Russell was a fastidious man. He was also, at this moment, a worried one.

Tim Carny was a big balding man with a stomach he could almost rest on the bar, if he didn't keep it securely wrapped in a wet foam-striped apron. At this moment he was wiping his hands as he fixed a careful eye on his favourite patron. That corner table, wooden and scarred, was Brock Turner's any time he wanted it. But he hadn't liked the rigid crossing Brock had made from the wall phone to his seat. The big man's glance was as shrewd as his sigh was gentle.

'You fixing to go home soon, Mr Turner?' Tim was adamant on addressing all his customers with a prefix. It gave the place class.

'Sure, Tim, sure.' Brock settled back into the embrace of his chair. Two things you could say about Tim Carny. He knew a man liked to be comfortable when he was doing his drinking. His plain wooden chairs had arms. The other thing was that Tim had never opened the swinging doors of his saloon to women. And that, at this moment, was very important to Brock Turner.

'. . . and closing hour as stated in my licence is four.'

'The shank of the evening, my friend, but a hopeful sign of character that you observe the legalities.'

'And further, I'd say, against my own judgement, that if you haven't the sense to go home, there's Sam's singles' bar across the street.'

Brock half rose in indignation. 'You go too far, comrade.' He sat down abruptly. 'Since when the hell do I need a singles' bar?'

'I'm glad to hear it.' Tim bestowed a mild smile on the corner table.

'You're right, Tim. You always are. But I can't go home yet. Company's coming. It'll call for another bourbon and branch for me and a double seltzer for my friend. If I misjudge not, he's had something of an evening.'

The big man lifted his eyes to the large, round white-faced clock. Set high enough not to trouble the regular customers, but conspicuous enough to be seen at closing time.

'And don't worry. We'll be out before the cock crows or your Third Avenue equivalent. Look, if I don't talk to Mort here and now I'll be trapped in one of those button-down network meetings in the morning. If I'm walking out, I want to tell him fast.'

'Mr Turner . . .'

Brock swept a beneficent smile around the empty room and raised an empty glass. '"I often wonder what the vintner buys, more precious than the goods he sells." *The Rubáiyát*. Ever hear of it?'

'The Ruby Yacht? Not being a sea-going man, Mr Turner – '

The door swung open.

You had to admit, Brock told himself, Mort Russell had savvy. He made an impeccable entrance, tasselled loafers, knife-edge grey slacks, navy blazer, pure maroon foulard scarf at his throat, matching foulard breast-pocket handkerchief. He had even shaved. Ragged but he had tried.

Brock rose, pulled out a chair with a sweeping bow, and signalled Tim Carny.

'Jesus, I ought to fire you, Brock.'

Brock pushed his chair in. 'Allow me.'

'What have you got to tell me that can't wait till morning?'

'Bags under your eyes, Mort. How was she?'

Tim Carny materialized with two glasses and a bottle, which he set before Mort.

'Seltzer! Jesus H. – ' Mort exploded, as he had longed to since he had been awakened. 'Look, Turner, you've run out of independence! That's final. I'm running the show. Carny, I'll have two double Jack Daniels and the bill's on him!'

'So little gratitude for so much thought.' Brock smiled dreamily beyond Mort. 'Do what the man says, Tim.'

Mort put his hands to his head. It was pounding when he needed it most. And that crack about bags under his eyes with a board meeting at nine in the morning. He could not afford even the relief of outrage. Brock was his special catch. He had to keep it that way. But he'd pour the whisky on the floor before he'd go back to the seltzer he craved.

'All right, Brock, let's hear it. I want to go back to bed.'

'I understand. In a nutshell – do you want it in a nutshell, Mort baby?' Brock counted the two seconds of silence that was always so effective in his news stories. 'I'm quitting.' He waited for what he counted to be nine seconds. He watched Mort Russell thin his lips and draw in his head, a gesture that had earned him the nickname of Turtle.

When Mort finally spoke, it was as quiet as anything Brock had ever heard from him.

'You can't.'

'I'll make the necessary contractual amends. Money. Whatever.'

'You can't.'

Brock's dreaminess vanished.

'What do you mean, I can't? I'm a free man. I'm through. That's what I want you to know. I'm finished. I've had it.'

'I see your point. But' – and this came even more softly and with greater finality – 'you can't quit.'

'Think you can stop me?' Brock began to wish he had kept this exchange until morning. It was not working as planned.

'I don't have to, Turner. You'll stop yourself. You traded your soul – most of us do in this business – for money, glamour, expense accounts, free-loading with the rich and famous, or whatever. You traded for a ticket to anywhere for your own private purpose. We made a deal. You delivered. I have no quarrel with that. Your stories were brilliant, most of them. Never dull. Even that cutesy last night. You're a personality – about as much as this network can stand. But we gave you the big chance, Brock, and in return you promised us the "Big Story", the Sunshine story, whenever you broke it.'

Brock reminded himself what he had almost forgotten – that Mortimer Russell had been one of the ablest newspaper editors in the country when he made his trade. He wondered whether Russell regretted it. But a good editor never forgets the smell of a big story. In a moment of weakness, a moment of 'trade', Brock had hinted at Sunshine. Russell would hold it over his head until he delivered. He had a right to, Brock thought grimly. In Russell's shoes he would.

'I haven't a lead on it, Mort. Both the *Estrellita de Oro* and the *Aztec Princess* came in clean in New Orleans. I've been in every port in this country . . .' He shrugged. 'I want to go private, Mort.'

'So would a lot of us. I can't. You can't. But I'll tell you what I can do. I'll give you a month off. Go take a rest. You look shot, Brock. And last night you sounded it.' The eyes grew sharp. 'What's the matter? That wife of yours giving you trouble again?'

'No.' Brock pushed his glass away. He knew now he had made a mistake. He'd been making mistakes since Lili's pale-blue note had been delivered to him at the broadcasting studio.

Go find an island. Take a girl who won't make bargains. I can overlook that when it's not business. You're a celebrity, Brock. You're still a married man. Sooner or later that catches up with you in the eyes of the great American public.

Mort Russell was enjoying himself, as he always did when he was winning. Brock was bone-tired. He did not need Mort's reminders of his life. He had Lili's wide, stricken eyes and the little-girl politeness of her note. He had gotten drunk on both, drunk enough to put himself at Mort's mercy.

Balance of power. That's what mattered. Why the hell had he lost it over a blue-eyed girl, too young for him anyhow?

'I'll think about that island.'

Mort smiled gently. 'But not for another ten days. Next Monday the President is giving one of his select White House luncheons for select newsmen. And you're select, Brock. Very, very select. Don't forget that, because the network won't.'

The afternoon sun that greeted Brock Turner hotly on the tarmac of Washington's Friendship Airport drifted pale and green through the curtains of Castleton House on New York's East Side. The seven-storey brick building was in all probability the last vestige of a fading morality. The brash new generation, intent on demolishing all hand-me-downs of structured living, now ignored it.

The narrow rooms with their prim single beds, and primmer warnings were often empty now. The green-carpeted corridors hushed, except for occasional wisps of music, faintly, unobtrusively classical. The card room boasted four solid oak tables for bridge or whist and in one corner a narrow table for cribbage. Each room contained a radio. But no TV. That stood cornered and detached in the room where Lili Roundtree now found herself.

Castleton House was for women only. Lili had arrived at its sheltered portals only because Aunt Josie had a friend who eighteen years ago had found it respectably safe. Lili was determined to give no more pain to the dear, fading chatelaines of St Charles Avenue.

Now she sat in the green-and-gold striped sitting-room, listening to the faint, intoxicating surge of New York's 57th Street traffic. She was waiting according to pre-arranged plans for the arrival of Mr Willard Roundtree, who, Aunt Clem had said grimly, would henceforth guide her destiny.

She was quite willing to sit quietly for these few shadowed moments and assure herself for the umpteenth time that she, Elizabeth Beaulaire Roundtree, was at last in New York City. Her closetlike room upstairs, a quarter of the size of her billowing, organdied bedroom at home, held the freedom of a mountaintop. She was rootless now. She had joined the world's free spirits.

She must stop thinking of St Charles Avenue as home.

It was a shame that this distant relative was making a long trip from some place called Thatcher on a false premise. But there had been no gainsaying the aunts. Lili felt herself smile. Maybe Mr Willard Roundtree had found that out too.

She would be polite, with all the courtesy she had been

taught. But the old New England farmer, if that's what he was, must be made to understand.

Yet in spite of her careful plans, Lili felt tremulous, unsettled. If she sat very still, she was even conscious of an irregular thumping of her heart. She knew the reason, determined as she was to ignore it.

Somewhere in this city Brock Turner was walking and laughing and living and being. Worse, in the corner of this very room, she could see whenever she wished the blank milk-white eye of the television set. She would come down here at six o'clock this evening, or any evening, snap it on, and see him, hear him . . .

'Miss Roundtree . . .?'

She jumped to her feet in surprise.

'Forgive me. I didn't mean to startle you.'

She saw a tall, lean, grey-haired man in a well-tailored grey suit, a discreetly bright paisley silk tie and with an air of thoroughly enjoying himself. He might have stepped out of the Boston Club in New Orleans.

'I'm Willard Roundtree.' He held out a neatly manicured hand and eyed her approvingly. 'We're cousins,' he added with some satisfaction.

'I know. I'm Elizabeth. I mean Lilith. Lili.' *Not cousins*, she thought. *He's at least my uncle or grand-uncle*. 'Won't you sit down?'

'Thank you,' he said solemnly, his steely eyes warm. She was Henrietta's blood all right. The same fine bones, the elegance, the reserve no man would ever quite plumb to the bottom. Not that this child looked like Henrietta. Not with those true-blue eyes and that straight light brown silk hair. Mouth a bit too wide, brow broad, cheekbones prominent. Henrietta, slight as she was, was rounder. Everywhere. Willard sighed to himself. What had happened to young women? From his unfashionable but very masculine six-decade perspective, young Elizabeth Roundtree could certainly use a few more pounds.

But she was breedy, damned if she wasn't. He sensed strength, untried stamina. Take a little doing to keep her in hand. But once reined on course, she'd take any obstacle.

She was also, Willard told himself, the most alone young woman he had ever met.

'Do you like New York, Mr Roundtree?'

He recognized finishing-school politeness. And disinterest. But he was wrong there and knew it. It was not disinterest. It was caution. This girl, for all her soft, lovely voice, proudly held head, and lifted chin, was apprehensive.

'I always like New York. Greatest place in the world to escape to. When you live on a farm. I'm in court at present in Boston. Defending a man who's on trial for the killing of another man.'

So Willard Roundtree was a lawyer too. They hadn't told her that. But they hadn't told her much of anything beyond St Charles Avenue.

'Did he do it?' Her solemn eagerness broke the thin awkwardness. It also made her eyes very bright.

'Mitigating circumstances, my dear. Always mitigating circumstances. That's my job. But the court schedule prevented my catching an early enough plane to take you to lunch. We should go somewhere to talk. Is there anything you like to eat at four-thirty in the afternoon?'

She would have thought there was no better place to talk than the Castleton House sitting-room with its tomblike stillness. Besides, she liked this surprising man. It would be kinder to tell him at once and finally that she had no intention of going to Thatcher.

He was fishing in his coat pockets. 'There's a place I know, East Fifty . . . they serve right through the afternoon. A superior Marseilles bouillabaisse if you like that. And the best chocolate cake I ever ate, outside Thatcher. What those ladies can cook up for the Firemen's Carnival is a caution. Of course they don't serve it with Paris murals.' He found a slip of paper. 'La Belle Époque, that's it. Not my Paris. But then the Nazis had that beautiful lady by the throat when I was there. Do you have to do any of those things girls fuss over before they go out?'

'No.' She hesitated. 'Mr Roundtree, there is something I think I should say.'

'I'm sure there is.' He drew a thick old-fashioned gold

watch from his vest pocket and snapped open the cover. 'But we have three hours . . . three hours and forty minutes. Don't deny me the pleasure of taking out a pretty girl.' He rose buoyantly, his eyes twinkling. 'It's not something I get to do very often. In Thatcher.'

Lili enjoyed herself.

In the dim, nearly empty restaurant she gulped down every mouthful of Willard Roundtree's recommendation, heady with the newness of it all. Through the revolving door her ears caught the muted thunder of New York's unceasing rivers of traffic. Through the rose-red café curtains her eyes were dazzled by crystal shards of light that glanced from the towering structure of glass and granite across the street.

She was alive at last! She had made peace with her conscience. And Willard Roundtree was obviously pleased. She would not spoil that. She would tell him, quickly, firmly, and very kindly, right after coffee. She would thank him for his trouble and go. Out into the pulsing excitement of this tremendous city. Out into freedom. Out – For an instant the pain of Brock Turner returned. But she managed a glowing smile.

'This is fun.'

He had seen the shadow on her face.

'I hope so. It is for me. Tell me, Elizabeth – Lilith – Lili. Out of that battery of names which do you prefer?'

'Lili.'

'So do I.' He would have agreed to Hepzibah-Euphronsia if she had said so. 'Anything else you'd like known about yourself?'

'Not really.'

There was, of course. Questions that had met silence in the big polished house of her girlhood. Uncertainties like cobwebs she could not brush away. Why her father had made her promise so long ago never to give up the name Roundtree even after she married. Why Aunt Clem, with closemouth finality that had lasted until ten days ago, insisted that she was a Beaulaire. Unless she chose to live under the bar sinister. To Lili, without understanding, that was as threatening as a plumber's pipe, suspended over her.

Now sitting opposite this merry, kindly man, it would be easy – She broke the flight of her thoughts. Family knots, ties that looked like silk and held like cables. Wasn't that what she was escaping? For ever.

She shook her head. 'There's really nothing, Uncle Willard.'

'Good.' He returned her smile, concealed a twinge of his own. *Uncle!* But Willard had never blanched at reality. Time was more assertive than cousinship.

The Vienna mocha torte arrived. Then would come coffee.

She tensed a little, but her face remained bright.

'Tell me about the man in that trial. Did he really murder somebody?'

'Oh, yes. Quite effectively. One blow of an axe. He hasn't much chance of a fair trial. I took the case to make sure he does. He's part Seneca Indian. I'll probably lose, but a few things should be said first.'

It was what Aunt Clem had continually warned her about the North. Half civilized, given to violence, no manners, and Abraham Lincoln the worst of it all. Tales of axe murders had occasionally floated out of the bayous, but here was Willard Roundtree, her own relative, defending –

'But if he did it?'

Willard Roundtree's eyes sobered. His defence might as well begin with this young innocent.

'Howie Crowfeather has a parcel of land in northern Massachusetts. All woods. Deer-hunting country. But Howie doesn't believe a man should kill except for defence or need of food or clothing. So he's posted his land against hunters. A man came on it with a gun. He might have been trying to scare Howie. I haven't proved that. But Howie had a doe there, penned in with her fawn. He had found her with a broken leg. The man shot them both. Howie went after him with an axe.'

Lili had gone pale. 'I'd do the same thing.'

'So might I. With Howie's ancestry and creed.'

A strange thing happened to Lili. She had a sudden longing to hold fast to this wisdom and warmth. She had been brought up too long by women. She was dimly conscious of the blood of which she was so unsure, pulsing through her, a primordial echo of open sky, billowing trees, rocks, and high winds. Or was it only the poetry in which she had steeped herself in the stifling confines of the convent?

She was aware that Willard Roundtree's face was weathered, his well-kept hands knotted and strong. His eyes squinted slightly with the look of a man at home with distance. Behind him she saw a measureless horizon, silvered, unknown, and of heart-stabbing beauty. The vision vanished.

They had finished their coffee.

'Uncle Willard, there is something I must tell you.'

His face was inscrutable.

'I know Aunt Clem went to a lot of trouble, writing you, explaining – asking you to meet me. And you've gone to a lot of trouble coming all the way to New York for me. Don't think I don't appreciate it. I do. And I feel very bad. I don't want to be ungrateful. I like you very much . . .'

She could not guess what he was thinking. But his expression brought a thickening to her throat.

'But you see – '

'Lili,' he lifted a warning hand, 'charming as you are, if you go on talking, I shall miss my plane. And no doubt you will be late for an engagement with whatever young man is lucky enough to take you out this evening.' She looked suddenly so near tears, he amended quickly. 'If there isn't one, there will be. I came to New York because I have something to say to you. If it seems unfeeling, you must forgive me. It's from a lifetime conviction.'

She felt rebellion flare. This is what she had wanted to avoid. Talk. Argument. Persuasion.

'Yes, but . . .' she began hotly.

'Will the court hear argument?' he snapped.

She was silent.

'Dear, dear Lili,' the mellow voice warmed. 'I have absolutely no intention of taking you back to Thatcher with me. Today. Or any day. Or even asking you to come. You could do it. Successfully. But it's not the place for you now. You are young. You are as alive as any ancestor of yours and mine could have wished. Stay here in New York if this is what you want. Or find your own place in the world. Get a job. Fall in love. Or out of it. But live! Be young! And live!'

In the silence, his eyes met hers. He looked away. He picked up the waiting check and pushed back his chair.

'I'd like to think you'll pay us a visit some day. I've a valley outside of Thatcher with a litter of the most rascally grey fox cubs that ever tumbled out of lair. You'd like them. But there'll be another litter, next spring. And another.' He permitted himself a wink. 'I'll write a very reassuring letter to Clementine Beaulaire.'

He helped her from her chair with old-fashioned courtliness. At the door of Castleton House he kissed her cheek.

'Live, my dear. True to yourself.'

As he walked into the sun-dust of the city's ending day, he heard in his mind the long-dead, imprisoned wings of Henrietta Roundtree, beating free.

CHAPTER TEN

Lili awakened to the strangeness of a narrow room, a narrow bed, and a narrow window through which no morning sun apparently penetrated. In the greyness that passed for light, she saw it was seven-forty. For a few moments she lay putting the pieces of her new life together.

She was free. She was alone. She could do exactly what she pleased with no one waiting, no one asking questions, no one expecting answers.

That was what freedom meant.

It also meant no fragrance of fresh-made coffee floating upstairs, no cheerful voices from the kitchen, no telephone distantly ringing, no knock on the door to tell her it was for her. And no plan that would involve the weighty decision of what to wear for the day. Or for the evening.

Lili would let the evening take care of itself.

She lay another moment, thinking of this freedom Willard Roundtree had so sweepingly bestowed on her. It seemed even more enormous in this tight little room. She had only to open the door and there it was waiting, a palpable void that she must fill. She, alone.

'Live,' he had said. *Live*. As if she knew how or where to begin. She felt her throat constrict as she saw again the fine, greying face, the shrewd eyes bright with understanding. Had she let go of something rich and warm that might have been hers in the place called Thatcher? For she knew now she could not go there until she had proved herself, made her own way, and kept faith with his trust in her.

'True to yourself.' When she knew what that self was.

Brock Turner. He was still too large in her thoughts. With a queer combination of relief and frustration she had returned to the hotel last evening too late to turn on his newscast. Would she deliberately avoid it tonight, tomorrow, the next night, until she could forget? Or would it be better to turn it on tonight, see him on the TV once and have done with it? 'He's married,' she told herself for the hundredth time. The words had begun to take on the numbness of a worn refrain.

Enough! She jumped from bed, pulled up the window shade, and saw why the room would be eternally grey. The window opened on an alley. The opposite wall rose blank and out of sight. By pushing aside the heavy net curtains and twisting her neck, she could manage to see high above a shaft of pale sky. Faintly blue with promise.

She dressed quickly. She had three objectives. A city map to tell her where she was. A newspaper that might list apartments and jobs. The third was less clear: to forget this was Brock Turner's city. More specifically, to stop wondering which corner she might turn and accidentally meet him.

'Good morning, Miss Roundtree.' The flowery lady at the desk had been impressed by Miss Roundtree's manners and even more by the gentleman who had called on her. One did not see his kind often these days. Not with the hippies taking over the streets. 'I hope you slept well.'

'Yes, thank you.'

'I expect you'll want to do some sightseeing. We have several tours – there, those folders.'

'I'd like a map of the city. Then I'm going to look for a job.'

'Ah, yes, of course. We have a service to help you with that. Miss Stockman, in the little office across the lobby.'

'What I want most, I guess, is to find an apartment.' It was a mistake and Lili knew it. The flowery lady pursed her lips.

'It is, of course, up to you, but we do advise our girls to know the city first before they undertake living on their own. You see, Miss Roundtree, this is not – uh – uh – yes, New Orleans. Things happen in New York.'

I hope so, thought Lili but she only murmured a pleasant thank you and picked up the city map.

On the way across the lobby she looked in on the helpful Miss Stockman, who was on the telephone. She motioned to Lili to wait. On the clean-swept desk Lili saw a plastic-bound listing of girls' schools and a larger leather-bound listing of libraries. Miss Stockman's back was straight, her blouse neat and white, her grey hair secure in a bun. When Miss Stockman looked up, Lili knew she would see Aunt Clem.

She smiled, waved, and walked quickly out into the sunlight of a fine New York spring day. And into a cacophony of morning traffic, a tide of human beings that made her stop and catch her breath. All of life seemed to be flowing past her out there. Exhilarated, she let herself be swept along. A sign said LEXINGTON AVENUE. It was wider than the street she was on. She turned without purpose, passing the glitter of small shop windows, splashed with colour, and discovered that within a few blocks she could buy western leather shirts, Tibetan prayer shawls, Turkish marzipan, French bikinis, fifty-four-inch 'cultured' pearls, potted tulips, hanging spider plants, and, next door, 'books, pictures, and postcards for the mature adult'. She paused, unaware. Instantly a heavily bearded young man stopped beside her, his hand in his jeans pocket.

She flushed, slid into the stream of passers-by, and realized the great city's first gift. Anonymity.

At a traffic light, forced to stop, she watched the tiny absurdity of a street hawker's shimmying topless dolls.

'One for forty-nine, lady. Two for a dollar.'

The light changed.

On the other side of the street she bought a newspaper from a blind vendor and marvelled at his quick change and his quicker, 'Nice day, young lady. Enjoy the city.'

Could even the blind tell that she was a stranger?

Light suddenly dazzled her eyes. The morning sun had at last risen above the buildings and now shone into the streets. She looked up the heights of the soaring buildings, shouldering each other into the sky, dwarfing even as they lured. She wondered who could occupy them all. Head thrown back, she felt their dizzying magnetism. And remembered that she had not eaten breakfast.

At a quick-food counter Lili chose a stool at the far end and opened her newspaper. At some remote time in her past life, her nemesis and only boy-friend, Chuck, at the university, had told her that if she finally decided to break away, she must do three things at once: Buy a newspaper and open to the want ads, find a place of her own to live, and find a job, any job. With that settled, Chuck had advised knowingly, you can wing it.

Wing it. The phrase had stayed with her. After Chuck had left the university, he married, invested in a filling station, and went to settle on Lake Pontchartrain nine miles out of New Orleans for the rest of his life.

Wing it! From her handbag Lili took the sterling silver monogrammed ball-point pen that had been Aunt Josie's graduation gift. Over a mug of coffee, a limp English muffin-and-pat-of-jelly, and something called juice, she began her assault. It would be difficult. Her map told her that New York's numbered streets ran east and west, the avenues north and south. A chequerboard.

Another muffin and three coffees later she was ready. From the long, fine-print column in the newspaper it would seem that this tremendous, bursting city had a place for everyone.

She would start at once . . . West 74th Street, fnshd std. apt. Which way was west?

On the fifty-sixth floor of a skyscraper Mortimer Russell sat at his enormous, kidney-shaped desk, its gleaming surface innocent of any evidence of the commercial world in which he laboured so strenuously. A rainbow of telephones lay concealed at his right, a bank of communication buttons and knobs at his left.

His round outside office, with unopenable windows in a half circle behind him, boasted several deep, lilac leather chairs and a four-section divan. The three-inch-deep grey pile carpet could trip up a secretary's high heels. This was Mort Russell's kingdom, an oasis of executive splendour, and the final evidence of corporate eminence in a world as uncertain as tomorrow's news.

Mortimer had designed it himself. On sleepless nights he would return to it, sitting in semi-darkness, listening to the ghostly strains of a stereo Mozart violin concerto, his fingers curled around a glass of finest cognac, the mighty city winking its thousand eyes around him. He had come raw to this city and conquered it. But the conquest had never quite erased for him the jangling nostalgia of a city editor's desk, the smell of fresh ink on newsprint, and the hearty fellowship. He missed the newsroom's 'You did it, Mort! Great story! You've got the whole lousy gang on the run.'

Days of youth.

A light on the left-hand panel brought Mortimer Russell back to the present. It glowed blue. The news executive picked up the blue telephone.

'Mr Turner from Washington, Mr Russell.'

'Put him through.' He sighed. The two-faced solid-crystal desk clock read four-fifty-eight.

'Yeah, Brock.'

'I had lunch with the President.'

'Is that what you called to tell me?'

'I'm catching the five-thirty plane to my island.'

'You've got a six o'clock broadcast.'

'No story, friend. No story. You can fill with crime

statistics, Soviet short-range missiles, or Disneyland. They've got a new joyride – '

'Brock, don't. Just don't. I got my ulcer under control and I'm going to keep it that way. You've got your month off – '

'No story, Mort. I've given you good advice.'

'You've been drinking?'

'Why should I? I've got my island – '

'I'm sitting here, Brock, till six. Then I'm going to hear every word of your broadcast tonight. Or else, so help me, I'll break you . . .'

'I'm just trying to do the honest thing, little brother. But it's an ungrateful world.'

'You're on for three minutes, twenty – '

'Two.'

'You owe us ten.'

The phone clicked off. The blue light went out. Mort returned the blue phone to its cradle. Turner was right, of course. He should handle Brock differently. He knew that. But each time he resolved to come down from the heights, the cheerful buoyance of Brock Turner's overblown personality needled him into tightening the screws. A show of authority. Envy? Or something less definable? An uneasy realization that Turner reflected back to him his own sense of failure.

Turner, his doppelgänger. His alter ego. The monkey on his back. He would like to find a reason to fire him. But that, too, would be an admission of failure.

A yellow light went on. He picked up the yellow phone. 'Yes, Turner's going on. He'll run four minutes.' It pleased him to stretch Brock's time. He would like to see the guy run out of words. Just once.

He swung around to the vast panorama of the city spread to the murky horizon. He would catch the six o'clock broadcast on the monitor.

He rose and went across the corridor to the newsroom.

There was never a time when Mort Russell did not find its clatter soothing.

The broadcast came on with a fast start.

'Hi, friends. Brock Turner here. The Samuel Pepys of the White House lunchbreak. I'll give it to you straight.' Brock Turner flashed a grin at his audience, dug into his pocket, and came up with a torn-off cuff, a lunch-size napkin, and two minuscule sheets of crumpled pad paper. It was the kind of showmanship his audience loved, and his boss, Mortimer Russell, despised. It would fill time.

'Here we are, straight from the salmon's mouth. And as it happened. Arrived at White House twelve-twenty-three. The President dislikes tardiness, but if you arrive too early his staff aides don't know where to put you. President looking fit. One could have Dubonnet or dry sherry. Big Bill asked for a martini and got it. Then food. Now let's see . . .' Brock shuffled the papers and smoothed one out, glancing at the clock. He was filling nicely.

'Cream of watercress soup. Salmon mousse. Cucumber and dill salad. Silver-dollar-size biscuits. Very tasty. An excellent Chardonnay. Strawberries in pink wine. Or pink wine in strawberries. Macaroons. I think. All exactly what old Andrew Jackson would have enjoyed before a good big plate of chitlins.'

He glanced at the studio clock and smoothed out the ripped-off cuff.

'The President believes that détente with the Russians can be maintained if firmness is applied. Ditto for the National Association of Manufacturers, ditto for the Teamsters Union, the sheikhdom of Kuwait, and the Society for Endangered Reptiles.'

With another glance at the clock he dropped the cuff on the desk and picked up a napkin, unfolding it to read it.

'The First Lady enchanting in yellow. Wish she had stayed around. New rug in the East room, blue as a girl's eyes. Rumour of a mouse in the Oval Office. No doubt a Republican mouse. The President was interrupted only twice. Once by the space agency, which had overrun its weekly allowance by ninety million. The President didn't think that was so bad for a slow week. Second interruption. The Attorney General had lost his tennis shoes.' Brock looked directly into the camera.

'That's it, friends. A little of thee and me. And then no

more of me and thee. Until I report back in a month my considered judgement whether any man can be an island, if he puts his mind to it. See you.'

The switchboard was flashing with calls coming in from happy fans. The producer muttered that they may have lost a few dozen in the South-East but they must have picked up a million in the North and West.

A news girl approached with a telephone message.

Brock smiled, ducked out, and in another three minutes was urging a pleased taxi driver to make time to Friendship Airport.

'I can't make time, any more than you can, Mr Turner, but I can sure give it the old try.' He happily rode the horn.

The Venezuela-bound plane was twenty minutes late for take-off. Twenty minutes was not what Brock Turner wanted on his hands. Or, for that matter, five minutes. He wanted no slack time to wonder whether anyone had turned on a back-room television set in an old pile of a house on St Charles Avenue in New Orleans. Or whether anyone ever would.

She was probably married by this time, with that big hunk of glitter on her left ring finger and a second ring to make it respectable. If that's what was so important.

'Dear Brock . . .' The blue-grey letter was still creased into his wallet. 'Dear Brock, I wish I didn't have to write this letter. I don't want to. I want everything to be exactly the way it was at Les Trois Piques. And on the river. But it never can be. I've thought about it all night. It isn't you and me, just us. You have someone else.' (She had crossed out 'wife.') 'I don't know where she is or what she means to you. Or what you mean to her. But it matters. I know how I would feel . . .'

The hell you do, Brock thought, *the hell you know anything, Elizabeth – Lili*.

'. . . and I just couldn't . . . I mean it's just no good that way, with someone else there . . . I hope you understand.' The squared, schoolgirl writing had continued. 'Because I'm not sure I do. I only know how I feel. And I have to be honest about that. I had a lovely time. I'll never forget it. Lili.'

There had never been any need since to take the blue-grey note from his wallet. Only to wonder where she was. He remembered how she dropped the diamond ring on the table and knew through some inner blindness that she had not married. Not that guy. He could skip the Venezuela plane at this moment and take the next flight to New Orleans. Find her, talk to her, tell her what a once-in-a-lifetime thing had happened to them. Or, maybe, just to him. That was the unknown quantity. He could hurt her ...

He crossed into the waiting-room. And froze.

The man with his back to him was unmistakable. The heronlike hunch to his shoulders, the long wrists dangling from black sleeves, the angular height, the almost completely round head. His face, as Brock knew it would be, was not white, not yellow, not brown, but the colour of a well-used meerschaum pipe bowl. The thin, close-cut grey hair, brushed straight back, lent respectability, except that Brock knew it was a wig. The gold-rimmed glasses were professorial; all but the tinted lenses.

Brother Sunshine. The Reverend Sun Chang. Professor Saul Chane. Importer Samuel Ching. Or the half-dozen other aliases, so similar as to be disarming.

Brock held his breath. And stifled an impulse to collar the man, feeling his own hands around that stringy throat. For what? The invisible seedlings of corruption Brother Sunshine spread and its attendant human anguish? Or Brock's personal vendetta for the warping of his own life, a warping made more explicit by his last glimpse of Lili's face and the quiet hurt that lay in a blue-grey envelope within his wallet?

He owed Brother Sunshine a lot and he would pay it. But not now. Not in helpless rage at evil for which he had no proof. Not in a public brawl that could end in nothing but damaging headlines. Brock swore, not for the first time. He was pursuing a man he could not pursue, a phantom in search of a phantom.

The man turned and walked down the long passageway to the boarding gates.

'Flight Two Twenty-six, San Juan, Caracas, and Bogotá, is loading now. Gate Six.'

Brock's plane. His month of escape. Of release. With his eyes still on the heronlike figure he mechanically dropped a coin on the wooden newsstand bowl, picked up a paper. Then he moved into the corridor in the Reverend Chang's wake.

'Final call for Flight Four Eighty-one for New York at Gate Two.'

The Reverend Chang joined the remnant of the line and looked around. Brock lost himself in a group of people moving past Gate 2. He had thirty seconds to make up his mind.

He could take a leisurely course to the Venezuela plane. To his island. And the sweet healing of nothing, for what it was worth. He had found and lost the girl he wanted more than anything his life had ever held. The burning need to avenge had already taken its toll. It was time to let go. To stop being a celebrity and, in his own sight, a trained clown. To forget.

'Excuse *me*!' The woman gave an angry stare, for Brock had abruptly swung around, sprinting headlong towards Gate 2.

'Ticket, sir?'

'No time. Any seats?'

The airline official smiled. 'No problem, Mr Turner.'

There was no forgetting, no changing course. There was no island in the world that could hold him for an empty month. He knew he was doing the only thing possible for him. He would hunt this man until he caught him. Illogically it would bring him nearer to her.

When the plane was airborne, Brock rose and sauntered through the aisle.

The Reverend Chang was not aboard.

For the young, who are the true believers in the stars, the twisted must inevitably be made straight, the opaque clear, and love, if it does not conquer, will endure in the tenderness of its wound.

Lili held to such faith and on this her first full day in New York, she saw six o'clock as the mystic hour of resolution. It was then that she would see Brock on the silent, staring TV screen in the corner of the Castleton House living-room. She would hear his voice. The nobility of that blue-grey note she had written in the security of her bedroom would not waver. Brock was married. But surely they could meet, they would meet once more, and their very sacrifice would bind them for ever to each other. Six o'clock.

The day was mellow with spring. Lili planned it carefully, cutting four clippings from the newspaper. Two for jobs: 'Good starting salary, no experience needed!' And two for apartments: 'Studio for young careerists.' The very word held the image of a new life. When she and Brock made their final tragic renouncement, she would go, head high, into the loneliness of her career.

Whatever it was to be.

She carefully listed the four addresses. She had already discovered that New York City was laid out in blocks. The streets were logically numbered from downtown to uptown. The avenues were also, if less logically, numbered. The deviations did not trouble her.

The time for soft hours of fantasy was over. Her young wits, long sharpened on skirting the obstacles of discipline, stood by her. She was not easily intimidated, and total freedom gave the day a dizzying excitement.

She would start by walking.

Textiles Futura proved to be a dim office with one dirty window on the third floor of a truck-filled side street. The empty receptionist desk held promise.

A fat man in striped shirt-sleeves beckoned her into the single inner room.

'Type?'

'No.'

'Steno?'

'No.'

He looked her up and down. 'What can you do?'

'I speak French.' She would omit the soufflés and the dinner setting for six courses.

'Not to our customers you don't, girlie. Know filing?'

'I thought this position was for a receptionist.'

'Our receptionist does everything. Everything.' He slid a

faint emphasis into the repetition. And looked her over again. 'Ever think of modelling? We don't use models here but I got contacts in the dress business.'

She moved imperceptibly back. She had *not* thought of modelling or of any other job that would take her on the road to herself. But her instincts had deep roots. Henrietta's granddaughter was born to know the look in men's eyes.

She smiled sweetly. 'Thank you very much. But I'm not really interested. I appreciate your taking the time to see me. I'm sorry I do not qualify. I hope you do find someone who is just right. Good morning.' The flood of courtesy left him without any answer. The door closed.

Lili quashed her anger and took out the next clipping: 'Sales, no experience necessary.'

The woman wore a bright red wig and was tightly encased in black satin.

'Ever sell before, dearie?'

'The advertisement says no experience necessary.' Lili had no way of knowing the soft, clipped refinement of her speech had an almost foreign flavour. The woman distrusted foreigners.

'There's no experience *and* no experience. How long you been in New York?'

'Not very long. Two days.'

'Where you staying?'

'I'm looking for an apartment as soon as I get my job.'

The woman bridled. *Her* job, as if she expected one cut out and waiting as soon as she walked in. She knew the type. All manners and couldn't sell a ham sandwich to a starving man.

Lili broke the silence.

'May I ask what you sell here?'

'Look around. Blouses, bags, novelties, and lingerie. Men come mostly to buy the lingerie. We feature specials.' She lifted from a rack behind her a drift of coarse black net explicit in cutouts and gilt. 'Think you could sell this?'

'I don't think anyone could.'

The woman burst into a laugh. 'At least you're honest,

dearie. Not that that will get you far in this town. Let me give you some advice. I came to New York thirty-five years ago from Boise, Idaho. This is as far as I got. If you come from a good place and know a good guy, go back. Nothing gets any better here.'

'I am interested in a job.'

The woman shook her head. 'I'm doing you a favour, dearie.'

On the street Lili decided to change her luck. She would look at the two apartments for 'careerists'. She had lost all orientation to Castleton House, but the street numbers still worked.

The first apartment was a third-floor walk-up with no bathtub, a hole in the living-room floor, and the stove in a closet.

The second, a four-flight walk-up, with a broken handrail and tacked-down threadbare carpets, across which she saw something dark scurrying.

She returned to the afternoon sunlight. It was dusty now with city air, and the tall buildings were lost in a haze. She was tired and she had had no lunch. But still the smells, the sounds, the very raucousness of the city, buoyed her. She would have to revise her ideas. The limited income that was hers did nicely at home in New Orleans. But here? The job must come first. And she felt desperately unqualified.

Suddenly she felt the loneliness of the great city pressing on her, alive, hostile. The impersonal faces. The jostling of elbows, the roar of the traffic, in which she was no one, no one at all. Lilith Roundtree. A ridiculous name when you took it apart. Nothing when you put it together.

She looked into the white interior of a cafeteria that might still serve lunch. At the rear she saw the moon face of a clock. Five-ten. At six Brock – Brock! She clung to the name like flotsam in this sea of indifference. She forgot her hunger, her resolution.

She resorted north and south, east and west, on the street signs. She walked until she came to a wide avenue with a busline. She would take it north to 60th Street. She joined the day's-end stifling crowd and pushed aboard and clung blindly to a strap. It seemed an eternity until the jolting vehicle stopped long enough to give her a view of street numbers. Sixty-six? Sixty-eight? She pushed her way out of the bus on to the sidewalk. She was in a cluttered commercial district, as far from the quiet street of Castleton House as turmoil from grace.

No one had told Lili that New York's most tempestuous avenue, Broadway, ran diagonally across the city from south-east to north-west. She had half the city yet to cross and only seven minutes before Brock's broadcast.

She hated public tears but now they stung her eyes. It was so hopeless, so futile. Pursuit of a man's face, a man she could never have. She glanced at her watch. Five minutes before six.

Then diagonally across the street, above a wall of traffic, she saw it. ABE'S RADIO AND TV SALES AND SERVICE. She could see the blank screen in the window. An oasis. How do you cross a street like this?

She darted between two taxis and a bus, followed by shouts, the squeal of brakes, a savagery of horns, and reached safety. The light changed. She ran crossways and into the store. In a clutter of shapes and sizes, cabinets and parts, she saw a shelf of six identical black-and-white TV screens, all silently busy with moving, wordless figures.

The boy sweeping the floor eyed her curiously. Her face, both strained and flushed, looked almost beautiful.

'Could I turn on the sound on one of those?'

'Sure. What d'ya want?'

She hesitated. 'The news. Brock Turner.' She had given a little of herself away.

'Why not? That's his channel.' The boy's head jerked towards the shelf. 'He's on at six.'

'I know. How do I . . .?'

'I'll do it.' The boy not unwillingly dropped his broom and flipped a switch on the first of the screens. A voice broke from the set. Lili leaned against the wall. Twenty seconds later six faces of Brock Turner flashed into focus along the shelf.

It was more than she wanted. Almost more than she could bear. It was a clarion to the world of her most secret feeling. When she reached her own room, she would cry. But right now, for this living, choking instant, in this shabby, dirty, public corner of nowhere, she was with him.

'Hi, friends. Brock Turner here . . .' The sharply knowing eyes searched hers, the grin was for her alone.

Then something odd happened. He began to talk. His eyes no longer smiled. He was pulling things from his pockets, paper, a rumpled bit of cloth. She heard the flippancy, the hard edge of mocking indifference, a voice tired of the very words it used. Was this the man she had met for one silver-spun evening, briefly? Yet for all time?

'That's it, friends.'

She would have turned away but his next words were riveting.

'A little of thee and me.'

Her poem! The old wisdom she had quoted to him that he had not known. Where had he found it?

'And then no more of me and thee . . .' He was talking directly to her. What she heard was a question, grave, delicate, searching.

Lili did not remember leaving Abe's Radio and TV Sales and Service. She did not remember thanking the boy with the broom, or somehow finding a cab on the traffic flood outside the door.

Once back in the cell-like room of her new life, she did not cry. She lay sleepless for a while and then she dreamed. Over and over she glimpsed Brock Turner through curtains of shifting, changing mists, sometimes finding him, sometimes losing him, never quite reaching him.

But always, before the mists closed again, he looked back, directly at her.

She awoke as thin light filtered into her room. She felt weighted with unrest and an inexplicable sense of desolation.

Then she remembered. From the barrier of that TV screen he had told her and the vast faceless audience of which she was but a shred that he was going away. To an island. To be an island. A body of land surrounded entirely by water. Which she could not cross.

CHAPTER ELEVEN

The empty month that Lili silently counted off until Brock's return proved emptier and slower in passing than anything she had ever known. New York's brief spring was engulfed in waves of early summer heat. The job market was engulfed in waves of brisk young students who could talk glibly of what they had done or wanted to do.

How did they all know so much? Lili asked herself as another office door closed behind her. The idea that they didn't know eluded her. She still took the world at face value. It was a part of good manners not to suspect the people one met. If she had, would she ever have lost herself so completely to a man she had seen once? But it wasn't once. It was her whole life compressed into one day.

She had also been taught that it was part of good manners never to discuss the price of things. She was in this fast, demanding city totally unable to put a price on herself.

An apartment of her own was now out of the question. An apartment to share? Where? With whom? She had made one friend, seemingly the only permanent resident of Castleton House beside herself. A small girl with bright frizzy hair, yellow rainboots, a wide smile. And a purpose.

'I'm into Egyptology.' Ginger's chatter was as bright as her hair. 'I go up to the Metropolitan Museum of Art every day and do the pharaohs. I'm in the Second Dynasty now — or is it the Fourth? With the mummy vats. My boy-friend Luther is in entomology up at Columbia University. You know — bugs. Our relationship got meaningful over scarabs. Dad let me come to New York for a year on the condition that I would live in this dump.' She grimaced. 'He says girls who come to New York and take apartments by themselves are after only one thing. He always calls it "one thing".' She giggled. 'What else? But that's all right. Luther's got a room up on Morningside Heights. So we make out.'

One day Miss Stockman beckoned her into the stark little office off the lobby.

'Miss Roundtree, are you enjoying New York?'

'Oh, very much, thank you.'

'Have you found anything interesting?'

'Indeed I have. Almost everything.' Lili's fervour was at least honest. Around almost every corner she imagined meeting Brock.

'I mean a position. I believe that's what you hoped to find.'

'Oh. No, not yet.' Lili wondered if Castleton House discouraged its guests who were not doing something. 'I'm trying, but nobody seems to think I can do anything useful.'

'Sometimes,' sighed Miss Stockman, 'we must tailor ourselves to what the world needs. I always thought the finest position in the world' – Miss Stockman never said 'job' – 'would be secretary to a distinguished and important man. Imagine talking every day to interesting and famous people, working beside a man who – ' Miss Stockman's cheeks grew quite pink. 'But my father, the Reverend Howell Stockman – no doubt you have heard of him – believed that the noblest endeavour was to serve people. So after working with underprivileged girls, I came here, through my college. It's had its rewards.' Miss Stockman did not specify them. 'Elizabeth . . . may I call you Elizabeth?'

'Of course.' An imp of protest, of rebellion, against all the narrow paths of all the Miss Stockmans of this world stirred in Lili. 'But it isn't my real name.'

'Really? I thought your aunt's application . . .'

'It's my given name. But not my own name.'

'I see.' Miss Stockman did not. 'What is your own name, if I may ask?'

'Lilith.'

'Lilith?'

'Elizabeth is my saint's name but Lilith I took for myself. I know she was supposed to come to a bad end. But maybe it wasn't her fault. Maybe she didn't fit in – where she was in the first place.'

But the discipline that drained Miss Stockman's pink cheeks had also drained her of humour. 'One always finds where one belongs if one tries, Eliz – Lilith. I'm sure it's a very pretty name. We'll change our records.'

Uncomfortably Lili saw that her flippancy had been a kind of rudeness, and rudeness, Aunt Clem said, was a way of hurting people. She took the secretarial-school folder Miss Stockman held out and offered her hand.

'Thank you, Miss Stockman. I'll drop by and tell you how I'm getting on.'

'Yes, do. That would be nice.' The flush had gone, leaving Miss Stockman's face settled to duty. Once she must have felt many things deeply, Lili thought. How did it all change? For an instant Lili saw herself, greying and alone, walking through a long corridor of time to a neat, narrow desk.

'I always have a cup of tea at four,' Miss Stockman added. 'I'd be happy to have you join me some day . . .' She hesitated. '. . . Lilith.'

Lili went to her room. Out of the improbable had come the unexpected. It was the first time anyone had ever solemnly addressed her as Lilith. She repeated it to herself. Lilith Roundtree. A portent? She saw fleeting, wordless images in the depths of her mind. Lilith Roundtree might do what Elizabeth Roundtree could not.

She looked at the marked calendar on her desk. Five more days.

Brock Turner did not return at the end of his month. In the Castleton House social room Lili snapped the TV on to a thin-faced stranger, waited through his briskly cheerful account of the usual glum news for a mention of Brock. None came.

That night she swung widely between her two inner selves. As Lilith she could call the network, ask for him, or ask his secretary. She would be businesslike, impersonal, but she would find him. She would go to him. As Elizabeth, no. Why would he even remember her? Had she not finally, irrevocably broken with him? Even now he might be with his wife. Or with another girl who would suit his temporary fancy. That was it, of course. He was away. With someone else.

The thin mirage of Brock, the dancing firefly of hope, had gone. The great city pressed its pulsing loneliness on her. Its heat, its strangeness, enveloped her. Time, empty as a vast uncharted river, spread around her.

Late afternoon and dinner-time were the worst. One day she went up to the Metropolitan Museum of Art to see Ginger at work, her frizzy young head bent over endless black-and-white sketches of monumental Egyptian kings, turned faceless under Ginger's earnest driving pencil.

Once Ginger invited her out. A double date with Luther's cousin, Calvin, Ginnie bubbled, on leave from the Peace Corps. Calvin turned out to be a bearded, lanky man who had adopted an orphaned baby aardvark and was anxious to get back to it. He presented Lili with a jar of dried grasshoppers, the perfect accompaniment, he assured her, to cactus-heart wine. If she would spend his leave with him, they would change the world together.

The purpose of the double date became clear when she found herself sitting at nearly midnight on a park bench, leaving to Ginger and Luther the discretion of the Morningside room. When a drizzle began, Calvin told her that, circumstances being what they were, he would have to sleep on the bench. Unless . . .

She explained as gently as she could about Castleton House and as gently said good-night. She promised she would think about changing the world. On the bus downtown she remembered the abandoned jar of dried grasshoppers. Calvin had meant well, and she had liked him for his solemn smile and his dedication. She had even laughed with him once or twice. As she entered the vicelike loneliness of her own room, she wondered if it were her destiny to be at odds with what was new and strange. Wasn't that what she had come here to find?

One less-than-golden opportunity came. Part-time demonstrator of Tru-Glo cosmetics in a drugstore.

The salesman's eyes were on the young creaminess of her skin. 'Haven't you ever heard of *selling*?'

'Of course I can do it,' said Lili. 'But I don't use all that stuff myself.'

Hour after hour Lili stood before a throng of questing, tired-eyed women with bundles, and rubbed, patted, and assaulted her own face with the mysteries of the green-gold jars. Three nights later her face was bright with Tru-Glo blotches.

'You're taking their money for nothing,' she stormed.

'If you think ten bucks for a jar of hope is nothing, girlie, you don't know women. You didn't tell us you blotched!'

One night in July Lili drew from the back of her desk drawer Miss Stockman's folder for stenographic schools. It was not the shining future she saw when she kissed her aunts goodbye or when Willard Roundtree understood her nameless needs. It would give shape to her days. It would sift the image of Brock Turner through and out of her thoughts.

She would meet him some day when she was chic, successful, indifferent. She would glimpse him across a room of chic, successful people. She would nod, distantly, only half remembering. Or she would meet him hurrying through an airport. She would pause graciously, distantly, but of course she was already late for her London plane. Or would it be Rome or Tokyo?

During the morning hours in the stifling classroom she attacked the hooks and angles of shorthand as if they were malicious barriers to her future.

In the afternoons she sought the solace of Central Park, that incredible two-and-a-half-mile-long spread of green at the city's heart, of trees and grass, lakes, woody knolls, and outcroppings of the primeval rock on to which the city was rooted. She walked its paths endlessly, innocently, marvelling that the massed buildings crowded to the edge and no further, that a city so overwhelming could keep itself at bay.

One overcast August afternoon she learned that it did not. She found herself on a path far to the north. Dead leaves mingled with the dust at her feet. There were no other strollers. Across an area of worn grass beyond a large boulder, a cluster of people stood staring up into the thinning branches of a tree.

They were, as Lili saw, an odd assortment, young, old, male and female, sensible, commonplace, and not without kindness.

'What is it?' she asked a small bald man at the edge of the group. He took off his silver-rimmed glasses, wiped them, and put them back in place before answering.

'*Charadruis pluvialis*,' he answered shortly. 'Very rare in this part of the world.'

Lili stared upwards.

A girl in a long peasant skirt, her feet grimy in sandals, turned to the blue-jeaned young man whose hand she was holding. 'It's the grey, isn't it?'

A tall, angular woman in a long raincoat and fuchsia turban, her throat wrapped in red and purple chiffon, turned sharply. 'No, no. It is a golden. You can't mistake it. It's been blown off course, poor dear. It will be gone by tomorrow. What a thrilling sight!'

Lili saw what seemed to be a plain brown-feathered bird, ten or so inches long, perched high on a limb, half hidden in yellowing leaves. It looked very ordinary to her. The little bald man's eyes danced.

'She's right. She always is. It's a golden plover. Migrates eight thousand miles or more. Alaska to Patagonia in the fall, returns by way of the Pacific in the spring. What a sight! I never hoped to add it to my record. The golden plover! A man could die happy after seeing that.'

Lili stepped to one side for a better view and caught annoyed glances as the leaves crackled underfoot. The bird did not stir. She moved more lightly beyond the group. It was then she saw the boy.

He was small. Shirtless, with ragged shorts and mismatched sneakers. His skin was coffee-coloured and his eyes dark and intense. He reminded her of Luis, who was already perhaps a leader of his people wherever he was.

Then she saw the slingshot. It was home-made from a branch. It fitted the boy's hand, and the heavy rubber band was wide enough for the stone in its grip.

The boy's eyes were on the tired bird. He lifted his

weapon, held it rigid, took aim. Lili sprang at him. Wildly she knocked the slingshot from his hand. She picked it from the ground and shook it in his face.

'Why would you hurt him? What good would it do you to kill the bird? Don't you know that killing – ' She caught her breath and knew that there were tears in her eyes. Her stifled emotions had at last caught up with her. She glanced back and saw the shadow of the bird still in the tree.

The boy was looking at her silently, his eyes shifting to the slingshot in her hand. Had he even understood? Or was he used to abrupt deprivation from an unjust world?

'Look,' she started to say, 'this isn't a toy. You could kill – '

'You steal that slingshot from my brother?'

She had not seen the youth approach. He was taller than average, a scar across his pallid face, his torn T-shirt revealing a scrawny chest but a muscled shoulder.

'It's no toy for a boy,' she said stoutly.

'You take it from him?'

Then she saw that a pace behind him the youth was flanked by two young men, not very different from himself. One carried something that glittered and slithered from his hand. It was a bicycle chain. The three moved slowly.

Instinctively she backed. She was now separated by the tree from the group bird-watching. The nearby boulder threw a shadow across her.

The leader of the three smiled and showed a broken tooth. The smile was more chilling than the chain.

'I'll pay him for it.' She opened her purse. It was a mistake. The small boy had disappeared. The trio was quietly advancing. She had once heard that if you stare a wild animal directly in the eyes it will turn away. But these were not animal eyes. They were furtive, scheming, male eyes. The youth with the chain was looking at her body. She backed again. She was beside the boulder now. Another step she would be behind it.

The third youth suddenly laughed.

It sent an electric charge of panic through her. Could she turn and run? Could she step back again? She saw no one near. She felt her heel catch in the dirt. She reached out and felt the boulder.

'Stay where you are.'

The voice did not come from the three confronting her but from somewhere above her. 'Don't panic.'

He slid down the boulder, a young man in dusty khaki shirt and pants, burdened with a load of cameras and equipment, brandishing a tripod like a sword. A whistle hung around his neck.

'That's all, you jerks. Move it.'

The three wavered in silent communication. Three to one. For the girl . . . blood lust boiled easily in the mindless summer.

'Get out!' The young man in khaki waited only an instant, then lifted the whistle. Its note was long and quavering and it split the quiet. Lili's tormentors fled. She leaned limply against the boulder.

Her rescuer set down the tripod.

'My name is George Rutherford Clarence. I am a photographer, among a good many other things. And you can thank your luck, or whatever you happen to believe in, that I was shooting from the elevation of this rock. You have ruined my last, best shot of a golden plover. You are obviously not bright enough to know that no girl who looks like you has any business walking alone in this section of the park.' He snapped the tripod shut, adjusted the bulk of cameras and boxes hanging from him. 'If you will tell me where you live, I will convey you directly to your door and advise anyone who happens to have you in charge that you are obviously not to be trusted out of doors by yourself.' He shifted the third camera, the one dangling from his shoulder, towards his back. That left one hanging from his neck and another at his waist. 'You might have been murdered. Or worse. Depending on your point of view. And you would have inconvenienced a great many busy people, including myself, in aiding the course of what passes for justice in our uncomprehending and unthinking society. Temptation is the other side of crime. And grows in direct proportion to cerebral deficiency,' he ended irritably.

It was no doubt all her fault, but Lili had no real idea what he was talking about. Yet the flow of scolding words slid over her like a comforting blanket. Her heartbeat steadied and with it her breath. She felt her dependable strength return and managed a half-smile.

'I'm sorry.'

'Would you like a glass of water? I always carry mountain springwater. Purifies the vision.'

Was he making fun of her? Behind his horn-rimmed glasses, with his tufted sideburns and his narrow nose, he had the look of a painéd owl. He removed his glasses abruptly.

'It's not polite to stare. Anyhow, they're windowpanes. That's all. Windowpanes. Keep the dust out of my eyes.'

Without them he was pure chipmunk. Amiable and hurried. He held out another of the artifacts suspended from his shoulder, a khaki-covered canteen bottle.

'George!' It was the lady in the fuchsia turban, chiffon scarves flying. 'I heard the whistle. What did you see?'

'Just the usual. A whitethroat, two pine siskins, two redpolls. But of course I was watching the plover.'

'What on earth did you blow for?'

'Maiden in distress.' He nodded towards Lili. 'Muggers.'

'I see.' The tall woman fixed a commanding stare. 'It won't do, girl. It won't do at all. You've not even armed. You can't go bird-watching in isolated sections of the park without a weapon.' She brandished a shooting stick she was carrying like a spear. 'I never sit on the beastly thing but it is rather lethal-looking, don't you think? I had the end that goes into the ground sharpened. What is your name?'

Lili was beginning to feel like one of those blobs the sister made her inspect on a glass slide beneath a microscope. She was tired of standing too. She was even more tired of being scolded.

'Lilith Roundtree. If you'll excuse me . . .'

'Lilith?' The fuchsia turban looked at her with interest. 'Lilith? A most unusual name. Your own?' The face was aristocratic, the large dark eyes heavily lidded and sharp.

Lili felt the curious weight of a powerful presence. It was easier not to explain.

'Yes, of course.'

'I'm Mrs Rutherford.' She waved George's attempt to introduce aside. 'George claims the same name but I am related to no one. Only to the heavens.' She glanced upwards as if acknowledging a friend. 'It must have been quite a shock to you, poor dear. But a golden plover is worth anything, is it not? I would invite you back with me for tea but most unfortunately I have an appointment at five. Private. George understands that and I must prepare myself. George, take Miss Roundtree – it is miss, isn't it? – somewhere for some refreshment and then see that she gets safely home. Where is home, if I may ask, Miss Roundtree?'

'Castleton House.' This city had chipped her identity into little pieces. The shock of its sudden violence had not yet worn off. 'I come from New Orleans.'

'Yes. Yes, of course. George, do bring – uh – Miss Roundtree to call some day.' The fuchsia turban turned away, then swung back.

'Lilith? Most unusual.'

Over a square-topped table in an ice-cream shop, Lili found it easier to talk to George Rutherford Clarence. Once he had settled his burdens on the padded bench beside her, his thin shoulders straightened and his smile warmed.

Lili ordered black coffee and a banana split and smiled back.

'You have to get used to Amelia, Lilith.'

'I can see that.' Normalcy was beginning to return. And with it what Lili considered her character weakness. She could never long be anybody but herself, not with someone she trusted. She found herself trusting this young man. 'Are you related? I mean, both Rutherfords?'

'She says blood relationship shackles you, keeps you earthbound. She'd never call on me as a relative. But as a – a – what do you call it – a sort of liveried footman, you know, I wear the house colours. I'm useful. Especially bird-watching. We both do it. She liked you.'

'I don't know why. I didn't tell her the truth.'

'She knew that.'

'I mean, my real name is Elizabeth. I'm called Lili.'

'She knew that too. I mean, she could tell.'

Conversation had been odd ever since Lili first heard his voice above her on the boulder.

'How could anyone tell all that?'

'Mrs Rutherford is a medium. She's also a prophetess.'

Lili had a momentary, disappointing vision of old Bessie with her fly-specked cards on used-up tea leaves in her dirty shack on Basin Street. For ten cents she would promise you a handsome stranger who would sweep you away in his yacht to a desert kingdom or a palace in Spain.

'Mrs Rutherford does not tell fortunes,' said George severely. But behind the windowpane spectacles, his eyes were bright. 'She would not thank you for saying so. Nor does she summon spirits. She says they have enough to do in their own world without answering everybody's questions in this one. She reads the future and she sees into space. You'll see when we go up to visit her. Would you like another banana split?'

'No, thank you.' The dust-shot twilight of August filled the street outside.

'Well, I would. I have a passion for desserts. And most people don't like to sit with me while I eat them. I suppose you wouldn't either.'

'Oh, yes, indeed. In fact I'll change my mind. I'll have another with you, if . . .'

For an instant George stared at her in disbelief. Then he gave a happy little smile. 'Lili, I think you're the most wonderful woman I ever met. What's the "if"?'

'If you'll tell me why you were so angry with me after those – those rough boys left. I was terrified.'

'So was I.'

'You didn't sound it!'

'That's part of my trouble. I'm actually very shy. My father – he was an elocution teacher, a success-maker. You know, up and onward with the George Clarence method. It never worked with me. He used to say, "Georgie, if you ever have anything important to say, which is unlikely, get mad or you'll never get through it." So I got mad.'

'I'm very grateful, George. You saved my life. And that's one of the biggest things that ever happened to me.'

On a gilt clock behind the cake and cookie counter, Lili saw it was twenty minutes to six.

Six. Maybe this was the night Brock would return. If she flew downtown . . . if she found a TV store . . . if . . .

George left his tip, paid his bill, and with all his encumbrances escorted Lili to the front of the restaurant.

'You sit here on this window bench. I'll hail a cab and signal you. Then you won't have to stand on the kerb waiting.' He looked at her almost humbly. 'I guess you're pretty tired.'

CHAPTER TWELVE

Somewhat to Lili's surprise George Rutherford Clarence did not call her. At home in New Orleans a young man would have called at least once after meeting her, otherwise Aunt Clem asked questions. 'We can't all be beautiful, Elizabeth, so we must do our best to be charming.' Lili would dutifully accept a second date and then dispose of the young man at a time of her choosing.

But then no one in New Orleans had ever saved her life. George evidently considered his social duty done. If she again walked up into Central Park, she would undoubtedly find him with his horn-rimmed windowpane spectacles and his outlandish burdens of equipment.

She hoped the tired brown bird was safe. She remembered someone saying, 'It seems to be all right. It will rest the night then wing on.'

Wing on. So would she. Wing on.

She did not return to the park. Instead her walks took her along the avenues, into the heart of the city's restless excitement. She was fascinated by Third Avenue, the bewildering clutter of its antique shops. She would stand outside their windows wondering who on earth would buy the gilt horses' heads, the ancient leather bellows, the chipped blue-and-white washbasins, clouded mirrors, and inevitable nudes supporting candelabra. She tried to imagine the rooms they would decorate.

She lingered outside the self-conscious boutiques, smiling at the flower-decked hats, the flounced skirts, the puffed and lacy dresses that Aunt Clem would have swept from her closet thirty years ago. 'The poor need them, Elizabeth, more than I.' From the price tags Lili doubted that the deserving would ever see these. She tried to imagine who would.

It seemed that on Third Avenue when people were not indulging in extravagances they were going into bars. Every block had one, sometimes two. Maybe the shoppers went in *before* they bought, Lili thought. That would explain a lot.

She would walk downtown along the east side of the avenue and uptown on the west side. She would pass and repass a curtained café, gaudily labelled in green and gold; SAM'S. Underneath in discreet black letters was: SINGLES. She had heard of New York's singles' bars. There had even been one in New Orleans.

In the early evening, when the curtains were still drawn apart, she would glance in. The place was quite bare, with small round tables and what looked like corrugated walls. As the twilight melted, Sam's would begin to fill up. Girls sat alone or together. At the bar long-haired young men stood talking, sometimes with a back to a girl, sometimes an arm already linked in hers. They all laughed a great deal. Lili wondered if she would ever walk in.

Then early one evening while the light still clung achingly to the sky, her telephone rang. It was George, his voice stiffly uncertain.

'You remember me?'

'Of course I remember you, George.' She had an impulse to reach through the telephone mouthpiece and pat his hand.

'My aunt – I mean, Mrs Rutherford – wants me to bring

you to see her Sunday afternoon next. Four-thirty. It means tea with her. Do you want to go?'

'I'd love to! How nice!'

'You don't have to if you don't want to.'

She had been brought up to keep too much eagerness out of her voice but those dos and don'ts belonged to a vanished world.

'But I do want to!'

'If you don't like it, we can leave.' His reluctance puzzled her. Perhaps it was George who didn't want to go. Perhaps that strong-willed woman . . .

'Why wouldn't I like it, George?'

There was a tiny silence. 'Lili, would you care – I mean would you grant me the privilege – I mean if you're not doing anything – Do you like Japanese food?'

Never let a young man know you have nothing else to do.

'I'm not doing a thing and I adore Japanese food.' She tried to remember ever having eaten any in New Orleans.

'I'll pick you up in twenty minutes.' The stiffness had gone. He sounded boyish.

She hung up before she realized that George Rutherford Clarence had not answered her question.

In an exotic Japanese restaurant an hour later she found herself sitting with George on an enormous square cushion on the floor, a pair of wooden chopsticks sliding and flipping between her fingers and what looked like raw fish slipping obstinately back into its saucer. Her knees had begun to ache.

'Having a little trouble, Lili?'

'George, I – well, I wanted to come here. I'm tired of being out of step with everything in this city. If you'll just tell me how to hold these things . . .' To her surprise his fingers were both strong and delicate. He showed her the balance, the easy pinch, of chopsticks, touching her hand so lightly that she wanted to clasp his in reassurance. Of what? Friendship? Gratitude for his kindness?

Suddenly they were laughing. He sent for a fork.

'Better than slow starvation, Lili. Next time just tell me. I'll try to do better.'

So there was to be a next time.

Three days later he took her to the Museum of Modern Art where she looked at huge chunks of sculpture and a roomful of shapes cut out in bright painted metal that fluttered and dangled from stands and walls and ceilings.

'That's what I do,' said George.

'What?' said Lili.

'I make mobiles. Sort of like those. Watch them. You don't look at the shapes, the separate pieces that hang on the wires. You look at the sculpture they make in space. It's what the eye does to the image you create. Like the sea, they're always in motion. Or like the wind. People say you can't see the wind. But you can. You can see the shapes it makes when milkweed seeds blow or a tree bends. Of course I don't think George Rutherford Clarence is ever going to be an Alexander Calder. But I have my goals and I do understand. I'd like you to see my mobiles, Lili. If you ever wanted to.'

His intensity surprised her. It also excluded her. It was the missing ingredient in her own life. She had known it briefly. It lay numbed now and buried within her.

In the semi-darkness of the open garden behind the museum, among the unrealities of soaring shapes, she found it easier to talk.

'But why do you take stenography, Lili, if you don't like it?'

'To get a job.'

'Do you need a job?'

Need. What had need ever to do with longing? She would have a bed, she would eat in any case. But a job had become more than that. It was an area in space she alone would occupy, an extension of herself, something to become. Like those mobiles. She needed outside currents to shape the space around her. But she could put nothing of this into words.

'Anyhow, I started the course and I'd be nothing at all if I didn't finish!'

She told him about her efforts to find work. She talked as gaily and lightly as she could, with the quick charm she had been taught. His face grew sharp.

'Whatever gave you the silly idea of answering ads that

said no experience needed? That's admitting that you don't know what you want to do, that there's nothing you can do, and you haven't got the wit to figure what you might do.' He spooned into a sherbet angrily. 'You don't find success falling out of trees. You've got to find it inside yourself. You're not a stupid child, you're a damned attractive girl who has a lot to offer, and if you took the time to make a list . . .'

Lili leaned back, warmed to a smile by his anger.

'Yes, George,' she said meekly.

George put down his spoon. 'There I go again, don't I? I'm not really mad, it's just the way it is with me. I guess a girl like you should do anything she wants. And it's none of my business.'

'I'm grateful, George. I really am.'

They walked across town to Castleton House in the softness of the night. Summer lingered. The city glittered high around them. Other people were walking, quietly, closely. The pinnacle of a skyscraper balanced a young moon. Even the traffic seemed sparse and subdued.

Suddenly the magic, the city's stark, soaring power, caught at Lili's throat. Brock was everywhere, a part of it, a part of her, his strength encompassing her like the brilliance itself. She was silent with the memory of him, his glance, his touch, the low passion of his voice, the sleepless hours when her mind, her body, would ache in the singleness of her bed.

A sense of disloyalty stung her. Of fair play. Brock was gone from her life, she told herself savagely. This kindly man beside her, trusting, eager to please, asking nothing, this man is a friend. A friend she was lucky to find.

On the brightly lit sidewalk outside Castleton House, George looked at her anxiously.

'You're quiet, Lili. Have I kept you out too long?'

'No. I had a lovely time. It was all so new. You made it so interesting.' It was what a girl said. Yet she meant it.

'Are you still willing to go to Mrs Rutherford's on Sunday?'

'Yes, of course. I said I would.' She heard the tightness in her tone. But why was he so patiently repetitive?

'I'll pick you up at two. She lives up on Riverside Drive. I live on the West Side too. Only a short bus ride. So it will give us time to see my mobiles. That is . . . if you want to.'

He was so careful of her, so deliberate. Why again did she want to cry at kindness?

Four o'clock. The door opened abruptly.

Mrs Amelia Rutherford, in the quiet contemplation in which she liked to sit, stared at her caller. He was a tall, commanding man and he had obviously pushed past the maid, who was gesturing from the hall.

'Thank you, Mattie. It's . . . all right.' If there was fear in her voice she veiled it with anger. 'I was not expecting you, Colonel Chadwick.'

'Oh, come off it, Amelia. You should always expect me. You know that. Lovely day.' He nodded towards the great shining river below her windows and the bold thrust of cliffs on the opposite shore. 'Finest view of the Hudson in all New York. No wonder you stay in this crumbling area. But you keep your style.'

His eyes travelled the long room appreciatively, the beige and blues of the deep-pile Oriental rug, the rich sapphires and crimsons of the velvet chairs, the crackleware and oxblood vases, the ivory and jade carvings that lay casually on small tables. Treasures the colonel understood.

At one end, cutting ten feet off the room, stood a ceiling-high screen framed in ebony and made of silk, embroidered in stitches so fine that the figures of phoenix and peacock, emperor and concubines, glowed with life. Mrs Rutherford watched the colonel's eyes narrow as they always did at the screen. In the reflected light of the shining river the curious singed-paper tone of his skin yellowed. She rose and drew sheer curtains halfway across the bank of windows. She loved all light but there was much she would shut out at this moment.

Colonel Chadwick dropped his lanky height into a chair. He had an air of confident prosperity, his light tan suit closely tailored, his deeply waved grey hair combed back to accentuate its fullness, his trimmed grey moustache military in its neatness. But nothing, nothing, Mrs

Rutherford told herself, could conceal the cannonball roundness of that head, the searching shiftiness of those narrow eyes.

'Sit down.' He swept a hand graciously.

She remained standing. 'I'm expecting guests at four-thirty. What do you want?'

'My dear mother-in-law – '

'Don't call me that!'

He shrugged. 'A position of honour, a matter of courtesy.'

'My daughter never married you. I know that!'

'With your splendid gifts of vision, Amelia?'

He was mocking her, as usual. Her only weapon was indifference.

'Naomi would not agree with you,' he continued. 'Like so many of our believers, she has passed through the bodily state of marriage to the serene and blessed state of release and service. Princess and handmaiden of Ishtar.'

'For God's sake.' Mrs Rutherford walked to the far end of the room, to the grand piano and its burden of silver-framed photographs. A little girl of ten with dark curls. At twelve, with her pony. At sixteen, in a white tulle party dress. At eighteen, her eyes wide with trust. Two years later . . .

When Mrs Rutherford turned, her face was expressionless, her eyes like steel.

'As I said, I am expecting guests.'

He rose, his smile gentle. He spread his long, thin hands palms up. 'I come in friendship, Amelia. You know that. Unfortunately Naomi has need of a few things . . .'

'The money I send never reaches her.'

'Are you implying . . .?' His voice deepened. Mrs Rutherford heard again an echo of its curious coercion. 'Whatever is given the temple enriches Naomi and all. If you choose to send nothing, then Naomi will be deprived.'

God alone knows where the evil in you came from . . . But Amelia did not say it aloud. She had said it too often, storming at him helplessly, only to surrender in the end, hating her final abasement, her fear.

'I'll go see her myself. And find out what she needs.'

'You are most welcome, Amelia. We are always graced by the visit of so aristocratic and distinguished a lady. Only Naomi apparently can convince you of her present serenity and happiness. But of course she was not brought up to hard work. She contributes very little towards the group. And she must live on the fringe, one might say, unless . . .'

Mrs Rutherford knew she would not go. The girl had faced her the last time with blank eyes and a radiantly empty smile, as if talking to a stranger, refusing any plea or command to leave the bleak mountainside. Her shabbiness had torn at Mrs Rutherford's heart.

'Five thousand would do nicely,' murmured Colonel Chadwick.

'Five! You know I can't – '

'I think you can. Your extraordinary talents, dear lady, rate high in the market.'

'I do not take money.'

'A pity.' His eyes lingered on the extravagance of the silk screen at the end of the room. 'A gift to the temple might take care of Naomi's simple needs. For quite a while.'

Mrs Rutherford went to a pearwood escritoire, gilt embossed, another segment of the elegance that was as life-supporting as breath to her. The elegance her only child had flouted. But some day that child would come home. Nothing, nothing must be changed.

She wrote the cheque quickly.

'A little cognac, to warm the heart, Amelia. Yours and mine.'

'My guests are almost due.' But she poured the liquor as he knew she would.

Colonel Sanford Chadwick stretched his long heron-thin legs before him and sipped slowly. Very slowly.

A single day can be an invisible door. Walk along the confines of daily existence and there it is, opening without warning, without prediction. Walk through it and no day, no hour, is ever the same again.

Lili had no such presentiment on this glowing Sunday. Summer seemed to be holding its last breath, autumn briskly at hand. Even the tumult of the city stilled under its cobweb of magic. People walked, sunned themselves, and on the street where George Rutherford Clarence now escorted her, they were sitting on endless brownstone stoops leading up to similarly endless brownstone houses. The entire street wore the same monotonous brown. To Lili, despite the day's gilded softness, all these city homes looked hopelessly dismal.

She was not aware of the curious, often bold glances that followed her. She had never been.

She followed George up the stairs, waited for him to unlock the ornate, but grimy, glass door. He took time to unlock a mail slot, one in a row, that bore the name Clarence.

'I used to take a lot of kidding on that name but not since I knocked the last guy down.' He took a single card. 'Ah, here it is. They hand-deliver to save postage. Meeting of the citizens' committee to restore shad to the Hudson. I'm very much involved. No reason why they can't do it. In London they've already begun to clean the Thames. I'll enrol you if you'd like to join.'

He opened the door to his ground-floor apartment. Lili walked in and drew a little breath of surprise. It was empty except for a thick colourless carpet on the floor and a cot along the side wall opposite the window. The walls, too, were colourless, not white, not grey. Yet the room pulsed with life. From the ceiling mobiles hung, a myriad of shapes, of wings, of bright balls of colour. The air current from the door sent them fluttering, meshing and parting, entwining and passing, restless as leaves, yet never touching, and never twice the same. Mobiles. The flow of space. She began to understand.

He was watching her. 'Do you like them?'

'They're beautiful. I never saw anything like them. Did you make them all?'

'Oh, yes.' He closed the door gently. 'I sleep on that cot and at night in the light of the street they come alive. My birds.'

He was oddly silent, and as there was no chair in the room, she stood watching the shapes. The quick current that had stirred them was gone; now they moved lazily as if to vibrations of their own.

'You'll do, Lili. I knew the first moment I saw you that you were right.' He took a step towards her. The overhead shapes spun and changed course. What an odd way to live, she thought. Every breath, every word spoken, every step taken, would be echoed up there, an extension of every mood.

'Will you see the rest of the place?'

He opened a door into a closetlike room. An iron-railed spiral staircase led upstairs.

He started up. 'Please come. It's quite all right.'

Her entire relationship with this odd, intense man had been built on trust. She followed him.

The room at the top was as completely furnished as the downstairs room was stark. Two deep chairs, a quilt-covered wide bed, a deep-pile rug, curtained walls in warm earth tones of terra-cotta and beige. Light poured in from the window.

'It gets the morning sun,' said George irrelevantly.

'It's nice,' said Lili. But of no matter to her, she thought. He was looking at her with that same unspoken concern that left her faintly uncomfortable and unsure.

'It's yours, if you want it.'

'Mine?'

'Oh, I know it must come as a surprise. But I don't use it. I've always thought of someone who might live up here. Who would be close and yet – yet could be distant. Who would understand me. And my birds. It's hard to explain. I've never tried to before. Someone light and gentle who would walk that way. Lili, I'd try to make you very happy here. Do you understand what I'm saying?'

She didn't. If it was a proposal, she had never heard anything like it. If it was not, she could not believe its implication. Not from this kindly young man, without warning, without even trying to kiss or to touch her. His face looked anxious in the bright afternoon light, yet beneath the anxiety she sensed something deeper. She had not realized until this moment that he was not wearing his glasses. His eyes, a light hazel, were fixed on her with such honesty, such intensity – She could hurt him, as she herself had been hurt.

'You would be happy, Lili. Comfortable. I'd promise that. You'd be free to do as you like. I'm away most days and nights. I rent a vacant lot behind a garage in Brooklyn where I make stabiles. That's like space sculpture too, only very large. And it doesn't move. I'll show you some day. Did you ever see Calder's "Arch of Sopelto"? That's my dream. And if you were here . . .'

For a moment the unspoken hung in the silence between them like one of his own slight mobile shapes. It might have fluttered one way or the other, but as suddenly as it had materialized, it was gone.

She saw what she might say, gently as the brush of a wing. Not to hurt. Never to hurt.

'George, it's a lovely idea and a lovely room.' She glanced around and let her refusal ripple on a small laugh. 'I didn't know any room in all New York could be so light and bright. I know you'll find someone to rent it. But you see, I couldn't. I've taken my room at Castleton House for six months. And it's where my relatives . . . my uncle' – for a reason she could not explain, Willard Roundtree came to her mind like distant wisdom – '. . . all of them expect me to be. Don't you see?'

George Rutherford Clarence put on his glasses.

'Of course I see, Lili. I guess it wasn't very sensible. But I just thought – well, you don't find a tenant who understands about mobiles. And you were sort of the right weight.' His smile was young and undefended. It could break her heart. 'Thank you for coming to look.'

'I've loved every minute of it, George.'

They walked in silence to the bus. He carried a camera and some other paraphernalia, which he busied himself adjusting. On the bus he began to talk. He talked about the scraps of iron and abandoned wheels and broken pipes and bits of wire fencing he accumulated in his vacant lot.

By the time the bus stopped in the still-leafy shade of Riverside Drive, Lili had almost forgotten the afternoon's purpose.

'Remember,' said George earnestly. 'You don't have to stay any longer than you want.'

He helped her down the bus step and she gave a small friendly laugh. 'George, you could spoil a girl!'

But something young, untried, and never-to-be had gone from between them.

'This is Colonel Chadwick, Miss Roundtree.'

Mrs Rutherford's manner was as impeccable as it was tight. She wore a long bronze silk dress of total simplicity. Around her neck hung a jade necklace ending at her waist in an enormous carved pendant. Only a woman of such presence could wear so bulky a weight, thought Lili. Yet there was something more unusual than her jewels. Mrs Rutherford, gowned and self-contained, bore no resemblance, except for the strong, prominent features, to the Mrs Rutherford who, gaily turbaned and wielding a walking stick, had come storming across the grass, words like her scarves flying from her.

Tea was served immediately. The angular, narrow-eyed colonel seated himself beside her.

'Roundtree. Roundtree. A southern name?'

'No.' In the room's quiet Lili felt oddly conspicuous. 'New England,' she said shortly.

'I should not have thought you were from New England, Miss Roundtree.'

'She's from New Orleans,' volunteered George, unnecessarily.

'Ah, of course. I should have guessed. The softness of speech, the brightness of the eyes . . .' His glance was openly admiring. 'New Orleans. Mardi Gras. Sanctity and flesh. Conscience and licence. Where a man puts on a mask to be what he is. And the given name, Miss Roundtree, would be romantic, would it not? Charlotte? Eloise? Lurette?'

'Colonel, I believe you said you had a plane . . .?' Mrs Rutherford started to rise.

He waved a long hand. 'When I can enjoy the summer of youth? Have I guessed accurately, Miss Roundtree?'

She felt uncomfortable at being placed centre stage by

this man. And with Lili discomfort became defiance.

'My name is Lilith.' It was sharper than she intended. And surer.

'Lilith.' The colonel's eyes, which seemed to be looking around and above her, returned with interest. 'Lilith. Your *given* name?'

Whatever Lili might have answered was gone. A rush of darting shadows swept the room. George sprang to his feet.

'There they are! I must get them! In this light!' He swung his camera from the table and was halfway to the hall. 'The key! Bring the key!' George vanished.

Mrs Rutherford rose. For the first time she managed a smile.

'Dear George. Such absorption. My neighbour in the next building keeps pigeons on the roof. George cannot resist photographing them when they are released. I have a little observatory of my own on my roof, but these days one must keep every door locked.'

It did not explain much to Lili. But it left her alone with a man for whom she had taken a growing, chilling distaste.

He leaned closer to her. When he spoke, his voice had a new quality, a subtle, personal urgency.

'Lilith. You interest me, Lilith. Why did you take that name?'

'I liked it.'

'Indeed. Yes, I can understand that. She became a demon, touching even the hearts of children with evil.'

'I don't believe legends, Colonel . . . Chadwick.'

'You must or you would not have taken the name. And since you've taken it, you have grown in wisdom. The doers of good are subject to others. The demons, the doers of evil, command their own lives. As you are beginning to learn.'

Lili longed for the return of Mrs Rutherford, of George, of the end of this compelling, close voice.

'But why are you so alone?'

He asked it with such quiet intensity that for an instant its truth stung Lili's eyes with self-pity. Then her normal healthy spirits rallied.

'I don't really know what you're talking about, Colonel Chadwick. Everybody is alone at some time or other. My aunt – I was brought up by aunts – used to say that you can only grow alone. So if that's what it takes, I've got it. I would like to see the pigeons.'

She rose and Colonel Chadwick rose with her. To her surprise his long left hand shot out and gripped her arm.

'Lilith, I already know you. This is not for you. Nor is – what is his name? – that pigeon-chaser on the roof. All too pale. You will know the iron of life, the testing, where the demons live. You are destined to grow alone. But sometimes the burden will become too heavy . . .'

His right hand fished in his pocket.

'When it does, when you can no longer bear it' – he handed her a small white card – 'call this number. Someone will hear.'

Mrs Rutherford's voice floated from the hall. 'But, George, you can't always expect them to fly in your direction . . .'

Lili took the card mechanically. The long dry hand released her arm. She backed away from him. But not before she had seen on the lanky wrist above the protruding wristbone a blue-black mark, a circle the size of a dime, coiled . . .

He saw her glance and dropped his cuff.

'Ah, you recognize it? The snake, symbol of renewal. Sacred to Aesculapius, he who heals, who changes.' He smiled, a shadow smile to Lili more chilling than his voice. 'Some day you, Lilith, will know.'

Mrs Rutherford was returning, followed by George, still working over his camera.

'Lili, why didn't you come!' He set the camera down tenderly. 'Magnificent. Silver-white. Translucent over the river.'

'Miss Roundtree has been kind enough to keep me company. An old leg wound. Troublesome at this time of year. Makes stairs difficult.' Colonel Chadwick rubbed his knee, straightened, and bowed to Mrs Rutherford.

'Dear lady, I am deeply obligated . . .'

He left as if Lili had never existed.

George was apologetic. He should not have left her.

'It's all right, George. Really. I understood. I didn't mind at all.'

'But the old man. Colonel whatever. Pompous type, wasn't he?'

Lili shrugged. It was part of the incongruity of the day. 'We . . . talked. Nothing much.' She felt as distant from George now as from this room. 'I'd like to go now, if you don't mind.'

Mrs Rutherford's farewell was kindly and distracted, as if she had just remembered Lili. 'George must bring you again another time.' Lili had a sense of incompletion. Nothing had turned out as she had expected. The day had fragmented, the pieces too small to pick up.

In her room at last Lili looked blankly at the white card Colonel Chadwick had given her. It bore a single word NEVAH. And a telephone number, a long row of digits, 800 . . . She did not bother to read the rest. Her impulse was to tear the card to shreds. The man had been outrageous in his self-importance. His pompous confidence. If she had come this far only to look forlorn and lonely to the first stranger she met, she had indeed made a mess of things.

The emotions of the day, as they so often did with Lili, exploded into anger, then defiance. She had never worn her feelings on her sleeve or her face. What had she let herself become? One of those helpless, vulnerable, mistletoe girls looking for the first strong oak to support her? She was where she wanted to be. The whole marvellous city was out there around her, crowded with people leading full lives. Self-pity was not going to put her among them.

She would forget Brock. Hadn't she already begun?

Lilith, you will know the iron of life . . . you are destined to grow alone . . . but sometimes the burden will become too heavy . . .

The words lay coiled in the depths of her mind. She would forget them too. Her life was her own now. Keep busy, Aunt Josie had told her, running mouse-like in unessential directions.

But in this searching hour Lili wondered if all the unchannelled busyness of women concealed secret pain. If in truth it was an opiate to honesty.

Later that night she spread the Sunday newspaper on the floor, knelt down, and opened to the help-wanted section. A single sentence jumped from the columns. IF YOU ARE UNDER TWENTY-FIVE, WITH IT, AND SPEAK FRENCH, WE WOULD LIKE TO TALK TO YOU.

She wasn't sure what 'with it' meant, but wasn't that the purpose? To fit into this alien world? She cut out the ad with growing peace of mind. At last she could laugh.

Lilith, for all you know you're on the way to becoming a demon. Now, wouldn't that be different?

It was a step. And it was away from Brock.

She was hardly aware that she had returned the white card to the folds of her handbag.

CHAPTER THIRTEEN

The phone rang steadily for a day and a half.

Bluefield's best-known citizen came home so rarely that when he did, word spread like a prairie fire. The last ring this morning came from the front door. Brock, sitting hunched at the kitchen table, looked up and shook his head.

Alice Turner sighed. She liked, she craved, this acknowledgement of her celebrity son. She found his reticence puzzling, even hurtful, though she would admit that to no one. At what point did a child become a stranger? His hair was as tousled as ever, his shoulders satisfactorily broad, with no sign of thickness anywhere. And he was famous. But he was no longer boyish. The casual sense of fun, the lightness that had been his father's despair and her own secret resource, had subtly changed, as if the world had touched him in ways neither she nor anyone would understand.

She returned from the door with an envelope in her hand.

'Telegram for you, Brock.'

'Thanks.' He started to rise, her hand pressed his

shoulder. 'Kitchen breakfast. Everybody stays put. Except your father, who never sat still very long anywhere. Remember?' Her eyes warmed. She found it increasingly easy to mention his father but not yet David.

'I remember.' He pocketed the telegram, unopened. 'Well, thanks to whoever delivered it. I didn't know they still did that anywhere.'

'Miss Hattie usually phones them. But our phone's been so busy that she couldn't get through, so she sent Glenda over.' Telegrams didn't come so frequently to Bluefield. When they did, you opened them quickly while you held your breath. But she didn't say that. She waited.

'Who's Glenda? Or should I know?'

'She had a crush on you in high school.'

'Good Lord. She's not still out there?'

Alice Turner's laugh, suddenly girlish, was good to hear. 'She wanted to come in. My goodness, she did. But I explained. Glenda's all right. She had her teeth straightened and she wears contact lenses and she's going to marry Al Viner who's a clerk in Beal's Hardware and will probably own it some day. I told her you were resting. You've turned me into a dragon, Brock.'

'Nobody could do that. Anyhow I'm grateful. I'm off duty, Mom.'

She asked no questions. Nor had she since he burst in two nights ago out of one of Bluefield's lashing September rainstorms. She had flung her arms around him, cooked him a hot meal, made up his room, and the plain clapboard house of her thirty-five years of marriage sprang to life.

'Brock, isn't that telegram important?'

'Not really. Only one guy in the world would have the gall to send it here.' He grinned. 'But okay. If you can't stand it any longer, you read it.'

She opened it carefully. '"Enough is enough."' She read aloud, separating each word. '"Back on the fifteenth or up yours."'

He took the telegram from her.

'Who is Mort?'

'Executive vice-president of my network, hell-bent on being president, chairman of the board some day. He'll probably make it. They like his language. Mortimer Russell. My boss.'

'I see,' said Alice. She had trained herself to placidity. She recognized the old streak of obstinacy in her first-born, as Scottish as his middle name. 'It's nice to be wanted.'

He had given her too little thought, he told himself. Her anguish must have been long and profound and lonely. How many times in a life do you keep on running when you should stop and look back?

A black cat jumped from the window ledge to the table. Another, striped orange, rubbed around his ankles.

'Where did you get these?'

'When Sargie died, I thought of another dog . . .'

Sargie. He had not thought of that. The splendid old half-collie, half Saint Bernard, who had warmed his youth and his bed. Sargie was mortal too. But for an instant it hurt.

'. . . but I'm used to big dogs. Anyway cats are more suitable at my age.'

His father had hated cats.

Brock scooped the black cat from the table and stroked it. 'What's his name?'

'Caliban, though I don't expect you to know why. You never did like poetry, Brock.'

'That's right.' Until . . . *a little of thee and me* . . . and the little dog-eared book he carried to surprise a girl – some day. 'Never saw much use in it.'

He lowered the black cat to the floor and picked up the striped orange one. 'And this?'

'Not so classical, I'm afraid. Her name is Minnie. But Minnie has a heart just as big as a whale.'

He gave the cat a whirl. 'Heigh-de-ho!'

'David used to sing that.'

She put both cats outside the door and busied herself.

David was his younger brother. The golden one. Beautiful, with his fine hands so suited to surgery, his quick mind, his gentle laugh. David with his professed ambition to follow his father. 'David will go far beyond me,' Dr Henley B. Turner would say. 'David's born to be a doctor,' Alice would add. 'A great doctor.'

That was until the night Dr Turner's car was found upside down in a culvert on a narrow curve. The speedometer had stopped at eighty-two. Dr Turner had been killed instantly. David, at the wheel, with the steering column penetrating his chest, had lingered. Brock, away on his first job as cub reporter in San Francisco, had flown back to watch his brother die. And to learn of the glassine envelopes found in David's pockets and the heroin found in his body.

Brock stayed with his mother during the investigation. 'David Turner a supplier,' the local newspaper had shrilled. 'Schools, youth clubs, campuses . . .' Alice Turner turned a deaf ear. Later, when she could no longer deny the evidence, she sat stoically, dry-eyed, in her living-room. 'The mercy is his father did not know.'

Brock never disabused her. Her acceptance had been too hard reached, the threads of her life too ravelled. Brock gave up his newspaper job, stayed home. He even thought of going to medical school. To practise here in Bluefield, to make up for David.

Alice Turner had turned brittle. 'No, Brock. Go back to your paper. Your life is out there. Mine is here. You cannot help by staying here. You must do what you are suited to.'

It was almost a dismissal, almost a hint that somehow he had failed. He called her from his various assignments, then less frequently. He returned one Christmas and was surprised at how well she was doing. She had lined her walls with books and her life with causes and she had become Alice Turner instead of the doctor's wife. The new role suited her like the brighter knits she now wore even if it did not take the deeper shadow from her eyes. Always, Brock believed, when she looked at him, she saw David.

That was the winter he became engaged to the prettiest, most eligible girl in town, Marcia Reeves, daughter of Judge Reeves. The judge had long ago forsworn the scales of justice for the headier realms of high politics to become a major power in the state.

The June wedding in the rose garden of the Reeveses' Victorian mansion was a glory of sentiment, sunlight, and imported champagne. 'Small bubbles, always remember that, boy! Small bubbles.' Brock could have done without the epithet, as he could have done without the overload of heavy faces, heavier jokes, of the herded politicos. He was left in no doubt of the availability of clout. Marcia's fairy-blonde beauty shining through a mist of white veiling gave the ceremony a near spiritual quality.

'Be happy, Brock,' Alice Turner whispered through her tears. 'It's all so perfect.'

The judge pumped his hand. 'You treat my little girl right and you can have the world, boy. You hurt her' – the smile vanished over prominent dentures – 'and I'll burn your ass.'

The judge was a widower, Marcia his only child. His well-known silver oratory tarnished in direct ratio to his consumption of alcohol. Brock had no way of knowing his ethereal bride could inherit her father's inclinations.

By this time Brock had joined the network. The couple honeymooned in Bermuda, set up housekeeping in a chic Greenwich Village mews.

'What's a mews, Brock?'

'It was at one time stables, remodelled into flats.'

'A stable! Sweetie-pie! You're asking me to live – '

'If J. P. Morgan's horses could live here, I guess you and I – '

She laughed. 'Brock, how you go on!' She kissed him in a flurry of scented ruffles and pronounced herself delighted with the four rooms, festooned in flowered chintz. She made herself delectable in the mornings before he left and even more delectable when he came home at night.

If the delectability proved more wrapping than content, Brock did not search his marriage too closely. He was rising fast in the network. He was travelling. His face and his voice were becoming nationally known. He had a wife who was lively and pretty when they went out, a goal to return to at the end of a trip.

'Good thing, Brock. She's all right,' said Mortimer Russell after a dinner for four when Mort's arm slid too often around Marcia's pretty, swinging shoulders. Brock told himself he should feel a gut anger. Oddly he didn't.

'A news reporter's like a travelling salesman, Brock,'

Mort continued, stroking Marcia's shoulder, who was as usual listening only to the music. 'He can have a girl in every town if he wants. And usually does. And I don't give a damn as long as he gets the story. But we're building you, Brock. You've got to have image. Reliability. Stability. When you say something on the air, people must believe you like the great white father. So, Brock Turner and wife . . . okay. Very okay.'

Much as Brock resented Mort Russell's crass use of his marriage, he knew himself that it was not only the urgency of his body that swept a more than willing Marcia into his arms those courting nights. It was a deeper urgency to get on with his life. His father and brother were dead. He lived. Within him lay the sediment of that fact, a compulsion to find their killer, his brother's corrupter. Somewhere there walked a man whose blandishments had brought David to his final destruction, and with David the decency of an entire family.

Yet Brock knew that compulsion could unravel his life. Marriage was the norm. A woman beside him, pretty and acceptable. A fulfilment that his whole upbringing demanded. Marcia, fragile, lively as a hummingbird, was his now to cherish – as the ceremony read. He learned patience with her sudden outbursts of excitability, her changeable whims, her craving to go dancing, which she loved above all things. He would watch her, swinging to the savage rock beat, her short skirts revealing her thin legs to the thigh. She would return to the table, face flushed, eyes unnaturally bright.

'Champagne, Brock! I'm a champagne girl! Small bubbles, remember?'

The afternoon he was packing for his most serious assignment yet, he found her dressing case thrust into a canvas tote at the rear of the hall closet. The case contained a fifth of Scotch whisky wrapped in a ruffled nightie. The bottle was half empty.

He reached Mort Russell at home.

'You've got to go, Brock. The White House has okayed it.'

'Bill can take the assignment.'

'Sure. So can half a dozen guys, and they'd jump at it. How often do you get a Geneva summit? Don't be a goddamned idiot!'

'Marcia's ill . . .'

'Then get a nurse or put her in a hospital. First pregnancy always gets 'em down.'

'She is not pregnant.'

There was a small silence. 'Your final decision?'

'Yes.'

Mortimer Russell should have hung up but he had a winner in Brock Turner and he wasn't used to losing. 'Look, you cement-headed blockhead! That little cutie's tough as a yard of wire. She'll survive. If she doesn't know that the news comes first, she'd better learn. I'll take her out to dinner. Personally. And explain. With three dozen roses. You'll go. Or else.'

'Then it's or else, Mr Russell.'

Brock hung up slowly. He saw the narrowing of the road. But he knew he would not leave her. Perhaps it was his fault in a way. She was used to protection. His absences had grown more frequent. It was his work, but some women could not understand a man's work.

He poured what remained of the bottle down the toilet. When Marcia came in, giggling and flushed from her afternoon, he said nothing. And asked nothing.

He requested a local news desk from the network and got it. He called home frequently, took her out more often, and indulged in a futile variation of hide-and-seek called find-the-bottle. He was not sure at what point she discovered that he knew, but her excitability increased. She announced she had enrolled in a modern dance class.

'Why, Marcia?'

'Because it makes me feel alive. And Mr Ronaldson said I have talent.'

'Then you better get off the booze.'

'I don't drink a thing except when I go out with your swinging friends. And then I have to be a good sport. Do you want a droop for a wife?'

She whirled around the room, lifting her skirt, and flung herself against him.

'Brock! Live a little! You're getting dull, sweetie-pie!'

For the first time in his life he felt helpless. He wondered how other men handled the problem, and then dismissed that speculation. The hell with other men. This was his. This was Marcia, the girl he had married. To solve a problem there had to be admission of one. Marcia continued to bubble like the champagne she drank in public in the evening, to rush off to her dance class in the morning, to sleep longer and heavier in the afternoon.

Until the afternoon when Brock, driven by unease, left the news tapes to come home early. He walked into a living-room littered with swing records, melting ice, glasses on the coffee table, and an empty bottle overturned on the floor.

Marcia lay on the double bed, nude except for a black half-slip. Her eyes were unfocused. The room was heavy with smoke, raspberry sweet.

She looked at Brock glassily. 'Hi, sweetie-pie.' Her smile was doll-like in its prettiness. 'Ronnie was here. So nice.' She slid into unconsciousness.

A week later, struggling against the bars of a hospital bed, Marcia called her father by telephone. He arrived in a silence more ominous than speech, refused to meet Brock, and took his daughter home. A letter reached Brock the following month. Marcia would never return. There would be no divorce. Any attempt on Brock's part would be met with a suit for criminal neglect, corruption, and abuse.

Judge Reeves had his little girl back.

Four years now. Or five?

Brock had given himself wholly to his career and reached a pinnacle that no longer interested him. He filled his needs with women as eager as they were available and always faceless the next morning. He had found and lost and found again the winding track to David's destroyer, but he was always a phantom when Brock caught up.

Then he knew that the drained, driven years had lasted long enough. Somewhere he had to find some direction. Not in lying on an empty beach but in movement, movement. For three months, bearded and dirty, he drove unseeingly endless roads that led nowhere. He stopped in seedy, small-town lodgings, in cheap motels furnished in plastic sameness with no questions asked, anywhere he would not be recognized. He searched his own life against the passing tide of plain, working faces, people who would never know his fame or his earnings yet who seemed rooted in daily satisfying priorities.

Priorities. That's what he sought now. Order in the frenetic speed of his days. A goal.

Then one day Brock Turner stopped fooling himself.

Somewhere west of Winnemucca, Nevada, in Mrs Carney's rooming house, he put in a telephone call. It was seven o'clock, six in New Orleans. But at least, he told himself wryly, the ladies of St Charles Avenue would not be listening to TV.

'May I speak with Miss Elizabeth Roundtree?' He heard his own huskiness.

'Why, Miss Elizabeth is not here . . . Just a minute, please.' The soft, obedient voice ended abruptly. Brock counted the seconds, a habit of his profession. No one knew better how long sixty of them could be. At the end of seventy-five he heard a different voice, sere as a leaf.

'Who is it who wants to talk with Elizabeth?'

'A friend of hers. Brock Turner from – '

'Elizabeth no longer lives here.'

'Can you tell me where I can reach her?' His mouth went dry. She was married.

'She's gone north. To New England.'

'Can you tell me – '

'I'm sorry. Good evening.'

The leaf fell. The branch was bare. Brock listened to nothingness and then hung up slowly. New England. Yet if she had married, she'd still be in New Orleans, with two carats on her finger and bridge at the country club. That is, if she had married that dolt.

Lili . . . Elizabeth . . . Lilith – changeable as wind, quick as fire, the careful innocence of those eyes, the darting intelligence of her, the obstinacy that both exasperated and challenged him. Lili – that was what he was both running from and running towards. Lili beside him for the rest of his life.

He refused Mrs Carney's corn stew and sought a bar. He took a corner table, looked past the frizzy-haired blonde with the round smile, the round legs, and the round cleavage. He ordered a double Scotch.

New England. It might seem to the Misses Beaulaire a pinprick on the rim of cosmic darkness but it included six states, all small, with a total area of sixty-three thousand square miles, population of ten million, the cod, the nutmeg, the pinetree shilling, cradle of liberty, hub of the universe, and under God's right sole on His footstool. Somewhere in all that clutter he might find Lili. Might? Hell, he would. He already felt her in his arms, light as a wing, passionate as a flame.

At dawn he left double the cost of the room on Mrs Carney's kitchen table. He drove through the day, the night, and the next day whipped by a purpose that lifted him from fatigue. He was hardly aware of leaving the mountains slumbering like wrinkled elephants behind him, of crossing the shadow-mottled wheat greens of the plains. He was only aware of the highway beneath his wheels, straight as a Comanche arrow to the heart of his dilemma.

Now he was alone in his mother's kitchen, and the moment had come. The cats purring around his ankles, the smell of good coffee warm on the air, steadied him. He drew a sharp breath, picked up the receiver, and dialled.

He was surprised to discover that he had not forgotten Marcia's telephone number. He was even more surprised when she answered.

'Brock! How nice! Why, I never thought – ' Then she remembered. 'What do you want, Brock?'

'To come over. See you.'

'I don't know what Daddy would say to that.'

'Is he there?'

'He went to Chicago.'

He was in no mood to wait. Perhaps it would be easier this way.

'Marcia, I would like to talk to you for just ten minutes.'

There was a silence. 'I don't know if you should, Brock, but I guess ten wouldn't hurt anybody.'

If he was shocked when he saw her, he tried not to show it. She was achingly thin. She had a blue bow in her listless mud-blonde hair and a fixed dullness in her eyes. The electricity had gone. He could only wonder what latent strain had surfaced in this only child. And where he himself had failed, if he had. But it was too late for that now.

'Sit down, Brock, won't you?' she said politely.

The room had not changed. The ponderous Victorian furniture still looked bolted to the floor. The Turkish rug was worn a bit thinner before the judge's deep brown chair and at his station of command before the marble fireplace. The Brussels lace curtains still hung floor length and immaculate. The loudest sound was the incongruous chiming of the century-old ship's clock on the mantel. Above it hung two crossed Civil War swords, their gilt tassels motionless and dun. The stuffed hare beneath the glass bell on the bookcase still had but one eye.

Brock hated the room. In the flowering days of sentiment he had seen Marcia as a bright little caged bird. Now she faded into the room, one with its dimness.

He masked his pity. He would be very gentle.

'How are you, Marcia?'

'Oh, very well.'

'Happy?' He said it as lightly as a bubble, important as it was.

'Oh, yes. Daddy takes me almost everywhere with him. But not this time because I've just come back from the mountains. I always feel so good after being there.' She smiled prettily. 'How are you, Brock?'

'Okay.'

'I saw you once on television and you looked just like I remember. We don't have a set now.' She waited.

'Marcia . . .' Gently, he told himself, gently. 'Have you ever had any desire to see me?'

'Oh, often, Brock.' Her face lighted. 'You were the best dancer in Bluefield. We had so much fun. Remember that winter we got engaged? You cut in on me three times at the Christmas cotillion and Annie Keecher said, "He's sweet on you, Marcia." And then she said I ought to be careful because you were David Turner's brother and everybody knew what he was. But I said I could forget all that any time I danced with you. And I did until all that happened in New York and Daddy had to bring me home. But I've forgiven you, Brock. Honestly. People can't help what they are . . . do you think?'

He was not prepared for the opening of the front door. Judge Reeves stood in the entryway. His face was a dark mottled red, the muscles of his right jaw worked feverishly.

Brock rose. For an instant the bare hatred in the older man's eyes held him. Then the judge went to his daughter.

'Who let him in, Marcia?'

'He telephoned.'

'Go upstairs. I'll rid the house . . .'

It was as if Brock were not there, not human. His gentleness vanished. The years of frustration, David's death, his mother's widowhood, the misery of his own exile, and the helplessness of his need for Lili blazed into one seething sense of injustice. And injustice was for Brock Turner, as it was for his Scottish forebears, the ultimate evil.

He stepped quickly between Marcia and the door.

'No, sir. I'll go when I've said what I came to say. And Marcia is to hear it. Very simply. Since she has not come back to me, since she has not lived as my wife for five years, since you have insisted she stay here and she tells me she is happy, I want a divorce. In fact the time has passed for wanting. I intend to start action and I believe any court in this country – ' He had gone too far and he knew it.

An odd smile spread on the judge's face.

'Marcia, your husband wants you to go back to New York.'

'New York?' She looked blankly up at her father. 'You said I'd never have to. You said I could stay here with you the rest of my life and I would never again have to . . .' Her hands went to her face. When she dropped them, Brock was startled by the change. Her wispiness was gone, her small face harsh and seamed. 'Do you think I'd ever go back to that, Brock Turner? All those nights when you left me alone. When all I could do was drink and drink. Then you'd come back and – and make me do things . . . again!'

He was appalled but he would be steady, careful.

'What things, Marcia?'

'Things I hated . . . you know what things. What a man can do . . . to force his wife . . .'

He stared at her. She had the face, the voice, the memory of a stranger. But he must know.

'Marcia, tell the truth! How long were you my wife – in any sense?'

'Turner!' The judge took a step towards him.

'No, no. Let me say it. I remember now. Everything. And why wasn't I your wife?' Her small teeth showed, not in a smile but in the rolling back of her lips as if she would spring animal-like at him. 'Ask them what I told them about you those days in the hospital. Ask them how I cried because I couldn't stop thinking and hurting. Ask Daddy!'

Brock began to understand. What brainwashing, what subversion, had gone on in the delirium of this child-mind? What poisons injected?

The judge was not finished. 'Marcia, would you be willing to give your husband a divorce?'

'A divorce! No. Never. Never! A divorce is dirty! It's wrong! It breaks the promise I made before God. No matter what he did to me, I'll never do that. I'll never soil myself again!' She wheeled on Brock. 'If that's what you've come for, why didn't you tell me? Sneaking in here when Daddy's gone, asking sweet questions, making me talk. No. No, Brock.' Another change slid over her face, shadow over water. Shrewdness flickered in her eyes and she looked old. Old and knowing. 'I'll never give you a divorce. Never, never! Nothing you can say will ever make me. I'm not afraid of you, Brock. I'm safe here. With Daddy!'

The judge put his arm around her and, without looking at Brock, led her from the room.

The enormity of it, the abyss into which he had been made to peer, distracted Brock even from his hopeless anger. Its finality left no crack in the closed door.

He left the house alone. He would not for a long time

forget the obscenity of that heavy arm across Marcia's thin shoulders. The barrier across his own life.

From an upstairs window Judge Reeves watched Brock's car wind down the road. He had long recognized the insubordination in those direct eyes. He resented Brock's growing fame that was beginning to make the judge feel old and out of touch in his own town. But most of all Judge Reeves hated, with an intensity that left him shaken, this virile young stud who had possessed his daughter.

The car turned out of sight. The judge let the storm within him subside.

All in all he was satisfied with the morning. As satisfied as he was with his Chicago trip. He would take Marcia with him next time. He would buy her pretty things. He would keep her beside him on his campaign, his devoted daughter. It would hold his enemy at bay. The voters would like it.

For Judge Reeves, now in his sixtieth year, was smitten with ambition. He had pushed many a man to Washington. Why not his turn now before it was too late? Old friends, cronies, men in his political debt, had not been surprised. Some had already offered to come into the state to help him become Senator Reeves. He liked the sound of that.

He also liked the cheques that had been written for his support. He drew four from his wallet. Three in payment of old obligations. The fourth still puzzled him. He did not know the tall, angular, greying man who had pushed through the crowd and asked to meet him. They had talked later. The man said he had been an East Asia importer. He had made some money. Now that he was back home, he would like to put it to the good of his country. He would like to contribute to the support of a man of proven principles and achievement. Congress had need of such maturity in its ranks. The judge had warmed to the stranger's intelligence, his cultivated manner. He found himself talking of his ambitions, of his widowerhood. Even of his daughter. He had been touched by the concerned understanding the man had shown in Marcia.

Now alone in his room, his house once more safe and the embers of his hidden fires cooling, Judge Reeves turned the cheque over slowly, contentedly in his hands. A new supporter, one of substance. A widening future. He had little to fear now from Brock Turner. He glanced at the cheque once more before putting it into his small wall safe. It was made out to the judge's election committee. The amount was five thousand dollars. The signature, Colonel Sanford Chadwick.

CHAPTER FOURTEEN

Under twenty-five, with it, and speak French.

Arthur Shallcross leaned back in his desk chair and surveyed the girl in the doorway. Under twenty-five? Probably. At least she wasn't thirty-five, making like twenty-eight. Speak French? Very likely or she wouldn't be here. With it? Neat red suit, skirt nearly down to the knee. Patent-leather shoes, also neat. And the blue eyes levelling on him without a flutter.

'Lilith Roundtree.' Voice was softly husky and refined. But what kind of name was Lilith?

'Sit down, Miss Roundtree.'

She sat and crossed her ankles.

'I don't know whether you're just what we're looking for . . .' he began.

A ten-watt smile. 'Neither do I, Mr – '

'Shallcross, Artie Shallcross.' Who was doing the interview? he wondered.

'Mr Shallcross, I am under twenty-five. I speak French as well or almost as well as I speak English. The sisters said I had to. I have only one question. So I don't take much of your time. Your advertisement said "with it". With what?'

The first applicant to ask.

'Today! Everything!' He gestured widely and sat up in his chair. 'I am starting a magazine. It's called *Young*. Because I believe that everybody, all over the world, under thirty – honestly under thirty – thinks the same about things. Fed up with all this' – he glanced at her and cancelled the expletive – 'all this stuff, like war, injustice not enough jobs unless we kill off enough people to make room, not enough money to do what must be done unless the government prints it up like toilet paper, and where does that leave everybody?'

Her eyes were wide and intense and of a colour he couldn't name. Heliotrope, maybe. He was a pale, serious young man with long straggly brown hair and a long straggly brown moustache.

'The young . . . we're the ones who are going to have to clean up the mess. The elderly can't tell us, Thoreau said. They shouldn't try. They've made all their mistakes, let the young make their own. That's going on the masthead of the magazine. We're going to publish it in as many languages as we can afford. And it's going to deal only with what young people think. People under thirty, because that's where the world's at now.'

Her steady gaze disconcerted him.

'We're not going to cover only politics and serious things but what we eat, how we dress, where we sleep and who with . . . everything that's right for us. All over the world.'

'I see,' said Lili.

She was different, all right. She knew how to listen.

'What can you do? Except speak French.'

Lili uncrossed and recrossed her ankles. 'I can type.'

'Shorthand?'

She drew a small breath. 'Yes. But I don't read it back.'

Unexpectedly he gave a small sound that might have been a chuckle, and the two girls watching from their desks looked up. There were no private offices. The large single bare-walled room had been converted from an apartment in an old building, which Lili had found with difficulty.

Artie Shallcross waved his hand, 'You don't need shorthand. We don't dictate much around here. Everybody does everything. Copy, layout, delivery to the printer, going out for sandwiches, the works. I ought to tell you our first issue comes out in January. Nobody gets paid until we're published.'

'I see,' said Lili for the second time.

'So if that won't do, say so. It's sort of a labour of love for all of us. But we think it's going to be big. I inherited a half

168

a million dollars and I'm throwing it all in to start up. We tread water for a while. With the first three issues we expect to touch base and then the money will begin to come in.'

'I understand,' said Lili.

'I'll show you. Dawn, hand me the cover layout, will you?' The girl called Dawn was slender, strikingly handsome, and black. She gave Lili a light smile.

Artie spread the magazine cover on top of his desk. What Lili saw was a field of faces, all shades, all moods, and all young: daring, angry, joyous, tearful, despairing, triumphant, sensual, tender, defiant. Across them a single, page-filling word that seemed hardly necessary. *Young*.

'In Spanish it will be *Joven*. In French *Jeunesse* . . . trickier to fit.'

Lili let a second beat by. 'But *jeunesse* does not mean "young" in French,' she said politely.

'What the hell?'

'It means "youth". The word for "young" is *jeune*, *j-e-u-n-e*.'

Artie counted with his fingers. 'Beautiful. Beautiful!' He gave her his first pale smile. 'Carla.' He beckoned to the girl at the second desk. She was plump, her black hair fell to her waist, and she wore a marvellous assortment of beads over a red and green shawl. Beneath it a sheer blouse revealed full, maternal breasts. 'Carla, you dug this up. Come over here and learn something.'

The girl's dark hair fell over Artie's shoulder. She shrugged, her good-natured smile widened. 'Win some, lose some. I thought it had class.'

A young man burst from an inner room. He was short, thick, balding, and excited. He wore bifocals, but the smoothness of his skin could only belong to the young. 'I've got it! Sensational!'

'Lilith, meet Hank, the best photographer under twenty-nine in the city. He's also office manager when he isn't out hustling ads. Hank, Lil's starting tomorrow. Find her something to sit on and a table until we get another desk.'

Hank saw her to the door, eyed her curiously. 'All you

need around here is staying power. If you've got it, right on! We start at nine. Art's here at eight. No shutdown time. Bring your lunch.'

Outside, gusts of cold autumn rain beat down on the street. Lili was hardly aware of them. She did not remember accepting the job, but now that it was done she felt an exhilaration unlike anything she had ever known. Part of it was the tingle of the soaring city no longer unconquerable. Part of it was the freshness of the wind-borne rain. But mostly it was a new self-knowledge. She was wanted, she was needed, she had work to do. She was Lilith Roundtree. 'With it.'

She lifted her face to the rain and walked the thirty blocks north to Castleton House.

The euphoria, of course, wore off.

Her first mistake was not to bring lunch because she had not taken the advice seriously.

'We brown-bag it here, Lil.' Carla had a soft, wide smile that belied her dedication. 'Unless you can afford to eat out.'

'It's my turn to go out for coffee,' Dawn, the handsome, distant black girl, said. 'It's around the corner. Their sandwiches are terrible but if you'd like to come with me . . .' She broke off the sentence indifferently.

'Could I?'

The work was frantic, repetitious, and head-throbbing. Artie Shallcross had more vision than order and the staff was busier demonstrating young enthusiasm than correcting errors. But the discipline that had taught Lili French knots, Latin verbs, and complete sentences also taught her survival. Quietly she found lost papers, reshaped bungled paragraphs, and slid the credit to other desks. She also bought two peasant skirts and strings of fake jewellery, and learned to smile through any and all exasperation, of which there was plenty.

After a week she and Dawn had lunch together. In a booth in a hero-sandwich cafeteria.

'You're doing all right, Lili. How do you like it?'

'Am I? I don't know much yet.'

'Do you think anybody does? We're all learning. Our problem is to teach Artie. Carla's into that.'

Lili glanced around the narrow jammed cafeteria. Dawn mistook the glance.

'I guess you wouldn't be doing this in New Orleans.'

'Doing what?'

'Having lunch with a black girl.'

To Lili this was as disappointing as it was embarrassing.

'If we were in New Orleans, I'd ask you to lunch, Dawn. If you'd come.' She gave a half-smile. 'But my Aunt Clem . . .'

'I know.' Dawn met her smile.

'She's nearly seventy,' Lili added, as if that explained everything.

The awkwardness slid away. In silence they began to eat. Dawn was the first to look up.

'I'm sorry about that question. It's the first time I ever asked it. Of anyone. But you're nice to talk to. I guess that's because you've got – well, what my grandmother calls listenin'.' The little laugh faded. 'I'm going with a white boy, Lil. He wants to get married. My father won't meet him. He says marrying Cass will make me a common girl. My grandmother says' – Dawn slid into deep dialect – '"The Bible tells us God created us all and the Constitution tells us we're equal and Mr Lincoln said we could all get paid when we could find jobs. But that don't make red into blue, cabbages into roses, or black into white. If God meant that, he'd pass another miracle. And you and Cass ain't going to provoke Him to it."' Her laugh was easy, but her eyes were misted. She slid a hand to a chain beneath her blouse. At the end of the chain hung a ring set with a minute chip of diamond.

Love could always touch Lili to the quick. 'Tell me about Cass.'

'He's an engineer with the Seabees. He builds roads and things. He says he's going to Vietnam soon now. He's not all that good-looking but he's the most wonderful human being I ever met. We used to go dancing a lot. We were really good. We won the Harvest Moon Ball once.' She looked into a distance of her own.

171

Lili did not ask why Dawn was working for *Young*, or why any of them were. Or why she herself was. But she began to sense in the bickering friendliness and the hopeless, good-natured clutter of the office, the threads of mutual dependence and hope stringing their lives together. As if with the publication of this unlikely dream, their paper dream, their own confusions would end and their lives would be resolved.

'Art's got a thing about people,' said Dawn after she and Lili had ordered coffee in the same cafeteria one evening a week later. 'If New York's a melting pot, it boiled up and spilled over in that office. Carla's Italian and Catholic. She lives with Artie in a loft over in Chelsea. No marriage. Because Carla says it's got to be for ever for her. And she's not that sure. Hank is Jewish. His family's Orthodox and they don't want him to marry his Reform girl-friend. He's trying to prove something and maybe he will. Artie's mother came to the office one day. All WASP: White Anglo-Saxon Philadelphia. Art read her that piece by Thoreau he's hipped on. About how the old shouldn't try to tell the young. She didn't come back. She was like a little grey-haired doll. Pearls and gloves. She'd have liked you, Lil.'

Lili felt a first sting of resentment. She forced a laugh.

'Not if she'd talked to my Aunt Clem first!'

'Look, I didn't mean anything. Except you're about the only one of us who hasn't got hang-ups. Maybe that gives you time to be nicer about things.'

This girl offered friendship but carefully. It was probably time to go. Yet Lili was not yet ready for the silence of her room, for the streets crowded with couples embarked on their own plans for the evening. It was easier to sit in this brightly lit cafeteria, surrounded by bright faces. Their laughter was a barrier against the night. And their talk against the silence.

Dawn glanced at her watch. 'He's calling me at eight. So I have time for one more coffee. Okay?'

'Mine, this time.'

'I'm sorry for what I said about the hang-ups.'

'It's all right. Really. I wonder what made you think I don't have any.'

'You don't act it.'

'How should I act? How do they think at the office I should act? Get mad? Fling things around? Cry?'

'You never talk about yourself.'

Lili found it a relief to laugh. 'Maybe that's because I spent a lot of years going to a convent. A real old-fashioned one with walls two feet thick. A long time ago they shipped girls from France to marry the men who had settled in New Orleans. The nuns came along to see the girls were proper. They're still doing it. In the convent if anything hurts, you stay on your knees until it goes away. I guess that's where I'm still at.'

'So there is a guy?'

Dawn's question was too sure, too soft. Lili would come apart if she thought too much about Brock now. But her need was deeper.

She caught her breath as if she were about to dive. 'There was,' she answered quietly. 'But I'm not going to see him again. I . . . can't.' She regretted the last phrase, but it was too late. 'He's married. So that's that.'

'But it isn't!' Dawn said it flatly, as a fact of life. 'That's a dead end, doll. Unless you're a one-man woman. And who is these days?'

A half-memory, a mere trail of mist, her father's face. His words when she had passionately refused to relinquish a broken jack-in-the-box. *'Don't ever fall in love, Lili, unless you're sure. Because it will be for ever. It's in the blood.'*

She had no answer then. Nor did she now. She was angry at herself for revealing what she had, for letting something so deep, so anguished, and so beautiful touch daylight. She had given Brock up, she had done what was right, but in this world of new confusions, maybe right and wrong no longer had any meaning.

Lili managed a smile and pushed her empty coffee cup from her. 'Shall we go?'

But as she walked into night she repeated the words.

Maybe, she told herself silently, savagely. Maybe *not*. Maybe they still had meaning for her.

That evening, in the clear cold of late October, when frost in the upper air turned the thousands of building lights to diamond hardness and her own breath to fresh cold vapour, Lili walked down Third Avenue. Past the boutiques, past the restaurants, past the antique shops and art displays and finally the windows of Sam's Singles. The curtains were half-drawn which left a view of the bar with an early scattering of sitters, and three empty stools in a row. They would be filled soon like the small wooden tables, the room close and noisy and warm with people.

She paused, looked at the empty bar stools again. Then she pushed the swing door open and walked in.

Lili would look back on that night as long as she lived. Its magic, its pain, its through-the-looking-glass aura. She did not believe in fate nor did she believe in stars, but she wanted desperately to believe in something.

She took the safer centre seat of the three that were empty. She felt bold, but not conspicuous, not as conspicuous as being alone at one of the still empty tables.

The bartender was a man of comfortable girth and a friendly smile. He was also a man who knew his customers.

'What'll it be, honey?'

Lili had not prepared herself for that question. Answering a bartender was different from answering an escort.

'Take your time.' He beamed on her and busied himself with ice shavings. He reminded her of Ed's father – rotund, kindly, who was once King of Comus and who might have become her father-in-law.

'A Ramos gin fizz,' she said, louder than she intended.

'I haven't made one of those for a long while. It'll take a little time.'

'I know,' Lili assured him. 'It's all right.'

The bartender was sure it would be. This girl wasn't looking for trouble or booze. She looked more like – the bartender searched his limited vocabulary and gave up – something bright, blown in on the cold wind. He'd make

174

her a good Ramos. One. She could live with it the rest of the evening.

Lili looked around. It wasn't so bad. Nobody bothered her and it was still early. She briefly met a few glances and looked away. You were supposed to show people if you wanted to meet them and she wasn't ready for that. The bartender was still shaking her drink briskly and when it was frothy enough, he set it down in front of her.

'It's supposed to take ten minutes,' Lili reminded him.

'Yeah, I know. But this ain't the Ramos bar, honey. So I only got time to shake it maybe two minutes. And that ain't whole cream in it, either. Half and half. Shall I throw it out?'

Lili laughed. She was feeling better every minute. Maybe she should give up being somebody else and be herself. She cupped the glass with her hands and took a long sweet swallow.

And that was her mistake.

No one had warned Lili that memory is a treacherous process. The least-suspected stimulus can send an impulse to jolt the mind, to shatter the defences. In this case it was nothing more than a single swallow of the famous Ramos gin fizz.

That first long sweet sip swept her headlong back to a star-spangled April night to a table in Le Vieux Carré, to the black glitter of the river. And the overwhelming wholeness of being with Brock. And the gin fizzes for two.

She set the drink down again carefully, letting emotion flood her and slowly subside. She would have gone to Brock that night. They had both known that, hadn't they, from the first hour? Or had it been only in the urging of her own newly impassioned body? She would have gone to him and it would be for ever. For ever, until he should tell her as casually, as lightly as rain, the truth.

A little of thee and me, Brock . . . a lot of thee and me, Brock . . . all of thee and me, Brock. Didn't you ever read that? You should, you know. I'll read it to you some day. Moon of my delight that knows no wane . . . all of thee and me, Brock. And then – and then turn down the empty glass!

The bartender watched her as she took a longer, deeper

175

pull at the Ramos fizz. It left a rim of foam above her upper lip. Like some kid, he thought, some starry-eyed kid who had no business to be there. Yet she puzzled him.

A young man slid on to the seat next to hers. He looked at her twice.

'Hi.'

'Hi,' said Lili from a distance. Her smile swept past him and stopped. A nine-inch TV stood on a shelf. 'That thing work?'

The bartender sighed. 'Yeah, unless the lady upstairs is running her dishwasher. Something you want to see?'

'Oh, anything.'

He snapped the picture on without the sound. The black-and-white screen filled with a drizzle of wavy lines, white dots, and perpendicular zigging. Through it ran shapes with eggs on their heads that suddenly catapulted into heaps.

'What are they doing?' asked Lili solemnly.

'Playing football. And the lady's upstairs getting her dishes washed.' He snapped it off. Nobody came to Sam's to stare at TV.

Her glass was empty. He grabbed a rag and wiped under it.

'I'd like another, please.'

'Another Ramos?' He looked at her hard.

'No. Not a Ramos. I'm through with Ramos. I'd like a Sazerac.'

'Not in my bar, you won't, doll.'

'If you can't make it, I know how. In fact my father-in-law – he was going to be but isn't, thank goodness – said I made a better Sazerac than the Boston Club. And that's saying a lot in New Orleans. So if you've got the absinthe . . . though I guess they don't use that any more. Anyhow, at the Comus ball, which I would not go to because I thought it was all silly by that time, they said the King of Comus had to supply the absinthe, although I guess that was a long time ago. But I can make you a Sazerac . . . and you'll like it. Everybody does.' She started to slide from the stool.

The young man took her elbow.

'Thank you very much.' She gave him a ravishing smile and regained her seat. 'Do you like rackasacs?'

'What's your name?'

'Elizabeth Beaulaire Roundtree, called Lilith.'

'Come again?'

'It doesn't matter, does it? What's yours?'

'Fred Bunce. I'm in computers.'

'Oh. I see. Yes, I do see. But computer me no computers, Freddie. For lo, the bird is on the wing. Where's my next Ramos, please?'

'I haven't made it,' growled the bartender. 'And I'm not going to.' His usual problem. Nice girls who don't know what they're ordering. 'Drink this and you'll feel better.'

'Thank you.' Lili's eyes melted him. 'Thank you very much. That's very nice. You know something?' She leaned across the bar. 'I'd like to feel better. I really would. I feel sorry for everybody tonight. Everybody in the whole wide world.'

Her voice trailed. She stared beyond him into the mirror behind the bottles. The images focused, blurred, focused again. She glanced away and came back to it. She felt her heart thud sickeningly against her ribs. A voice, female, shrilled from somewhere . . . 'You *are* Brock Turner . . .?'

Other voices. 'I heard your broadcast from Saigon, Mr Turner' . . . 'Gee, Brock, you tell it like it is' . . . 'Can I have your autograph, Mr . . .'

Lili turned slowly. And looked into his face.

'Brock . . .' But no sound came.

She felt her arm gripped, pulled from the stool and past dozens of faces.

'Come on. You're getting out of here.'

It was oddly not Brock's voice. Not the way she remembered. But there was nothing left inside Lili for speech. Or for tears. He was here.

'You don't have to pull me,' she said with dignity. 'I can walk.'

Once she was on the street a rush of cold air cleared her head. He released her arm and hailed a cab.

'Where are you living?'

She gave the address. In the seat beside her he neither looked at her nor touched her. The glance she slid at him showed a rigid line of jaw, a stiff set of mouth. She let two traffic lights pass.

'But I don't want to go there! I mean back to my room!'

Then, for the first time, he seemed to see her. His face was thinner than she remembered, his eyes brooding with some kind of inner pain. But through his anger she saw all that she longed to see, a caring so deep that it seemed to hurt her even as it enfolded her.

'What the hell were you doing in a place like that?'

He rapped on the glass partition. Huskily, he gave the taxi driver another address.

It was part of the night's magic that Lili would never again see in the same way the flagstone walk leading to the house, the dark panelled door, the elegance of the coach lantern above it, and the dim ground-floor corridor through which Brock led her. A door opened to a large square room, in darkness except for the silvery wavering light on walls and ceiling, reflected from the river. Through tall windows Lili could see the incredible spangled arch of a huge bridge, soaring almost above her into the night.

In the centre of the room stood a kingsize bed, a tufted bench at its foot.

She stood at the window, numb and small within the overpowering unreality of it. She heard him close the door, cross the bare, polished floor. He took her coat from her shoulders. The room was sweetly warm. Slowly, wordlessly, he swung her to him. He held her face in his hands, searching it silently, as if a word spoken would shatter the binding promise. Slowly he opened her dress and slid it to the floor. She stood motionless as the river's tide seemed to slide across her. Her eyes met his and filled with tears. With the sigh of a child at last safe she lifted her lips and her breasts to him.

Long after the city had quieted, the rippling silver played through the room, illuminating the triumph of their love. Sleep was no part of this unearthly night. They sought each other again and again, as if time would run out before their hands, their lips, their bodies, healed the anguish of separation.

When the river-white dawn at last pressed at the window, Lili slept. She awoke to the dazzle of the morning sun and the completeness of this, her new being.

She was alone. On the tufted bench a note was pinned, torn from a pocket notebook. It was brief. 'Good morning, darling. Be here when I get back.'

Beside it lay a key.

Her new life had begun. Unsolved. Unknown.

CHAPTER FIFTEEN

Mortimer Russell glanced at his solid-crystal desk clock as the office door burst open.

'Ten minutes late,' he observed shortly.

Brock gave an easy laugh. 'Why don't you give up, Mort? Save it for those poor slavies who haven't the clout to talk back. When they do, you'll be out of a job.' He perched on the edge of Mort's cleared, polished desk and swung a leg. 'You ought to buy me a lunch except that I'm busy.'

'I'll buy you a dinner.'

'I'm busier still. What's the problem?'

Mort left his cushioned executive chair and sat down on the divan.

'Take the weight off your feet, Brock. I've got a few things to talk about.' He waited for his maverick newsman to sink into the other end of the sofa. 'I suppose you know that was one helluva story you filed from Saigon.'

Brock nodded. He could be uncertain about his life, but not about his work. He was good because he had worked to make himself good. He could always get the story because he didn't give much of a damn what happened to him. And because he found that when he was honest with people they trusted him. His one job now was to get her to trust him too. The memory of the night stirred within him.

'Glad to see you smiling, Brock.'

'Nice day, sir. One of your better ones. What's on your mind?'

It was a different Brock. Mortimer Russell was puzzled. Some of the strain had gone from the strong features. Yet Mort sensed a distance. And a restraint. He could match it. You didn't handle Brock Turner by asking questions.

'A great job,' he repeated. 'You've been back now how long?'

'Three days.' Three dragging days – until last night when he had walked past Sam's singles' bar and looked in. Christ almighty. A singles' bar. And some guy who looked like a chipmunk beside her. She hadn't explained that yet. He couldn't bear to think of any man –

'We want you to go back, Brock.'

'What?' He had missed something.

'Saigon. That's where the action is.'

Brock abruptly snapped back to the present. 'Sure, and where it's going to be for a long time until somebody turns off the madness. The whole place is rotting, like termites. Lean on anything and you fall through. The CIA is running all over the place with fingerprint powder in one hand and ground-to-air missiles in the other. The politicos are talking about acceptable casualties. And nobody from a first lieutenant to a brigadier general knows what a jungle is. It's flypaper land. Get in it and you're stuck.'

'I assume that's a personal opinion?'

'Yep. The personal opinion of every reporter out there. Only they don't want to hear it back home. They might learn something.'

'Okay, okay.' It was not what the vice-president wanted either. Objective reporting was what he wanted from Brock, what the board of directors wanted from Mortimer Russell, and what Washington wanted from them all. But Brock's strength was that he would tell it the way he saw it. 'So how soon can you leave?'

'For where?'

'What's the matter with you, Brock? Haven't you heard me?'

Brock's thoughts ran truant up a slant of sunlight to the deceptive blueness of the late autumn sky. 'No.'

'Saigon. How soon can you get ready to go back?'

'You're kidding.'

'I asked you a question.'

'Then make it a year. Minimum. Maybe five. I covered everything fit to cover out there. The place is jumping with newsmen shooting each other down. You get more footage per day from that sink than three networks could use. Besides, I've turned up something else.'

Mortimer Russell's eyes hardened.

'The old hang-up, eh? Brock, you can turn up the Great Wall of China if you want to. On your time off. But I've given you all the leeway I'm going to, for a personal vendetta.'

'Okay, if that's the way it looks to you. But I have one more week coming to me before I start anywhere. I'll be out of town.' *If she'll go with me*, he thought. 'I'll give you my answer when I get back.'

'On Saigon?'

'On a lot of things, Mort. I like my work. I like this job. The network's been good to me. But for the first time in my life something else comes first.'

'Brother Sunshine?'

'Him too. Don't worry. I'll call in. If you need me, I'll listen.' He grinned. 'Just don't send dirty wires to my mother.'

Mortimer Russell remained seated on the divan. He stretched his short legs, clasped his hands behind his head.

Brock had changed. Mort knew the explosiveness bottled up in that racing mind. The involvement, the passion for honesty, the quick temper, the quicker resentment. Hell to live with. But it was what made Brock Turner great.

Let him take one week. Two. Mort smiled to himself. Brock would be back, begging for the first assignment to take him on the road again.

For another moment Mortimer Russell gave himself up to the luxury of longing. To be thirty again. To be alive. He found himself wishing not for the first time that Brock would find a woman. A woman to steady him. And to steer him to that destiny that time holds for all men. The dismal destiny of staying put.

Brock returned to the newsroom, found a desk, and took off his coat. He had nothing to do until five o'clock. He would not be returning to his six o'clock news slot for another ten days. But the staff seemed glad to have him around. With a difference, of course – the difference between being his own man and somebody else's. Or in the worn-thin, overworked banality of this business, a star. He was far from that, he knew. He could burn out as fast as he had come on.

Lili. He wished he had asked where she worked. He would call her now. And on the hour. Every hour. Anyway, she would be at the apartment when he got back. He felt sure of that. He had to feel sure. The 5.00 p.m. appointment would not take long. He opened his wallet and looked at the sheet of Bangkok rice paper he had folded there. Thin as tissue paper. He was glad he had not told Mortimer Russell any more than he had. Mort's executive hide was thickening. From here on Brock could do better what he had to do, alone.

He thought again of the scene in Bangkok. The hotel crowded to the doors in the deepening crisis. Everybody talking, nobody listening. The bar jammed as if the apocalypse were coming with room service. And the Thai boy there waiting in his room to ask if he wanted some silk shirts made. He always wanted shirts made. The shirtmaker not only had interesting sources of information but he liked Brock. The American never questioned the price even when he was charged double for a shirt when a little news went with it. Brock had gone at once to the shirtmaker and found the place shuttered, blinds down. But the door was opened at once. The little man was all in white. His face was as long as a noodle and the room reeked of incense. Somebody was dead.

The shirtmaker thrust a two-day-old English-language newspaper into his hand. A bus accident north of Bangkok. The gas tank had exploded. Four escaped. Eleven injured. Three dead, burned beyond recognition. The shirtmaker nodded towards a newspaper picture, framed in flowers and white ribbons. It had taken Brock not more than three seconds to recognize the deceased, although the round head was covered in a straw hat, and the thin mouth was smiling. It must have been taken long ago.

'Peace to Buddha.' The little man held his hands, palms together, to his forehead.

Brock knew his grief was not for the late Reverend Sun Chang. But for the rows of blue cotton coolie coats newly made and piled in boxes to be shipped to Hong Kong, where they would be padded, lined, and given to the aliens the reverend helped, without benefit of immigration authorities, into the United States. When the aliens arrived at whatever port they had managed to slip through, the reverend was there to spirit them into faceless anonymity. And to take back the coats. The opium hidden in the padding was always first grade.

It was a nearly flawless system without visible trail. Brock could understand the shirtmaker's grief. Still, the little man should have known that circumstances being what they were in South Asia it could not last much longer. Brother Sunshine would know when a good thing was up.

Brock nodded his head solemnly.

'Three shirts. I will pay double. Have them at my hotel Thursday.'

Now, idling in the newsroom, Brock folded back into his wallet the thin paper that had come with the shirts and glanced at the clock impatiently. His five o'clock appointment would answer his one question. Then freedom. His own life with Lili. At least for a week.

At four-forty-five he called the river-edge apartment. He imagined her coming in early, waiting for him. There was no answer. Promptly at five he entered the downtown office of Mr Franklin Mee, certified public accountant and collector of rare jade.

Lili unlocked the door of the apartment and pushed her way into the almost dark corridor. She shifted her bundles and moved towards a grey square of light. If she had not forgotten to close the door to the room at the end, she would be in Stygian darkness now. What a way to live! The kitchen a mere closet. A half icebox containing exactly one stale English muffin, a tin of smoked clams, three bottles of beer, and two chocolate covered Popsicles on ice. And all that furniture, except the oversize bed, built into the walls.

But when she looked at the river, the room became silvered with beauty and remembrance.

She found the lamp switch and the curtain pull. She drew the curtains, and the room became cosy. She promptly pulled them open. She sensed that for this impetuous, casual man who now held the very fabric of her life in his hands, cosiness could be a danger signal, the hint of imprisonment. As for her, she had fled the safe life of Elizabeth. As the first Lilith fled that same treacherous web of Eden.

She put away her grocery purchases in the miniature kitchen. Then she turned out the single lamp and threw herself on the bed's midnight-blue cover. All day she'd been carried along on imagery until she had begun to make mistakes. To a few curious looks she smiled absently and left. She had planned in detail their first dinner, in candlelight. The wine she would leave to him. She imagined him rushing out, hoping to find a store still open. Dinner would be late. At the thought she grew warm. First they would share again the wonder of their love on this the beginning of their new private world.

She must have fallen into a light sleep, suddenly awakening, aware the room had grown cold. She switched on the lamp above the bed and saw that it was ten minutes past eight.

He had said he wanted her here when he came home. But he had set no time. She had only assumed . . . she shivered. In the empty strangeness of the apartment, her new being evaporated, she was Elizabeth Roundtree. Had she forgotten? She jumped from the bed, smoothed it and went into the kitchen. Her supply of groceries looked pretentious and absurd. The artichokes, thin slices of veal, watercress, whole cream, eggs, chocolate, huge oranges, and coffee, fresh ground. Like Christmas ornaments she remembered packing into little boxes, garish and out of place, from a tree grown suddenly gaunt. The river flowing silently outside told her full night had come. She had waited too long. She had assumed too much. She had forgotten that he was not and could never be hers in any real sense. If he was now free at last, he would have told her. At once. He had said nothing. He had not even asked about her own life, her work. He had been angry beyond reason at finding her in Sam's singles' bar. But what did that mean except that he was a man who was used to having his own way?

Tears so ready stung her pride. But Lili never let her doubts flutter long. She found it easier to act. She would give him ten minutes more. No, fifteen. No, she would not. She walked to the window and looked up at the soaring bridge suspended like a necklace of pale green lights over her head. Exactly like last night, it had the fragility of a dream.

She left Brock's key on the bed and closed the door softly behind her. She was not sure where she was but once on the street she would start walking, always away from the river.

Mr Franklin Mee, an immaculate stick of a man behind rimless spectacles, waved his visitor to a chair. He had kept Mr Turner waiting forty-five minutes and that should put things on a better bargaining basis. Mr Mee's downtown office had none of the antiseptic and faceless efficiency of uptown. There he was: Franklin Mee, C.P.A., twenty-eighth floor, Chrysler Building. But here his office bore no legend. It was a quiet room, a serene room. The room in which Brock Turner sat waiting bore no legend on the door. A polished refectory table, three straight-backed chairs, and a single glass cabinet holding one very small jade vase completed the furnishings. They added up to a serenity as timeless as it was surprising behind the building's façade on congested Mott Street, the pulse of New York's all-knowing, all-concealing Chinatown.

Brock waited. The game to be played was familiar, and as ancient as greed. Mr Mee's American face, American clothes, and American ease in no way changed the rules.

'Well, Mr Turner. How have you been?'

'No complaints.'

Silence drifted like dust.

'I regret keeping you waiting.'

Brock waved an indifferent hand. He thought of Lili and cursed himself for not anticipating this staging. It had happened before when Franklin Mee was most curious.

'I listened to your broadcasts from South Asia, Mr Turner. Most interesting. I envy you your colourful life. Even though it does not always lead you to the truth.'

'Does anything?'

'Ah. Like me, you have become a true non-believer. Except in what is real and actual. Like jade. And refreshment at the end of the day.' He clapped his hands abruptly and a houseboy entered with a tray on which he carried a fat porcelain teapot and two shell-thin cups.

Brock sipped and waited. He did not dare glance at his wristwatch. Mr Mee would be waiting for that. At last, with the tray gone, Mr Mee leaned forward.

'It is always pleasant dealing with you, Mr Turner. You are one American who understands the value of silence. Well, does this amiable visit have a purpose?'

He knew damn well it did. But Brock took his time.

'I happened to pick up a bit of jade in Hong Kong. I don't know if it has any value.'

'I'd be delighted to look at it for you.' He stretched his hand eagerly for the envelope Brock took from his inside pocket. He opened it quickly and let two small green chips slide on to the table. Not quite an inch long, they were two halves of a scarab, the back and underbelly. Fitted together they made the whole beetle.

'Excellent colour. The true emerald-green of jadeite, the most valuable of all jade.'

Mr Mee held the two pieces in his hand, stroking them with a dry forefinger. 'Jade is the most interesting substance in the world, Mr Turner. It is the only stone that bears the essence of life. Its English name comes from the Spanish word *ijada*, which means "loin". The Spaniards found it in Mexico and Peru, though of course it is the Orientals who understand it best and carve it with the most skill. When it is powdered and mixed with water, it is a powerful remedy for all kinds of human disorders. It gives

186

strength to the bones, it prevents fatigue, and it prolongs life. Taken before death, it prevents decomposition.'

The hard narrow chair had begun to cramp his legs, but Brock sat as stiffly as his host. They were coming to the heart of the matter. Mr Mee pushed the jade bits across the table to Brock, who made no move to take them.

'Let me show you something.' Mr Mee rose and went to the glass cabinet, unlocked it with a key from his pocket, and took out the five-inch-high jade vase. The surface was carved into a labyrinth of tiny entwined serpents, yet so thin that it was nearly transparent. 'A thousand years old, Mr Turner. It once contained the birthing ointment for an empress. Listen.' He struck the rim with a fingernail, and a single exquisite note floated pure as a bubble. 'In some parts of the world jade is called the colic stone. But the finest is called the sounding stone. Life and music. What more could any substance offer man?'

He returned the vase to the cabinet and resumed his chair. The two pieces of jade lay like barter on the table.

'The Chinese poet T'ang Jung Tso said it for all time, Mr Turner. The magic powers of heaven and earth are ever combined to form perfect results; so the pure essences of hill and water become solidified into precious jade.' He smiled for the first time. 'What is it you want from me, Mr Turner?'

Brock drew out the tissue-like piece of paper that had come with his Bangkok shirts. He spread it with the black brush characters upmost on the table. 'What does this mean?'

'It means *snake*. Symbol of renewal.'

'Slips out of one skin and grows another.'

It was not a question. It was a statement. Nor was Brock surprised. *Snake* was a word David had whispered again and again in the fading delirium of his life.

Mr Mee's eyes were on the two pieces of jade. Finally he picked them up and turned them over. 'It is extraordinary that you should find these pieces, Mr Turner. They go back to the Seventh Dynasty. They are very rare. Almost unobtainable. Occasionally one might pick them up. Stolen from some collection. You know, of course, what they are.'

'I was told they are life stones. Whatever that means.'

Mr Mee looked into the distance. 'Life stones are small pieces of jade that were once placed on the tongue of a dead man before burial. They guaranteed resurrection. These stones – the divided scarab might have been carried in the mouth of a dead ruler.'

He set the jade before him. Brock stirred impatiently. The game had gone on long enough.

'Lucky our friend had no need of them.'

'What are you asking me, Mr Turner?'

'You know what I'm asking you. You profited by the business – '

'That would be difficult to prove.'

'Everything is difficult to prove. I'm not looking for proof. Just one piece of information. If the Reverend Sun Chang has slipped his skin as such, what is he now? And where?'

The bits of emerald-green jade seemed to hold all the light on the table. Brock watched as obsession battled caution behind the rimless glasses of his host. Finally Mr Mee took a pad from the table drawer and printed one word on it.

'Where?' Brock repeated.

Mr Mee shrugged.

Brock had learned all he could. He rose and with a hint of a bow left the office. He did not see Mr Mee suddenly lean forward and snatch the two pieces of jade from the table. The small shielded eyes lit for an instant as with a curious ecstasy as Mr Mee lifted the two tiny pieces to his mouth and slid his tongue beneath them.

In the street below, awash with humanity, Brock could find neither telephone nor taxi-cab. He settled for a five-block walk and the subway. In its rattling whiteness he glanced once more at the slip of paper. It bore one stark word. NEVAH. The wry humour of it struck Brock even as understanding cut with an edge like broken glass. It was the last word David had uttered, incomprehensible until this moment. It turned his long search into something subtle, personal, and silenced. Brother Sunshine had slipped from him, and this was his final taunt.

NEVAH. It was not difficult for a man long used to printing-type to read the word in reverse. HAVEN.

Mr Franklin Mee, in the solitude of his quiet rear room, expected no more visitors this night. He had locked both front and rear doors and now, in a loose black robe, he gave himself to pleasure. Among the carvings of jade on the table before him lay a contoured shape of pure white jade, not quite as large as his hand. His eyes closed, Mr Mee's fingers stroked the smooth convolutions, yielding to delicate sensations at once cool and erotic.

He did not hear the rear door being quietly unlocked. Nor was he aware of a tall, angular figure entering noiselessly. In fact so lost was Mr Mee in the pounding fantasies in his brain that the man might have stood waiting had he not chosen to speak.

'Rather debilitating, Mee.'

Mr Mee's eyes flew open. In one gesture he reached for his rimless spectacles and jumped to his feet.

'Sun Chang!'

'Colonel Chadwick, as you well know. Sit down.'

The colonel's connoisseur's eye swept the table. Three of the jade pieces he knew well, the deep-green unguent vase, the seamless chain of links cut from a single piece of striped jade, and the voluptuous white carving. The fourth, a tiny emerald-green scarab in two parts, held his attention longest.

Then he spoke softly. 'The winds of the Northern Hemisphere blow harmony from east to west. Air currents from west to east, on the other hand, bring discord. You are aware of that, of course, Mee.'

Mr Mee sat stiffly in his chair, perspiration starting on his forehead.

'You know, too, that a man's skin is renewed every seven years. And with his skin, his body. But not his brain. His mind grows wisdom like the rings of a tree. For his years and his wisdom he is reverenced. But the man who cannot change his skin and increase his wisdom . . .'

The colonel had elected not to sit down. Rather he

drifted back and forth as if outside the cage of a small animal whose eyes never left him.

'There is a plant, Mee. Very green, very prevalent. It grows almost everywhere in the world. It is poisonous. It can choke a man. No way has been found to stamp it out. It has long underground runners that surface far from the mother plant. It bears the same leaf.' A widening of the thin lips might have been a smile; otherwise the colonel's face was expressionless. 'The plant is called betrayal.' He paused. 'You are acquainted with it?'

'No, no! I swear . . . Sun . . . Colonel . . .'

'Stop drooling, man, and wipe the sweat from your face. The plant recently surfaced in the shack of a very excellent shirtmaker in Bangkok. A pity. His workmanship was of the best. His death was, I am sure, a loss to Americans with expensive tastes.'

The colonel stopped pacing. He leaned across the table. 'Your half-brother, Mee. Did it grieve you?'

Mr Mee stiffened. He was a believer in destiny. A man's years were numbered on the Wheel of Heaven. But now when life had become sweet, when the long servitude to Sun Chang was over, it came hard . . .

'I did not know of my half-brother's death.'

'You lie!'

The colonel swept the green scarab halves into his hand. 'Where did these come from?'

'They were given to me.'

'By whom?'

'By a friend who knew my interest in . . . jade.'

The colonel indulged in a genuine smile. He saw no reason to further terrify his victim. What he had to do was as necessary as it was inevitable. Those who live by the sword die by the sword. Not true, as anyone knew who ever watched a general die in a comfortable bed. But those who live by treachery die of the same venom. Sooner or later. Mee was one of the lucky ones. His turn had come quite late. And might not have come at all had not the American made his visit.

'I will not ask the price you paid for these stones. I already know. As I know the shirtmaker's price for his betrayal. He was stupid. The few dollars could scarcely have mattered that much. But you were the clever one. I had great hopes for you when I put you on that stinking cargo ship long ago. You, I believed, had the gift of survival. And survival was valuable to me. I could not then guess your ambitions, or your corruptions.'

The colonel glanced again at the table, then fixed his eyes on Mr Mee's face. He moved imperceptibly closer to the chair.

'You knew what these jade stones meant. These life stones. They were a warning. It must have cost your half-brother all he possessed to send them. Your recent caller, Mr Henley Brocklebank Turner, proved a convenience as well as a source of revenue. He also proved to be a fool. Brock Turner has yet to be taught what you are now learning. The Reverend Sun Chang is gone for ever. He is to be forgotten. But he is not to be betrayed!'

The colonel's long arms shot forward. His large hands closed around Mr Mee's throat. A gasp slid into a small squeak as the powerful fingers found and applied pressure to the vital double pulse below the jaw.

Mr Mee slumped forward, his head on the table among his jade playthings. In a few seconds his heart stopped.

Then Colonel Chadwick performed his last act as the Reverend Sun Chang. He thrust his hand into his pocket and felt the reassuring halves of the tiny dark-green scarab. He straightened up and, as soundlessly as he had entered, left the room.

In the limousine to the airport Chadwick leaned back, the flicker of a smile on the narrow hawk-face. It was done. The last of his betrayers was silenced, those distant figments of himself, Brother Sunshine, the Reverend Sun Chang, banished like the smoke phantoms he had peddled. As for his nemesis, Turner, let him go on blundering like a hound on a cold scent. Colonel Chadwick emerged now in full light, gentleman, patron of the arts, benefactor to humanity.

The smile faded. In the passing anonymity of headlights and traffic, a subtle change possessed him. He stood now at the threshold of the secret goal he had so long nurtured.

Not the ugly traffic of dark alleys, filthy lofts, bewildered human flotsam that had brought him his wealth. But a higher goal, known to a few, accomplished by ever fewer.

He shivered with almost sexual excitement, as he remembered those long-ago news films of the crowds, seas of faces raptly upturned, arms thrust forward in mindless loyalty, mouths open in a single shout to a small man on a high podium who would do with them whatever he wished. Their leader. Their master.

That was the obsession of Colonel Chadwick. To stand on a stage of his own creation, look down on creatures of his own choosing and know that they were his, bound to him by ties of black mystery and erotic promise that had, since time, lured and enchained the human spirit.

As the airliner carried him, first-class, into the night and the western hills that encircled his retreat, Chadwick yielded to a rich sense of well-being. No longer the quarry, but the hunter. No longer hireling, but master. His mind went further. Godhead.

But because no man can change the texture of his soul, Colonel Chadwick added three words to his contemplation.

At a profit.

It was ten minutes to nine when Brock unlocked the door to the apartment. A bone-chilling darkness met him. He turned on the lamp. A key glittered in the centre of the bed. The apartment was empty. For an instant the reality numbed him. He had been so sure, so full of apology, so buoyed by anticipation.

He tried to grapple with the meaning of her absence. Why didn't she wait? *Why shouldn't she?* Last night had been the first night of their new life. If her words, her lips, had not meant that, if her body – How little he knew of her. An image, a face, carried in his mind – of his own making? For the moment he could not even remember where she lived. He found himself opening doors, looking for her as if she might be hiding. It came to him abruptly. Castleton House. He picked up the phone.

He felt a quickening of anger. Her room phone was busy.

You don't know her, boy. You know only what you want to know. And you've had that before.

He waited three minutes and called back. A female voice was sorry but there was no answer from Miss Roundtree's room.

Brock slammed out of the apartment. He started to walk. He needed a drink. He thought of his regular saloon. Then his subconscious reminded him that would take him past Sam's singles' bar. But she would not be there, not if she had a date. A cab slowed and he hailed it. The address came to him automatically.

Willard Roundtree sat in the stiff sterility of Castleton House and surveyed Lili thoughtfully. Though she had obviously not expected him, she sat polite and contained. She looked thinner, he thought, if that were possible. Her eyes looked larger. If that were possible. But where was that brave show of independence, like a young-rebel call with manners? Something less obvious, less outgiving, had replaced it, something that eluded him.

'I called you last evening, my dear. You were out, as I should have expected of any attractive young woman. But I certainly couldn't go back to Thatcher without some news of you. They all ask.'

She wondered who 'they' were.

'In fact, they consider it quite reprehensible that I haven't managed to fetch you back with me yet.' His eyes twinkled. If Lili had not been so deeply involved in her own turbulent thoughts, she would have seen their sharpness. She did not yet know how far Willard Roundtree could see into her. But she liked him and she was painfully aware of her distraction.

'You're very kind.' Her smile was faint. 'How is your Indian?'

Willard was disconcerted. This girl with her quick surface glintings was like spring water. She slid through your hands.

'Charlie Redwing? My dear girl, he is not my Indian. Or any other man's. You'll know that when you meet him. He

193

manages my farm only because he does it better than I do and feels sorry for me.'

In spite of herself Lili laughed. If life had not suddenly wrenched her into a new being, she would have liked to claim this man as a relative.

'I meant the Indian who is in prison, whose deer was shot.'

Good girl, he thought. She has heart. 'He got twenty-five years. We're appealing, of course. Takes time. Wheels of justice . . .' He glanced into the lobby and abruptly stood up. 'I just want you to know, my dear, that if you will come to Thatcher for Thanksgiving, everyone in the family will be delighted. It's always held at the farm. I do the cooking. And the praying.' He glanced again at the lobby. 'I'm better at the first than the second,' he finished quickly.

A broad-shouldered, roughly handsome man was filling the doorway, his eyes on Lili. As long as he lived, Willard told himself, he would not forget the sudden radiance in her face.

'Excuse me, sir.' The man seemed to thrust himself between them. 'Good evening, Lili.'

Cold, Willard thought. *Whoever he is. Maybe a little too cold.* But he saw that the tone brought Lili to herself. Her eyes could flash as quickly as they could melt.

'Why . . . good evening, Brock.' Willard must have imagined the tremor, because her head was high. 'Willard, this is Brock Turner. A – a friend of mine.' A flush came and went. 'Brock, this is Willard Roundtree, my . . . cousin . . . my second cousin – Willard, what are you, anyway?'

'Let's say another member of your clan. Glad to meet you, Mr Turner.' Willard thrust out a firm hand to have it taken and dropped. He was glad to note the handshake was strong if reluctant.

'Brock's a news reporter on TV. He's very famous. You must have seen him.' Lili had found an uneasy footing.

'No reason you should, Mr Roundtree.'

Willard knew now where he had seen that face. But he saw no reason to admit it. He had yet to make up his mind about Brock Turner. 'I'm afraid the advantage is yours, Mr Turner. I live on a very old farm up in Thatcher,

Connecticut, sir, where all the Roundtrees hail from. At least the ones who haven't amounted to much. We're in the habit of relying on newspapers. Guess that's the reason.'

'Brock, don't believe a word of it. Willard is a brilliant lawyer.'

Willard saw Brock's eyes sharpen with something like interest and something even more like irritation. He knew he was now in the way but he had a few more things to learn.

'I don't get to New York very often, Mr Turner, but when I do, I have to check up on Elizabeth here. Ever since she started calling herself Lilith. Can't ever tell, when a girl takes on that way. Right now I'm trying to persuade Elizabeth to come to us for Thanksgiving. Do you know Thatcher, Mr Turner?'

'Can't say I do.' Brock heard his own abruptness. The resentment stored against Lili was transferring itself to this old man who hadn't the sense to leave. Yet Brock knew that Willard Roundtree was measuring him with a sharpness few men had dared.

'Well, Thatcher is an experience, Mr Turner. We don't make much news but we get along. And have for nearly three centuries. Come and see us some day. Eliz – uh – Lilith, my dear' – Willard turned a benign and searching look on her – 'if you'll come at Thanksgiving, I'll meet you in Hartford. Thatcher is better arrived at by degrees. Glad to have met you, Mr Turner. Good-night, my dear.' He gave a warm peck to her cheek, his eye on Brock. 'Good-night, sir.'

Never, Willard told himself as he walked into the city's alien night, had he sensed such a binding current of human emotion between two young people, as embattled as they were aware. This was a new and unexpected Lili. Not vulnerable. Willard had had enough of vulnerable women. This was Henrietta's child, as eager to live as she had once been lonely. He wondered if Brock Turner knew what he had found.

'So that's why you walked out!' Brock barely waited for Willard's departure.

'I walked out, as you put it' – Lili found her own unspeakable relief in anger – 'because I'd waited long enough. When you left the key, you might have told me when you were coming back!'

'And you might have left a note!'

'I didn't know you would ever come back.'

'Didn't you trust me?' Brock knew he was talking too much. Beneath his frustration his mind was running like a mouse in a maze for a way to break the circuit of anger and take her in his arms.

'Trust you! Do you realize I've only been with you two days out of my whole life and you – you –'

'I come looking for you and find you with another man.'

'A cousin!'

'The first time I ever saw you in that old spook of a house in New Orleans there was another man. You never explained that. And then the singles' bar.'

'Brock, if you think . . .!' They were quarrelling in earnest. Another few words and the damage would be done. Lili caught herself. Tears would come if Brock looked at her like that. Tears she did not want.

'You might at least thank me for the food I brought.'

She was so slight, so proud. Brock felt his need of her twist like pain in his chest.

'I will thank you. When it's cooked.'

'Even raw it's a lot better than a tin of clams and two Popsicles!'

'By the way, where are the Popsicles?'

'I . . .' Defiance was melting. 'I ate them.'

The chatelaine at the lobby desk looked up to see the broad-shouldered man sweep young Miss Roundtree into his arms and kiss her. The woman tried to look away. She would not stare, but late that night and other nights, she would remember.

'Brock!' Lili gasped and slid from him. 'House rules! I'll send you a booklet.'

'Don't bother. I make house rules.' He grinned at her. 'But not here.'

They had hurt each other. He must not let that happen again. She was young. He was wiser. He loved her beyond anything he could understand, yet beneath the crossflow of

196

his emotions lodged one persistently disturbing thought. Other men would want her.

'You can be quite a hellcat, can't you? Come on, let's get out of here.'

They went to a side-street bar and ate sirloin steaks, he quickly, she thoughtfully, aware of all that had not been said.

'Brock, what are we going to do with all that food at the apartment?'

'Do you care?'

'It was very expensive.'

'Rick will be delighted.'

'Who's Rick?'

'The guy who owns the place. He lets me use it when he's away. I gave up my own apartment a while ago.' He did not add it was at the depth of his hopelessness about her. 'Rick's an inventor. He doesn't invent very often but he likes to eat. Why the hell are we talking about Rick? Maybe it's time to talk about us.'

It was long past the time, just maybe. But there must be no more unnecessary words.

'Lili, if there's one thing we should both have learned in the last twenty-four hours, it's that this is for keeps. Right?'

She nodded, almost imperceptibly. She could not bear to spoil the closeness.

'So we begin there.' His hand covered hers on the table. He did not try to keep the pain from his voice. 'Lili, I am married. I can do nothing about it.'

'She loves you.'

It was not a question. It startled him. It had been a long time since he had thought about Marcia in such terms.

'No.' The single syllable was firm. Perhaps too firm. Too much protest was evasion. But whatever Marcia had wanted from him she no longer wanted. That was enough. 'No,' he repeated. 'It wasn't like that.' If the direct blue eyes, fixed on him so unblinkingly, held a question, he hurried past it. 'She's not well, Lili. She isn't able to go through a divorce.'

Lili drew her hand and herself a little from him.

'My darling, you don't understand. There's nothing I

want to keep from you. It's a long, unhappy story. She chose to go her own way. If I could help her now, if I could do her one bit of good, I would. But I can't. And I can't turn my life off.' He leaned across the table, caught both her hands tightly, his voice deepening. 'I love you, Lili. I want you with me. Every day, every night. Now. For ever. I can only offer you half a life. But everything I am and have is for you. I will swear before God to love and cherish you as long as I live. But I cannot swear it before the laws of man. Do you understand . . . a little?'

It was as if the table, the room, the world, hung suspended; she saw the road ahead. A life luminous with love. Or for ever without him. She met his eyes once more. She could only nod.

Their lovemaking that second night held a new intensity, beyond their first frantic need of discovery. Their bodies melded with the serene confidence of commitment. When at last Brock fell asleep, Lili lay awake beside him, tracing this new destiny in the spangled bridge arching into the darkness beyond the window.

She would love this man always. She had seen his jealousy. She knew his passion. She would never know all she wanted to know about him. Perhaps that was the price paid for the life that was now beginning for her: the dismissal of easy doubt, a tightrope of determined trust. He stirred beside her.

'Still awake, my darling?'

'A little.'

He took her in his arms. A fantasy of spangles played across the ceiling as they reached towards each other.

PART THREE

MASKS

CHAPTER SIXTEEN

It had not been at all what Lilith had foreseen. As she watched the fog thicken from the window of the smart little apartment on Wilton Place in London, she could look back to those first months with Brock so long ago and almost laugh at young Lili's uncertainties, her misgivings, her inadmissible guilts growing, when she permitted them, in the dank rigidity of her upbringing.

She was beyond all that now. Her constant triumph had been not letting Brock know what each new step had cost her. Renting their first apartment together in New York. The agent had cast only a glance at her, but that glance told her how he saw her, how everyone saw her. The man at the bank with whom Brock had opened an account for her, appreciative eyes sliding over her. The tradespeople, too easy with their emphasized 'Miss Roundtree'. When Brock came home and took her in his arms, it no longer mattered. Until it no longer mattered at all.

She had become used to, after the first shock, seeing her name in the news columns, even her picture, as Brock Turner's 'constant companion'. If at times she longed for the mystical security of the word *wife*, she found herself hardening at last against it.

As if all doors were closing on her former life, the magazine *Young* was predictably stillborn. Nobody seemed to mind much. On the last day Artie Shallcross served champagne. 'It's still a great idea. But nobody's going to get it off the ground on just flower power. You're okay, Lili. Though you had me fooled at first.' Before she left, he showed her with a last fling of pride the four new subscriptions that had come in that morning. 'Four thousand and we'd be home sort of free.' She stared at it.

'What's that?' She pointed to the third name.

'NEVAH?' He shrugged. 'Box number, San Francisco.

Means you send the magazine the subscription price and never hear from them again. One of those flaky youth groups. Grow like crabgrass out there. And only the boss makes money.' He sailed the list to the waste-basket, missed it, and let it slide to oblivion on the floor.

At the door he gave her a half-grin, both knowing and sad. 'Remember our motto, Lili. "Never trust anybody over thirty." Peace.'

She did not mention the card Colonel Chadwick had thrust on her. That was behind her too. Each new unfamiliar day held its own discovery.

Brock was unmoved by the demise of *Young*. Even caustic. 'Now go out and get a real job, Lil. Not hippy and hare-brained.'

'It wasn't – ' She caught herself. Brock, she knew now, was ten years her senior. She never thought of him that way. What difference could time make between them? But she saw that patience as well as discretion was needed. After thirty . . . 'What kind of job?'

'Anything you want to do. Sure, I make enough, more than enough for both of us. But I don't want to come home and hear about the price of lettuce.'

The implied criticism added another layer to the thickening around her sensibilities. If she had once thought making life good for the man you loved was destiny enough, she quickly made up for that error. To her surprise she found a job almost at once with a young group called The Best who conspired to sell chic to anybody who wanted it. It was not long before Lilith Roundtree became known for her low-key fine taste. Fashion magazines, retailers, decorators, the melee of hard-pressed novelty seekers, sought her out, not least because of her interesting and publicity-valuable life-style.

If at times during Brock's frequent absences Lilith questioned the shallow routine, the fragile structure of her life, she put the question away when he walked in the door. In the deep and constant passion of their nights she was able to forget. Or at least to ignore.

'Brock Turner and Lilith Roundtree . . . fascinating!' 'I'd say she's got it made!' 'I'd say the other way around!'

'Another picture, Mr Turner. Give us that smile, Lilith!'
'What eyes that woman has!'

Early in their life together a letter came from Thatcher. A sombre reminder of the reality that Lilith was determined to shed. She waited to open it until Brock came home. His quick jealousy could embrace any aspect of her old life.

'It's just an invitation, darling. The annhversary of Edythe and Martin Roundtree, whoever they are.'

'I think you should go.'

'You can't mean that! I don't even know them.'

'You don't have to. You're a Roundtree. You know the old man, Willard.'

'Brock, I'd be miserable. Suppose they ask questions?'

'Tell them the truth. Is there anything disgraceful in living with the man you love and who loves you?'

'They're an old family in a small New England town. Why, they'd look on me as a scarlet woman.'

Brock came to her, took her by the arms, and searched her face. 'Is that the way you look on yourself?'

She avoided his eyes. 'No, not here in New York. Of course not. I'm . . . used to it. Doesn't – doesn't everybody?' She tried for a laugh and failed.

He released her, crossed the room, and turned back.

'I think we'd better talk about a few things, right now, Lil. What you've just said means you can't honestly face up to your life with me. If that's so, it isn't much catch for either of us. If you'd be miserable up there in – what is it – Thatcher, then you can't be entirely comfortable here with me. If all this – if our wonderful life together means anything, you won't hide it from anybody.'

She was near tears. And he saw it. 'Lili, Lili, what century did you grow up in?'

'I don't know!' She brushed at her face defiantly. 'And it wasn't my fault anyhow. All I'll ever want is to go on living with you. Why should I have to go to Thatcher to prove it? You met Willard Roundtree. You disliked him on sight!'

'I'd dislike any man I found you enjoying. Actually I thought he was quite a guy. Not a man I want to lie to.'

In the end she went because it was the last hurdle. It must be taken.

In the perspective of time, that first visit to Thatcher was not at all what Lilith expected. It was to become instead a disturbing revelation with one unforgettable impression.

She repacked her single bag twice.

'Lil, what's the matter with you? Anything you wear will be good enough for that town.'

'I wish you were coming with me, Brock.'

'Do you?' He looked at her quizzically.

'That'd be worse, I guess.' She forced a laugh and dropped a kiss on his head as he sat watching her. He caught her in his arms.

'It's us against all of them. Don't you know that? Nobody up there can hurt you, unless you let them.' He kissed her. She drew his hand to her breast, then saw him glance at the bedroom clock. She slid from him quickly.

'Time for your plane?'

''Fraid so.' It had become increasingly like this but she would not say so. Nor would he. *When you're married,* thought Lilith, *you can fling out. When you're not, you have to be careful. So careful.*

'I'll be back in a week. Call the London office if you want anything.' He cupped her face with his hands. 'Oh, my darling, my darling ... it's a crazy life for us. Only you make it workable.' His kiss was so long and deep, she wondered why she ever doubted.

'Tell 'em about French knots, darling.'

'Get your shoes shined, my love.'

They always parted like this, little reminders of themselves, little hooks to their fragile closeness.

She took the train to Hartford because she wanted time. Time for the transition. Time to brace. She thought of herself as Elizabeth Roundtree of New Orleans coming to unbend some rather prim-faced, backward relatives, until she remembered that sage and gentlemanly sophisticate, Willard, and laughed at herself as he would. She saw herself as a woman of the world, charmingly tolerant of a town that had probably never even heard of Brock Turner and Lilith, his 'constant companion'. Play-acting, all of it. She could only be herself. And that was a quietly nervous, strikingly smart young woman in a short mink coat with a royal-blue wool suit that made her extraordinary eyes glow as Willard Roundtree came down the platform to greet her.

'So glad, Eliz –' He brushed her cheek. 'By the way, what is it? Elizabeth, Lili . . .?'

'Lil will do. Short for Lilith. That's me now. The liberated woman.' She said it lightly, but he recognized her need to be honest.

'Good girl.' It cleared the air.

He said almost nothing on the drive to Thatcher. He let her watch the country unfold, the long roll of the dark, leaf-bare hills, the masses of iron-grey clouds sent billowing across the sky by the lofty winter winds, the sudden rifts of blue reflected in a lake, then gone. In her city-spent life, Lilith had never seen such open and tumultuous sky.

'We should have snow, but this has been a curious winter. Cold and bare.'

They crossed a single two-way bridge that spanned a grey ice-choked river. From it issued an appalling rumbling and crackling, a demon-like thunder.

'Ice beginning to break up,' said Willard cheerfully. Lilith looked down and saw jagged grey slabs piled against the bridge's rusted stanchions. 'It'll hold, they say. Trust in God until the next budget time.'

On the other side of the bridge a white wooden sign with a scrolled top heralded Thatcher, 1741. Ahead, a slender white church spire thrust into the ominous sky, a finger of judgement.

Lilith, to her surprise, found her senses stirred by the wild emptiness of the land and that single thrust of defiance. Defiance she could understand. As Willard foresaw, the long drive had done its work. Her nervous uncertainty seemed gone, her eyes were large with anticipation, her face glowed. *She will do,* he thought. *She will do very well.*

In the years to come Lilith would remember little of that winter's day drive, the town drawn within itself against the cold hills, even the anniversary reception. What she did remember would torment her for ever with the crosscurrents of inevitability and guilt.

Willard made two turns off Main Street and stopped at a large rambling house of white clapboard, dark green shutters, and the grace note of a fanlight above the front door. 'The ancestral home,' he murmured with a sidelong glance, which she missed.

It was unlike any house she had known on St Charles Avenue, or which carefully groomed St Charles Avenue would tolerate. It spread without definition into a background of bare-branched maple trees creaking in the sharp wind. It was belted by a wide veranda. One side bore evidence of a cupola recently dismantled. Two peeling shutters complained bitterly against an upper window. The entire house needed paint.

Despite the cold, the front door stood wide. Against the light a thin man in a well-tailored navy blue suit extended his hand. His bow was courtly. 'Martin Roundtree. Welcome.' The woman beside him, with soft curling hair, soft smile, soft as the long peach chiffon she wore, bent forward to kiss her.

'Elizabeth, my dear! At last! Welcome to Thatcher. And to West Street!'

But the intelligence in the china-blue eyes told Lilith that Edythe Roundtree saw a good deal more than she revealed.

They were already dressed for their reception still two hours away. Behind them Lilith caught a blur of faces, curious, watchful. Too well-bred to stare? Not quite. Somebody led her up the handsome polished staircase to the room that was to be hers for the night. Pine and calico and a single four-poster bed.

So it was to be Elizabeth after all.

In the heated press of people Lilith was not left alone. There were Roundtrees, seemingly, everywhere. Long training had taught her to smile even when it became brittle; to talk the quick, bright nothings of a crowded room, the small graces that had so long amused Brock until she had won him to their importance, then disappeared.

206

She heard phrases like smoke rings beyond her. 'Charming' . . . 'the French side' . . . 'Henrietta' . . . a man's knowing laugh . . . a girl's stifled giggle . . . 'such a pity'.

She began to listen for the hall clock's chimes. She wished she had asked Willard to brief her on names, children, dates, but she had been too self-involved. She saw herself now in an air-spun cage marked STARING PERMITTED. It would all be over tomorrow. But Brock would not be there when she reached home, when she would need him most.

'So you're Lilith.' The voice was deep for such a young man. Robustly built, his eyes dark as his nearly black hair, and oddly shrewd, his expression sullen until he smiled. Then she was aware of a momentary but powerful sensuality. She could not guess his age.

'I'm Michael. Sorry not to have done the honours earlier. This must be pretty awful for you.'

'Not at all.' He was too young to condescend. 'I don't know many people, but that's always a challenge, isn't it?' She flashed a brighter smile that seemed to take in the room.

'I think you've got guts.'

'I should hope so. That's what puts teeth in the tiger and shell on the shrimp.' Nothings. Always keep it light. Lesson One. Then she saw uncertainty in his face. 'You're kind to come to speak to me. And I know who you are. Michael, the oldest. Right? Then John. He's the quiet one. And Lowell. She's sweet. I think she's in love. With that high school boy Duncan? And Claude. What is she? Ten, eleven? And a beauty already. Kim's the youngest, isn't she? The one with the white mice. You see, I've done my homework.'

'Look, Lilith – '

'How did you know that name?'

'I know a lot of things. I'd like to talk to you.'

'Lovely! Why not?'

'Not here.' His glance brought the walls close. 'Nobody can talk here. Uncle Willard says you're leaving tomorrow noon. Would you drive around Thatcher with me in the morning? I'll show you the whole town, the whole

Roundtree bit.' His laugh had the harsh edge. 'You may never come back. But you'll know.'

His glance slid to her dress where the blue-green silk swelled. But when it returned to her face, he was suddenly boyish. She did not like Michael Roundtree, she decided. But she could recognize the hint of young desperation. She had been there herself. Besides, being with Michael would save her awkward questions and, worse, awkward silences in this all-too-encircling family.

'Are you up by nine-thirty?'

'Of course.'

The wind had died. The morning sun beneath a lifting mass of purplish clouds silvered the rim of the hills and glittered off the granite monument that dominated Thatcher Cemetery.

Lilith breathed the cold, still air as if her blood, her pulses, had too long been deprived. 'Are all of them here?'

Michael, hatless as she was, leaned on his knee, his foot on the squat granite cornerstones. In lumberjack coat and boots he looked solid and compact, his neck short and strong, his hands hard.

'God, your eyes are blue, Lil.'

She drew her red coat close. 'I asked you, is this where all the Roundtrees are buried?'

'Where the elephants come to die?' He grinned. 'Oh, no. There are Roundtrees all over. Boston, St Louis. The richest one is out in San Francisco. Simon. Worth millions. That's where I want to go some day. Only the more respectable ones are here. That leaves you out, Lil.'

'I don't need that, Michael.'

'Don't get sore. I told you I thought you had guts.'

'I think my private life is my own business.'

'Who said anything about your private life?' Her surprise gave him an advantage. 'Look, Lilith. By the way, I like that name. Suits you. I know all about you. I make it my business, like I told you. I know you're . . . you live with that news guy Brock Turner. Okay. More power to you. Maybe a few other people around here know it. But our local sheet, the *Thatcher Standard*, doesn't carry the syndicated stuff, the dirt.'

'Let's either change the subject, Michael, or go home.'

'Wait a minute, will you? I'm trying to tell you something. That's not why they're giving you the once over. It's because – God, don't you know? Because you're the bastard branch of the family.'

'The *what*?' Another triumph for him. He was enjoying himself now. He no longer felt her junior.

'Sure. Henrietta and Isaac Roundtree had ten children on the record. Only nine of them were the old thunderer's. Amos, your father – '

'What about him?' The question was mere form, her mind was probing. If it were true, if she were not a Roundtree, she would be released for ever from this sharp-eyed tribunal that was Thatcher, even if her tentative sense of anchorage was gone. What difference did it make now? She had Brock . . .

Michael was still talking. 'That's why Amos never inherited. Not that it would make any difference. The year after old Isaac died at a ripe eighty-four, his whole bundle went down the drain. The big bust of nineteen-twenty-nine. Nobody knew he was into that. He got even with his wife. Didn't even put her name on the monument. Just Isaac Roundtree. And you know why? Because she isn't buried there. Nobody knew what happened. Or wouldn't say. But everybody talked. Said she was drowned in a basement flood. Some said she ran off with a travelling man. Isaac must have been rich. But nobody asked questions, not of old man Isaac. He was the town. I guess everybody believed in the end he murdered her. He died crawling up the wall to get the devil off his chest. Gave himself that epitaph.' He pointed to the lichen-deep words in the granite: ALL MEN SHALL CALL HIM RIGHTEOUS.

The sun had slid into the cloud mass. Lilith shivered. This faded past had nothing to do with her. She was anxious to return to Brock, to their private, closed world. She moved from him towards the path. He caught her arm.

'I've talked too much, haven't I? I wanted to impress

you. But that wasn't why I asked you to come out here.'

She shook gently free. 'Then why, Michael?'

'I asked you because you've made it! Don't you see? You broke free! You're yourself, Lilith! You've done what I want to do. I can't do it your way, maybe, but there's some way I can do it! You don't know what it is here. Everything is Roundtree! Old Roundtree! The library, the community house, the charities . . . God knows what. My father is a Roundtree of Roundtree and Roundtree, Main Street attorneys. I'm supposed to go into that. And all I can think about is getting out. Before they do to me what they've done to him, to all of them. Ossified them!' He drew a long breath. He was not talking to her, he was talking to the openness beyond, his face dark with rebellion.

'Did you see Sputnik, the first one up there in that sky? I was only a kid then but I was up on that ridge with a pair of binoculars I had swiped. I saw it! I saw that pinprick of light going around the world every hour and thirty-five minutes! Around the world, and I still hadn't finished my schoolwork. Glenn and Carpenter and Shepard. They were my heroes. They'll be on the moon before nineteen-seventy! And I'll still be here . . . *here!*'

The bitterness was only a prelude in the weighted silence.

'Is that what you want, Michael? To work in space?'

'No! That isn't what I want! That's being done. I've missed it. I was born too late. But there are other things. New. For my time. Where a guy can make a million bucks, or ten million or even a hundred. It's not the money for itself. I want it so I can forget it. So I can . . . hell, how can I say it?' His strong hands were clenched. 'Be myself. Do what *I* want! Whatever it is!'

She was too wise to ask what stopped him. She had learned herself that the real barriers always lay in one's own mind.

'Look.' He whirled on her. 'I'm going to say something I've never said to anyone. You've met them, my parents. My father and his manners and his uptight suits. My mother doing things his way. She says he's not strong. That's not my funeral, is it? If it's his, that's the way it works. But I can't stand here and wait for that. How do you walk out, Lilith? Just walk?'

She drew a long breath. The biting air, fresh as ice water, told her again that she was not alien to this world of Thatcher. This black-browed young man, battling the loneliness within him, sensed it. He was asking her for more than attention. He was asking her to share his defiance. Like Artie Shallcross and the others, so young in their failed dreams.

The old generation have made their mistakes – the young have the right to make theirs.

'I can't make your decision, Michael,' she said at last.

'Do you think I want that? I've already made it.'

She sensed that wasn't true. She sensed also that somehow she had become an instrument. She shared at this curious moment not only his defiance but his youth.

Then Lilith did something surprising. She opened her handbag and the wallet inside it. She ruffled through the cache of credit cards, artifacts of her success. From among them she drew out a bent-cornered greying card. Why she had kept it so long passed her own understanding. Except that it represented a time in her life she did not wholly want to forget. She never told Brock. The past too often opened tiny scars of jealousies. The present was theirs. She had let the card lie there, year after year, like a pebble in a shoe.

'This was given to me, Michael, by someone who said when things got too rough, too lonely, use it. I never did. But maybe you . . .'

He glanced at the single word NEVAH, but it was the telephone number that interested him.

'Eight hundred . . . that's a free call. The area code is San Francisco. I know that one.' He pocketed the card. His smile puzzled her. 'Thanks. That's the roll of the dice for me.'

Suddenly he kissed her, his lips too parted, too moist.

Wordless and provoked, she walked down the slope from him. By the time they reached the car, Lilith could define her uneasiness.

This young man had made her a conspirator. The end lay beyond her vision.

CHAPTER SEVENTEEN

Ground visibility 2000 feet and worsening.

The plane had been in a holding pattern over London's Heathrow Airport for forty-five minutes, making wide sweeps over the estuary, the channel, and the greening, invisible countryside of the midlands.

Brock, belted into his first-class seat, damned the fog and his luck. Once again he had cut it too fine. He had a reason, of course. But then he always had a reason. Lilith would be dressed and waiting, beautiful and tense, in their Wilton Place apartment, watching the fog obliterate the street below and turn the white façade of Belgravian houses into a ghostly mirage. There would be the sorry-darling phone call from the airport, the missed engagement, and the final passionate relief from his chagrin and her contained anxiety. But it was happening too often. Though neither of them would admit it, it was an erosion, inevitable as the soaring of his career. Lilith had her own success. She had greeted their move to London with joy. The great city encrusted with centuries of self-confidence had provided her with anonymity and room to grow. She found she could market her own sense of elegance, and her work was stamped with a style as unique as her first name. Lilith, Brock realized, had become a person of her own. Imperceptibly she had remoulded, too, his prairie-boy roughness. If she still had doubts about her life, he never saw them. After his all-too-frequent absences her eyes met his with the same warmth, the same desire. They had made work all they had promised each other. Until now.

'Attention, all passengers. This is the captain. Due to heavy fog over south-east England, Heathrow Airport is now closed in. We have been rerouted to Prestwick. We shall do everything we can to find you comfortable accommodations and to see that you are taken on to London at the earliest possible hour.'

Brock unfastened his seat belt and peered at the white night, thick against the plane's window. He had failed her. This was the night of Mortimer Russell's big gala in London. Royalty would be there. It was a command performance for Lilith and himself. He should have left Washington sensibly two days ago, yet what he had done, he told himself, was for them both. Not that that would make it easier now. Well, Mort would escort her and jump at the chance. Mort had never concealed a kind of lustful admiration. Lilith had managed a sophisticated balance of charm and distance that had kept Mort where he belonged. Yet the more Brock thought about it, the less he seemed to know of this girl who had shared nearly a decade of his life. Lilith managed so many things while revealing so little of herself.

He was battling his demon of jealousy now. As he resigned himself to the captivity of the plane, Brock was aware of a deeper sensation. He found himself almost grateful for this brief interlude of suspended time, this respite from responsibility. What he had to tell Lilith on his return was the most momentous news of his life, of their lives together. Yet the telling would not be easy.

He relived the scene, as he had done dozens of times since it had happened. The White House was not new to him. Off and on, the press room, the East Room, had been familiar stomping grounds, for him as for hundreds of rival news gatherers, bristling with credentials and self-important questions. It had been his custom to sit back, let it come. Eventually some small chink would reveal itself in the prepared statement or official answer. Brock would have what he wanted.

Three days ago he was met at the press door and conducted down a long corridor that he knew led to the Oval Office. The door was opened. The President of the United States rose, shook hands, and gestured him to a comfortable chair, taking the seat opposite.

'How do you like London, Brock?'

'News is news anywhere you find it, Mr President.'

'Or make it.' The presidential smile removed the sting.

'I tell it only as I see it, sir.'

'With twenty-twenty vision. Or better.'

'I see what any other reporter could see, Mr President, if he looked far enough.'

In the few seconds of silence Brock groped for a direction.

'How would you like to be on my side?'

An answer seemed to be expected.

'I was not aware that I wasn't, sir.'

'You're a gadfly, Brock. If you know anything about ranching, that's the big one that torments the cattle.' The presidential spine leaned back into the yellow cushion. 'What I'm talking about is a position I've had in mind for some time. A new one. Not a press secretary. I'm adequately served there.' He smiled. 'What I need is a man on my personal staff who knows the news business worldwide. Who is objective. Independent. A man who can spot the phony stuff, watch for the traps. A man who will be a liaison for me with all the media. Everywhere.'

There was another silence. The President was skilled in the art of fly casting. Brock had a moment to himself, to see the hazards, and the rewards. And to conceal a sudden surge of emotion.

'You have the qualifications I need, Brock. Would you like to think about it? Talk it over with whoever you talk things over?'

Brock answered carefully. 'I don't have to do that, Mr President. I am honoured.'

They shook hands.

The summit of his career. After this, if he made no mistakes, the world was his. He walked slowly out into the early afternoon sunshine that glistened on the great columns. He nodded absently to the guard at the gate and found himself in Lafayette Square. A few pigeons fluttered from the walk. He knew the scene as well as he knew Bluefield's Main Street or New York's Sixth Avenue. Yet subtly it had changed. It was light-struck. He wanted to call Lil at once. He remembered London time. Not quite five-thirty. She would not be home yet. Besides, he had something to think about, something sparked by the small phrase the President had used: 'with whoever you talk things over'. Meaningless, of course, jocular, nothing – as well as ungrammatical. But it had flicked on a running chain of thoughts.

By the time he reached the network offices, the conclusion stared him in the face. More than anything in the world he wanted to bring Lilith with him to Washington as his wife.

In the increasing pressure of his work, in his happiness with Lilith, he had put Bluefield and his marriage behind him. Lilith, with her infinite tact, had never mentioned it. She had not even asked the name of his wife. She had accepted and adjusted, and he was deeply grateful.

But now it was different. He tried to remember what he had heard of Judge Reeves. The old demon had lost his bid for Washington. He lived on in the big house with his daughter. Then Brock's mother had moved to Florida and the trickle of Bluefield news had stopped.

But if the judge were still alive, he must have lost much of his clout. He would recognize, too, that Brock now possessed it. Marcia might be reasoned with. She might even have found another life.

Brock boarded the three-thirty plane to Kansas City feeling like a kid with a new set of dreams. He would buy Lil a ring (she had always refused to wear them). They would be married in London. The registry at Caxton Hall. Or a church, if she wanted it. He felt his chest tighten with his love for her. 'Mr President, my wife, Elizabeth . . .' and surprised himself. From what deep-buried association had that name floated up?

It was half past eight when Brock drove his rented car through the little prairie town. The street-lights showed him changes. Judge Reeves's old Victorian pile was no longer on the outskirts. A shopping mall and a gas station had pushed nearly to its gate. The house was dark except for a single light over the doorway, which revealed the neglect of chipped paint, a dying wisteria vine. But somebody was home.

Brock walked around the house and saw a light from the kitchen window. He could see a figure in a rocker. It was

Hattie, the long-time housekeeper, 'Miz Hattie', as she was always known, which was neither servile nor gentry but satisfactory in Bluefield. She was placidly sewing on a lapful of white stuff, and to Brock it was a good sign. He knocked lightly. She rose without excitement, opened the door, and peered into the night. The brown coiled hair he remembered was white.

'Miz Hattie, it's me. Brock.'

'Brock! Henley Brocklebank Turner! Where in the world . . .'

He stepped into the kitchen. She threw her arms around him, then drew back shyly. 'I forgot you're famous now, Mr Turner.'

'You don't forget anything, Miz Hattie. I'm Brock and I'm no different. How are you? You look great. I was driving through. I thought – '

'She's here.' The voice cooled. 'Reckon we ought to get that front doorbell fixed. Then folks wouldn't have to walk clear around in the dark. You come to see her?'

'I came to see the judge.'

'You didn't know?' Her look was suddenly careful. 'Judge Reeves died. Three months ago come next Thursday.'

'I'm sorry . . .'

'Guess you're about the only one who is. He had the bottle real bad. If it hadn't been for that friend of his who came here regularly, I don't know what we would have done, Marcia and me.'

Brock didn't like to think of the sprawling old house with these two women in it alone. Marcia, who was always afraid of the dark. His journey had taken an unpleasant turn.

'Is Marcia keeping this place alone?'

'Not for long now. She's come through it, Mr Brock, pretty well. You'd be surprised. It was the colonel who helped her. He was here the night it happened. They found the judge in the library with his heart stopped. Guess it was the best in the end. The colonel took charge of everything. The Lord bless that man, Brock. He was like another father to Marcia. The judge must have seen it that way too. He left

216

a big piece of money to the colonel and this house, too, on condition the colonel would look after Marcia, take care of her.'

Miz Hattie, Brock realized, was talking as if she couldn't stop, as if the weight of it had broken through a silence held too long.

'And he will too. He's a fine man and he's going to see that Marcia has a lovely place to live in, in California. A place she'll be happy. After this house is sold. He'd be here now only he's got his own business to attend to. I'll be going to my sister's then. But I'd even like to think . . . I shouldn't be saying this. But I know how things went for you and Marcia. And I was sorry. My, you two were the prettiest pair I ever saw at a wedding, and I guess it's grieved you, because I haven't heard about you finding anybody you ever wanted like Marcia. But people shouldn't live alone all their lives for one mistake. I like to think now that maybe Marcia and the colonel . . . oh, he's much older but what difference does that make? He's such a fine gentleman and so tall and well educated. And he lost his wife, they say – '

She put her hand to her mouth. A board in the upstairs hall creaked. And creaked again.

'She's through with her meditating, as she calls it. I'll tell her you're here.' Miz Hattie hesitated. 'You might find her a little changed. But she's – she's all right. You go right into the library, Brock. We don't use the front part of the house any more.'

He did not have to wait.

Marcia entered quickly, lightly. She wore a long unbelted brown robe, flowing to the floor, unadorned except for a black embroidered scroll at the throat. Her ashen hair fell curling to her shoulders. Her eyes looked beyond him but her voice was warm and held no surprise. She held out both hands.

'Brock! You're here. At last! I didn't know when it would be but I knew you would come. I'm alone now and that's good. I must make the decision myself. It's ordered in the second circle.'

She smiled and his uneasiness deepened. It was not the

little-girl smile that had once captivated before it destroyed. Her manner was serious and contained.

'Marcia, I didn't know about your father. Miz Hattie just told me. I'm sorry. It must be quite a loss to you.'

'Yes. But I was not unprepared. It was the sacrifice of the third circle. When it came, I was ready to accept it. He died right in that chair, his head slumped over the desk on his papers. I still see him sitting there. But I am taught not to need him. Through him I moved into the second circle.'

There was nothing in her confident poise to suggest madness. He knew of the proliferation of strange cults that brought peace to the insecure. She was no longer hysterical or flighty and showed no signs of illness. He wondered about the judge's 'good friend'; he decided not to probe. If Marcia had found a protector, so much easier his own problem might be to resolve. He had, after all, only one question to ask her.

She gestured him to a chair and seated herself beside him.

'I know you have many things to say to me, Brock. And I'm ready for them. You have been very patient too. I know now what must come.'

She was making it almost too easy. He reminded himself again that it was no business of his what had happened in this house. If she were willing to listen, to agree . . .

'Miz Hattie tells me you will be moving out of this house.'

'Yes.' Her face lit up. 'When I have made my atonement of the second circle. Then I will go to a different life. The life of the first circle, where I shall be prepared.'

It seemed to him that for an instant doubt flickered across her face, making it childlike. Then it was gone. She laughed gaily.

'We've been separated so long that it must be very funny for you to hear me talk so seriously. I was such a silly-head, wasn't I? I loved to dance. *He* told me I will dance again.' She jumped up and began to sway, stretching her arms out, letting the robe sweep around her. As abruptly she stopped. 'But not yet. That is wrong. Not until I've passed through the circles of sacrifice, atonement, and release.

And I am ready for the whiteness of Ishtar. She who wears only light.'

Marcia returned to her chair and sat with the palms of her hands together. 'Do you understand?'

'I think I do.' He found himself shifting impatiently. A little of this could go a long way. Yet something he could not identify tinkled like a warning bell within him. 'It means you are free of the past.'

'I will be, Brock, when I have passed through the circles.'

'So our life together, our marriage, has no meaning for you. And never will have.'

'There is no marriage in the second circle.'

'Marcia.' He spoke intensely but quietly to cause no ripple in the room's dim closeness. 'Will you let me get a divorce?'

She looked at him curiously. 'Where there is no marriage, how could there be divorce?'

'But I don't live in these circles of yours. For me there are laws.'

'Laws? Between you and me? What laws? You owned part of my life. You still do. I can only win it back by purification. By giving it to you again in atonement.'

She jumped from her chair, bent over him, and kissed him on the lips. With a single gesture she let the brown robe drop to the floor. She was as nude and desiring as the first night he had taken her.

'You have waited a long time, Brock. I am ready to go back with you when you will have me.'

The normalcy of his return to Washington, his office, the humming news tape, and the solidity of the white dome beyond the window dimmed the outrageous scene in Brock's mind. He marvelled, looking back, that he had not shaken the clouds of absurdities from her or taken her to bed.

He had stomach for neither, and so she had triumphed. No judge on earth would give a divorce to a man whose wife had been ailing and who now asked nothing but a reunion. Those were facts, yet he could not dismiss the thought that, had he stayed longer with her, there was something to be learned. Something hidden, evil, engulfing her, engulfing them both.

But as Brock had reminded himself often, or excused himself perhaps too often, he was a newsman. His life was what other people did. If he touched down any place too long, he would lose the next story. And the next story was what he was paid for. Delivering it had brought him to the White House. Christ, he asked himself uncomfortably, when had he had time to stop running?

He called Lilith and reached her.

'Hold on to your hat, Lil. I've got big news. Very big. Get yourself gussied up. Tell you when I see you. I'm taking the day flight but I'll be there. Plenty of time. Don't worry. Tell Mort his company isn't needed. Or wanted.' He heard her laugh, sweet and near. 'Sure. Jealous as hell. Any man would be, with a woman like you. I love you, darling.'

As he put down the receiver his hand slid half automatically to his empty pocket and the non-existent ring he might have brought her.

'Fasten your seat belt, please. We shall be landing at Prestwick in fifteen minutes.'

Brock opened his eyes. The night was clear, the stars polished, a half-moon hung in the cold Scottish sky. She would have left the apartment by this time with Mort Russell, his hand slipped cosily under her arm, handing her into his limousine, elbowing her through the crowd, presenting her to the royals.

Fatigue? Frustration? Or simple anger at the trickery of life? Brock had the taste of ashes in his mouth. Even the splendid sunlit memory of the White House greyed in his mind. Had he been too quick to accept? There was a rumour that the President might be under fire before the year was out.

But he was a newsman, wasn't he?

And yet what did a guy just past forty do if he found he'd made a mistake?

He wondered what dress she'd be wearing, then resolved not to think about it.

And then . . . who or what was Ishtar?

The fog that drove Brock's plane north settled deep on London, muting traffic, erasing modernities, dissolving present into past. The great clock on the Parliament building hung four faint moons above the mist. The Houses floated fairy casements into the night. The river moaned of the fog and lapped at Thames-side wharves.

The fog fingered, too, the ghostly crevices of the old city. The long-dead stream of the Fleet, bearing its medieval burdens to the river. The rotted pilings for the rivermen's boats that had daily ferried two thousand eager Elizabethans across to Southwark whenever Mr Will Shakespeare and the Chamberlain Company unleashed murder most foul, magic most rare, love most ripe.

Up Ludgate Hill it swathed again the ghostly, gibbeted bodies of the beggars at history's unequal tables and dressed with mercy the scars of fire and bomb, greening monuments of London's survival.

With the wisdom of time it probed twenty feet below the teeming modern pavements, the last silent shards of brick and timber, pottery and bronze, of that splendid pagan town and pride of imperial Rome, Londinium.

Lilith, sitting slight and elegant in Mortimer Russell's limousine, her face turned to the window, was hardly aware of all this. But she loved it.

For a few brief hours the city was surrendering, as she would like to do, its artificial, bright bravado to the mystery of invisibility, to anonymity, to its own secrets. As the car inched along, the fog had become her refuge.

Mortimer Russell shifted restlessly.

'Sorry it's so slow, Lil.'

'I think it's marvellous!' She turned a radiant face to him.

'You'd think by this time they'd have found a way to get rid of the stuff. What on earth do you see out there?'

'Bear-baiting.'

'What?'

She laughed. She felt happier now that she could escape into this milkiness. How could she tell anyone what she was seeing beneath this polished rectangle of narrow streets and lofty houses called Mayfair? The open meadows had given it its name. Rollicking Londoners once gathered here for their beloved May's Fair to loosen their jerkins and their spirits, to heal their blood with honey mead and dancing, to whet their savageries with pit fighting, animal baiting, and to bed their lusts behind hedgerow and hayrick.

Lilith now perversely let these imageries flood her mind. She and Brock, bare-legged, young, free. She was caught in his arms, swung against him, her dress falling.

The limousine stopped. The fine old hotel materialized, pouring misted light on to the pavement. From London's black taxis were debouching knots of people. A red carpet ran to the kerb.

'My God, they're not here ahead of us!'

Lilith remembered the evening. 'Who?'

'The Royals. This is Command, I tried for the queen. Or a princess. But I'm satisfied. Why doesn't the fog slow them down like us?'

Mort had grown portlier with success. But no less anxious. Having had her secret private fling, Lilith would succumb to graciousness. Brock would expect it.

'Maybe they know how to plan for it, Mort.'

'Look, I don't like to do it this way, Lil, but I better take a quick look inside. I'll send Roger or Jim out. It'll be another five minutes before you get to the entrance. Okay?'

'Perfect.' Lilith smiled. 'Don't worry, Mort. Just don't worry.'

He hesitated only an instant. 'You're stunning, Lilith. A lot more than Brock or any man deserves. I'll be right there at the door to meet you.'

'Thank you.' Graciousness was the key to this evening.

It turned out not to be Roger or Jim, whoever they were in Mort's hierarchy, but a tall reddish-haired young man who came to the limousine at the kerb.

He handed Lilith out gravely and offered his arm.

'I'm Dennis Cason. I'm Australian, I don't raise sheep, and I'd consider it a privilege to escort you.'

'That's very kind. Mort had to see to the Royals.'

'I don't know who Mort is and I'm quite sure nobody has

to "see to" the Royals. But I'm delighted to meet you, to find you alone and to – Who are you?'

'Well, really!'

'Quite honestly. I'm not here very long. I have a ticket to the benefit. Two, in fact. My pal can't stand benefits . . . and when I see an unescorted lady . . .'

They had reached the entrance to the hotel. The lobby was thronged. Lilith looked around. Mort was not in sight.

'You see? You need me. We'd better find seats. I'll take your wrap. If you can part with it. By Jove, that is mink! Leave it to the Americans, we Aussies say. Flair. Savvy. Know what to do with money. If not with themselves.'

'I'll wait. Thank you for your trouble.'

'Ah, coolness is the note. Righto! But you obviously can't stand here with the crowd pushing in. So if you'll trust me with five minutes more of your time . . . Look, here's my card, utterly respectable. May I tell you you look like Lady Hamilton? If I don't get a better name, I'll use that. Here's a programme. Mortimer Russell presents – in not too-small print. If that's your gentleman, he will indeed be seeing to one royal cousin and an even more royal great-aunt. So, Lady Hamilton . . .'

'Oh, do for heaven's sake stop!' Lilith laughed in spite of herself. The man was impossible but he was here. 'My name is Lilith Roundtree. Mort has a box. I'll meet him there.'

The Australian's sharp blue eyes held hers.

'Why?' he asked, softly.

Mortimer Russell was coming towards her. Dennis Cason turned and disappeared. But the strangeness of the encounter stayed with her. As if a stranger could see at a glance her vulnerability, the thinness of her protective shell. Lady Hamilton, mistress of a duke? Why that?

'Sorry, Lil. I was detained. You all right?'

'Of course I'm all right. What a crowd! Mort, your evening is going to be fabulous!'

'I had Joe call Prestwick Airport. Brock's plane isn't in yet. But it's expected soon.'

He took her arm. Mort's hands were always moistly warm. But she knew her evening's role.

Together they entered the ballroom shimmering under crystal chandeliers, roses in all shades of pink draped from box to box, pink velvet-back chairs filling the floor space, and at the end of the room a built-to-order stage of gilt and mock-crystal, tented with huge swags of pink-and-rose chiffon.

God, thought Mort, don't they ever do these affairs in anything but pink? But Lilith's eyes glowed. She sat straight-backed on her little gilt chair, her head high, the glittering white of her ballgown giving her a radiance few women ever matched. She swept up glances like a net of silverfish.

'God Save the Queen.'

The audience rose. The evening had begun.

Mort's evening. He glanced at Lilith. She belonged in a setting like this. She needed it. She would always attract men. Brock was a fool to leave her like this. But Mort was at this moment very, very grateful for his foolishness.

The entertainment part of the evening was over. It had been a smashing success. Perspiring performers and singers, watchful-eyed stars, the orchestra leader, and anyone else who might conceivably have the right were arranging themselves to meet royalty. Receipts would indeed aid the needy gentlefolk and Mortimer Russell would rise another notch in a world he had so unsparingly battled.

He stood now at one side of the ballroom watching preparations for the dancing ahead. He could see Lilith still in the box, surrounded by a group of men younger than himself, younger than Brock. Young bluebloods with titles.

Titles. As chief network executive, he commanded power that few titles in this room could claim. They came to him now in the luxurious hotel suite, the lavish spread of his London offices, the titled, the multi-millionaires, the foreign magnates, all had something to sell or buy from Mortimer Russell.

Yet he was honest enough with himself to admit that it was not wealth, not power, alone that satisfied him tonight. It was the realization of a childhood dream. As a boy coming home from school on Chicago's shabby South

Side, he would stop to press his nose against a toy-store window, to watch a procession of leaden knights on horseback, bearing gilt-paper standards, riding splendidly from a cardboard castle.

'Have you heard anything more, Mort?'

Lilith had left her admirers and stepped into his momentary reverie.

'You're gorgeous tonight, Lilith. You look absolutely – '

'Mort, I asked you a question. I thought we'd hear something before this.'

'Oh. Oh, yes. The plane landed. Brock's at Prestwick. They're putting the passengers up for the night. Brock will be here in the morning.'

'I'm very grateful, Mort.'

He believed it. She had been grateful too long. It was all he had to go on and the very truth of it made it unpalatable.

'Then come and be presented. The talent's done with.'

'Must I?'

'Of course you must.' He tried to keep irritation from his tone. The evening was stretching too far. Already he began to feel her slipping from it.

She silently accompanied him.

The ageing cousin held out a white-gloved hand. A duchess only a little older than herself smiled warmly. Lilith made a small curtsy, a credit to St Charles Avenue.

'How do you like our fog, Miss Roundtree?' The ageing lady was known for her infallibility with names.

'Oh, it's exciting. I come from New Orleans, where we have lots of fog.'

'But that is clean fog, I'm sure. In my day the London fog was mustard-yellow and everything, drapes, upholstery, our very clothes, had to be cleaned afterwards.'

'Lilith Roundtree.' The young duchess leaned forward. 'I've seen that name. You're a fashion adviser. Tell me, is that name Lilith usual in America?'

'No, I just took it for myself.'

The young duchess laughed. 'I envy you. I have four given names and every one of them is a hand-me-down. I had absolutely no choice.'

Lilith would have liked her for a friend.

A few more pleasantries. Mort escorted her to the supper room. She would make it anywhere, he told himself. The one woman to crown his own career.

The orchestra began an Offenbach pastiche. Voices rose, pink lights glimmered. A mercifully short speech. A grand finale of pink bombe glacé with strawberries. The dancing would begin. The Royal Box was empty.

Mortimer appeared with Lilith's mink wrap.

'Ready, Lil?'

'More than.' Her relief was almost too apparent.

'Good. My duty's done.'

Outside, the fog was beginning to lift. Mort gave an unfamiliar address to the chauffeur.

'No, Mort, please. I really want to go home.'

'Honey, I'm taking you to the most exclusive club in London. Costs me seven thousand a year just to belong. It's the only place I know where champagne starts at a hundred bucks a bottle.'

'I'm sorry, Mort.'

She heard the irritation as he changed the address. She remembered what Brock used to say. 'He's a chameleon, Lil. He can be the best friend a man has. Or the worst.'

At the apartment Mort took the key from her and opened the door himself. His euphoria had faded. He was not a willing loser and he understood timing.

'I want to talk to you, Lil. For a few minutes. It concerns Brock and it's important. I think you'll be interested.'

She was home now. And happier. She felt Brock's presence. She was where Brock could reach her.

'Of course I'm interested. Brock always calls when he's delayed like this. That's why I wanted to be here.'

She let Mortimer slip the mink wrap from her shoulders. 'I know he'll be glad that your benefit was such a success. You've been such a good friend to Brock and me. I thought after all these years I'd stop worrying about his late planes. But I never do. I hope it didn't show too much.'

'You were the most beautiful woman in the room, Lil.'

'Thank you. I'll tell Brock that too. It will be good for him. But I really don't think you looked around too much.'

'No. I didn't have to.'

His tone brought a flush to her face. She knew both the powers and the intensity of this man who directed Brock's destiny. It was a tightrope she walked. He was watching her closely, with an expression she could not read.

'Would you care for a brandy?'

'I'm not staying that long, Lil. When I said I wanted to talk, it's really more simple than that. I came in to congratulate you both.'

'On what?'

'Didn't Brock tell you?'

'Tell me what?'

'That makes my little visit even more important. Then you don't know.'

'I don't know what? Oh! You mean – no, I don't know yet. Brock called me from Washington just before he left and said he had news. Very big news.' She laughed; excitement made her face girlish. 'You know Brock when he says that! Of course I never know whether it's an election in Rhodesia or a trip to China or a week's vacation. What is it this time? He won't mind. If he'd been home on time, I'd know. Besides, he should be taught a lesson about cutting things too fine. Shouldn't he?'

A great many lessons, Mort thought. He wanted this radiant woman. He wanted to possess her. But more than that, he would give half of all he had to have such a woman waiting for him, the glow, the elusive patina, she could give to a man's life, the bewitching combination of childish enthusiasm and worldly sophistication. He wondered if any man would ever know all there was to Lilith Roundtree. But he at least could give her the setting, as he had tonight.

Yet, she had shed it like rainwater at the mention of Brock's name.

'Well, are you going to tell me?'

'The President wants Brock on his staff.'

She stared at him. 'You mean the White House?'

Mort nodded, his eyes measuring her. 'He's to be the President's personal liaison with all media. Worldwide.'

She took in the enormity silently. He wondered whether anything in the world could break that inner restraint.

227

'You're sure, Mort?'

'I should be. I arranged it.'

In the silence he saw that she understood. He had not meant to say it, but the night's frustration had begun to grate.

'When is he to start?'

'He'll tell you all that.'

'Can't you give me an idea?'

It had gone further than he intended, yet not far enough.

'He must be in Washington the first of the month.'

'Less than two weeks? To leave London? To move? To find us a place to live? But I can do it. Oh, Mort, I don't know what to say. Washington. And Brock coming home every night. And a regular home!' That glow again. 'I'll be waiting up all night for him. Oh, it's so great for him. Why, Mort, he could become – '

He should have let it go at that, but her untouchability stung him.

'You haven't had time to thinkthis out, Lil.'

'Think what out?'

'Washington. Brock. And you.' She was waiting, her enormous blue eyes fixed on him. 'Washington is a political town, Lil. Nothing else. Prestige is built not on achievement but image. Nearness to power. Vote-getting usefulness. It's a society of strangers, shifting continuously. They haven't much in common so they cling to what they can share. Conventions. Little securities.' He paused. She wasn't getting it. 'Your life with Brock isn't exactly . . . conventional.'

'Mort, will you say exactly what you mean.'

'I'm talking about Brock's image.'

'What about it? He's the best-known news – Oh . . . you mean *I* could affect – '

'You could affect his upward mobility, his progress.'

'Because we're not married? I thought people today – I mean, after nine years . . .'

'I'll give it to you straight, Lil, because there's no other way. And because maybe Brock won't. After nine years there is still Marcia, Mrs Henley Brocklebank Turner.

228

Brock's legal wife. And that is wha4 the wives who run Washington won't tolerate.'

He had to give her credit. She had courage and the devil's pride. She'd break before she bowed. When she spoke at last, her voice came low and tight.

'Marcia. Did you know her?'

'What difference does that make? Yes, I knew her. Lil, I'm sorry about this. I know it hurts. But somebody's got to tell you the facts of Washington life. Brock's moving into a big arena now.'

She held up a hand. 'I understand. I really do. Brock will tell me.'

'Maybe he will, maybe he won't. But if he says anything different, he's lying. Lil, for God's sake, wake up! Nine years! Brock has given you everything on earth except the one thing you should have. The one thing any woman wants in the end. If she's honest.'

She walked towards the door, as if not hearing. But he knew from the whiteness of her face she had heard.

'Marriage, Lil.' Mort picked up his overcoat and met her eyes. '*I* could give you that.'

It was past midnight. The telephone had not rung. Wrapped in a fleece robe, Lilith sat huddled before the coal-fire grate, listening to the silence. She had no need of sleep. Sleep was an escape. There would be plenty of time for that. Tomorrow. The next day. The day after.

She would lie in Brock's arms once more. There would still be time for that. And perhaps again. But in the flickering blue of the flames she saw what had to be seen, what every alerted sense told her, what her woman's intuition already knew: The time was now. The parting preordained.

She fell asleep and awoke to the ashes of a fire, a greyness between the drawn drapes, and the unlocking of a door. Disoriented, she saw Brock enter. She lifted her arms to him, even as her mind shaped another woman, faceless but real at last. Marcia, his wife.

PART FOUR

THE GHOSTS OF THATCHER

CHAPTER EIGHTEEN

The spring tilt of the planet that layered London in fog, twisted human destiny, and made restless the human heart, struck savagely at Thatcher.

For almost a week its citizens, lying in their beds at night, listened to the distant crackle and thunder of breaking ice. Then the river rushed free. Strong, reborn, it hurtled down from the hills, past Deerford and Pinesville, past Thatcher and Juno's Landing, past clusters of Yankee homesteads, their roots in self-dependence, their faith in a tidy tomorrow.

At eleven-twenty on a Tuesday morning Hazel Haskell opened the windows of the Thatcher Library to the sun. Mr Slater set a bale of damp newspapers out to dry in front of his stationery store on Main Street. In Thatcher High School distracted youths stole delighted glances at spring's perennial revelations, budding nubility, and long young thighs. And everywhere to the opening of green-shuttered windows, women, their heads in kerchiefs, emb!rked on spring's second rite, house-cleaning.

At eleven-twenty-five everyone in Thatcher heard the roar. The old bridge bent, cracked, and succumbed to the power of the river. In its plunge it carried with it two vehicles. One, an out-of-state, overweighted truck. The other, an all-too-familiar grey sedan. Within two hours a black-bordered *Thatcher Standard* blared the headlines:

CONDEMNED BRIDGE COLLAPSES
THREE ROUNDTREES AMONG FIVE KILLED

Before the day was out, the story would be picked up by the *Boston Transcript*, *The New York Times*, the *San Francisco Examiner*, and the wire services.

Martin Roundtree lay as neat in death as in life, in a dark

blue suit, his face fine even more beneath its powder. Only his thin, folded hands, witness of his orderly days, bore the scars of their struggle against ice and steel.

'. . . lost his heroic and hopeless fight to save his daughter-in-law, Hester, wife of John Roundtree; and one-year-old Susan, daughter of the Reverend Duncan Phelps and his wife, Ariel, cousin to the Roundtrees. All bodies were recovered.'

A stunned Thatcher, reliving its long outrage over the neglected bridge, swung wildly between loud indignation and mute grief. The unfortunate truck driver and the hitch-hiking youth with him were no less victims of tragedy but they were outsiders. The Roundtrees, whatever they had been, good or evil, targets of gossip or esteem, were Thatcher's own. The town pressed its ownership. Everybody had an idea of what should be done. The three Roundtrees should be buried together. They should be buried separately. The caskets should be closed. They should remain open. Privacy would be kindest to everyone. Martin Roundtree should lie in state.

In the end Edythe Roundtree stood firm in her widowhood, her softest word carrying through the comings and goings, the lowered voices, the protective bustle that garments death. The sprawling white house on West Street filled with flowers and relatives. The smell of fresh coffee was as pervasive as the lilies. The inevitable stream of neighbours poured through the kitchen, loading cupboards and refrigerator with pies and preserves, roasts and salads, with which Thatcher always met death.

Tall John Roundtree, face gaunt, eyes shadowed, asked to bury his young wife separately, quietly. Later the same sun-warmed afternoon Duncan and Ariel Phelps carried their only child in a white box up the hill to the Roundtree plot. The iron chain had been let down, the raw spring earth lay waiting and sweet.

Martin Roundtree, as befitted the head of the family, would indeed lie in state in Community Hall, his coffin closed, his guard a rotation of Thatcher's citizens, humble and high, who found in rigid silence the only way to express the inexpressible.

Now nothing more was to be done until the last of the far-flung Roundtrees had assembled. And the last of the questions asked.

Which could never be answered, Willard Roundtree told himself. The 'whys' never were. He stood on the porch of his farmhouse looking over the new softness of the valley. Then, shading his eyes, he saw the young, blossoming figure of Kim, Martin's youngest daughter, at the pasture fence. A young bay colt nuzzled her arm. She listlessly patted his nose and walked up the path to the house.

'Go meet her, Clancy,' Willard commanded the huge red Irish setter at his feet and watched him bound off to the girl. Clancy's muzzle was greying but the dog had never lost his faith in human nature. A man could endure anything, Willard thought (not for the first time), with a good dog and a fine young horse, and the image of youth to sustain him. What was Kim now – sixteen, seventeen? It did not matter. A man's years falleth like leaves but for the young . . .

'I feel awful, Uncle Willard. Just awful.'

Kim had a little more flesh on her bones than the others, Willard noted gratefully. She was straight of back, broad of shoulder. Her love for all things living had already set her apart.

'We all feel awful, Kim. It's the time. Don't be afraid of it.' He sat down beside her on the step, which was damp, but the sun was warm.

'I'm not afraid of it. But I feel worst of all.' Her thick brown braids fell forward as she traced a ring in the old wooden step.

'Are you sure about that?'

'It was my fault. Partly.'

'I don't quite see that, Kimmie. It was the fault of a lot of people, or to be honest, the indifference of a lot of people that let the old bridge stand until it rotted.'

'It isn't the bridge. I know all about that. But you see, I was the one who was supposed to drive Dad and little Susan to Bollington. Then I found out that Larry was coming home.' Beneath the freckled skin he saw a tell-tale red. Larry Higgins, the young pediatrician with his black eye patch, his crooked smile, adored by children. But why not? 'I wanted to talk to him about veterinary school. So Hester said she'd drive in my place.' Her face crumpled. 'If she hadn't . . . if I hadn't – '

'Kim, let's go take a walk.' Willard got to his feet more slowly than he liked. 'I want to show you something.'

He walked her up the incline behind the house to where an irregular stand of trees was growing to meet the meadow.

'Do you know what a cull is?'

'No.'

'It's a tree whose life span is already fixed. It may be a very old tree. Or merely mature. Or a very young tree. It may have been injured or become diseased or touched by nothing more than some whim of nature. This a good forester recognizes. He girdles the trunk with a deep cut. When its time comes, the tree will sleep and fall over where it was girdled. It will never know who the forester was. Nor why it was chosen while others lived on. But it leaves an opening to the sky and a richer soil for all life. It is the way of forests.'

The stillness was alive. Branches creaked, leaves rustled, something small and timid scurried past their feet. He breathed the recurring peace and wonder of this valley that he could find nowhere else on earth. She was crying now, soundlessly and full. Good. Good. There had been too much of Roundtree restraint. Crying would do them all good. All who still could.

The sound of an approaching car startled them.

'It's John!' Kim brushed at her face.

'Go ahead with Clancy, my dear. I take a bit longer.'

He stood for a moment, alerted by another sound, wild, strident, and familiar, from the sky. Then he saw them, stencilled against the thin sunlight, a black wedge of great birds, circling lower and lower until he could hear the powerful, pulsing whisper of their wings. Wild Canadian geese returning early to the valley. A good sign.

He straightened his shoulders and walked down the incline. An old man's tears must wait.

*

John Roundtree, the second of Martin's two sons, stood leaning against the paddock bars. His grief was the hardest to bear, perhaps, as Willard himself once knew. Was it sixty years ago? The loss of a young wife, at the flood tide of love, the shimmering brightness of their future. John and Hester had been married little more than a year.

Hester had gone dutifully with John to Washington, a not quite comfortable wife of a freshman Congressman. But always she had been happiest returning to Thatcher, as if Bantam Brady's Irish daughter had found her security at last in Martin Roundtree's reassurance, his growing esteem. John had caught the lilt in her voice that last morning of her life.

'Your dad's asked me to drive him to Bollington, John. We're taking little Susan with us. He takes such joy in that child. Then he looks at me with that glint in his eye. I told him he'd have a grandchild as soon as you'd settled on what you wanted, boy or girl. He says he thought a sound Irish girl like me could make up her husband's mind for him. And I said that would be the day, *acushla*, with the devil's own will runnin' in all of ye!'

John remembered her laugh, as full and hearty as her startling beauty and her vigorous body. She was long past Brady's Pub brogue, but she returned to using it when she saw that it delighted Martin.

The bridge. For the thousandth time John flung his silent curse at himself and his stars. If he had played the politician's game, if he had voted for their disastrous nuclear bill, they would have given him the new bridge.

He came back to the present. Kim tugged at his elbow.

'John, you're not listening to me!'

'Guilty. What's the penalty, nature girl?'

'And don't call me that. All I want to know is whether you want me to wait and go back to the house with you. I mean, I have my motorbike, but if you'd like company – I mean – '

He looked down at this youngest Roundtree girl. Half child still. So rich in kindness. So untouched. He caught the ends of her two long braids and looped them under her chin.

'Oh, John . . .! For Pete's sake!'

'My apologies, Miss Roundtree. When did you grow up?' But he was glad she was there. 'You go along, Kim. I'll stay here for a while. You might stop at Ariel's. Just to stop.'

She understood. The relatives were pressing close at the big house. The funeral services were still twenty-four hours away. He watched her pause at the paddock gate. The young horse came trotting to her, his whinny soft and demanding. Hester's colt, Mischief. Kim had added Sir. 'Sir Mischief,' she had explained. 'For when he's big and handsome. He'll need it.'

'Kim'll take care of that colt, John.'

Willard had joined him. John knew there was no need to answer. Not with his throat half closed with emotion. The two men watched Kim drop a kiss on the colt's fawn nose, before he wheeled and romped away.

'Like to come in, John?'

'This is okay, thanks.'

Willard nodded. John gazed down the long valley. Patches of snow lingered between the boulders. Marshland and gullies still glittered in coatings of winter ice. But in the ooze beneath, the turtles would be stirring, frogs spawning, the silvery cycle of life beginning. A muskrat might be making his way beneath the warmer water at a pond's edge, a sprig of new green in his teeth. John loved the valley more than his own life. Now it seemed to hold the only purpose of existence.

'I need help here.' Willard seemed to be talking more to himself than to John. 'Charlie Redwing can handle the farm, but over the years I – well, I bought another eleven hundred acres out there. Against Martin's advice. He could be right, yet. But' – he glanced at John – 'an old man's craving. Keep the land. Make it richer. Protect the trees. Shelter the wildlife. Best thing a man can do with the end of his years.'

'And the beginning!' John's face hardened. It would be craggy some day like the land. 'You don't have to drop hints to me, Will. Hester and I talked about coming back. I haven't told my mother this . . . or anybody else. But I'm not going to run for office again. I'll never make a compromiser, a wheeler-dealer. I don't understand the political power game and I don't want to. I had ambitions once. Bring industry here, make the town hum, build over the land. The whole bag. But that fight over the nuclear plant taught me something. People would come here and measure the whole valley in terms of how many parking lots it will hold, how many supermarkets, and subdivisions. I don't think that's Thatcher's destiny. I've got other ideas. That Ridge up there . . .' He was alive to his subject now. He pointed excitedly up to the long spine of rock that bordered the valley on the south, past a huge glass and granite house, empty and exposed through leafless trees, and on up the Ridge. 'Remember the old cave up there, Will, where we all used to go because we thought it was haunted? Below it on the other side is that long slope of rock that catches the full sun from the south, as much as anywhere in this part of the state. I'd like to build a solar-energy station up here. A battery of solar cells, tilted to catch the sun's heat. Sure, it sounds impractical. It's so expensive, it's almost pipe-dreaming. Every cell is manufactured. And needs silicon. But there's silicon everywhere! In the sand, the rocks, the earth! A way will be found to get at it. And to mass-produce the cells. Why not here? I'd go to the governor, the legislators, the power boys. We're owed something for the bridge. If we can prove that this far north solar energy can be collected and stored . . .'

John looked out beyond the valley, further than the older man had ever looked. 'Will, ninety-nine per cent of all earth's energy comes from the sun. Ninety per cent of that is reflected back into space. They say that if a battery of solar cells eight miles by eight miles were launched into space it could supply all the energy needed to the city of New York. That sunlight out there. That's Thatcher's destiny. That's what I see. And nothing would touch the land, change the valley. I'm no scientist, Will. But I'm not a politician either. I believe in what's here. I'd live for that.'

Willard's answer was so low that John was not sure he heard it.

'I'd die for it, John.'

Clancy's barking restored the present. The squirrel the ageing dog had treed scolded from an upper limb.

'I haven't even gotten around to telling you what I came for, Will.'

But the old man was still nurturing a warmth that had begun to grow inside him, the first warmth since the mindless tragedy of the bridge.

'Michael's come back, Will.' In the afternoon light John seemed to have aged again.

'Your mother will be glad.'

'Maybe.' The word cracked like a pistol. 'Maybe not. Why after all this time would he come? To see Dad in his coffin when he hadn't so much as called in these ten years?'

There were layers here Willard would not probe. Layers deeper than the wild night Michael had flung out of his father's house in hot fury. Then the three lost years of total silence before word came that Michael had surfaced in San Francisco with the richest of the Roundtrees, his Uncle Simon. What lay deepest for John was that Hester had been Michael's girl first. And that the shadow of Michael had fallen across his youth, his love, his brief happiness in marriage.

The past. Did it ever let go? Willard glanced at the younger man's set jaw.

'He has a right to be here, John.'

'Not this way. Not as if he'd never left. As if he'd take over just as he used to.' John caught himself. 'Guess I'm carrying on today. There are bigger things now. I was wrong about his coming on strong, the way he used to. He's changed, Will.'

'We all have.'

'Not like this. Michael's different. As if he were apart from other people. As if he knew things we don't. He asked me only one question. I couldn't answer it. Maybe you can.'

'What is it?'

'He wanted to know where Lili Roundtree is.'

For a moment Willard did not answer. When he did, the

words came quietly. 'I don't know, John. I wish to heaven I did.'

Overnight the face of March had changed. In wind and rain, against scudding clouds and ragged sky, they brought Martin Roundtree from Community Hall to the church. The young Reverend Duncan Phelps stood on the altar step waiting.

In the front pew beside Edythe, Willard watched the procession come up the aisle. Michael and John walked together, expressionless but contained, as was expected of the Roundtree brothers. Lowell, the eldest daughter, content (Will hoped) beside her rough-bearded archaeologist husband, who had abandoned conformity to the parched dust of his diggings. Then Claude, the family beauty, who had exchanged the first rush of her stage dreams for marriage to the masterful man beside her who loved her too much to manage her. Claude was now even lovelier in her silver blondeness, her body thickening with life. A grandchild that Martin would not see. Last came Kim, as quick in laughter as in tears, young Dr Larry Higgins beside her, a man's dignity gracing his awkward face and black eye patch. Their grief a bewilderment through which shone a shy new awareness of being together.

'Duncan doesn't look well.' Edythe's whisper brought Will back from the acute intimation of his own mortality. Duncan, no less sure of his ministry than when he came to it five years ago, too pale, too stiff-jawed. Willard saw perspiration on his forehead. Ariel, Duncan's beautiful but haunted-eyed wife on the other side of Edythe, leaned forward tensely.

Only Willard knew that late last night Ariel had called him to the shabby little rectory. He had found Duncan slumped at his desk, a photo of his lost child in his hands, a glass and a half-empty bottle of whisky beside him, his words maudlin. 'There is no God, little Susan. He does not live. He never did. No God takes little children. You know that now. There's nothing. Only the ice and the water . . . the end . . . the . . . the nothing!'

They had gotten him to bed.

By morning he had forgotten. By afternoon he was at the church, ashen but correct, welcoming the three other clergymen who guided Thatcher's faith. For no one was to be omitted from Martin Roundtree's last rites.

The small stone church was crowded. Outside, townspeople stood on the soaked, trampled lawn. They would hear the service, courtesy of loudspeakers from Billy Haskell's Electronics Service. Through the open door Willard saw that the rain had slackened. Mentally he thanked Duncan's denied deity.

'We have come to give thanks for the life of Martin Roundtree . . .' Duncan began, his voice thin and loud. 'In the midst of life there is death, in the midst of death, purpose, in the midst of purpose, hope. Hope . . .' he repeated. Willard could hear the congregation stir. 'Hope. What hope? What purpose? I ask you that, all of you sitting there! For what purpose did that honourable man, the young wife, an innocent sweet little girl . . .' Duncan faltered, started to sway. Reverend Nichols, the Methodist, took his arm. The voice of Father Flynn, the cheerful little priest, soared confidently.

'"I am the Resurrection and the Life . . . ye that believeth in me . . ."'

The congregation settled back. Duncan sank heavily into an altar chair. The choir launched Martin Roundtree's favourite hymn to the vaulted roof, and like a vast sigh of relief, the people of Thatcher joined in. 'Mine eyes have seen the glory . . .'

Whether they had or not, Willard told himself, the week's agony was at last past. The service so ineptly named For the Dead was completed. The reassured living could resume their ways, their lives.

He held needlessly, tightly, to Edythe's arm. She walked dry-eyed, head high. In the arched doorway ahead he saw the two brothers, Michael and John, framed for an instant together against the low clouds.

In the last pew at the side of the church he saw Lili.

CHAPTER NINETEEN

Work began immediately, mercifully, on the anguishing wreck of the bridge. Thatcher's citizens grouped to watch two cranes rushed from Bollington lift the dripping, twisted metal to waiting trucks. And to see the emptiness grow in what had been their one link to the highways to the east. The other bridge over the Birch River was twenty-two miles downstream. It seemed disrespectful to talk so soon of a blighted future. The town needed new life. What they had now was isolation.

There was rumour, too, that young John Roundtree would not return to Congress. Another link gone. But no one blamed him. He would head the family now. As a lawyer, he should take up the family practice. Thatcher could not remember when Main Street had not carried the circumspect lettering: ROUNDTREE & ROUNDTREE, ATTORNEYS AT LAW.

There was the surprise of seeing Michael Roundtree back. Tightened lips showed what Thatcher thought of any son flinging ungratefully from his father's house. Sharper than a serpent's tooth . . . Worse, Michael had in a few hours left no doubt as to his prosperity. When it was said he had inherited money, the older citizens shook their heads. It was well remembered that long ago Simon Roundtree had gone west and made a fortune in California. Thatcher viewed with distrust that distant, gilded mirage. Heaven knows how money was come by out there. But they were polite to this new Michael Roundtree. And careful.

'Elizabeth . . .'

She came back to the present, to the billowing white curtains, the polished mahogany, the gleaming old silver, the fireplace and the portrait hanging over it, the Roundtree dining-room. A tall young man stood in the doorway.

'Sorry, I didn't mean to startle you.'

She gave a half-laugh, more as cover than relief. She wondered how much of her emotion showed on her face.

'I don't startle so easily, John.'

'Then you did remember me?'

'Of course I remembered you.' She had not, until she had seen him in the church. It was Michael she remembered and so far Michael had not come near her. Once on the return to the house he had looked squarely at her as if they shared a secret. It had left her uneasy. But then any thought of Michael left her uneasy. She had never known what he had done with his 'young rebellion. Now that he was mature, she saw his brooding intensity was fixed. She was relieved that it was John coming towards her.

'But nobody calls me Elizabeth.'

'It's a nice name. Okay. Then you're . . .?'

'Lili.'

He held out a hand. 'I want to thank you for coming, Lili.'

'I wanted to. Your father was so courteous to me once when I was here before.'

'He never knew any other way to behave.' John glanced at the heavy armchair at the head of the table. 'He'd sit there, look up and down the table at us, and say, "Remember, anything you have to say at this table, say it pleasantly. Good manners aren't going to solve all problems but they certainly make them easier to live with. Now, John, what have you to tell us about your day?"'

'Did he really?' Lili liked this tall young man with the engaging warmth.

'Oh, yes. Sounds odd today, but if you'd grown up in this house you wouldn't think so. We had to keep our fights away from the table.'

'Where did the others sit?' The fine old room had suddenly come to life.

'Well, Mom sat down there at the other end, nearest the kitchen door. Lowell on her right. Claude opposite. And Kim, when she was old enough, on Dad's other side.'

'And the two other chairs?'

'Company. We could always bring somebody home.'

'It must have been a wonderful way to grow up.' No

mention of Michael, but she would not probe. She was outside of it. In another day she would be gone, putting the pieces of her own life together.

'In some ways it was good. But it always boils down to the old question: the individual or the group? You either give to it and diminish yourself, or you take from it and diminish the group. In this house you gave to it.' A quick tenderness lit up his face. 'Hester – my wife – tried to learn that. But the Irish don't bend easily. In the end, stubborn as they both were, I think she was Dad's favourite. I don't know the moral of that. And I'm certainly boring you with family stuff.'

'Oh, no.'

He seemed unwilling to end the interlude. 'I guess you know who that is.' He nodded towards the portrait over the fireplace, a glowing young woman with an abundance of dark curling hair, and a richly red silk dress.

'I should, John. That hung in our living-room in Dauphine Street, in New Orleans, until the house was closed. My father, Amos, painted it of his mother. I used to look at it and think if I could only grow up and look like Henrietta Roundtree.' Her laugh was bright and welcome. 'I didn't get anywhere near her. But I'm glad that picture's here.'

'So am I.' Some of the strain lifted from John's thin face. 'And I'm glad you're here. All of us are.'

'Why, thank you.' She was genuinely surprised.

'That's what I came in to say. Before I ask a question that really isn't my business.'

'What question?'

'Do you have to go back – wherever you're going – soon?'

Yes, of course, she thought. Have to? Why? Did she have to go anywhere or do anything . . . soon?

'Why, John?'

'We were talking it over.' He didn't explain the 'we'. 'Lowell and Steven are leaving for Ankara. Claude and Hutch live in Denver. He has an air-freight business out there. And a ranch. A baby's coming. Ariel was going to come stay with Mother but Duncan – well, he needs care. She wants to take him to Virginia – there's a place near the seminary he went to. I'll be going back and forth to Washington for a little while longer. Heck, why am I going through all this?' He grinned and suddenly the bond of family, of need, was visible. 'That leaves you, Lili. If you could stay here for a while. Maybe through the summer – here with Mom. She likes you. She's too proud to ask you, but if there's no place else you have to go . . . I mean, right away . . .'

He was stumbling like a boy. But she saw. They must have talked about her more than she guessed. They must have known that she and Brock . . . had they kept track of her all these years? Were they willing to overlook the irregularity of her life when they needed her? Could she fit into this house, this pattern, this gossipy town, even for a week?

'Why me, John?' But she didn't say it. She had had too many self-doubts for too long. He was still talking.

'. . . it's asking a lot. You're a pretty sophisticated person. We all know that. And you have a career . . . and Thatcher's not much for a woman who – I mean a girl who is used to a different life.'

Her laugh came, quick and sudden. 'John, you're making a terrible botch of things. You've asked me something very sweet and very touching. If you're trying now to say that it won't matter if I've lived with a man without marrying him for nearly ten years, why, thank you very much. But I have nothing to hide, nothing to run from. I loved Brock from the day I met him. I still do. I will never be ashamed of my life with him.' The words were coming faster now, as if by affirmation she could hold to a fading reality, as if she were talking beyond this room. 'That's what I want you to understand, John. All of you here. My whole life has been different. I could feel it, sitting in that church yesterday. I could feel it here in this house, meeting more Roundtrees than I ever knew existed. Maybe I'll feel it all the rest of my life. Women who live as I have were once supposed to be – what was it? – Scarlet? Fallen? That's what my own aunts believed. Today it's modern, even chic. Well, it isn't any of those things. Nothing has changed about love or separation. We're still women. I was one of the lucky ones. I've lived for ten years with the one man I wanted. I can't help him now. I could hurt him. So I'm alone. If I can be of use to anybody, why, I'll try. But I won't be forgiven. Or "accepted". I'll be myself. Whatever life I've lived is part of me.'

In the small silence the clock chimed from the hall. She was aware that the voices had gone, the bustle died away. She was also aware of John's eyes gravely on her.

'I like brave women, Lili. I married one.'

She laughed, because it hid the thickening in her throat. 'I'm not brave, John. I've been scared more often than you know.'

'You don't know the definition of bravery.' He smiled. 'I like honest women too.'

Later, alone, Lili threw a coat over her shoulders and walked out on the wide veranda that ran around three sides of the sprawling home, a Victorian addition that would no doubt be removed some day to please younger eyes. Venerable maple trees rose black and stark against the melon-green twilight. From somewhere came a shrill piping that she would learn were peepers, the tiny tree frogs in the vanguard of spring. Neither street lights nor house lights were yet on. In the distance the hills rolled purple and mysterious to meet the night.

She had committed herself. For some indefinite time this house with its more than two centuries of births and deaths, ecstacies and hurts, forgotten passions and pain, would be her home. She almost regretted her defiant words to John. It was up to her to adapt here. Nothing so weighted with time would bend to her.

A shadow detached itself from a post at the end of the veranda.

'I've been waiting for you, Lilith.' He came towards her with that knowing half-smile she had seen before. 'I think it's time we said hello. If you still know me.'

'You're Michael. Of course I know you.' He had taken her by surprise.

'We have a lot to catch up on, you and I.' A gesture seemed to dismiss everything but the moment. 'It's also time I said thank you.'

'For what?' Perhaps it was the light; he looked sombre, older.

'For everything. For whatever I have. And am. You gave me the courage to get out of here. Remember that morning? I drove you around, up Cemetery Hill, showed you the Roundtrees, dead and alive. You said, if you want to leave, leave! You haven't forgotten that?'

She hadn't. Nor had she forgotten her uneasiness, nor the sudden rough kiss.

'And you showed me how. That's what I'm most grateful for, Lilith. I don't know whether you knew it at the time but you gave me the way from hell to heaven.'

He reached into his pocket. In the dusk the small card glimmered white and immaculate. When he handed it to her, she saw it was creased, dog-eared, and worn. But she could read the letters. NEVAH. And the telephone number.

'Yes, I remember this too. But I didn't think it meant anything. I don't remember what it was for.' She searched her mind. So long ago. 'A sort of friendship club. When you got lonely?'

'Not friendship. It was the door. I walked through it.'

'I don't know what that means, but if it helped you, that's fine.' His intensity made her uncomfortable as it had once before. She wanted to forget the incident with its sudden supercharged intimacy. It could not matter now.

'I served a long apprenticeship, Lili. Then I went to my uncle's house.' He spoke slowly, carefully, as if the words had already been thought out. 'I waited. It was foretold that on my father's death I would be ready. And that you would be here.'

His face was gaunt, his voice almost disembodied. She tried to keep her own voice light.

'That wasn't hard to guess, Michael. All the Roundtrees were, I think. Besides, your father had been kind to me.'

His hand gripped her arm. 'Don't mock me!'

'Michael, I'm not mocking you. I don't understand what you're talking about.' She slid her arm free.

'No, of course not. How could you? Yet.' He brushed at his forehead. 'I'm sorry. I have so much to do. It's been a

248

shock to all of us. I've been away so long. You're cold.'

'A little. Let's go inside, Michael.'

He walked along the veranda beside her. Abruptly at the door he stopped. 'Lili, don't try to go against me now. The first step has been taken. I'm here. You're here. As it was planned in the scrolls of – ' He broke off. 'I read too much, Lilith. That's what happens when a man spends time by himself. I'll have to do better. Live it up a little when all this is over, right?'

Lights went on in the living-room windows. In their glow Michael Roundtree had the face of a man who had never been young. He saluted her and turned down the porch steps into the darkening street.

Lili had not been cold but she shivered as she went into this closeted, time-ridden house.

It was agreed that Lili would return to New York, pack the clothes she would need, and close for a time her small apartment. Like a chapter in her life, she told herself. She put the chilly scene with Michael out of her mind. She had given Edythe her word. There was nothing she could do. She had not seen him again and Edythe had told her Michael's loyalties were in California with his inheritance. She could come to appreciate Edythe Roundtree's balanced objectivity. It was not part of the Roundtree passion for involvement, and it was welcome.

Tidying and storing her belongings, Lili had no sense of regret. Only a sense of passage, of inevitability. The two smart, neat rooms held nothing any longer of herself or of Brock. She had had no heart to fill them with the artifacts of living, of life flowing through them. Crumpled pillows, tossed magazines, shoes kicked under the divan, pictures chosen together, the wall map that had made Brock's life hers. The apartment was sterile now.

Winging on. The phrase came to her from nowhere. From her first months in New York. Her job failures. The group of bird-watchers in the summer dust, the eruption of small ugly violence, George and his cameras. George who loved the sculpture of space and perhaps Lili herself if there had been time. Mrs Rutherford, her chiffon scarves floating. And through it the hidden fires of her longing for Brock that had brought her both despair and courage.

And then she remembered, rising from an inner darkness, a bubble, an echo, a phantom, the crumpled white card in Michael Roundtree's hand. The tall, angular man with the round head, his hand touching hers, lingering. 'When you can no longer bear the burden of loneliness . . .' Had Michael reached that stage in his flight? But she could not imagine it. He was too purposeful, too grasping towards goals. More likely he had picked up the telephone one long-ago, defiant day . . .

Colonel Chadwick. The man's name returned like the imprint of a finger on sand. She had never told Brock. It had no bearing on their life. As nothing before that life had for her. And no bearing on her future. Nor had Michael. He was unlike the others. Yet she knew so little of them all. If legend was right, she was only half Roundtree, Henrietta's half. Once she had fulfilled this quickly-made promise to Thatcher, she would be free. She smiled wryly at herself. Free, for whatever it meant. Did she, any better than the next, understand that misused, overworked word that had all the illusory light of a fleeing mirage? Free to forge new fetters of loneliness and self?

She was past thirty. It had not taken her many weeks to learn that the frivolities of her work lived no longer than its fashion. Without her celebrity, her bright, chic, young customers would flock somewhere else for their new, sensational, consuming trivia.

In reality Lili minded none of this. Her mirror told her she had changed. The prettiness showed by all youth was gone. Her features, her wide, mobile mouth, tilted nose, high cheekbones that had never seemed to go together, had fined into an elegance. What was it someone had said? 'When you're forty, Lili . . .'

She was not willing to go that road yet. Her eyes were still wide and enormous. Some day she saw them heavy lidded and, hopefully, mysterious. Like an ancient Russian actress. She was not ready for that either.

Actually, when she could forget the persistent ache of Brock's absence, Lili could smile at herself. She was quite unaware that through the depths of that love, that anguish, she had emerged a stunning woman. Other women covertly watched her, trying to fathom the secret of her elegant, electric impact. Men attracted by her quick intelligence found themselves held by the banked promise, the startling depths, of those eyes.

But introspection was no more Lili's forte than self-pity. The apartment clean, the closets neat, her few mementoes packed away, she was ready. She tried not to think of its appalling emptiness. She had never really lived here. It was a shell against a storm. She would keep it. As a shell.

She thought of calling Brock. Then, with the self-honesty that was so often self-wounding, she knew she was grasping at an excuse. Their last goodbye had been complete with tacit understanding. He could not offer her marriage. She could not be a part of this wider world. Love had taken third place. For one wildly foolish moment she thought of pinning a note to the pillow, as she had so often done against his unexpected return. 'Brock darling. Thatcher for a while, care of . . .'

In the end, of course, she did not write it. She drew the blinds against the warming sun and locked the door behind her. 'Brock darling, no more of me and thee.'

'Lili, I'm giving you the south-east corner. Lovely in the spring. This was Henrietta's room once. That's her actual slipper chair beside the lounge. And her rose water and lavender bottles on the dresser with the silver stoppers. She liked nice things. You're right next to the little room where your father slept as a small boy.' Edythe's smile was grateful but not courting, as if she sensed this younger woman's need no less than her own. 'I hope you won't find us too dull. We're so very glad you're here.'

Lili was relieved to learn that, for the time being, Michael Roundtree had left Thatcher.

Meanwhile in the March winds the flag on Thatcher's green snapped at half-mast. Black bunting draped the Roundtree Community House in still-shocking newness.

In the big old house on West Street the last of the

relatives were taking leave, duty done, their own lives to be picked up, their own mortality flowing back. Edythe stood with her son John in the wide hall, enduring the flutter of goodbyes, the quick embraces, the promises to write, the invitations to visit.

Lili, on the fringe, drifted alone into the dining-room, wondering why she had allowed Willard, then Edythe, to persuade her to come to this house. It had been no part of her plan. She had read the newspaper report of the tragedy. On an impulse deeper than she could explain, she had taken her car and found her way to Thatcher. She had intended to stay only for the funeral of that slight, courteous man who had once made her welcome. Now, forty-eight hours later, she was still here.

And every hour made her return to her New York apartment more difficult. On her last and only other visit to Thatcher, Brock had been home waiting for her, to ask questions, to laugh away her doubts, to understand her feelings, to hand her their evening martini, and to wrap her in their private world. This time she would unlock the door to two darkened rooms, switch on the lights to silence, and turn up the stereo to blot out the unasked questions, the unheard laughter.

There had been no real parting in London.

The day following his return they had spent together. They walked along the Serpentine in Hyde Park, drifted past the shops in Sloan Square, dined in their favourite hideaway pub beneath the sign of a royal guardsman. She had never heard him so ebullient, so boyish, or seen him so eager. He had always been casual about the future. Now he seemed to be rushing to meet it.

When they returned to the apartment, he slid her dress from her shoulders. She slipped from him.

'We must talk, Brock.'

'About what?'

'Washington.'

'We'll find a place to live.'

'Not about us. About you. Your work.' She drew a little breath. 'Your wife.'

'My God, Lil. That? Now?'

'Washington is different.'

'What are you asking me? Yes, Washington's different. What of it? Are you asking me about a divorce? It's your right, of course. But now . . . is that what you're really asking? Again?' His anger was so sudden that she knew he had been thinking about it. The 'again' so sharp, so untrue, that she knew he had been stung. 'If you want to hear it all, I'll give it to you. There's nothing that can be done. Nothing. If there were, you wouldn't have to ask.'

She knew. 'You've seen her.'

A little of the youthful excitement drained from his face, leaving something she did not at once recognize.

'I went out to see her. Do you want the whole story?'

'Whatever you want to tell me.'

'I didn't want to tell you any of it. Nothing has changed. She won't give me a divorce. She said . . .' Later he wondered why he had added this, but now he was like a man fighting through cobwebs. '. . . she said that before she'd give me a divorce, she'd come back to me.'

The coal fire hissed. New moonlight slid between the drapes to the floor. Lili drew her dress close.

'That's pretty final, Brock.'

'Only if you make it so.'

He returned to Washington ahead of schedule. He kissed her goodbye at the apartment. She rolled up the wall-size map where for nearly ten years she made little check marks on the places he travelled. She packed away the guide books that told her the streets he walked, the hotels where he stayed: Vienna, Prague, Frankfurt, Casablanca, Tel Aviv, Delhi. 'Brock Turner reporting' – slipping in when he could that surreptitious promise – 'a little of thee and me.'

Her lies were light as he was leaving. 'I have my own work, Brock. I'd like to take a small apartment in New York for a while . . . until you know. Until we both know.'

He had agreed quickly. Too quickly. She recognized at last the new expression in his eyes. The distant look of a man who had found his one big chance.

CHAPTER TWENTY

Michael Roundtree was driving too fast. He always drove too fast, impatient of delay, irritated at being passed or outdistanced. Now as he swung the low-slung red sports car from the highway north of San Francisco into a winding mountain road, he felt a sense of exhilaration, as if destiny awaited him. Which in a sense it did.

He knew every twist of the road as he knew every room and hall of the huge pseudo-Gothic mansion on Nob Hill, where he had lived for the past six years and whose outrageous splendour was now his.

The death of his uncle, Simon Roundtree, had left him untouched, though it had been momentarily awkward. Bachelor, womanizer, possessor of uncounted wealth and an overtaxed heart, Simon met his abrupt end in the arms of his svelte and lusty Washington mistress. A phalanx of expensive lawyers had stifled the story. When Michael had at last emerged from their oak-lined offices, he stepped not on to the solid pavement of Market Street but into an intoxication of light and space dizzying in its future.

Specifically, the Washington mistress, Christina, received Simon's yacht, his private Bahama island, his Paris apartment, and an added million, all designed to keep the lady from surfacing. In a Gordian knot of trusts, corollaries, and sundry legalities, Michael inherited the bulk. So great had been Simon's longing for an heir, he had elected to see only Michael's presence in the cavernous house, not his absences.

Following this convenient demise Michael flung himself into Sybaritic indulgences that included long visits up this same mountain road and, at the house, an upstairs suite hung in cream chiffon for a doll-like creature, half Malaysian, half French, porcelain of face, perfect of body, with the most beautiful hands Michael had ever found, white moths as skilful as they were exquisite.

His long-time friend and mentor, one Colonel Chadwick, had discovered her. 'No, no, Michael. You must have her. We are brothers. NEVAH brings all things to its believers. That was the promise I made you long ago.'

The colonel had shown an increasing awareness of his affairs.

Matters might have continued in this drift but for the shattering abruptness of Martin Roundtree's death. His own father. To Michael it was more than inconvenient. It was a summons to the past. It carried an element of the unknown. Michael had steadily refused to go back to Thatcher even when his uncle Simon had shown an ageing interest in Roundtree roots. Michael himself had no need of the town, its present, its past, its prying.

For a few hours he was numbed by indecision. While Noet lay sleeping beside him, a spent flower within the chiffon hangings, Michael saw what he must do. He was the eldest son. His place was assured, his grief was expected. The very size of the catastrophe would keep questions at bay. And his father was dead. Never again would he have to stand at the study door to hear the carefully tempered voice, to see the thin aristocratic face beneath the green lamp-light. 'We're all waiting dinner again, son. Perhaps later you will explain.'

Michael turned from the memory in such savage rebellion that he awoke the delicate Noet. Without protest she let him reach for her once more. When at last he flung himself on her, she could not guess that he had come to the turning point of his life.

He would go back to Thatcher. Conquering.

Now, as he gunned the red sports car recklessly up the mountain in the afternoon light, he told himself it was not the lust for conquest that he had brought back. It was a vision. Standing at his father's open grave, he had looked beyond the tired old cemetery monuments, to the Ridge. There he had caught the glimpse of a house, new, glittering, and commanding. His own NEVAH. At the heart of it he saw the face of a woman. The one woman he knew now he wanted. Lilith, the woman who had shaped his destiny since that day long ago when she had pressed into his hand the small white card bearing the word NEVAH. He remembered still how her extraordinary blue eyes had turned glacial when on an impulse he had kissed her. He wondered whether they still would do so.

As the car reached the final curve of the mountain road, Michael glanced at the clock. He must have driven like the devil. He was early. And that was the last thing he wanted.

Around the next curve the grilled gates would rise. They would open at his approach. And they would be watched. He stopped the car, let the motor idle, and looked out over the empty mountainside. He had a few minutes left to contemplate the three lost years of his life.

NEVAH. Michael could smile now at the childish reversal of letters. But not at the unfading memory of that dark, wet night soon after his arrival in San Francisco. Unwilling yet to seek the shadowy uncle who bore the Roundtree name and probably the Roundtree discipline, Michael had chosen first to sample the youthful debaucheries of the city. Then, his funds gone, his appetites blunted, he had finally sat on a damp kerbstone, a helpless refugee. It was then he had pulled the sodden white card from his pocket and made the telephone call. There was no surprise at the other end. Instead, after a wait, a tall angular man with a small round head, had come striding towards him, his raincoat flapping like wings in the mist.

For the next three years the place called NEVAH had been his shelter. The days had flowed in a hazy succession of peace and languor, interrupted only by the mysterious rites of renewal.

Daily, in the afternoons, twenty or more figures sat cross-legged on the floor of the vaulted temple, tilted their drained faces up to the great golden scroll, a coiled serpent on a black curtain. In a black robe, arms outspread, stood the colonel. His deep voice rose and fell like the dark surf. Michael still remembered the prescribed incantation.

'O mighty Ea to whom we give ourselves. Send Ishtar, thy beloved, lady of the gods, into the darkness to find her lost lover . . .'

'O mighty Ea' came the returning chant.

'. . . and let her return in her nakedness to fertilize the Earth.'

After that the followers prostrated themselves. The Lady Ishtar rose from her place on the first step to stand before the great curtain. She would drop her white robe, her only garment, and entwine her arms to follow the serpent's golden coils. A sigh, a current of wind before storm, would sweep the hall.

So time passed at NEVAH, time without measure. He forgot why or whether he had left home. Where he was going. The emptiness of the days, the nearness to power, the faces of others young as himself, blurred and focused in a contentment he had never known.

At last he was summoned to the Haven itself. He passed through the beamed and vaulted hall. He entered a small windowless room that must have been cut into the mountainside itself. The dim illumination was eerie. Above it the colonel's dark robe melted into the shadows.

Michael, he said, had passed through the first circle. He was ready for all that had been promised and would be given. All would be permissible. Without guilt. Without remorse.

A door at the rear of the room stood ajar. He was directed to pass through it.

Now Michael came out of his reverie and started up the engine of the red sports car. The rites he wished to avoid must be over by now.

Michael drove around the last curve. The grilled gates opened before him, and he found himself sweating. But this time he would win.

The man who called himself Colonel Chadwick could see the red sports car long before he heard it. He switched off the closed-circuit television, pushed shut the library-table drawer on its paraphernalia, and swung his pale leather chair around to the view beyond the rear window. It always soothed him. The jade-green peace of the lawn, its softness defying the drying winds of the mountaintop, the free-flowing shape of the pool, aqua light glinting among myriad flowering bushes and the bordered paths.

It was all a testament to his success, like the closets full of Savile Row suits, the dresser drawers of monogrammed silk shirts, the endless mirrors of cut crystal, rose quartz, and white jade reflecting the subdued light that was neither sunlight nor lamplight.

The colonel might well survey his Haven, his NEVAH, with pride. It was a monument to his sagacity, to his daring, and to his hard-earned experience of the eternal human dichotomy. On one side, the earthbound human animal filling his stomach, building himself shelter for survival. On the other side, emptiness, the void around and within himself. Herein lay his weakness, herein was his susceptibility. Thus he could be made pliable by nothing more deadly than his own dreams. Given food for those dreams, he could be made submissive.

Like every creator of illusion, the artist, the poet, the preacher, the magician, Colonel Chadwick understood this vulnerability. He made practical use of it. Gratefully the lonely, the lost, the failed, and the fearful, all accepted his promises. They came to his mountaintop. With sensible foresight he chose only those whose satisfactions they could pay for.

Money? The very softness of his voice was persuasive, money was the prison of the earthbound. Those attaining the realm of Ea would have no further need of it. Here lay not superstition but truth.

Yet, beneath the autocratic flow of his own words, the colonel felt uneasy.

He disliked confrontations. In Michael Roundtree's telephone call the colonel sensed a note of defiance, not deference. It could be dealt with, of course. But the colonel was no longer young. He had eluded all of his enemies. He wanted no more.

He heard the crunch of wheels on the gravel. The red car had passed through the gates. The colonel glanced around the room, satisfied. It was the living-room of a country gentleman, except that it was sound-proof. Natural stone, redwood panelling, sand-coloured leather chairs, filled it. A curved divan embraced a stone fireplace. Everywhere were the books. Walls of books: travel, philosophy, the occult. Closer inspection might reveal some of the fine bindings to be false, but their hollow interiors contained many of the essentials of the colonel's business.

A heavy Spanish refectory table bore a single ornament, a dark jade serpent, six inches high, so life-like that its glistening coils seemed to move in the light.

The colonel opened the table drawer and slipped a glass object into his pocket. A casual stance before the fireplace suited his superior casual tweeds. His left hand felt in the pocket of his jacket and toyed with the two halves of a jade scarab that he nowadays always kept with him. He did not relish this test of its infallibility.

'Welcome home, Michael.' It was only with the privileged that the colonel used real names. In the groves of NEVAH, guests knew each other only by given titles. 'Dushu, created son of Ea,' he added and made the palm-to-palm greeting.

Michael returned it perfunctorily.

The colonel gestured to the curved divan and sat down. Michael seated himself opposite.

'I expected you earlier, my boy.'

'I had things to do.'

'More important than – '

'A good deal more important, Colonel.'

The colonel understood. Michael was fencing, wanting to be drawn out. The colonel was expert at that.

'I was sorry to hear that your father had passed beyond.'

'Were you?' Michael paused. 'I wasn't.'

'Excellent. Will you have a drink?' Refreshment was unrestricted in the first circle.

'No, thank you.' Michael seemed to draw himself together. 'I came to tell you I'm going back to Thatcher.'

'Ah. Then you were welcomed. Very good. But I would think one visit enough for the time. You have no need to return.'

'Whether I have or not, I've decided to go back.'

'For how long?'

'As long as I choose, Colonel. That's what I came to tell you. I want to cut free of all this.'

'I can understand. And we agreed that since your

inheritance you must live a more open life. But you have not forgotten, I am sure, your debt here.'

'I've paid that a thousand times over. My God, look at the record!'

'Your indebtedness to NEVAH is not kept in books. It is kept in your soul, your peace of mind. Everything that has been given you. May I remind you where I found you? Without hope or direction, without friends or funds. I took you in.'

'For Christ's sake, turn it off! I'm not your creature. I paid you back. But I want my own life now. Free!'

'No one is free, Michael. Except here within the circles of Ea. I promised you that. Your freedom here. But no one, no one, can leave NEVAH on a whim. You know that. And if you try . . .'

'And if I try, Colonel?'

The colonel was on his feet, remarkably swift and strong for his years. With a single gesture he gripped Michael's wrist, below the serpent tattoo.

'If you try, Michael, you know you will fail!'

Michael saw the hypodermic needle materialize in the colonel's long hand. It would be easy to give way, as he had done before. But this time something bright and struggling was taking shape within him. Something he wanted and could not name.

He twisted out of the colonel's grip, spun around, and caught the colonel's shoulders, forcing him back upon the divan. It was only a step to an armlock on the round head. Then his fingers found the carotid artery, as the colonel himself had once taught him. *'It will require only eight seconds of resolute pressure to subdue your enemy. With finality.'*

He heard the colonel gasp, a stifled rattle. The long heron legs thrashed out. Then Colonel Chadwick slowly slid to the floor, a hypodermic needle rolled from his hand, a jade fragment, one half of the scarab, fell to the carpet.

Michael looked around.

Silence. Nothing disturbed, nothing heard. He stooped and picked up the piece of jade.

It would be four hours before the rites of Ishtar would

take place. And another eight perhaps before the followers dared to invade the colonel's privacy.

He was without emotion, even a sense of deed. He walked to the front door. For one instant he thought he caught a glimpse of a face reflected in a hall mirror. Then it was gone. His imagination. The residue of the NEVAH's fantasies.

He drove the car through the gates, which closed automatically behind him. At the bottom of the mountain he swung into highway traffic and let his thoughts settle to normalcy.

For ahead, on a long road, lay Thatcher. And the girl who could heal him of this inner hell. Lilith.

The end of one more of California's cult leaders attracted little attention in the press. A Washington paper gave a quarter of a column to the unique collection of jade found on his premises. Los Angeles papers gave it space on page nine, after two Hollywood paternity suits and a rape-strangulation assault. San Francisco papers all but bypassed it.

Besides, the city editor of San Francisco's feistiest daily was heartily sick of cults and the poison-and-sunshine image they gave the state. He was far more interested in the caller who sat waiting in the reception-room while he leaned on the telephone, listening to the relentless monotony of his boss's voice. It was over at last. He picked up his coat and went out to meet his visitor. A broad-shouldered man, greying at the temples and careless about his clothes. To the editor's sharp eye there was more than a hint of stubble on the chin.

'What the hell! Brock! God, I'm glad to see you!' He would normally add a 'How've you been?' But he knew.

'Good to be here, Phil.' The handshake was strong, the clap on the back hearty. But the famous grin had the hint of a twist and two new lines deepened the corners of the firm mouth. For a man only slightly north of forty, Brock Turner looked old. But his laugh was quick. 'Okay, now that you've finished inspection, where do we eat? It's on me, you old warthog, so pour it on. I'm out of touch with the town.'

Phil Black had been a newspaper editor too long to hurt a man's pride. He named the most expensive restaurant on the wharf and ordered Alaska king crab and a Grand Marnier Mousse.

Brock Turner began to relax. It had not been an easy decision. He had made headlines when he was fired from the White House. This time he was summoned not to the Oval Office, but to the office of a presidential adviser. Nor was he asked to be seated. The man was blunt, and Brock detected a certain satisfaction.

'You don't know how to take orders, Brock.'

'Not when it comes to opinion.'

'Opinion's not the name of the game here. We work together. What's mportant is image. Solidarity.'

'Sure, sure.' The whole thing was a waste of time. He'd forgotten more about newsmaking than these guys would ever learn. As for liaison, it hadn't taken him two weeks to discover that meant compliance, cover-up, patsy, fall guy. Brock's big chance was doomed from the beginning. In the final blaze of anger and frustration he walked as gratefully out of the White House as he had walked into it four months earlier.

The real shock had been Mortimer Russell. At first the great man was out of town. Once he was tied up with a six-million-dollar client. When Brock understood the message, he quit trying. After a couple of two-hour expense-account lunches with officials of other networks, he saw the whole picture, which in the end did not surprise him. Television, a gigantic tuning fork to every quaver of client mood, did not like failure. Especially in sensitive places. The most sensitive spot on this planet to every aspiring, jittery executive was the Oval Office.

Brock laid down his napkin, glanced out at the brilliant waters of the bay and the soaring reassurance of the great bridge, and grinned. This time it was freer, Phil Black noted. He liked this big bulky man from the day he had hired him, twenty years ago, as a cub reporter. God knew Turner wasn't easy. But he was honest. Like other men who had suddenly been forced to take the road down from the heights, he was a victim of that honesty.

'I guess I'd better level with you, Phil.'

'Since when?' The little editor had his own humour. 'But it's your nickel.'

'Have you got any need for a middle-aged reporter of vast experience who'd like to feel the pavement under his feet again?'

'You mean it, Brock?'

Brock held to his mood. 'Willing to work, not quibble. Given to late hours, sure stories. Salary not first consideration. Guarantees a good fight when he disagrees with the editor.'

Black saw the muscles in Brock's jaw tighten.

'Don't push it, Brock. You know damn well if you want a beat or a desk or a column with us it's yours. The pay's lousy.' The editor was enjoying himself. 'On the other hand, we don't have a can of Pan-Cake make-up in the place and you can go out to dinner without your autograph pen. When do you want to start?'

'Day after tomorrow. But I'd like a press pass today.'

'Why?'

'I want to go up to that cult centre. NEVAH.'

'What in hell for? That's locked up and under guard. There isn't anybody around now. It's finished.'

Brock hesitated. A man in his position had to spill his guts whether he liked it or not. He'd leave Lili out of it, although she had been with him, in his mind, these last few weeks as if she'd never left. A fading image. He'd never bring his kind of failure to her. He had a few ends to clear up. Then San Francisco would suit him fine. Middle age. She was still young . . . so young . . .

'Look, Brock, I'd better tell you. We're not covering NEVAH. We don't want any part of it. The kind of kooks who go in for that don't need any more publicity or encouragement. We'd like it forgotten.'

'I'll forget it, don't worry. But I knew someone Chadwick took up there. I ought to make one try.'

On the long drive up the mountain, he envisioned Lili's face dancing in the windshield, in the flow of clouds on the rim of the sky. He supposed it would be like that for a long time.

He stopped his car at the locked gate, flashed his press card, and tried to think about his purpose in coming. He knew there would be no records. Only first names, if any. There would probably be no trace of Marcia. But he had to know.

As he had to exorcize his private demon. To discover who or what had thinned his life and deprived him of his single, long-sought goal – the final confrontation with Brother Sunshine.

CHAPTER TWENTY-ONE

The news spread through Thatcher like spring wind, brightening eyes, freshening talk, and in an odd way stirring the bereft town to a sense of wholeness.

Michael Martin Roundtree, eldest son, bearer of the name, possessor now of a fortune that could be looked on as a rightful blessing, was coming home. The *Thatcher Standard* hinted that he had seen his duty properly. The *Bollington Eagle* speculated that maybe now the badly needed bridge would be hurried along.

People remembered Michael. But now they began to see him in new ways. He had always been a wild one. Stubborn as he was wild. But Martin Roundtree had pretty strict ideas even for Thatcher. As they thought about it, Michael had just been a little more headstrong than the others. No one could remember when a strain of wildness had not run in one or another of the Roundtrees. They talked now of Michael's dark good looks, of the sombre grief in his eyes as he walked with John beside their father's casket. Of what must have been his lonely years.

Young women and the mothers of budding girls noted, too, that Michael was still a bachelor. Heaven knew he had always been attractive to women. Young married matrons recalled with a private sigh his compelling attentions, remembering easy, purposeless surrender, and wondered why they had not waited for him. At least, it was agreed, Michael had had better sense than to marry the Irish bargirl who had flung herself at him. It was left to John to make Hester respectable. The town had accepted that marriage but in the privacy of its bedrooms had seen it as a sign of weakness. The same weakness John showed when he failed to wring out of Congress funds for a new bridge. Thatcher, when its emotions were stirred, had a way of overlooking uncomfortable facts. But John had his come-uppance. Hester had paid for her sins. Nobody wanted to speak ill of the dead.

Now Michael was returning, a new Roundtree – rich, strong, and with a titillation of mystery. With all that money Michael could live anywhere. He had chosen to come home.

The next rumour on the town's seismograph was that Michael, even before he arrived, had bought property. He had chosen for himself the huge granite-and-glass house on Thatcher Ridge. Built by the ambitious Orlinis (whom Thatcher had always looked on as intruders), it had stood empty for two years, an eyesore and a reminder of past evils. There was an old superstition that no one prospered who tried to live on the Ridge. But maybe Michael Roundtree would turn the stark structure into a place of hospitality and pleasure. Thatcher liked to remember when balls and receptions were given long ago in the big white Roundtree house on West Street. Maybe now . . . Of course Michael would need a wife. It could be lonely up on the Ridge for a woman.

The rumours brought John back from Washington. Michael had still not arrived. Sloshing through the April thaw of the valley floor, Willard silent beside him in high boots and mackinaw, John squinted up through the leafless trees at the granite-and-glass house, brooding and poised like a giant bird.

'Do you believe it, Will?'

'You have to believe a transfer of deed. It's been recorded.'

'But why? Why in God's name would Michael want that house? If he is coming back – and I don't believe for a minute he'll stay in Thatcher – why doesn't he do the decent thing and live in our house? Mom rattles around in it now. I don't think she likes all those empty rooms. Even with Lili there. Lili's been great. But I don't know whether Thatcher's her dish for very long.' He looked up at the harsh angles of the big house. The light glanced silver-cold from its glass walls. 'That house, Will. Everybody in Thatcher hated that house before the roof was on it.'

'Long before that, John.'

'I know. They never forgave Orlini for cutting down the old Thatcher oak up there to build that house. Neither have I. Three hundred and fifty years old, that tree. Thirty feet around. It was here when the Indians owned this valley. Sometimes I see it like a ghost, as if the house were paper thin and could blow away. But it won't. Now my own brother is going to live up there. A Roundtree in the Orlini house!'

Willard watched the big red Irish setter bounding ahead. He understood John's outburst, torn out of the long feud between the brothers, concealed only by the manners of good breeding at their father's funeral. He knew, too, the dark demons in Michael's genes. But there comes a period in a man's life when time must be weighed and wisdom portioned out carefully. He watched as the dog went splashing over tussocks of wet weeds and the startling bright green of unfolding skunk cabbage. Spring was the one constant.

'Nobody enjoys a good thaw like Clancy. Look at him! Mud from tail to head. Go after it, boy!' But the crow flapped away and Clancy leaped in joyous frustration to drier ground.

John was still staring at the house, his eyes narrow with anger.

'Michael hasn't said he was going to live there, John.'

'What else would he do with it?'

'He's applied for a variance to buy fifty more acres beyond the house along the Ridge. Or did you know?'

'Fifty! That would take in the old cave. And the slope

beneath it. That's where the solar-energy station is to go – if it's to work at all!'

'He's only applied, John. I think the town will stand with you. When Michael gets here, you can reason with him.'

'Reason! I haven't talked to him in nearly ten years. Look, maybe I'm still raw. I know I'm raw. Losing Hester and all. I can't face Michael, much less reason with him, knowing what he did to her. And to Dad. Maybe he doesn't know Dad had a stroke after he ran out. Maybe he doesn't know I stayed on . . . when it was his job to do so!' John's left boot slipped in the mud. He caught himself and his breath. 'Sorry, Will. I thought I had better control. I'm a big boy now.'

'No man is too big for his feelings. Go ahead. Shout 'em out. But then you'd better begin some cold thinking. I don't know any more than you do what Michael is after, but if that slope is important to you – '

'I'll fight him for that, Will. Even if I can't fight him for a lot of other things. That slope is not for sale to anybody.'

They turned back to the farmhouse in silence. The walk was serving its purpose. Will noted that some colour had come to John's strained face. He counted on John. A steadying man, when his own years were shortening.

'After all, maybe Charlie Redwing has it right.'

Some of the tension in John eased. 'I never knew when you could prove him wrong, Will.'

'I will when I know as much as that old Indian. He says that the Ridge belongs to no man. The gods of his people live there. They will strike down any invader.'

John managed a grin. 'Orlini should have heard that before he built that monstrosity. Michael can have it if that's what he wants. But the rest of the Ridge and the slope? No! This is one fight, Will, that I'm going to win.'

Lili sat on a slab of rock and turned her face up to the sun. A few yards below, the Birch River, still at crest, flowed sparkling and clean. Clean as the washed blue of the sky. And the streets and lawns of this small incredible town that knew exactly what and who it was. And who everybody else was.

She had grown used to that. She had been in Thatcher now more than five weeks. The townspeople nodded to her, some greeted her, some stopped to chat. Then, she was sure, they hastened along to whisper behind a hand. A new Roundtree, young, head-high like the rest, with those enormous blue eyes. She certainly didn't look like the others. And there had been a man but she had never married. Henrietta's blood there. Everybody knew that story.

Not that Lili minded any of it. The calm routine of Edythe Roundtree's days swept her along, as did Edythe's special stamina.

'Jim Cartwright, our old doctor, wouldn't have dared! But that young man right off gave me a capsule and pills. I asked him what for and he said they would soothe me. I gave them back and told him I didn't want to be soothed. I loved my husband, Lili. I want to live my grief as I lived my life with him. Why do people these days want to deprive you of your deep feelings?'

Sometimes at night Lili would hear Edythe's light step. Sometimes there would be a cocoa cup on the kitchen counter. Martin had liked hot cocoa before bedtime. Sometimes Lili would find snips of coloured wool beside the living-room chair where Edythe always sat with her needlepoint while Martin read. Sometimes, when a young moon dappled the lawn's darkness, a french window to the wide veranda would be found unlocked. Lili asked no questions. Edythe was *living*.

Lili searched for her own healing. Her first New England spring burst with an intensity unknown in the steamy warmth of New Orleans. Thatcher's spring came in a sudden storm of yellow forsythia, a silvery alert of pussy willows, the overnight surrender of snow to crocus spears, and the sweet-smelling delights of garden mud. It came with the fife and flute of swamp frogs, the piping of chickadees, woodpeckers' riveting, the liquid yearnings of cardinals and wood doves, the sudden alightings of flocks of robins. And most magic of all, the veil of red mist on the hills, the first budding of the northwoods. An alien April that brought to Lili, as it brought to every living creature in and on the earth, a sweet restlessness.

She had walked a tightrope of self-discipline against Brock's silence. The temptation to call him was fading. She no longer turned on the television set or opened a newspaper, half hoping. His success must be as great as it was secret. Only at night did she find herself thinking of the solid years of loving, building, enduring that Edythe Roundtree had known. She was still young, she told herself. Young enough for what?

Edythe eyed her closely.

'There's an old saying, Lili: You are either born a Roundtree or you become one. I'm not sure that I ever really made it. But you belong. Oh, yes, my dear. You come straight down from Henrietta. And that is no small matter. I never believed all that gossip. But if Henrietta had another man, I could hardly blame her. In fact, I think it would be rather encouraging for the family genes. Isaac was a most difficult person. How she endured him through all those children I'll never know, but they do say she was mad for him when they were married. Poor Isaac and his Bible. It must have been a centreboard in their bed.' Edythe laughed. It was something she would not have said to Martin. She liked this girl, with her independence. And her concealed hurt. 'Anyhow, I've always held that Isaac took some understanding too. His father was the town miller. When he wasn't grinding flour down by the river he was up on Preacher Hill, behind Willard's farm, preaching fire and brimstone, carrying on until he set the whole countryside by the ears. They say the cows bawled and the horses spooked. Well, after a good session of that everybody promised to do better, but I don't believe for a minute they ever did. I think in those days they liked to have the devil around and were perfectly willing to pay for their sins by hearing out old Ezra.' Edythe put down her needlepoint and wiped her eyes. 'I came from New York City. I thought I wanted to be a singer, mostly because I was in love with a young baritone. Instead I married Martin. Thatcher wasn't easy, my dear. It never has been for outsiders. The townsfolk are always right. Even when they're not, they're firm. And that's worse. I had to learn the Roundtrees. Like the begats in the Bible. I began with Isaac. He was a farmhand and a Civil War soldier. He got away from old Ezra, but his Mattie couldn't stand it. I can't say I blamed her. She finally went up and lived in the cave on the Ridge, poor woman, until she died of exposure. She was a little mad, but who wouldn't be? Isaac made a success of things but to the day he died, I think the devil was as real to him as his own wife. Maybe more so. Well, that's in the blood too . . .' Edythe let her voice trail with her needle. She had said more than she had intended.

'Where's the cave?' Lili asked for something to say.

'Up on the Ridge. I always thought it was dangerous. There's no real bottom to it. It just goes into an opening, a fault, when the slabs of rock were thrown together millions of years ago. I never liked the boys to go up there. But Martin said all the Roundtrees played up there.' Her eyes suddenly showed mischief. 'If you knew this family, you knew that settled it.'

She rolled up her wool. 'I talk too much, Lili. Old people never know how they bore young people with the past. I must think of things for you to do.'

But Lili wanted nothing more than these slow days, the long walks, the enveloping old house. Now, sitting high on the riverbank, she watched the lovely water, free as a running mare. The half-completed pillars for the new bridge rose on either side, framing only light and air. This land, like her own life, was cut sharply in half. How or when it would be bridged she had no idea.

A car stopped on the road above her. She did not turn.

'Well, well, well! Hi!'

He was coming down the slope towards her, handsome in a white turtleneck sweater, an obviously expensive tweed jacket, and smartly cut slacks. On the road above stood a new foreign-made sports car, all quite unlike Thatcher.

'Hello, Michael,' she said carefully.

He slid like an athlete the few remaining feet to the rock where she sat.

'My lucky day!' He held out his hand. She took it and found it not quite easy to release.

'Don't tell me you weren't expecting me?'

'Oh, I heard you were coming.'

He sat down on the rock beside her. 'Is that all?'

'What else is there?'

'I thought you might be a little glad to see me.'

She was used to this parry and thrust. Brock had been an expert. Yet this made her uncomfortable, as if in itself it contained a trap.

'Of course I'm glad to see you, Michael. Edythe will be too.'

'I wasn't asking about my mother. Though she's well, I hope.'

'She's splendid. I wish I had her courage.'

'She'd be better off with yours.'

Lili started to rise.

'Hey, wait a minute. Where are you going?'

'I was just starting back.'

'What's the hurry?' He laughed and took her wrist, pulling her down beside him. 'I've got a few things to say to you. In fact I've been thinking a lot about you while I was out west. Sit down and tell me what's wrong.'

'There's nothing wrong. Everything's fine. I know your mother will be glad to see you.'

She was annoyed with herself and with him. She was behaving like a schoolgirl. Michael Roundtree was a distant cousin, that was all. And she had begun all wrong. She had fluttered and given him an advantage.

'Then relax. Where's your car?'

'I walked.'

'A mile and a half?'

'Three, round trip.'

'A country girl! By heaven, I wouldn't have believed it. Okay. So I'll drive you home. My luck's still running. But then it always did. I'm the lucky one in the family. You know why? Because I make my luck. Like Napoleon, I make circumstances. But I'm always grateful. You know, actually, that you were responsible for my clearing out of this town?'

'That's not true. You left because you wanted to.'

'But you gave me the push and that neat little card telling

me where I'd find a welcome. NEVAH. Some day I'll tell you about that too. Anyhow, if it weren't for you, I'd be sitting on Main Street right now, Roundtree and Roundtree, Attorneys at Law, settling old man Blodgett's suit over a broken chicken-wire fence. Fee, fifty bucks. So don't knock it. Meeting you changed all that. I tried to express my gratitude at the time, if you remember.' He gave her a sidelong glance, and to her irritation she felt her face flush. 'I guess you do.'

'I'm glad things worked out,' she said shortly. 'I'd like to start home.'

'Right. Come on. You'll break the shock of my arrival. I'm the prodigal, Lilith. But unrepentant. This town goes for that. A little sin always livens things up around here. And with you at my side – '

'I wouldn't count on that, Michael. I won't be here all that long.'

He grinned. 'While you're here, I'll make you famous. Or infamous.' He picked up a string glove she had left on the rock and touched it to his mouth. 'I'll wear your colours in the jousts, my girl – or don't they teach anybody to read about things like chivalry any more?'

As they drove through Thatcher, she saw a few townspeople turn and look.

Michael waved cheerfully back. 'That's Hazel Haskell, the librarian. She always told me I'd come to no good if I didn't return the books I borrowed. There's old man Slater. Runs the stationery store. I used to swipe the dimes people left outside for the newspapers when I needed them. He'd see me do it. But never told Dad on me. I used to hate his guts because he *knew*.'

As they turned into West Street, Michael's tone lost its banter. 'Tell me, has my esteemed brother, John, established residence yet?'

'If you mean does he stay here when he's not in Washington, yes.'

'Is he here now?'

'Yes.'

'What a merry little group we're going to be. All under the family roof. Never mind. Tomorrow I'll take you up and show you the house I've bought. It's quite a place.'

His grin returned. 'Actually, Lil, I'm a nice guy when you get to know me.'

John did not return for dinner that night or the next. Young Kim dashed in about five-thirty and out at five-forty, with a Larry's-taking-me-to-the-goat-farm. Or so it sounded. Michael, to Lili's relief, was occupied with his own affairs. Edythe had become subdued.

On the third afternoon, near dinner-time, Michael flung into the house and hurled a newspaper on the hall table. Lili, in the living-room with Edythe, caught a glimpse of his face, dark with anger. Edythe rose quickly.

'Where's John?' he called.

'He hasn't come home yet, Michael.' Edythe's voice was soft. But Lili heard nervousness. 'He said he'd be here for dinner.'

Michael stood in the entrance, the paper again in his hand.

'Did you see this?'

'Not yet, dear.'

He thrust it at her. 'Then read it. Read it! And see what this goddamned nothing of a town is trying to pull off. A town meeting to "consider" the sale of the Ridge property to Michael Roundtree! "Consider"! Don't they know who the hell I am? I've got the right and the money to buy anything I want in this town. If this is John's idea . . .!' He seemed to see Lili for the first time. 'Hello! Sorry, Lilith. The Roundtrees never wanted to wash their dirty linen in public, but you might as well know how things are in this house!' He crossed the room and stood looking down at her. 'I didn't keep my promise, did I?'

'Promise, Michael?'

'I told you I'd take you up to see my new place. I've got the house, all right. It's the fifty acres beyond it I want. How about now?'

She had hoped he had forgotten. She was now quite sure she did not want to go anywhere with Michael. His confidence, his way of looking at her, the challenge he seemed to make of everything. She had known men before who were volatile, compelling, sure of themselves. But in Michael there was something else, something that left her uneasy.

'It's a little late, isn't it?'

'For a six-mile drive and back? You've got to be kidding!'

She glanced at Edythe.

'There's plenty of time, dear. Dinner is not till seven.' There was almost an urgency in Edythe's voice. Still Lili hesitated. Beneath the quiet running of this settled house she sensed old and hidden hostilities; in the ticking of the hall clock a hundred long-kept secrets, like mice scurrying in the walls. But Lili knew she had the overblown imagination of an only child in a house of adults.

'All right, Michael,' she said lightly. 'Why not?'

He drove fast and she liked it. She liked the way the smart little car hugged the curves of the road, the wind loosened and stroked her hair, the scent of pine and warming earth rose to meet her as he turned up the Ridge road. In the headiness of spring she almost forgot the man beside her. She was moving, living. She was young. Her long, dutiful weeks would soon be over. There was a world beyond this, even beyond Brock, for Lili Roundtree. A world she would make for herself. She was winging on.

He glanced at her, her lips parted, her eyes bright, the slight irregularity of her features that gave her at thirty a surprising beauty. He reached over and put his hand over hers.

She came back from spring's entrapment. She slid her hand carefully away.

He grinned and with a flourish swung the car out of the woods and on to a gravelled turning-circle.

The house took her breath away. Glittering, soaring in the still-bright April day, it thrust two great angles of glass and granite into the mild sky. Below lay the valley and the toylike roof of Willard Roundtree's farmhouse. To the east the white spire of one of Thatcher's four churches pointed the way to God. To the west the mauve hills rolled limitlessly to a pale horizon. But it was the house itself that held her. Whoever had built it flung defiance at this placid world.

'What do you think of it?'

'Spectacular.'

'I thought you would. The fellow who built it, Orlini, a wheeler-dealer type, had nothing but trouble here, so he finally put it up for sale. There's a lot of local superstition about it now, mainly because the town hates it. There used to be a three-hundred-year-old oak tree where we're walking. The town never forgave him for cutting it down. What the hell is one tree? The woods are full of them. The day I saw this place I bought it. It says everything.'

She wondered what. They crossed the gravel to a brick path, chipped and cracked and sprouting grass. A broad terrace overlooked the empty pool. Weeds sprang from between the tiles. The floor of the pool was damp with dead leaves. Eight marble pedestals rimmed the pool like blind eyes.

'Orlini liked big marble nudes. Thank God, they're gone. I like mine living.' The youthfulness had returned to his face, the bravado to his talk. Michael Roundtree would take a lot of knowing. It was not for her to try.

'Let's go in. I want you to see the house itself.'

The sun, lower in the sky, lit one glass wall with flame. The others had turned silver-cold. Suddenly she saw this house not in its arrogance but its loneliness. Whoever had lived here knew anguish.

He unlocked the glass doors that led into the living-room. She stepped through twelve-foot white drapes and again caught her breath. The vaulted room was furnished in stark blacks and whites, broken only by blood-red strokes of terra-cotta. Thick white carpeting emphasized the black wrought-iron staircase that spiralled the double-storey height. Yet it was frozen, as if life itself had stopped at the threshold.

He led her to the flame-touched glass wall.

'Now look into the room.'

'At what?'

'Can't you tell? Can't you *see*?'

He was staring up to the Gothic apex of the room.

'Don't you get it? It's more than a house. It's like a temple. To the sun god. To Ea.'

'I don't know what you're talking about, Michael.'

He rubbed his hand over his face. 'I get to seeing things sometimes. I suppose it's being by myself so much. I mean, inside. I'm a loner, in a way. I think you are too. That's why I wanted you to see this place. You'd understand. But nobody has to be alone, you know. There's a way.'

He turned and looked out. Through the leafless trees she saw the rise of the Ridge. 'That's where I want fifty more acres. There's a cave out there. I'll show it to you some day. It's not very big. But it could be made bigger. Like a grotto. Like the place of . . .'

He was looking at her intently. He stepped back as if to see her in a better light. 'Like the place of Ishtar . . . lady of the gods . . .'

She saw a film of perspiration on his forehead. His face looked clouded, old. She heard herself laugh nervously. 'I'm sure it's all very romantic, Michael. But I don't know what it's all about. Can we go?'

'No! No, Lilith. Stand there. Just where you are. There in the light.' His voice was not his own. His eyes were blank, as if he were searching for something far, far in the distant depths of his mind. 'Lilith. Ishtar! You *are* Ishtar . . . lady of the gods, beloved of Ea. Ea is dead . . . Lilith . . . Ishtar . . .'

He came towards her. She must not panic. She had read somewhere that human fear gives off a scent that can infuriate, even madden.

'Ea is dead. I am his prophet! You have gone into the darkness, O Ishtar, to find your lost lover. You have returned with the Waters of Life.' The chant was coming faster. 'Show me your nakedness, O Ishtar, that all creatures may call to each and in their coupling . . . in their coupling . . . renew the earth!'

Then at last she understood. Even in her fear, she felt a terrible pity. This was Michael, the dark seed of Isaac, who long ago had hurled himself at the devil on these same hills. This was the worship at Carnival time. Abandoned to ecstasy. This was the young nun she had once seen prostrate on the stones in her secret climax with the Bridegroom.

The ancient need to fill the void that lives in all creatures, the pagan terror of the unknown that flickers through civilization's shallow crust. Michael held out something that shone.

'For you, O Ishtar, immortal life . . .!'

It was a fragment of the darkest green jade in the shape of a scarab. One half of a scarab.

It was then she heard the car, faint but unmistakable.

'Michael . . .' she said softly.

He dropped the jade into his pocket. His powerful body seemed to slump. The glow had faded from the glass wall, leaving a grey mist tinged, like his eyes, with sadness.

'It's time to go,' she added gently.

He nodded. 'You must be cold, we've stayed too long.' The words came, tired, normal.

The car reached the gravelled circle. The engine cut out. Michael parted the white curtains and pushed open the glass doors. Lili moved quickly past him.

On the brick path a tall figure came towards them. He glanced sharply, first at Lili, then Michael.

'Would you wait in my car, Lili?' John said quietly. 'I must talk to my brother. Alone.'

CHAPTER TWENTY-TWO

The course of ordered days resumed in the old house. Lili carried the burden of her secret. She dreaded the hour when Michael would return. But that hour did not come. John had left for Washington. He would be back for the town meeting.

Whatever had happened on the Ridge had not changed the town's determination to hear out the case between the brothers. Half the town believed that Michael Roundtree should have anything he wanted. He was a man, they said, who would get things done. The other half said that John should be given his chance. They had not much faith in solar energy. The sun in Thatcher's history came when it had a mind to and not when any man willed. Still, it was better than the nuclear business that John had managed to halt.

The meeting was set for the last Saturday afternoon in April. It was a good omen. That was Thatcher's spring rite, Arbor Day.

'You must come, Lili.' Edythe had maintained questionless calm, sitting at her needlepoint. 'All the Roundtrees are expected. A sort of civic duty. Martin always took charge. John will this year. They always plant a tree. For years they planted an acrostic of the town. Tulip tree for T, hemlock for H, aspen or ash for A . . . spell out all kinds of things, names of battles, Victoria's Jubilee, and a whole avenue of trees for a poem. What was it? Oh, Browning. "The best is yet to be, the last of life, for which the first was made."' Edythe's laugh was good to hear even though the chatter seemed to be filling a sieve of silence. 'But Thatcher was never quite up to that, so they settled on the town name. They ran out of R's. So this year they're going to plant an oak tree. A sort of memorial for the one we lost. Though none of us are going to be here to see if it, too, lives three hundred years. Anyhow' – Edythe snipped off her wool as if it were a personal enemy – 'you must come. And to the meeting later, I hope.'

Lili did not answer. The meeting had become M-Day. She had another life she must find. Firm ground against these quicksands. She was now past thirty. In Thatcher thirty meant two children, maybe three – and springcleaning. Life hadn't brought her that. Yet with Brock . . . She slept restlessly and found she could still ache for his arms. She set herself a departure date.

The night before M-Day young Kim knocked on her door.

'Lili, would you mind if I talked to you?'

'I'd love it!' Kim's face was as radiant as it was troubled. Lili shook off a feeling of age.

'Lili, what's the matter with Michael?'

'Why do you ask me, Kim?'

278

'Because you went up to his house on the Ridge. Nobody else has. He doesn't want anybody up there. He's living up there now, but you never see any lights. Last night Larry said he saw little lights up near where the cave is. What could he be doing up there?'

'I haven't the faintest idea.' It had a hollow ring. And Kim caught it. She gave Lili a sharp glance.

'Okay. But I wish he'd never come back. It was awful all those years he was gone. But it was better than this. He and John never got along. Not about anything. And when John married Hester, Michael's girl – Well, I'm just sort of worried, I guess. About a lot of things.'

Lili gave her the warmest smile she knew. The girl was young, so young, after all.

'Yes. Larry.'

'Oh. He's a very nice young – ' Lili caught herself. She could hear Aunt Clem. Is that how one slid from youth to middle age, suddenly hearing oneself? She laughed and it felt better.

'What about Larry, Kim?'

'He wants to marry me.'

'Do you want to marry him?'

'No. I mean – Well, he said he'd wait. Wait! Isn't that grim? I'll be eighteen in a few months. You can't *wait* for things when you're that old. I just don't want to marry him. I couldn't say this to Mom. Or anybody. But you didn't get married, did you?'

'No.' Lili saw it coming, plain and clear.

'But you lived with him all that time. Don't look embarrassed. I knew it. I knew everything that went on in this family just because I was the youngest and nobody thought I heard. I used to watch Brock Turner on television and think how divine for Lili. She just lives with him and doesn't have to bother with anything else, or what anybody thinks. That's what I want with Larry. He says no. It's not going to be that way. I'm a nice girl. I'm sorry . . . I mean, anyhow, Larry says he wants to wait . . . until I'm ready. I'm worth it . . . what I mean is . . .' The words trailed.

Lili looked into something distant. And long gone.

'Do you ever want to marry him?'

'Yes. But not when I'm young. I want to be free. I want to know the real me. Don't you see, Lili?'

'Of course I see. That's what I thought too. Once. When I was engaged. Tell me, Kim, would you mind if you lost Larry?'

'I'd die. He's the only man – I mean he understands everything. How I feel about animals, how I cried when I found the pony tied up and starving. I mean, Larry – he's just all I'll ever want. I love him. But getting married? *You* didn't. And you have everything. I thought maybe if you talked to Larry . . .'

Lili felt her face tighten. Then she laughed. She found something quite dreadful happening. She could not stop. She discovered she was crying with great shaking sobs. This girl, so shining with her own love, was looking at her.

'Don't, Lili. Don't, please! I didn't mean to say anything. I thought – I don't know what I thought. I'm just stupid, I guess. Everybody learns to do things and say things and I was just always tied up with my guinea pigs and gerbils and frogs. I'm just a cluck! Don't cry! Please!'

Kim's arms were around her. Lili stopped shaking. She straightened, found a handkerchief, and managed a tight smile.

'I'm all right, Kim. Honestly. Maybe I needed that. You just made me sentimental. Or something.'

'I'm a stupe. You see, I thought after all those years and everything, it was all just beautiful to end like that. I mean, you so smart and independent and Brock going back with his wife.'

'What did you say?'

'Oh, I knew that too. Beth, my girl-friend, gets all the gossip magazines. We read Brock Turner found his wife somewhere in a retreat or some place, and took her away. I thought, well, you'd just done everything right and you're still free and beautiful and . . .'

A second, a century, passed.

'Kim.' Lili's voice came wire-thin but steady. 'I can't help you with Larry. You have to know yourself. If you love him, that's the opposite of being free anyhow, isn't it?'

Long after the door closed, Lili sat slight and numb, as the house grew colder. She had no tears left.

Brock and Marcia.

It was the one thing she had not thought of.

Lili slept badly, awakened by dreams she could barely remember and pain she could not at once identify. John had come in after midnight. She had heard the car stop, the front door open, Edythe's light steps run down the steps. Subdued voices, then the creaking non-silence of the old house, restless as herself.

A thin greyness shaped the window. She heard the patter of light rain. Arbor Day. No part of her life. But what was her life now? Where could she get hold of it, where to begin, when the heart of it had been cut out and she was past thirty? She lay sorting the fragments of dreams. Brock. She knew now that she had lived through the months of separation confident that she would meet him again, confident that eventually . . . Brock, in her dreams, coming towards her. Brock, frozen on a white screen. Brock and a woman, her back to Lili and going towards him. And everywhere glass, soaring glass walling her from him. From Brock and the woman.

She sat up abruptly, pushing at the darkness. Six-ten a.m. One more day to go through. Then she would leave. Whatever she had imagined, she was no more a part of this place than a part of Brock. Or of any of the unsubstantial, baseless places they had shared. Winging on . . .

She turned back the bedclothes. She would dress and fix breakfast and do whatever else she could. It would not be easy. But she would – it was almost a prayer – forget Lilith Roundtree. There was time later to pick up those pieces.

To her surprise John was in the kitchen before her.

'I thought city girls – '

'Didn't eat breakfast? Well, I'm starved and furthermore I'm an excellent cook.' She tied a large, striped apron almost double around her. It fitted like a sheath. She was, John thought, a woman who could make anything look chic. 'Stand aside, man, there's a woman working. What'll it be? *Café complet?*' She flashed a grin and John found the kitchen brighter.

'Also a couple of eggs over, some bacon, a plate of sausage, and toast light.'

'You can get out the plates.' She saw his face was grey with fatigue but his strong, craggy looks, his long, thin frame, gave a steadiness, a normalcy, to the new day.

She worked silently. The kitchen warmed to the sizzle of frying and the aroma of coffee. She sat John down at the table and poured out his first cup.

'Oh, boy!'

'Anything wrong?'

'Up-country, they'd call this a wedge of iron.'

'Good. Get you on your feet.'

Then she opened the refrigerator and took out the remains of a cold pot roast and a half of an apple pie.

John took one look and threw back his head in laughter.

'Right on, Lil! You're in. You've made it!'

'This is New England, isn't it?'

'It sure is. And if you'd add a pot of baked beans, a platter of hashed brown potatoes, some Birch River bass, and a rabbit pie, I could go out and get some ploughing done.'

She giggled and felt good. This man had a kindness, a humanity. She let him finish his breakfast in silence.

'Thanks, frontier woman.' He pushed his chair back and looked down at her. 'I'm glad you're here, Lili. I'll always be grateful.' At the door he turned. 'And by the way, I wish you'd get rid of all those Lili's and Lil's. Elizabeth's been a good New England name for a long time.'

'I'll remember that.'

He had made no mention of seeing her with Michael on the Ridge. It left a curious rift in the morning.

By eleven o'clock the rain had stopped, the clouds began to break up, and slits of blue let down a watery April sunshine on the crowd gathered on Thatcher Green.

A speaker's stand stood before the library steps. Beyond the granite monument to Thatcher's three centuries of war dead, a truck was parked. On the flatbed lay a two-year-old oak tree, its roots balled in burlap.

At the lower end of the Green, where two ancient elms had fallen and the sunlight came clear, a large hole had been dug.

Town dignitaries gathered on the stand. John, centre. Beside him a round fussy little woman worked at a large, drooping hat.

'Flora Macwinnie,' whispered Edythe. 'She wrote the Arbor Day song too.'

On John's other side sat Thatcher's new mayor, a bulky man with his hands on ample knees.

'Mayor Wright,' came Edythe's whisper. 'He used to be called Big Moon, down at Juno's Landing. John's going to recommend him for his seat in Congress.'

Beside the mayor sat a tiny wizened man whose bright eyes darted warmly over the crowd.

'Rabbi Melton from Bollington. Will says he knows more about trees than any man east of the Mississippi. He goes to the Holy Land once a year to plant trees and always comes home discouraged. But he says when the forests are back on the deserts, there'll be no more trouble.'

Oddly enough Willard Roundtree was not present.

The high school band trumpeted. Young voices rose shakily.

'Thatcher, may thy trees remind us of the glorious past
   behind us.
May they endure and proudly stand, symbols of this lasting
   land.'

The crowd found itself and the children followed, high and thin.

'Leaf and fruit, wind and bird, may thy messages be heard.
When each of us our course has run, may this tree still see
   the sun.'

Four men lifted the young oak sapling from the flatbed and tilted it upright beside the hole. The mayor rose.

'We dedicate this new tree to the victims of the bridge.' That was all. The national anthem was sung. It was over.

Except, to everyone's surprise, John Roundtree came forward on the platform and held up his arms. There was a wind rush of whispers, as if the gossip that lived so close to Thatcher's surface was escaping like steam.

'My good friends!'

The crowd quieted. For all their carping, they knew John was a sound one. He never talked without a reason.

'What I am going to say is not part of Arbor Day. Yet in a way it is. A while ago we lost an oak tree up there on the Ridge. It was three hundred and fifty years old. We hope the tree we are planting today will live through the next three hundred and fifty years. That, my friends, will be the year 2324. The point is, what are we, here in the middle, going to do to see that this young tree survives?'

The crowd shifted. They were never comfortable with reminders of their own mortality. If John was talking up his solar-energy cause, they weren't exactly clear about that either. Not if it cost money.

'Or to see that this town itself survives?' The crowd halted, rock still. 'For the last two weeks I've been travelling and listening. Do you know what they're saying in Washington? In Hartford, our own state capital? In banks and boardrooms? Do you know why that bridge is still half finished? Why there's no new highway planned to include us? Because they're saying *this town will die*. Then they say *let it*!'

John loosened his collar. 'Well, I won't. The Roundtrees have been here, rich and poor, warts and all, since the first settlers. Maybe some of us have been better or worse than others. But we've worked, we've tried. We believe in this town . . . and this state.'

'Attaboy, Johnnie . . . !'

'Thanks, Caspar!' John waved. 'Maybe you ought to know why we believe in Thatcher. Maybe you don't know because you've not taken the trouble to find out. We're famous here in this state. For one thing – clocks. For another, schoolteachers. Our clocks tell you the right time. Our schoolteachers tell you what to do with it!'

There was a ripple of laughter and a scattering of applause.

'That's only the beginning. Connecticut had the first democratic articles of law in American history. The Fundamental Orders of sixteen-sixty-two came with the charter from Charles the Second. In sixteen-sixty-two we had the first public election. You had to be moral to vote. We had the first cotton crop, the first cotton gin. And in eighteen-thirty we made the first American hoopskirt, though I'm not sure what that did for civilization.'

'It sure cut down the rate of population,' shouted a male voice. The crowd roared. They were enjoying themselves now. 'More, Johnnie!'

'There is more. In eighteen-fifty-six we made the first successful condensed milk in this nation. And, my friends, in nineteen-oh-one we set the first American speed limit for automobiles. Twelve miles an hour in the country. Eight in the city!'

They continued to laugh. There was nothing at this moment that John Roundtree could not have.

'There's only one thing we didn't achieve. When King Charles gave Connecticut its charter, he set the western boundary of this state at the Pacific Ocean. I'm afraid we blew that!'

The applause broke like a storm. The laughter came in waves. Thatcher had always an earthy good nature.

'Give us time, Johnnie!'

John held up his arms again. 'Time is what we have, friends. All we need now is a chance to make history. Or a chance to go down the drain. I've brought back with me the promise of a grant of one million dollars from the Fund of the Future . . . if in two years we can make this solar-energy experiment work. Another first for Thatcher, a first for Connecticut – and for all of us – the way we want to live.'

The silence was so sudden that John shifted awkwardly, almost boyishly.

'I've kept you all pretty long. I just thought you ought to know.'

Edythe turned her head, but not before Lili saw the glint of tears.

'I wish Martin had been here,' she said softly.

But Lili saw something else in her mind's eye: Michael at

the soaring glass window pointing along the Ridge to his cave.

Willard Roundtree's caller looked out at the view, then settled himself in an armchair.

Willard would now miss the Arbor Day ceremony. It was just as well, he thought. Time for John to take over for himself.

He set out two crystal wine-glasses and a cut-glass ship's decanter. 'Madeira, sir? Or do you prefer something stronger?'

'Not during business, thanks.' Mr Riccardo was a stocky man, black hair a little too long for Willard's taste, striped suit a little too tight-fitting, and western boots with a decided yellowish cast. But he had the sharpest pair of eyes that Willard had seen in a long time. Entirely compatible with his business card: DETECTIVE RAOUL RICCARDO, SAN FRANCISCO POLICE DEPARTMENT.

'Nice piece of land you have here, Mr Roundtree.'

'We think so. But then any land has its quality if it's respected.'

'Right.' Mr Riccardo measured his host. 'You're a reasonable man, Mr Roundtree.'

'I'd consider it a lifetime achievement, sir.'

Mr Riccardo nodded appreciatively. 'Then I'll begin by being direct, because there doesn't seem to be any other way to do it.' He had a notepad in his hand; he wrote rapidly on it and handed the slip of paper to the old lawyer. 'Ever seen this word?'

Willard read it, looked puzzled for a moment, then smiled.

'I think so. It's a proper name. Anatole France used it, if I remember, for the guardian angel in *The Revolt of the Angels*. And Padraic Colum, I believe, describes it in *Myths of the World*. Ishtar was an ancient Babylonian goddess, said to have re-fertilized the world.'

'Would you believe a cult?'

'My dear fellow, I'd believe anything today.'

Detective Riccardo sighed. 'That makes it a lot easier. My business is to believe nothing until I see it. But I've seen it. That's why I'm here.' He shifted uncomfortably. Legwork was a lot more to his taste than sitting in the presence of this elderly gentleman, with what he had to say to him.

'Mr Riccardo, if we're going to discuss the occult or the – what do the young people say today? – flaky, we should at least fortify ourselves. I urge you to try the Madeira. It's especially fine. I'm not sure we'll find this quality again.'

Mr Riccardo changed his mind and accepted the small glass. It was everything his host had promised. And warming, besides.

'I'll come straight to the point, Mr Roundtree, although it isn't my usual style. I'm from homicide, in Frisco. It seems we've had another oddball California murder. At least we have reason to think it is. The chief wants an answer, fast. Ever hear of a man called Colonel Chadwick? Sanford Chadwick?'

'No.' If Willard had an uneasy premonition, he would wait. Time, as he had learned long ago, was on the side of cautious delay.

'Chadwick, under a dozen different names, has been known to police departments for a long time. Opium trader, alien smuggler, con man, cultist, you name it. He's made a bundle of money and always managed to slip away.'

Mr Riccardo paused and let his gaze wander to the calm, springtime loveliness of the greening valley. It made his own task more awkward.

'Three weeks ago Colonel Chadwick was found dead in the fancy retreat he had founded up in the hills outside Frisco. It was diagnosed as a heart attack. The police went through the house because of the man's record. They found everything. Underground passages, black altars, fetishes, symbols, and, in one underground room called the Grotto, enough LSD, mellow-yellow frenquel – that's bananas, in case you're not with it – morning-glory seeds, and enough other junk to keep an entire cult high for a year. It cost a thousand bucks a week to stay at his place for the "cure". The colonel played for big stakes. They closed up the joint and sent the thirty-five "guests" home, if they had one. Otherwise to rehabilitation centres.

'Now comes the clincher, Mr Roundtree. A newspaper reporter went up there on assignment – Brock Turner, if you remember the name – I guess out of curiosity, looking for a story. They let him in. He found a woman living there in one of the hideaway rabbit warrens. Pretty well shot, I guess. But she had a story. She said Chadwick had promised her she would become Ishtar. When it didn't happen, she broke one of the cult rules and went to his house. She was hiding there in one of the hallways when a man came in. The place is loaded with mirrors and she could see into the living-room. She claims the man suddenly jumped at Chadwick and crushed his head. Then he stooped, picked something up off the floor, and ran out.'

For an instant Detective Riccardo wondered if the elderly gentleman was listening. He seemed to be studying the pine panelling of the wall.

'Yes, Mr Riccardo?'

'The murderer, she said, was one of the cult members. His name was Dushu, son of Ea. That lost us. It seems everybody was given weirdo names at NEVAH. And of course the colonel's head was not crushed. There was no mark of violence on his body. But anybody familiar with the effect of pressure on the carotid artery . . . As I said, I believe nothing. On the other hand, as Sherlock Holmes said, when you've eliminated everything that is possible, you have only the impossible left. You begin to believe that. We put her in a hospital. Then we talked to her again. She remembered after a time her own name, Marcia.'

'And the man's?'

'We didn't get that. But we learned what he had picked up off the floor.'

The detective fished into his wallet and held out a small object. An inch-long piece of dark green jade.

'It's one half of a scarab. Seems the colonel carried both halves in his pocket and played with them like dice. When he fell, they must have slid to the floor. The murderer, if that's what he was, must have picked up one half, the top, and missed the other half.'

Willard sighed. 'So you traced it?'

'We went to every jade dealer in San Francisco. Just on

the chance. Maybe he needed money. Maybe anything! We found an old Chinese in a back-alley shop. He said a young man had come in with half a scarab. He wanted a hole drilled in it so he could put it on a neck chain. The little Chinese guy wouldn't drill it. The jade pieces were life stones, he said. Drilling a hole would mean death. He was so upset, he peered out the window as the young man was leaving. Saw the licence plate. We had what we needed.'

Willard stirred, pulled on his pipe.

'So you came here to Thatcher,' he said at last.

Detective Riccardo briskly returned the jade scarab half to his wallet. His notepad and pen went back to his pocket.

'As a lawyer, Mr Roundtree, you know we don't have a case yet. Too much that's circumstantial. Most of that based on the testimony of a sick, disordered woman. If Michael Roundtree did kill Chadwick, he had his justification. Plenty of other men have wanted to do it before him. But – '

Willard rose. 'But you must obtain whatever further evidence there is. Quite properly you think you may find it here. I agree. If Michael did this thing, he is sicker than I supposed. Somehow he must be relieved of that burden. But he cannot be relieved until he faces it. You have enough evidence to take him back with you?'

Mr Riccardo could only admire the tight-lipped old lawyer. It could not be easy to confront weakness or madness in one's own blood.

'I have a warrant to bring him back with me, sir.'

'Would you give me twenty-four hours?'

The detective's eyes hardened. 'For what?'

'I think the evidence, if it exists, is obtainable here. But I think your own job will be easier if it is obtained with the least possible publicity. This old town has its old loyalties. And its gossip. The Roundtrees have been loved and hated in their time but always looked on as town property. There is, they would think, a matter of invasion of privacy here, without concrete proof. Thatcher privacy. If Michael is what you suspect, I will be the first to accept the evidence. To understand the danger.' The old lawyer looked out to the reassuring greening of his valley. 'And to endorse the processes of justice. Where can you be reached?'

Raoul Riccardo in his yellow boots was not the first man to feel in a way he could not have explained that he had gone down in defeat to Willard Roundtree. Yet he liked this man. More than that, he trusted him. Had fate turned up a different coin, Willard Roundtree was what the detective had once dreamed of being, a polished and compassionate lawyer.

'I'm staying at the Pinetree Motel. On the Bollington road, sir.'

Willard saw his visitor to the car, waved a friendly farewell, and signalled to the big copper-coloured dog lying on the porch.

'Things to think about, Clancy. Let's go for a walk.'

The ageing dog chose not to bound ahead. More and more often these days he walked sedately at heel. The old man patted the sleek head by his side.

'As Mark Twain once said, Clance, "Old age is endurable only when you consider the alternative".'

The town meeting, held at the Community House for lack of larger space, took exactly twenty minutes. The citizens craned their necks to see John and Michael sitting together at the board table. Edythe had not come, nor, oddly, Willard Roundtree. Just as well. There had always been bad blood between the brothers. Anything could happen today.

They were wrong. Calvin Appleby gavelled for silence, announced that the decision would be read for approval by a show of hands. At the end of it Michael Roundtree rose, bowed to the citizenry and the board, with a twisted smile nodded to his brother, and left. Few could remember afterwards how he looked or what, if anything, he said.

John hurried out to his car.

Willard was forking leaf mulch under his lilac bushes when John's car turned in.

'Well, how did it go, John?'

'We missed you, Will.'

'I just about ran this town for too long, my boy. It's time you and everybody else found it out. This morning I had a visitor. This afternoon I had some things to think about. I don't know which aggravated me the more. What happened?'

'What I wanted to happen. Michael now has permission to buy the twenty-five acres adjoining the house. The other twenty-five, including the cave, I'll get. That's all we need on top of the Ridge. We have the whole south slope for the silicon screens.'

'Sounds fair.'

'Oh, I don't think Michael liked it. But he let the old charm hang out. I don't pretend to you, Will, that Michael and I are ever going to get along. I'll never forgive the way he treated Hester. But you've got to let go of the past some time, I guess. As they say in the slicks – this is or ought to be bigger than both of us. If I can live with it, so can he.'

'I'll just put this old haying-fork back in the barn, John.'

'Sure. Funny, Will, it was exactly the solution I proposed to Michael before I left for Washington. Yesterday I drove all the way up to that glass heap to talk to him. He turned it down flat. Said he had uses of his own for the Ridge and he'd see me in hell before he let any of it go. I'd have argued it out but I couldn't keep Lili waiting up there.'

'Lili?' Willard's tone was sharp. 'She was up there?'

'She drove up with Michael. She's a damned attractive girl and Michael has never yet let one go by. Maybe it did her good to get out a little. I've never met anybody so alone in my life. But this town is no place for her. I've told myself that a dozen times.'

Willard gave his young kinsman a second glance. The spring wind, it seemed, blew in many directions.

They entered the musty sweetness of the barn. In a shaft of mote-filled sunlight, Charlie Redwing sat in Indian silence, a stoic mending a scythe. Man eternal, thought John. Like Willard, a shield of the land.

He felt good.

'If Michael had seen it my way at the beginning, a lot of talk and publicity could have been avoided. But he had to go the whole route to learn that. This town doesn't hand you anything just for being a Roundtree.'

'Never has.'

It occurred to John that Willard was oddly unresponsive. Maybe that, too, happened with years.

'When he passed me on the way out of the meeting, he said, "You won't get that land, John. Now or ever." He never was a good loser.'

They were out in the sunshine again, the incredible new warmth with which April could surprise the north hills.

'Will, why don't we drive around the Ridge on the south road and take a look at my slope? This is the kind of day when I'm absolutely sure the solar project is going to work out. I'll bet that slant of rock is heating up right now to seventy degrees Fahrenheit. Got time?'

Willard had time. But his mind was not on the slope.

CHAPTER TWENTY-THREE

Lil was packing, quickly but carefully. She wanted to leave no trace of herself in this house nor take any part of it with her. All that she really wanted now was her own life and all of the outside world she could find. Adventure without ties. Her own wits, her own flair, to be used for herself. She would not call it liberation. That implied chains and most of her chains were of her own making. Besides, no one on earth could ever start a day, any day, without chains to something. A house, a desk, a child, a lover. Life imposed them from the day one was born.

What she sought was fulfilment of herself. No more postponing. No more idling of her own energies. Age thirty-some was not a put-down. It was the beginning of self-knowledge. The preparation, the blundering, was over. The years had been used or misused. She would live with their scars but not with their horizons.

She glanced at herself in Henrietta's century-old pier glass and wondered again about the beautiful, doomed woman it had once reflected. And the chains that had held her to this house from the day she had come as a bride to the unguessed violence of her death. Her ten children. Her Roundtree name. It was said she could gallop a horse like an Athenian youth over these hills. It was said she had once taken a lover. It was said she had brought hot Creole blood to mate with cold Calvinism and every one of her ten children showed it. But in the end shawl and bonnet waited. Perhaps, in an odd way, it was Henrietta's ultimate fulfilment.

Lilith knew she was her descendant. Lilith, too, had paid the price of that impassioned Creole blood. But she was beyond that now. Her young, still-supple body was her own. Her future empty and wide as the sky.

She would first break all old ties. She would sell the house in New Orleans. Then she would set about earning her own living, the beginning of that shadowy fulfilment. Perhaps in Paris, where her French would help. Perhaps Rome, where her style would be recognized. Perhaps – She was folding a second, unworn dinner dress into her suitcase when she heard the front door open.

'That you, Edythe?' she called from the upper staircase.

Then she saw him. He was standing in the hall, darkly handsome as always against the afternoon light. He was looking up at her with an expression of unfathomable sadness.

'Michael!'

He brushed his hand across his forehead in the gesture she had seen before. He seemed confused.

'Oh, that you up there, Lilith?'

'Yes. I'm packing.'

'Why?'

'It's time for me to leave.'

He seemed to have difficulty taking that in.

'Yes. I guess it is. Would you come down and talk to me?'

She hesitated. She had not entirely lost her fear of Michael or her awareness or the painful memory of that half-hour up on the Ridge. Yet now there was something different about him. The banter was gone, there were lines she had not noticed before in his face, and that brooding

293

sadness was again in his eyes. She had seen the quick changes of his moods before. She felt uneasy, yet there was always time for a little kindness. Even to this strange man with his abrasive air of possession. But she would not be afraid.

She came down the stairs quickly, as if trying to brush away the scene that lay between them.

'Thank you. The conquered hero needs a kind word.'

In the living-room she sat down gingerly with the odd sensation that she was both guest and hostess.

'I came to see John. To congratulate him. He won, you know. I lost.' Michael's eyes were on her more intently than the words justified.

'I thought it was a compromise. Very fair.'

'Did you, Lilith? Then you don't understand this town. When they want you, they don't compromise. I came back for two reasons. One, to find out how much they wanted me. I've got money enough to put the whole town on its feet. My way. But there was John. So they compromised. There's no such thing as compromise, Lilith. Not with the things that count. It's either yours or it isn't. Right?'

'No, I don't think so. I don't think twenty-five acres is all that important.'

'If you got half of what you wanted, would you think it was okay?'

'It would depend, Michael.'

'Don't quibble with me, Lilith. You're too smart for that. What do twenty-five goddamned acres mean? Or even that glass house that nobody else wants? It's something else.' Again his hand rubbed across his forehead. 'It's an old score, Lilith. A man isn't a man if he doesn't settle them. It was always John or I. My father had an elder-son complex. You know. The crown prince. I was to carry the ball some day. But it was John he really liked. The old man used to sit in that chair you're in, waiting up nights when I went out. He'd always ask me where I'd been. Mostly I wouldn't answer because I found out that annoyed the hell out of him. Or else I'd say Rosie's cathouse down at Juno's Landing. He never hit me. He'd just say one thing. "Bad seed. You're bad seed, Michael." Then I found out what he meant. Old Isaac, founder of our clan. Up there on the cemetery under granite. Hot as a poker in bed, fighting the devil when he wasn't. Mad as a March hare when he died. That was the bad seed. That's what I was.'

This was a new Michael. Talking half to himself, half to the silence that pulsed around them. She did not interrupt. She had lost her uneasiness. Even the moments of nightmare up on the Ridge seemed figments of her own imagining. She did not understand this man, yet she saw that even her listening seemed to ease the torture in his eyes.

'Somewhere, Lilith, they tell me I have a son. I've denied it. His mother is dead now. John knows where he is. But I'd see the boy dead, too, before I claimed him as mine. Nobody's going to tag that kid "bad seed". Whatever I have, he'll get. Some day. But not whatever I am.'

'What's his name, Michael?' She asked it gently, almost for something to say. His eyes warmed for an instant, then he brushed the question aside. 'That's no more to you than to me, Lilith. I want to talk about something else. You didn't ask my other reason for coming back.'

This was the moment she did not want. She felt a faint chill of premonition.

'Oh, I have moods, Lilith. I imagine things. Not the way other people do. But I don't like people getting in my way. Or in the way of something I want. Sometimes I blow that myself. When I can't help it. It's not the way I want to do things.' He paused. He seemed to have forgotten what he intended to say. 'I came back, Lilith. For you.'

'Michael!' It was a protest, a plea, a search for some way not to hurt him.

'No, don't say anything. Let me talk. You probably never thought of me again when you left Thatcher. But I never stopped remembering you. I read everything I could about you. I hated Brock Turner every time I saw his face. Once I hurled a shoe into the television screen at him. I lived with my uncle, hoping he'd die so that when I got his money, I'd find you.'

He was out of his chair, pacing. He made no attempt to touch her or even come near her. Torment twisted his face.

He turned to the window. So empty, so needing of love herself, she wanted to help him through this hurt. But she could only stand helpless, astonished by the depth of his emotion, this man she had feared.

'I wouldn't ask you to marry me, Lilith. Though I used to have fantasies about that. I wouldn't even ask you for love. I don't think you could love me. And a man can buy the other kind anywhere. I want you with me. To end the loneliness, the dark. I'd give you anything you want, Lilith.'

It seemed that the old house, with its ghosts of generations past, stood listening. As it had listened to a century of passion and despair, hopes and abandoned dreams. Listening and waiting for the impossible answer. For human kindness to transcend love.

In spite of herself Lilith shivered.

Michael saw it.

The sadness drained from his face, leaving it harsh. The short laugh came, bitter edged. 'Get on with your packing, Lil. And don't believe any man who lays his life at your feet. You're a woman I'd like to sleep with. But there are plenty of others.' His cruelty was uppermost now. 'Younger.'

At the door he turned, as if unable to leave, as if wanting to say something, anything, to hold them both there.

'Tell John I wish him luck. He'll need it. As kids we used to believe that cave he's got went down to China. A little dynamite inside it could blow the whole Ridge to hell. He owes me a debt for not trying it. I love you, Lilith. Thanks for that.'

She heard the front door slam, a car roar off.

Her life led elsewhere, but here lay the full dimension of her heritage. She had touched its strength and its tragedy.

A telephone rang.

'Lilith, is Michael there?' She heard Willard's precise voice.

'He just left.'

'Do you know where he went?'

'No.'

A slight pause. 'Are you all right?'

Lilith heard in the question exactly what Willard wanted her to hear.

'Yes.'

'Is there anything you want to tell me?'

She let a pulse-beat of time pass. Kindness or conformity? She had never conformed.

'No,' she said. 'Nothing.'

It was mid-evening when Michael at last drove up the Ridge road to the stark loneliness of the house he no longer wanted. A show of bravado now, a burned-out match. He would leave in the morning. Destination? He would figure that out. He always had.

His headlights swung around the gravel circle and picked out a car parked at one side. Two figures stood silhouetted against the darkened glass. One, he recognized as Willard.

'Good evening, Michael.'

'Evening, sir.'

'Michael, this gentleman would like to talk to you.'

Riccardo fingered the handcuffs in his pocket. Uncertain. The moment had an odd texture.

'He is Detective Raoul Riccardo of the San Francisco Police.'

Somewhere within Michael a hidden vein seemed to open.

'Yes, of course.' He looked out across the valley. A few stars were pricking the night. There would be more. 'Come in, will you, Mr Riccardo? I'm ready.'

'I'm coming with you, Michael. You'll need legal advice.'

Michael met the old man's eyes. And wondered why he had not met them sooner.

If the San Francisco press had not been almost totally bemused with the abduction of a local heiress, the case of The People of San Francisco versus Michael Roundtree, in the death of Colonel Sanford Chadwick, might have splashed blacker ink into the headlines. As it was, a brief sortie into history by an enterprising stringer reporter revealed that Michael Roundtree was a distant New England relative of one Simon Roundtree, who had come west nearly a century ago and had made a formidable, if tainted, fortune out of the earthquake-devastated city.

But history's candle guttered in the neon light of the present. Old Simon Roundtree was long dead, replaced by more voracious predators. His son, Simon Gideon, was also dead and the shadowy bulk of the fortune sunk somewhere in the growing monoliths now ringing the bay and blocking the view.

Besides, there were pressures far beyond Roundtree interests not to look too closely into the Chadwick homicide. He had left a collection of ancient jade carvings, beyond statable value, to the city's museums. Plus a private 'guest' book containing some highly recognizable names of those who had found solace in the colonel's esoteric hospitality. The book lay sealed in a private safe of interested parties.

All this was as obvious to old Willard Roundtree as it was relieving.

Daily, on the phone to John, his voice grew more buoyant.

'Don't think of coming west, John. We don't need any more Roundtrees on the scene. Michael is all right, if remote. His claim is self-defence. The state seems to have a weak case against that. I'm not worried. There's a general urgency here to get it all out of the way. A can of worms nobody wants to open. And that's good for us. Tell your mother anything she wants to know. But nobody else.'

Willard had confidence in Edythe's resiliency.

On the telephone to his long-standing friend, Frank McQuade, editor of the *Thatcher Standard*, Willard was equally blunt.

'We're keeping it low here, Frank. I've got a newspaper man helping do that. Just watch the New York and Boston papers for us and keep it out of the *Standard*.'

A fine time in life, Willard told himself, for an old respectable lawyer to descend to such pressuring.

The afternoon light from the bay was flooding his hotel room. Four p.m. He pulled down the window shades. He'd have just enough time for the furtive nap he seemed increasingly to need. His caller was due at five o'clock. At that time, Willard fervently hoped, Brock Turner would have the answer he wanted. The man who might just have the answer he needed. He closed his eyes and saw again the uncompromising set of Brock Turner's jaw when he had first seen him so long ago at that hotel, what was its name, in New York. Lili – Lilith, she was transitional then – had looked at Brock with summer in her face. Dammit, he had liked the man from the beginning. Neither he, nor God Almighty, could stop people from tangling up their lives. It was probably right as the world judges those things that Brock should go back to his wife. The ailing woman who might just have been the last person to see Colonel Chadwick alive.

Willard let his mind drain. He was no detective, nor psychoanalyst. He was a defence lawyer and his one job was to get Michael out of the unholy quagmire into which, with some ancestral aid, he had slid. At this juncture, sentiment was softness.

The telephone burst at him. The voice at the end of the wire brought him to his feet, much too fast for a man of his age. It was all that he did not want now.

'I'll be right down. Yes. Yes. Of course I understand.'

Edythe Roundtree was sitting, neat and cross-ankled in an oversized chair in the lobby. He was thankful that she did not seem near tears. But then Edythe in crisis was always dry-eyed.

'I had to come, Willard. Michael's my son. Where have they got him?'

'Let's go where we can talk.' He pointed to a small empty coffee lounge.

She followed, meekly enough until they were alone.

'Where is Michael?'

He sighed. This, after all, was what had bound them all together so long. Stiff-spined, resolution against all the outrages a haphazard fate could deliver. The Roundtrees did not give way. They were one family. It showed in the light blue eyes of this small, defiant – Willard found an old-fashioned word satisfying – lady.

'They haven't "got" Michael, Edythe. There was a

hearing, an indictment. All circumstantial evidence in my opinion. The trial . . .'

She brushed it aside. 'Where *is* he? Now. This minute?'

'He's staying with the Jesuits at a retreat. He seems to find a quiet there he needs.' He tried a smile. 'The Roundtrees always seem to find God a complying presence. When they need to.'

Normally she would have met the thrust. Now she was as single-minded as a lioness stalking a lost cub.

'Willard, did Michael – do you believe – did my son kill that man?'

This was obviously where it must be said.

'He told me he did.'

'Oh, God . . .'

'Edythe, listen to me. You've come here without warning, against my advice and my concern for you. Against my wishes.' The warmth that was the old lawyer's trademark softened his voice. 'Of course, my dear, had I been you, I'd have done precisely the same thing. But that is not the issue. Michael claims self-defence. I believe him. In twenty minutes I am to meet a man who may, and I think will, prove Michael's case.' He held up a hand. 'No more questions now. Please. Have you a room?'

She nodded.

'Good. Go up to it. Rest. I'll call you at six and buy you the best dinner on Fisherman's Wharf.'

Edythe was armoured against even kindness.

'John told me that Michael – what Michael had gotten into – some insane cult or group out here. Drugs – I don't know what. How could he? Or was it our fault in some way? Something we didn't see – something . . .' She put a handkerchief against her lips. 'Let me go to him!'

'To ask him those questions?'

In the silence he seemed to hear the shuttle of time, the weaving and crossing of light and darkness, of love and evil, that had brought them to this moment.

She seemed at last to understand.

'No. No. If Michael's quiet now – at peace with – with himself. It's better, isn't it?'

He saw her to the elevator, shrunken, but contained.

In a reclining chair in her hospital room Marcia Reeves Turner petulantly shielded her eyes against the sun.

'It's of no interest to me, Brock, whether Michael Roundtree hangs for Colonel Chadwick's murder or not. Why should it be? Roundtree was *her* name, wasn't it? Oh, I know. You don't have to tell me. I read the papers. It was really so *cheap* of you, Brock. That woman and you. So common, letting everything be so public. But then the colonel taught me that only when we can rise above other people's flaws do we gain purity.' Her voice trembled.

Brock closed the louvred blinds. He had reached a state of controlled gentleness that was now forged into a kind of armour around him.

'You mustn't go on grieving, Marcia. It isn't good for you.'

'I know.' A half-smile flickered, a little girl's smile. 'I'm not really. Shall I tell you something, Brock?' He nodded. He knew the game.

'I was almost – almost glad. Even when I was watching it happen. From the hall in that mirror. Glad! There. I've said it. He had promised me Ishtar. And then it was always somebody else. Brock, he had *promised*!'

The big man nodded again. 'It was wrong, Marcia. I understand how much he hurt you. A gentleman does not break his promise to a lady.'

'No, he doesn't, does he, Brock? That's what Daddy said. Funny to hear you say it now. That's what the colonel did. He broke his promise. That's why I wasn't sorry.' She sat up straight and plucked at the pink chiffon folds of her dressing gown. 'That's why I couldn't cry out or say anything. Even when I saw the – the syringe in the colonel's hand. I saw him spring at Dushu – at Michael. I thought Dushu would kill him. And I would be glad.'

'Don't you want the world to know how the colonel wronged you?'

'Yes. Yes, I do!' A sudden fierceness lit the pale blue eyes. Then the wary, childlike smile returned. 'I know.

That's just a trick. To make me say I'll go out there into court and tell them what I saw.'

'No tricks, Marcia.' For an instant Brock withdrew into his own pain. In another half-hour he would meet with Willard Roundtree for the last time. He had failed. It was the last thing he might have done for Lilith, wherever she was now. For the Roundtree name meant nothing except for the one woman in his world who bore it. He returned to the present of this hospital room and the role he had set for himself.

Marcia's eyes were swimming with tears.

'My dear girl!'

'He had promised, Brock. *Promised*!'

'Try to forget, Marcia.' He picked up her thin hand, the nails badly bitten. Her fingers curled around his.

'You'll help me?'

'Of course. I'll ring for the nurse now.'

'No, Brock, no. Not yet. You're not going to leave so soon.' The thin fingers tightened around his. Her other hand clutched at his jacket. 'Brock, you can't. I have nobody else.'

'I have an appointment, Marcia. I'll be back.'

'But you say that and you don't come back. Not for ever so long. I'll scream. I'll call the nurse. I'll tell them I can't live without you!'

'And you know what will happen then.' His voice was so low, so endearing, he barely recognized it as his own. 'You're getting better, Marcia. Don't spoil things now.'

'Things – for us?'

'Perhaps.' He would still not bring himself to make a promise he could not face.

'Why perhaps, Brock? You're going to take me away from here, aren't you?'

'We have to talk that over. But I'm going to be late if I stay any longer. Have a nice supper and a good sleep.' He dropped a half-kiss on her faded hair.

She let him get to the door. 'Brock!' It was a thin, piercing wail. She was out of her chair, clinging to him. 'Brock, if I – if I go into that court and tell them everything

I saw, will you promise never to leave me, not for one second, ever again?'

He intended to unclasp her arms from his neck. He hesitated. 'You would do that, Marcia?'

She tightened her clasp. 'Yes. Yes. If you would stay with me. In a little house for just the two of us. With lots of sunshine and little trees growing around. And a porch to sit on. And you would be there with me. Always, Brock.' She held up her face. 'Would you promise?'

The nurse at the hospital reception desk watched the big man cross the lobby, his shoulders sagging, his face and his temples grey. He still had that masculinity, she thought, traces of the rugged good looks that made a woman glance twice. She remembered Brock Turner vaguely from his TV-idol days. He was older now, she thought, like a mainspring had broken.

They said the faded, complaining little woman upstairs was his wife. Well, some women never knew what they had until they ruined it. She nodded as he passed. But with her own youth strong, she dismissed him without curiosity.

In the time-cluttered offices of the *Thatcher Standard* editor Frank McGee rose impatiently from the pile of newspapers on his desk.

As he knew they would, the yellow press peddled sensation. The big dailies, if they covered the case at all, relegated it to inside coverage. But for a week, Thatcher gave itself over to the satisfactions of titillation. Words like drug-cult, cult leader, hideaway of sin, sex orgies for paying guests and other closet fantasies ran loose as mice behind the neat front doors. The faithful took comfort in the old thunder . . . 'Vengeance is Mine . . . but for him who repents the crooked will be made straight, the sinner healed . . .' Someone painted an obscenity on the Roundtrees' white picket fence. Kinder hands washed it out.

Most pervasive of all was the solid judgement that the dark side of the Roundtrees had reached bottom. Everyone who had grown up in Thatcher knew the dusty legend that Isaac Roundtree, patriarch and progenitor, in his final madness had murdered his wife, Henrietta. Michael had inherited his great-grandfather's devils as surely as he had inherited his sombre, brooding eyes. There was no help for that.

But the solution left them uneasy.

Michael was freed. He chose his final oblivion in a Jesuit retreat among the vineyards of California. Edythe, thinner and quieter on her return, announced it with head high, and a wry inner smile. In the deep roots of Thatcher's inheritance, popery was no substitute for penance.

Talk might have died there had it not found a new target. Curious eyes glanced at a slender open-faced boy seen in the company of John Roundtree. Edythe faced the matter bluntly and at once.

'Michael's son. Brandon. My grandson. He's come to live with us. You must meet him. We're having a party. Mrs Salter, do bring Tommie and little Lynn. He doesn't know many young people.'

With that the door on all questions closed. Thatcher would never know the search, the bargaining, the legalities, the price. Brandon was where he belonged. The boy's red hair, quick laugh, brash honesty might have led to speculation. But in this the town was kind. The Roundtrees were a ravaged family.

John, showing the boy the fields and woods, kept his own anguish buried. He saw Hester in every change of the boy's face. Michael and Hester so long ago. He would live with it. The boy was his as surely as if Hester had made him this gift. As perhaps she had. For what he had of Hester, his lovely wife, was brief. But it was all the love, all the beauty of mind and body, a woman can give to a man.

From the farmhouse parlour, warmed by the fire he increasingly needed, Willard watched John and the boy cross the spring-wet fields. He should be out there now to show him the first wild green of the skunk cabbage, the silver of pussy-willows. Time too for his old muskrat friend.

From the depths of his rolltop desk, Willard drew a rusted tin box. Gently he unfolded the tissue from a crumbling suede-covered book, and opened it to the last page Henrietta had written . . . 'I hear Isaac moving downstairs . . . whatever my destiny . . .' Beneath it lay a folded yellowed piece of paper that Willard had long ago slid there. It bore Isaac's scrawled and dying writing . . . 'God forgive me my sins of the flesh . . . I have consigned this woman, my wife, to the darkness from which she came . . .'

The past. The past had no claim on the future. The future did not lie waiting in old books, old walls, old men. The future was out there, getting its sneakers wet in the marsh.

With the sureness that had won his last case, Willard hurled diary and confession into the fire. He watched the fingers of flame pry open the pages, watched them blacken, curl, shred and vanish upward in spirals of smoke.

He picked up his walking stick and whistled for the quivering-nosed young setter that lay in old Clancy's place.

Outside, the spring freshness played him a trick. He saw for an instant a luminous, unforgettable face with remarkable eyes. Elizabeth – Lili – Lilith. There was fibre! There was a woman! Henrietta's own kind.

He wanted so much that she be happy.

He would like to see her once more. But then – he smiled at himself – he expected most men would.

CHAPTER TWENTY-FOUR

Mardi Gras had come again to New Orleans, that perennial ecstasy and farewell of the flesh, when anything could be done and everything was forgiven.

An early morning, pinkish mist floated over the still-empty streets as Lilith stood looking down from the balcony of her hotel room. In another hour these narrow streets of the French Quarter, with their wrought-iron balconies and fraying reflections of the past, would seethe with people, masked and unmasked, jostling, dancing, singing, pushing their way out of their inhibitions.

She had known it all once, long ago. Now as she traced

with one finger a lotus blossom in the ironwork filigree of the balcony, she wondered at the urgency, the vicarious excitement, the sense of anticipation of pleasure real and imagined, that had brought her to New Orleans two days earlier than needed and deposited her alone on this balcony with Mardi Gras opening like a lost fan before her. No one was alone on Mardi Gras. Yet a nostalgia for youth was hardly company enough for a woman who had suddenly reached a turning point in her life.

For nearly two years now her life had suited her as much as life ever would. Her work as translator in the Paris office of NATO had brought her stability. Her small apartment off the avenue Victor Hugo was a home of sorts. Her talents as hostess at small chic dinners, as guest at larger, glittering affairs, had won her recognition. Not that she sought it. Not that it could ever fill the inner emptiness at the core of her life. This she concealed with wit and with charm. It was, as she told herself, like this silent morning hour, to be filled with make-believe.

She had met men. The hot-eyed Argentinian million-aire, slightly younger than herself, who took her disco dancing, offered her fifty thousand acres of pampas, and wanted to live with her.

'Only as long as you like, Leeleet. One must have love. No? Yes? I will be in a convent – no, a monastery – until you tell me.'

There was a Georgian prince, with the face of a tired whippet and the sad eyes of a spaniel. 'I would like so much to make you empress of my country, Leeluth. But I am poor. I have no country. And you – you are a snow-woman!'

Not quite. But her aloofness gave mystique as well as strength to her life-style. She wondered how long a woman must live to discover that truth.

Then Sterling Marshall. Silver-haired, Oxford-educated, diplomat, financier, adviser to his government – and the foreseeable culmination of her own success. Widower, wealthy, 'the best catch in Paris', quivered the gossip columnists. Lilith enjoyed long walks with him in the Bois, quiet dinners at quiet restaurants, quiet talk, choice seats at the Symphonie.

Then he had asked her to marry him.

She had asked for time. Yet there was no real reason for that. Love could change to kindliness. Companionship, a sharing, could make a life too.

A letter from her New Orleans lawyers provided an excuse. They had found a suitable buyer for the Dauphine Street house. When could she come?

Sterling Marshall sensibly protested. 'It can all be handled from Paris, my dear. Or, if you prefer, by my own lawyers in Boston. If you really feel you want to go to New Orleans, I would like to be there with you. A woman shouldn't be bothered with those details. I like to think I'm taking care of you.'

It was obvious that this fine man had already taken her plea for time as consent. She was so near to giving it. And yet – just a little time. For what? Farewell to a past she had already put behind her? To a youth made restless by the Creole blood that still flowed in her veins? Or to relive alone for a few brief, secret hours the passions, the fantasies, of the one love that must sustain her the rest of her life.

She had selected the day after Mardi Gras for the closing of the sale. In the end Sterling Marshall had consented to her going alone. Wisely he had not pressed for her reasons. Perhaps he sensed, with an older man's insight, that there were doors that must ever remain shut until she chose to open them.

'If ever I cease to love . . .' Lilith leaned over the balcony. Groups of people were wandering into the street. A rowdy voice had begun the absurd little song, made famous a century ago by a flirty little Broadway musical-comedy singer, of whom the visiting Archduke of Russia was enamoured. Both singer and song had been transported to New Orleans for the imperial pleasure and gleefully adopted by the Carnival crowds. The song had become the enduring Mardi Gras theme.

'If ever I cease to love . . .' Lilith found herself echoing the silly words from the street below. '. . . may oysters have legs and cows lay eggs . . .'

She felt younger already. If Sterling had come, they would be properly attending the Comus Ball tonight; as a

Beaulaire, she would be invited. Instead the day and the night lay empty ahead, as she wanted.

'If ever I cease to love . . .' Maskers were beginning to appear in the crowd. The inevitable dominoes, she remembered, the red devils as mischief-making, as uncatchable, as sparks; the huge, grinning, sexless heads; the girls in tiny masks and tinier skirts, long slender legs provocative as a wink. Lilith remembered other hushed stories of her girlhood. Ladies, masked and curious, sneaking into Storeyville brothels; wives masked and seeking one-day lovers; debutantes street-dancing in the powerful arms of sailors. The mask was the heart and the pardon of Mardi Gras.

A jazz group set up on the street corner, its beat soft and compulsive.

Lilith turned restlessly back into her room. She could stay here and watch it all from the safe seclusion of her balcony. She could answer the latest of Edythe Roundtree's devoted letters; it had come just before she left Paris. It still lay in her handbag.

My darling Elizabeth,

How dear of you to keep me informed of your busy life. And how good to know that you are well and happy. There is always news from Thatcher, of course, though I'm sure it fades in a sea crossing. John's solar screen is at last installed. I doubt that it's going to light up Thatcher yet, but it has brought us all kinds of attention.

Lilith had read it all on the plane, yet she read it now, as if to postpone decision, as if to reassure herself with this last, sweet tie. Edythe's fine hand flowed on:

They've found an unusually good source of silicon – whatever that is – at the far end of the valley. Willard says it could make us famous (if anybody wants that). One strange thing happened. When they blasted near the cave to even out the slope for John's screen, the explosion carried right through a fault in the Ridge, a crack that ran the whole length of it. Down went that monstrosity of a house, Lil. It's gone, granite, glass, and all. Willard says who knows, another oak tree might grow up there. And Charlie Redwing just held out his arms and said the sun has brought the return of his people's gods. I hope so. They seem like nice, friendly spirits as Charlie tells it.

Lilith drew the breath that she knew Edythe had taken at this point.

But, Lilith, I've saved the best news of all. Kim and Larry are going to be married. I was half-braced for a 'meaningful arrangement', but Kim said no. They want a home for an abused pony Kim found. Would you believe she wants a full-scale wedding with all the trimmings? It will be in the fall, so it won't detract from the solar tests, she says. She might be right. As Kim sees it, the sun orbits entirely around her these days. You will come for the wedding, won't you? We're counting on you, dear.

Elizabeth . . . Lili . . . whoever they thought her, they were counting on her. The page blurred a little. She would go, of course. As Mrs Sterling Marshall? Her mind closed to the idea.

Assorted sounds filled the room. The crowds in the street were thickening. More players joined the jazz makers. Lilith's foot began to tap. She wondered whatever would be thought if the future Mrs Sterling K. Marshall were discovered masked and giddy in the streets.

She found she could still giggle.

On Bourbon Street she bought a mask. A sly-smiling, white kitten face with green glass eyes and a tiny silver crown. But she did not put it on. She carried it. A souvenir, she told herself. For Sterling.

She drifted through the narrow, familiar streets of the Quarter, sometimes with the tide of people, sometimes against them. Jackson Square was jammed almost to the levee. She passed a young, long-haired couple lost in their own world; the girl playing a flute, he a bass violin. A baby was strapped to his back. From the canvas belting floated the green, gold, and purple colours of Mardi Gras.

At the French Market she pushed through the crowds to an empty bench along the river, now glinting with streaks of silver and blue. Always the rivers. Her life seemed made up of rivers. One night, long ago, this river had been black as tar, shining with promise. One unfinished night. With Brock.

The din around her was mounting. She would go back by way of Dauphine Street. One more glimpse of her father's house.

A last, private farewell to her youth.

In the sober offices of Clare, Lemoyne, and Kelley, the balding, round-bellied little lawyer tapped a gold pen irritably and wished his caller would leave.

It was the custom of the firm to close at noon on Mardi Gras. Already Canal Street was solid with people. At any moment Rex, King of Carnival, would loom in the distance on that silver-white monstrosity, the royal float. Traffic would be barricaded for blocks.

Mr Kelley disliked Mardi Gras, as he disliked all confusion. He wanted to go home, put on his joggers, and shape up. In proper order.

Yet here was this caller sitting before him as solid as the legal tomes along the walls. Crumpled tweeds, wilted collar, not at all the type to be involved in any affairs of the Beaulaire family, in his considered opinion.

'I can't answer your question, sir. I don't know when Miss Roundtree will be arriving. Or where she will stay in New Orleans.'

Brock Turner leaned back in the chair.

'And if you did know, you wouldn't tell me, right?'

'We respect the privacy of our clients, Mr Turner.' Mr Kelley remembered the name vaguely now. A broadcaster. A TV newsman. Didn't look the same, though. Not quite so – Mr Kelley rarely gave himself to slang but there was no other word he could think of – sharp.

Brock sighed. A long chance. He had seen the notice of the house for sale in the New Orleans papers he still, obstinately, read. A little digging had turned up the family lawyers. And the closing date. Why? Nearness to her, the reassurance of her being?

He rose from the discreet leather of the Clare, Lemoyne, and Kelley chair.

'I'll drop by tomorrow, Mr Kelley. See if you know anything more.'

'It would be quite futile, sir. Most unusual, I assure you, to divulge any information about a client.'

'Miss Roundtree is an unusual lady, I assure you.'

Brock pushed his way roughly through the crowds. There had been no reason to torment that innocuous little man when what he really wanted to do was to take savage slices at himself.

Hare-brained, he told himself, the whole trip.

Well, he had done what he could. If not for her, at least for the name she bore. Not graciously, to be sure, but because it was inevitable when Willard Roundtree had called him in San Francisco. He, Brock, had hated Michael Roundtree's guts from the first moment he saw him. The dark scowl, the quick petulance. He wondered if Lilith had known him. If so, how well. He had even deeper reasons for his resentment. Casually, it seemed, and without motive, Michael had come from left field to deprive him of his own personal vengeance. Colonel Chadwick, or Brother Sunshine, as Brock still preferred to call him, was dead. Half a lifetime of pursuit, of planning, of the white heat of revenge, had ended, like his own career, in nothing. And ironically, bound him to a sterile and hopeless future.

For Marcia had indeed exacted her price. Her testimony had been more a wincing than a confession. Sitting shrunken and trembling in the witness chair, she had stripped her own feelings as if they were her body, baring every shredded emotion to a glassy-eyed court.

In the end Michael was acquitted. The last Brock had heard was that he had withdrawn to a Jesuit retreat, to immerse himself in books. And bathos, Brock thought spitefully. Willard had gracefully written Brock his thanks. Brock had not answered.

Marcia. He dutifully took her to a cottage in a fruit-farming valley south-east of San Francisco. There she had clung to him, silent and watching in the evenings, her hand dry as a leaf in his. Time stopped. His horizon fenced a half-acre. One Saturday afternoon, in the thin light of late autumn, she stood up, looked around, opened her pale blue eyes wide, and turned on the stereo to rock. Swinging her hips, she sashayed across the room.

'Let's go *somewhere*, Brock. I'm bored!'

He had read the Paris gossip. Lilith was to marry. A man Brock knew he could never match. Centre stage, social establishment, a career as solid as his name. Brock privately labelled Sterling Marshall 'grey spats'. In his clearer moments he knew it was where Lilith belonged. He would do nothing to upset her life.

Then perversely, contrary to all his self-promises, he had come to Mardi Gras. 'I know the town, Phil. I'll write you a hell of a story!' But he would not upset her. One glimpse of her, one moment of nearness. Hare-brained or not.

'Watch it, buster!' He heard a whistle, jumped back from the hooves of a police horse, and remembered he was in New Orleans.

He would find a small bar, a little peace, no regrets. Maybe he'd take a look for the last time at that expensive piece of real estate where he had first met her. Maybe not. He could almost see those enormous candid eyes measuring his interference.

The afternoon was half-spent when he finally reached Dauphine Street. The exterior of the house was neat with the blankness of a home awaiting new occupants. He pushed open the front door. That it was unlocked did not surprise him. They let everything hang out at Mardi Gras. Maybe there were house painters inside or cleaning women.

There was, he found, only silence. The thick walls reduced the crowd noises to a distant surf. Through the wide dim hall he saw the daylight of the patio. No board squeaked in the polished floors. Everywhere order prevailed in shapeless bulks beneath pale dust covers.

Enough! He was as empty of life as these rooms, snatching at something that was as irretrievably gone as the music he had not quite heard the first time he saw her here.

But there were sounds. Faint scratchings and scrapings from somewhere. Mice? Through the door to the parlour, slightly ajar, he could see a single straight-backed chair with something white lying on it. White and soft-looking. If it was a cat, it was loafing on the job.

He silently pushed the door wider.

Lilith was crouched on her knees before a cabinet, her face smudged, her hands grimy. A dust cover lay in a heap beside her. She seemed to be shaking, twisting, poking, at what looked like a cluster of costumed figures inside the cabinet. Two lay at broken angles on the floor. They had animal heads. Above the rattling she must have heard something.

She looked up. Her face, beneath the smudges, went ash-white.

He said the only thing he could think of.

'Having trouble?'

'It – ' her eyes were enormous, her voice small. 'It doesn't work.'

'So, you've learned that?'

'Oh ... . Brock!' She was on her feet and half across the room when he caught her. Then she stiffened.

'Are you – I mean, is there anyone . . .?'

He held her from him. 'If you mean Marcia, say so. I'll give it to you now. All of it. She has been with me for two years. She is better. She is going to replace me with a guy who raises lemons for a living and tap-dances for a hobby.' He saw her eyes warm, but he was not through. 'And you?'

She shook her head numbly.

'What about grey spats?'

'What?'

'The ambassador, the fellow you're going to marry?'

'Brock! That's awful. He's – ' The eyes glinted. 'Why didn't you tell me? Why didn't you ever write or call or let me know?'

He pulled her to him.

'Time for that, Lil.' He bent his head. 'Tomorrow.'

TOMORROW ... AND TOMORROW

The young man strode up the path. When he reached the door, he remembered and looked back at his companions.

'Take your time, sir.'

Willard waved his cane. When a man passed ninety, it was about all he had to take. Besides, he had a pretty girl on his arm and that was enough for now. A girl with a hand that was gentle but with eyes on the young man ahead.

Elizabeth Roundtree opened the door. A beautiful woman, her dark hair streaked with grey, drawn austerely back, her elegance unfaded, her face chiselled as if by winds, to a transparency. Yet she was a whole woman. That lay in the understanding of those depthless eyes.

'Brandon!' Her glance swept his uniform. 'Nice!'

'I don't think that's what the Air Force had in mind, Aunt Lil.'

Brandon Roundtree, Michael's son, stood tall, red haired, with a smile that creased his left cheek. Every gesture showed John Roundtree's careful stewardship.

'Lynn and I want to say goodbye.'

'How kind. Come in.' Elizabeth held out both hands to the girl. She, too, was in uniform, the wings on her collar bright and new. Her left hand wore a narrow gold band. Marriage was back in fashion.

The haven Elizabeth Roundtree had at last made for herself in Thatcher contained all she needed from the world. A rosewood cabinet, a pearwood escritoire, a long brightly chintzed divan. A table held only a framed photograph of a rugged, grey-haired man in open-throated khaki shirt and rakish Army fatigue cap. Beneath the picture was inserted a newspaper clipping. 'Henley Brocklebank Turner, war correspondent, killed in action,

Kabul, 12 March 1982. He gave his life to free a stranger.'

A year and a half ago. At the beginning of what the safely distant politicians termed escalation.

Young Brandon lit the fire against the first September chill. Elizabeth brought out wine, and a special Madeira for Willard. He thanked her with a wink.

Her glance turned on the young couple sitting close on the divan.

'And when you come back?'

The girl's face glowed. 'We're going to farm! Right here in Thatcher. We love the valley. Uncle John's taught us so much!'

Elizabeth rose and returned with a long envelope.

'Read it together. It's yours now.'

The paper was creased and yellowed, the handwriting spidery.

My dearest children,

You will be grown when you read this. And I will no longer be here to separate for you the honest from the false, the beautiful from the mean.

Wear the name Roundtree proudly. It bears no stain. I loved the man I married with all I knew of love. But it was not he who taught me the truth of love. It was a man who came briefly to love me and to bring its tenderness, its sacrifice, its meaning, beyond passion. If I could leave that wisdom to you, my children, I would die enriched. But each must learn for himself. Thus the heart makes no progress.

Forgive your father for what he did. The devil he fought so long lived only within himself, instilled by those who also lived by fear.

Be kind in your judgement of him. As I pray my children's children will be, in the century ahead.

Oh, my unseen, my future darlings! I would that I could know you! You are my flesh, my blood, my soul! Hold to your dreams – to the fires in your heart – to the ecstasy of each sun's rising, the longings of each new night. And to your secret horizons that I share but will never know.

This alone can I bequeath you. And now do.
                    Henrietta Beauclaire Roundtree
                    Thatcher
                    4 November 1900

Young Lynn Roundtree broke the silence. 'I wish . . . oh,
I wish . . .'
Brandon put a finger to her lips.
Willard in his chair opened his eyes. He had not been
asleep. He was looking through time.
What he saw would endure.